For the Love of Mia

For the Love of Mia

B. A. Osahor

2008

For the Love of Mia

OTHER NOVELS BY THE AUTHOR

My Forever Love
Still Breathing

ACKNOWLEDGMENTS

Without the help of my family, this novel would have never come to be for this been one heck of ride for me! To my family, I thank you for your encouragement and your love. Arric, thank you for your valuable and creative insight. Joe, and Dee, thanks for your much needed contribution. Kate, I owe you many thanks (as well as coffee, lunch, and dinner) for your assistance. To all my readers, thank you for your emails and your blessings! Thank you all for giving me the emotional support I needed to complete this manuscript, I love you all. To S.L. in Long Beach, you know who you are! I would like to thank the *Creator* for giving me the opportunity, along with the knowledge and strength to complete this novel. To all my old friends and my many new ones! I love you all! Keep on reading. Mom, I did it again!

Much love, joy, and romance to you all!

B. A. Osahor

To my knights in shining armor
Michael Anthony & Geoffrey Maurice
Thank you for your inspiration!

PROLOGUE

I am drawn to you like a mosquito to the fragrant aroma of warm flesh

Like a fish to cool crystal waters

Like the lust of an addict for their needed fix

Like a honeybee to a flower's sweet nectar

Like a moth to the amber dancing flame

Mia, you are my blood, my water, my drug, my nectar, and my light on a cold dark night

Mia, I will be your knight in shining armor

I shall be your knight forever and always!

I awoke to a lazy summer day, basking in the warmth from the rays of the golden sun shining high above in the bluest of skies. As if in a dream, I lay floating on a bed of white feathery clouds. The air about me hung heavy with the sweet pungent scent of flora. All around me lay the bright colors of red, yellow, pink, and white, of a whimsical garden filled with flowers and other plant life. Alive, the whole garden was alive. The rhythmic buzz of insects mingled with the trickling of water from a nearby fountain surrounded by a stone wall, enchanted my ears. I was as light as a feather as I brought my hand up to my face as gentle swirls of warm air tickled my nose; while honeybees swooped and dived from flower to flower collecting their sweet bounty. The warm summer sun, radiant overhead, was harmony to this peaceful place as all things alive flourished in their magnificence. Muted voices in the distance drifting across the garden were barely audible above the natural beauty and noise of this place. Peaceful, it was all so very peaceful, and I did not want to depart from this splendid garden so full of life and warmth. The day wore on, and the sunlight began to fade, and in its place the moon raised high in the sky enveloping me in a lustrous wave of light. The repetitive dance that was the day, changed to a symphony of crickets that was the night. Nothing mattered in this place and my desire was to stay in the peacefulness and the stillness of this warm night enjoying the fragrance of my serene garden. As the sonata of crickets faded into the night, the voices in the distance grew louder. I strained to hear, and as I tried to turn to look into the darkness from where the sounds emanated, I discovered I was immobile, held fast to one spot for there was heaviness upon my chest preventing me from moving. All of a sudden, dark clouds moved swiftly across the sky, hiding the glow of the moon, as eerie shadows took flight across the darken skies. From the spray of the fountain, the garden air was filled with mist, which seemed to come alive with spirits; writhing and thrashing a sinful dance along the ground. Heinous shapes lurched from the mist clawing at the tops of the rounded rocks as if the dead had awakened. As quickly as the spirits had risen, a strong wind swept down from the heavens, brushing the spirits away and vanishing them from sight. Then the reflected light of the world revealed its radiance through the clouds, cleansing the wickedness from the sky, and the moon's love was felt once again. The full moon emerged from behind the clouds and in its place a glass of red wine, blood red in color as if the heavens above were offering the gift of life to me once more.

Suddenly the splendor of my garden vanished, and the peacefulness of the night was shattered, like a mirror crushed into a million pieces, scattering my thoughts to the four corners of the garden as a wave of hopelessness and sorrow washed over me, taking me deeper into the darkness until the colors of my tranquil garden faded to a cold black. The distant voices turned to shouting, and someone was shouting my name. The voices grew louder, and the night grew to pitch black. The air around me turned bitterly cold, chilling me to the bone. The pressure upon my chest grew heavier. I struggled to breathe; gasping for breath which refused to come for the air about me was as thick as a blanket as I lay there in the shadowy void gasping for air like a fish out of water. The darkness carried the noise of unfamiliar voices and of someone crying. All around me there was a sense of urgency, as footsteps pounded up and down the stairs. Voices. Sirens. Sonny. Sonny, shouting my name.

"Mia, don't you die on me! Do you hear me? Stay with me, fight! I love you, Mia! Fight for me, baby! Fight it, Mia. *MIA!*"

"Sir, you're going to have to step back and let the paramedics do their job."

CHAPTER ONE

Recuperating from a failed relationship can take a lot out of a person, but after much soul searching I was finally ready to move forward with my life, and to be part of the human race once again. I thought I had put my heart into my last relationship to a respectable man, but that relationship was now over, putting me back into the dating game again. At this time in my life and at my age the thought of dating again was positively nauseating. I certainly didn't relish the idea of going through the dating *gauntlet* again, particularly since most men my age were already paired with sufficient others be it male or female. This made pickings rather slim for unlike orange trees, there was not an abundance of eligible men in San Diego, California.

I don't care to go into the tedious details of my last relationship. Let's just say that two years of our on again off again relationship, and Randy's indecisiveness about whether or not he wanted children, sort of sucked the fun right out of it for me. I am already the proud mother of two teen age sons from my first marriage and was not about to have more children, and Randy knew this from the very beginning. So on a scale of one to ten, our relationship went from a six to a one real quick once Randy had announced to me he was ready to start a family. As an economics professor at the University of San Diego, Randy and I had had many heated conversations about his comments on how a woman's place was in the home. Randy felt if women stayed at home and raised their children while the men went to work, this planet would not be in such chaos. So it was by mutual consent that we ended our relationship for good. I was a bit saddened over the fact when it was all over and done with. Not heartbroken, but saddened. I had cared for Randy, but deep inside I'd also known he was not the one with whom I would spend the rest of my life with. Call it woman's intuition.

For a few months following our so called "breakup," I would occasionally allow Randy to stop by my place once or twice a month for a visit. Sometimes we'd take in a movie, or meet someplace for dinner. But no matter how our outings started somehow our dates always seemed to end up the same way, his bed or mine. I was not blaming Randy, for I was as much to blame as he was, but I knew we couldn't continue on this path; it was just prolonging the obvious. So after a couple of months of our on again, off again connection, I finally came to my senses and put a stop to Randy's congenial visits.

It was becoming a bit confusing by not ending our *involvement*. I call it that because that's what it had turned into, an *"involvement"*, for we were no longer in a relationship of the *heart*. My feelings for Randy were still on the surface, but, I knew if I was going to move on with my life, *"we"* meaning *"me"* could not continue on like this. So I had to be the adult and bring an end to Randy's wavering. I wanted to come clean, to break what was left of the emotional bond between us. It was a tad more difficult than I had anticipated, for I was far too weak of a person to let go of the intimacy side of our relationship. It was pathetic, because Randy was not the greatest lover in the world, but he was dependable and a warm body. In spite of his faults, Randy was someone I was comfortable with, and as I'd mentioned before, I was *not* ready to play the dating game again. And to complicate matters even more, Randy was aware of my weaknesses and as long as he continued to come around I would keep on letting my emotions fool me into believing we had a possible future together. I kept falling into the trap of letting my emotions rule me to satisfy my sexual needs each time he came to visit and I knew I had to put a stop to it.

Prior to meeting Randy, I'd been celibate for nearly a year and I knew I could abstain from sex. Male chauvinist or not, Randy was a nice guy and he knew how to treat a woman. Now don't get me wrong, simply because I enjoy making love to a man doesn't make me a *nymphomaniac*. I think of myself as a normal human being with a healthy sexual appetite. After all, I wasn't spreading my legs wide for every man I met. To me, sex wasn't pleasurable unless there was an emotional connection between me and my lover. If I'm not feeling it in my heart, then I'm not feeling it any other place. I was relieved, when after three months of our initial *"breakup"* Randy finally accepted a teaching position in Spain. Anyone else would have thought that was the end of it all, but it didn't stop Randy from trying to give it one more shot. He pulled out all the stops, inviting me to join him in Spain, even claiming he no longer wanted children. But it was way too late for us by then for the emotional bond had been broken.

So, much to my disappointment and after all was said and done, here I was, thrown back into the dating game only to realize the rules of dating hadn't changed much from two years ago, except the players had gotten a lot younger. I was searching for what most women seem to be looking for, a strapping knight in shining armor to come and sweep them off their feet and carry them off to a large castle on a hill where they would live happily ever after; talk about a fairytale. I'd given up on the knight, but still, I didn't want to settle for just any man, like some of my friends had. But then again, when I think about it I believe that was exactly what I had done with Randy.

In my opinion it seemed the majority of African American men in California had a certain attitude toward African American women who were not of a certain skin tone. It appeared to me, African American men were still in search of the perfect *"African American"* woman who could pass for white, or with a certain percentage of white blood in their ancestry or as my son Anthony referred to as *"Caucasoid."* These so called African American women had to come equipped with all the perks of a White Woman, such as long flowing hair, thin lips pumped up with collagen, and green, blue or light brown eyes on any given clear day. Now, don't get me wrong, I'm not knocking African American men for wanting White Women. But like the saying goes *"to each his own"* and I do applaud African American women who have finally realized that men, like women, also come in different shapes, sizes, and colors. As I had once explained to a coworker, there seemed to be a shortage of decent Black men in the area, and it was becoming commonplace to see couples of different races together these days; not just Black men, but also Black women. Me, I really didn't care about the race thing especially since it looked like it was going to be a long dry season if I sat around waiting for my *Black* Knight to come and sweep me off my feet. My only criteria, besides the fact that he had to be kind, loveable, educated, and employed, was that he would also have to be a part of the human *race*. But on several occasions I could have sworn a couple of my dates behaved as though they where from a different planet.

As far as my looks, well, I've never been considered a knockout "drop-dead" beauty and I definitely wasn't in the *Caucasoid* group. My skin is as dark as a cup of strong roasted coffee, with a touch of cream, and my lips, well let's just say there is no collagen in these babies, my lips were naturally full. My hair is kinky, and after two children, I'd lost my *girlish* figure quite some time ago. Now don't get me wrong, I'm not hard on the eyes. I control my kinky hair by chemically relaxing it, and thank God and modern science for the invention of African American hair care products. If I could, I would send a kiss to all my hair stylists with whom I had visited in my lifetime for, thanks to them I've never had a bad hair day, so my hair is always whipped. And because of my visits to the gym I was toned in all the right places and my waistline wasn't bad either, plainly due to my daily workout at the gym. Be it far from me to admit this, but due to childbirth and my age, my breasts had lost their *spunk* quite some time ago. But thanks to a very gifted plastic surgeon and quite a bit of money, my "C" cup was back again, and my *girls* had regained their perkiness!

My clothing was the best I could afford to buy on my salary, which wasn't too shabby as Senior Marketing Director for a large recruiting firm, and I dressed appropriately for my size, so my size twelve body was always well draped, and with my height of five-feet-eight inches in my stocking feet, I looked like I weighed a lot less than I actually did. I definitely knew how to work with the package God had given me, and had learned to embrace my looks along with a little help from my friendly neighborhood plastic surgeon. Regrettably, as a teenager, I was not as confident in my looks as I am today. Growing up I had always felt I was the tallest girl in my glass, and at age twelve I was taller than most of the boys my age. I had always felt tall and awkward and only realized in my college days that I was not an ugly duckling. My grandfather used to tell me I was tall and stately like my grandmother, whom I had only seen in very bad black and white photos of her. My grandfather had passed away during my first year of college, but during visits home for the holidays, my grandfather had his way of greeting me by saying, "baby girl, you sure are easy on the eyes."

I have two wonderful sons, Anthony and Maurice, fathered by my ex-husband of five years, and although I had been the one who had initiated our final separation, which eventually led to divorce, my ex-husband was the one who had been sleeping around with other women. Talk about being stupid. I would never forget the statement he'd made the day I walked out on him. He actually had the audacity to tell me how he had screwed up before and how I hadn't left him on those occasions. He'd even had the nerve to ask me why I was leaving him this time. Well, I didn't know what had opened my eyes and prompted me to leave his butt that day, but now I knew why I'd called it quits; I grew up. I mentally grew up. After all was said and done, I'd come to the conclusion that all I ever really wanted was to be happy in my life here on earth. I'd decided life was just too damn short to wake up miserable every morning, which was exactly what I'd been doing for those five years of my marriage. There was a whole world out there of new experiences and caring people and I wanted to be a part of the universe, or so I had thought. I soon discovered that I wasn't as prepared as I thought I was. Needless to say, in the beginning, life on my own proved to be quite difficult, especially with two young children. But, I've always been honest in telling people how I have never regretted a day since I left my ex-husband and I would do it again in a heartbeat if I had to. Those five years weren't a total lost though; my two sons are living proof to that.

CHAPTER TWO

Today is one of the many reasons why I live here in San Diego. The sun is high in the clear blue sky with an occasional cluster of white puffs of clouds thrown in and the view from the Egg Roll, which sits on a hill facing downtown, and the way downtown was situated on the ocean, with it's skyscrapers, and on a clear day such as today, the view was even more striking. It was just warm enough to sit outside and enjoy the afternoon sun, but still chilly enough to need a sweater or light jacket if you should get caught in the shade of one of the many tall buildings spotting the downtown area. But today, my coworker and friend, Claudia and I where sitting inside my favorite Chinese restaurant, "The Egg Roll," which just so happens to be owned and operated by my long time good friend Sonny Steward.

Claudia is the perfect depiction of a *Caucasoid*, the so called *perfect* African American female, whose father is African American and mother is European. Claudia doesn't consider herself to be either White or Black and for some strange reason *"claims"* she despises Black men, especially those whose skin tone is not as *"light"* as her own. I've met her parents on several occasions and know her father well enough to say his skin is so dark, black clothes look brown on him and I'm still trying to figure out how Claudia came to the conclusion she was of neither race.

Claudia and I had met on the job, becoming co-workers first, and then happy hour buddies. Claudia was the type that likes to invite herself to gatherings if she thought it would be in her best interest. Claudia could be very interesting at times and the girl could come up with some of the craziest sayings I'd ever heard. Claudia would go from making you laugh to getting on your last nerve, but after a while Claudia's little antics sort of grew on you, and we all learned to tolerate her. In the early years Claudia had been fun to hang out with, but recently she had become too much to take, During the past few months something had changed in her life and I couldn't quite put my finger on what had caused this change in her. Whenever I questioned Claudia about this change, she would always fringed stress or issues with her parents, or as in most cases Claudia would simply change the subject. Claudia has always been coarse, but lately her coarseness had grown worse.

But with having so much on my own plate, being busy keeping my two teenage sons on the right track, and working on starting my own recruiting office, I had let the subject drop. After all, what could possibly be troubling Claudia? She had it all. Claudia was from a very prominent family, and she had no children to stress over. Claudia never struggled a day in her life. She had no debt to worry about, everything she owned was paid for, so what did she have to worry about? Everything had been given to her on a silver platter either by her parents or her grandfather. Recently my life had been one big struggle and babysitting Claudia was not my idea of fun.

Waiting for our meal to arrive, I thought I'd pass the time by filling out the required release forms for my youngest son Maurice, to attend basketball camp this summer. Even with my head down I could feel Claudia's eyes on me and I knew she was probably wondering why she was not the center of my attention. I had almost completed the paperwork, and was about to convey this to Claudia, but as I looked up, a fine looking Black man caught my attention. He was being shown to a table in clear view not far from the table were Claudia and I sat. A quick look around the room, and I noticed several other women in the room had noticed him as well. I glanced over at Claudia just in time to see her roll her eyes skyward, as she made her habitual sound, which was irritating as well, loudly sucking air in through her teeth. I took a deep breath, bracing myself for what was to come next. Lowering my head and going back to studying the application, I feigned disinterest as I waited for Claudia to say something negative about the man.

"Now what the hell is that ugly *termite* staring at? I can't go fucking anywhere and relax without some *termite* staring at me like he ain't ever seen a woman before. Shit, I swear. I get so damn sick and tired of grown men behaving like idiots. Don't you? Mia?"

"What?" I'd heard Claudia the first time, but I wasn't in the mood to deal with her negative attitude at the moment. Sometimes Claudia's attitude was so bad it made her an ugly person, and Claudia was anything but ugly. But once she got going on a subject she would go on and on about every petty little thing.

"What the hell are you doing anyway? Damn, I thought we'd agreed not to bring our work to lunch," Claudia said with a nauseating expression.

I wanted to say, *"Girl, please don't make that face,"* but instead I said, "It isn't work," which it wasn't, "this is Maurice's application to attend basketball camp this summer," I finished my statement without as much as an upward glance, as I heard Claudia smacking her lips, clearly, disgusted with me for working on what was supposed to be her time.

"Correct me if I'm wrong, but, ain't Maurice old enough to fill out his own damn paperwork? I swear, Mia, you treat those boys like babies instead of their ages. How old is Maurice anyway, 18?"

I silently counted to ten before speaking, as I placed my pen down on the table and gave Claudia a long penetrating glare. A look I normally held in reserve for my sons whenever they got out of line. It was just long enough to cause Claudia to glance away and mumble something incomprehensible, and I knew I had succeeded in making Claudia uneasy from my scrutiny. Claudia looked down and began fussing with her place settings, as she rearranged the fork several times. I took my time replying to her question, choosing instead to neatly place the application back into the large white envelope, all complete for Maurice to deliver to his school the next day. I spoke slowly with a shake of my head to each word. "Maurice is 16 and he needs a physical this summer to prove he is fit for the rigors of training in basketball camp," I replied, repeating the exact words that just so happen to be the first sentence listed on the application. Claudia gave up her fidgeting and attentively set back. "I don't mind filling out my son's application since I know his medical history better than he does," I said, as I briefly closed my eyes and rubbed the bridge of nose. I watched Claudia from beneath my lashes as she gave a loud sigh, before leaning forward in her chair, as she prepared to speak. I cut her off with a question. "What is it to you anyway, Claudia? I'm not putting you out by filling out these forms. Our lunch isn't even here yet," I finished, as I turned my head to one side for a quick glance around the busy restaurant.

"Shit, then why the hell did you invite me to lunch, and then ignore me?" Claudia asked, folding her arms across her chest, lowering her head and looking intently into my eyes.

"I'm not ignoring you," I replied, adding a little humor to my voice, shuffling away the rest of the paperwork that littered the table before me. "I thought I'd get this out of the way before we ate. There," I said as I stuffed the last of the papers back into my old tattered briefcase and snapping it shut. I decided to lighten up a bit; after all, Claudia didn't have too many people she could call friends. "You have my full attention now, Ms. Claudia." I slid my briefcase out of the way, placing it on the floor between the wall and the table, and with a contemptuous look I gave Claudia a big smile.

"I thought Sonya was joining us?" Claudia asked, suddenly in a better mood now that she was my focus.

"Nope, she had to leave early today, her daughter's sick," I replied as I took a sip of my iced tea.

"Damn, she is one sickly child. What's wrong with her ass this time? Oh good, *finally*, here comes our order. Is it me, or are they slow as molasses today? Damn, I could have made this shit myself and I can't even cook," Claudia said quite loudly. Her complaint summoned the waiter to step up the pace as he moved toward our table balancing a tray of food high on his right shoulder.

"I didn't ask Sonya what the problem was this time," I replied as our waiter sat our lunch out onto the table. I hadn't realized just how hungry I was until the familiar aromas from the hot food bathed my senses with their delicious fragrance making my stomach rumble in anticipation. I had ordered my favorites, fried rice, cashew chicken, and broccoli beef. This was the only place to be in San Diego for good Chinese food. The food was always superior to any other place and the servings plentiful.

"Oooh, I'm gonna gain *fifty* pounds from eating all this shit if I'm not careful. I don't want to have to turn sideways like Sonya to get her big black ass through a doorway." Claudia remarked chuckling as she served herself large portions from each of her dishes.

I shook my head, here we go again, time to stroke Claudia's ego. "What you meant to say, as big as Sonya and *me!* Anyway, Claudia, you don't have to worry about weight gain. You're one of those small boned people." Small boned with a big mouth, I thought, serving up some rice on my plate.

"Uh-naw, Girl, you're nowhere as *big* as Sonya. At least you try and work out once in a while. Damn I'll have to do an extra step class after this meal," Claudia proclaimed with a loud laugh.

Uh-huh, here we go again. She's in her element now I thought to myself as Claudia went into her daily workout routine and how at our age we had to work out…blah, blah, and blah. I'd heard this so many times before I could write a book about it. I drifted off to my own little world while giving Claudia an occasional head nod punctuated with an '*oh* or *yeah*' or some other agreeable sound to appease her. Claudia would talk about her workout routine for hours before noticing my eyes had glazed over. In fact, on a few occasions when Claudia had called me at home, and if I sensed it was going to be one of her long drawn-out calls, I'd place her call on speaker phone, freeing my hands up as she chatted away. During these calls, I would reply with a *"really"* or *"stop it"* every now and again and Claudia would talk about herself for hours. Typically, Claudia called right around bedtime and I can usually roll my hair or polish my nails while she went on about her latest conquest or how bad the sex was. Rarely did Claudia call me to talk about the last time she had good sex.

With Claudia tuned out, I begin to enjoy my lunch, with an occasional glance around the crowded dining room to keep me alert, thinking how much in popularity this place had grown in the last six years. I was so happy and proud of the way Sonny had hung in there and made this place what it was today. Sonny had created a diamond out of the rough. The building had been purchased dirt cheap, because it had been in such bad condition and Sonny had practically rebuilt it with his bare hands, along with help from his family, and me and my two sons. We had spent many weekends helping Sonny tear down rotting walls, dig up old mildewed and warped floorings, rebuild, prime, and paint until we were black and blue. I remembered the way the restaurant looked ten years ago when Sonny first opened it, and how slow business had been in the beginning. But now reservations were needed for lunch and dinner every day of the week. I felt fortunate because no matter what day or time, there was always a table ready for me. I guess all of our hard work had really paid off.

I don't know what it was, but despite my efforts to be polite, my eyes were constantly drawn over to "Mr. Good-looking" seated in the corner. I guess you could say my eyes were the needle on a compass and he was the magnet and I was meant to head in his direction. A flash of delight ran though my body when he caught me checking him out. I felt embarrassed but, I had also noticed how he kept glancing over at our table as well. Probably had his eyes on Ms. Claudia and I couldn't blame him.

Claudia's dark brown thick wavy hair flowed midway down her back, reminiscent of the 80s' Vogue girls. This look didn't seem appropriate for this day and age but it drove men wild. Her breasts, courtesy of our friendly neighborhood plastic surgeon (Claudia had decided to go with implants), also seemed to be disproportionate to her petite frame and slender waist, but she loved the attention from the men even though she complained about the stares. Claudia never seemed to notice the men always introduced themselves to her breasts first. Her waist, which was made slimmer by her nice round *Black* booty(I'm sure a gift from her father's side of the family), which was not too big to scrape the doorway as she passed through it, but just big enough to catch the drool as it dripped from the mouth of men in passing. Today her hair was pulled back into a bun, which highlighted her magnificent face, showing off her full ruby red cherubic lips, large round eyes, flawlessly lined and her long lashes lengthen even more with black mascara. And, in the middle, her long nose perfectly aligned after her last nose job. Claudia was the "super model" you could bring home to mom and not get into trouble for dating a *White* woman. That is until she opened her mouth. It was rare for Claudia to speak in a complete sentence without using a four-lettered word. She spoke like an angry sailor going down with the ship. It appeared every fourth word which poured from her mouth was a four-lettered word usually starting with, "*Fuck.*" It wasn't the way she talked, but how she would say certain things. At work, we usually had to stop her from finishing her sentences, or remind her she was in public, or if there were any young children present in the room.

"Mia? Damn, are you listening to me?" Claudia asked, clearly annoyed as she interrupted my train of thought, waving her napkin at me like she was flagging down a taxi on one of the busy downtown streets.

"Yes I am," I replied as I took a long drink from my glass of tea, to hide my smirk and put the last five words I'd heard from her into a usable sentence, but before I could speak, Claudia went on a different rampage.

"What the fuck is that ugly *termite* looking at any way?" Claudia asked as she leaned in closer to me.

"Claudia," I began, as I glanced around the room. "I wish you wouldn't use that word."

"That man don't know what the hell I'm talking about, duh?" Claudia said as she sat back in her chair crossing her arms and looking down at me. "Anyway, that's what he looks like with his beady little black eyes—a fucking termite."

"Claudia, you wouldn't know a termite if it bit you. Who are you talking about anyway?" I asked scanning the room. *Termite* was the word Claudia used when referring to what she deemed as an unattractive and unemployed *Black* male.

"Shit, Mia, are you blind or what? The *termite* sitting over there in the corner, over there," she said with a quick nod of her head. "Look at him, with his black ass. Staring at us and licking his big old rusty lips like he just got out of prison or something. *Girlll,* he's looking at us like he wants to eat us up or something."

I shook my head. How did she come up with this stuff? "Sweetheart, you need to put your glasses on because that man is not ugly, he doesn't look poor, and there is nothing wrong with his eyes either."

"Uh-huh. I know his type: minimum wage job, no money, and anyway, all he probably wants is a damn booty call, and most likely he expects you to pay his ass after it's over. What the fuck is he doing in an upper class neighborhood in the middle of the day anyway? There must be a damn rent-to-own furniture delivery truck in the parking lot, and I bet you any minute now we'll see two of his furniture hauling ass homeys giving him the signal his fucking break is over and it's time to get his black ass back to work."

I shook my head, embarrassed at her words. "The man is probably here for the same reason we are, *having lunch*. How are you going to assume he can't afford to eat here because he's Black? Sweetheart, look at the way he's dressed, does that look like a uniform he's wearing?"

"Trust me on this one, Mia; you don't want to get involved with him. I know his type, broke and homeless. Somebody's baby's daddy, probably with ten kids, by ten different women no doubt, and I bet you big money he still lives at home with his mama, the fucking *termite*."

I slowly shook my head. "You are too much. How do you come up with these things anyway? And as far as him checking me out, he's hardly looking at me, not with you sitting here next to me. You know how Black men always go for *your* type. He has his eye on you, *Ms. Thang*, not me."

"No he ain't," Claudia replied with a shake of her head. "I hope not cause honey he will definitely get his little itty bitty feelings hurt today. *Shitt*."

"Claudia, what do you have against Black men? I mean after all your dad-"

"I know my daddy is *Black!*" Claudia replied as she shoved her plate across the table as she turned to the side to look away. "I never said I didn't like Black men, and I have nothing against them as long as they are not lazy fucking bums sitting out on the porch or standing on the corner all day long sucking on a fucking 40-ounce. What's wrong with me wanting an intelligent good looking man with a *good* j-o-b? Hell, so far all the ones I've ever met wanted me to support their lazy asses."

"Claudia, you'd better stop your lying," I said as I threw my hands in the air.

"Well maybe not all of them, but half the guys I've dated were lazy ass good for nothing bums."

"So? And whose fault was that? No one told you to choose them."

"I'm ready to go," Claudia said grabbing her purse from the extra chair at the table.

"Ladies, how was lunch?" A deep familiar voice asked.

I looked up into the violet eyes of the handsome man smiling over me. I return the smile of my friend Sonny Steward. He was not your ordinary chef, he was tall, well built and with years of martial arts Sonny had crafted his body into a strong and muscular fighting machine, which was how Sonny always described himself. Sonny resembled his Korean mother with his slightly almond shaped eyes, and his golden skin, very striking against the whiteness of his teeth. His tall stature was inherited from his European father. Sonny kept his hair cut close to his perfectly rounded head, almost bald. Sonny always boasted how he had the best of three worlds, an Asian mother, a European father and an African American best friend. His motto on the wall outside of his restaurant bragged it was the best place in town for Asian food with a touch of soul.

I loved his smart style; his clothes were always pressed and fit as if custom made. Today his black dress slacks with cuffs, fit him so well the crease in his slacks ran straight up and disappeared just below his firm buttocks. He wore dress shirts in various styles and always with a fashionable tie, hanging on his muscular chest. When not at work, Sonny wore polo or Hawaiian style shirts and khaki pants or jeans, he was always so neat. His shoes were always the loafer type, and he sported sandals or tennis shoes during the warmer months.

Sonny taught martial arts at his parents' dojo when time permitted. He also volunteered at the Community Center twice a month, working with inner-city children. Sonny had trained with Anthony and Maurice at his parents' dojo, and was trying to persuade my oldest son Anthony to join the staff as a full time instructor when Anthony wasn't busy playing football. There was no doubt about it; Sonny was the nicest, kindest, sexiest, even-tempered, and the bravest man I'd ever known. Just watching him and seeing his smile, lit up my day. I was truly lucky to have such a friend as he.

"Here you are, my favorite chef. Sonny, the food here is always great," I replied as Sonny leaned over and gave me a light kiss upon my lips. The familiar scent of his cologne brought back many pleasant memories of our time together. "How've you been and how's Macey?" I asked, and I could have sworn Sonny blushed. "How was your honeymoon?" I teased. Sonny had recently returned from a short break from the restaurant, spending time with his new wife, Macey.

"I'm good, and Macey is doing well, thank you. Taking an additional week off from this place was exactly what I needed. Oh, Mia, before I forget, Macey and I are having a little get together next month, you're coming right?"

"Sonny, you know I'll be there. Baby, I wouldn't miss it for the world," I replied as I gave his hard arm an affectionate squeeze.

"Claudia, what about you, do you think you'll be able to grace our humble event with your loveliness?" It was no surprise to anyone who hung out with our little group that Sonny had a knack for getting on Claudia's wrong side, and Claudia couldn't stand Sonny either.

"Maybe, I'll see. We were waiting for our check," Claudia said rather impatiently.

"It's already been taken care of," Sonny said as he bowed his head at me and smiled.

"Well, thanks, Sonny. Now I know why this is my favorite restaurant, and of course it can't hurt to know the owner," I said with a chuckle as I began to gather my own things.

"Oh, don't thank me, it was taken care of by the gentleman right over there," Sonny said as he pointed toward the table in the corner where the chocolate brother sat.

"Thank you," I mouthed, along with a nod of my head and a smile, as I rose and prepared to leave the table.

"*Whatevah!*" Claudia hissed under her breath as she snatched up her blazer and was out the door before I had chance to gather up the rest of my things. "Mia, I'll give you a ring later on, maybe we can catch a movie or something," she called out as she headed for her car.

As I was unlocking my car door, I heard my name called out. On looking up, I discovered Sonny jogging across the parking lot toward me, with my old battered briefcase in his hand. "Thank you," I said as I reached out for my old case.

"No problem, babe, and this," Sonny said, as he placed a business card into my hand, "is for you. It's from the guy who picked up your lunch tab. He wanted me to make sure you, and only you received his card. See you at the game tonight. "Oh, and by the way, your invitation is in the mail, and, Mia, please don't forget to read your invitation. I know how you like to leave everything to the last minute." Sonny said as he gave me a quick hug before turning and walking away.

I glanced down at the business card, noticing it was for a landscaping and pool care service. The card boosted the company had been in business for over seven years, and the owner's name was Blair J. Freeman. I slipped it into my purse; just as my cell phone rang. "Hello?"

"Hey, I forgot to ask if you were coming back to the office after your meeting this afternoon." Claudia asked. We had taken separate cars for I had an offsite meeting to attend which would keep me out of the office for the rest of the day.

"No," I replied shaking of my head. "I won't be back today. Can we do the movie thing tomorrow night? Sonny just reminded me Maurice has a basketball game tonight."

"Sure, girl, no problem. What did old nosey ass Sonny want?"

Talk about the pot calling the kettle black. Claudia had always been envious of my friendship with Sonny. From the first time I'd introduced them, she wanted to know what Sonny and I could possibly have in common, especially after Sonny had shown no interest in Claudia whatsoever. "He returned my briefcase which I'd left at the restaurant. Here's something interesting, Sonny gave me a business card from the guy who treated us to lunch," I said as I pulled out of the driveway and onto the busy street.

"Well, honey, I don't want it," Claudia said, her voice filled with disgust. "You can keep the damn thing."

17

Her distaste for the man in the restaurant was quite obvious. At first I was just going to let Claudia's little comment slide, but I just as quickly changed my mind. "Oh, I intend to keep it, and from what I understand, Sonny was instructed to give the card to me and only me." I smiled, thinking how I would love to see her face right about now.

"Well excuse me. I'll call you later then, bye."

"Right." Claudia will definitely have an attitude tomorrow night. As far as Claudia was concerned, if a man wasn't interested in her, then something must be wrong with the man. Claudia played the same old game. First she would put the guy down, dog him out and then label him a poor lazy ass loser, wiping out her competition in case she thought someone else was interested. Then the next day Claudia would brag about how the guy had begged her for her phone number, and how she had decided to give him one of her "trial runs." It never failed; it was always Claudia's way or no way.

As I headed for my afternoon meeting, my thoughts drifted back to my friend and co-worker, Sonya and her twelve-year-old daughter, Tameka. I decided to give her a call to ensure all was well with her daughter. "Call Sonya, home," I said to activate the voice mode on my cell phone. Tameka had a severe case of asthma, and although she frequently used breathing machines on a nightly basis, and had recently begun taking steroids, her condition seemed to be worsening instead of getting better. This was Tameka's third trip to the emergency room this month. Sonya wasn't in, so I left a message, offering my services if she needed anything. I was feeling a little sad for Sonya and her daughter Tameka, so I said a quick prayer for them.

"Mom! Uncle Sonny! I'm glad you two could make it," Maurice called out as he ran up the bleacher steps to where Sonny and I sat, and took a seat down beside me. Maurice reached around me to shake hands with Sonny. "When did you get back, Uncle Sonny?"

"Yesterday. You played a damn good game tonight, Maurice. I was telling your mom what an excellent player you've become. I remember the first day you joined my Cub Scout troop. You were this round chubby little boy with a big head, and now look at you, you're as tall as a tree, and you play ball like one of the pros," Sonny said while shaking Maurice's hand.

"Thanks, Uncle Sonny," Maurice said with a big blushing smile. "And just for the record, Uncle Sonny, you don't always have to bring up the Cub Scout story, okay?"

Sonny laughed, as he pulled Maurice into a bear hug with me practically in the middle as I leaned back to avoid being crushed. "Hey, what kind of an uncle would I be if I didn't embarrass you from time to time?"

"How about just being my favorite uncle? Mom, is it okay if I go out with the team tonight? We're going over to Jimmy's Grill to grab a bite to eat and hang out afterwards for a little bit."

"As long as you get home before curfew," I replied, not wanting Maurice to stay out pass his curfew. It wasn't that I didn't trust him, but groups of male teenagers had a tendency to get into mischief when hanging out together no matter what their social status was. My biggest fear was to read about how some ignorant person would drive by and shoot into a crowd just because they found their parents gun under the mattress and they had nothing else better to do that night.

"Mom, it's Friday night, and it's almost nine now. By the time I hit the gym for a shower, and make it over to Jimmy's it'll be ten. Come on, mom. Please, make it twelve and you've got a deal," Maurice pleaded.

"Here's the deal, eleven o'clock, take it or leave it, Maurice," I said, giving him fake grin.

"Dag-"

"Maurice."

"Okay, see you at eleven then," Maurice said as he planted a wet kiss upon my cheek. "Catch you later, Uncle Sonny."

"Your sons grew up to be good young men," Sonny said later on as we strolled to our cars.

"You helped," I replied reaching out for his hand, as I remembered how much of a hand Sonny had in the raising of my two sons, for with his guidance, my sons were headed in the right direction. Sonny had been in my life a long time. We met when we were neighbors, living next door to each other and at one time we even shared the same apartment. It was during the time we were struggling, Sonny just out of college and trying to open his restaurant, and me, a divorcee with two young children. We became as close as a man and woman could be without becoming intimate. Once or twice, we had considered that type of relationship, but somehow, the time was never right for us. It was always one thing or the other. When I was involved with someone, Sonny was free, and when I was free, Sonny was involved. Then when Sonny started working on his business full-time, he was putting in long hours, seven days a week. Some days Sonny didn't even have time to sleep and eat, not to mention starting a relationship. He would come home exhausted, sometimes in the wee hours of the night. Poor baby, I remembered when I used to do his laundry along with the boys because he was often to busy to keep his clothes clean. And when I finally got my dream job, it was long days of working overtime for me. Eventually our friendship grew in a different direction, and we had grown to be the best of friends. But, through it all, we've always been there for the other.

"You call him yet?" Sonny asked as he placed his arm about my shoulder, pulling me close to his side.

"And who would that be?" I asked, as I leaned into him laying my head on his shoulder. Sonny had been the earthly foundation of my life for so many years that being this close to him was quite natural for us. Whenever we happened to walk together we would usually hold hands, or walk arm-in-arm, or like now, with his arm about my shoulders.

"Blair. You know, the guy who bought you lunch today."

"Do you know him well?" I asked, pulling back a bit to look up at his face.

"Well, sort of. He teaches classes with me at the Community Center. You should call him, he's a nice guy and he's available."

"Really?" I asked cocking my head to one side, and giving Sonny a long look. "How long have you known him?"

"For almost a year now, don't you remember me telling you about him?"

"No. You've known him for almost a year, huh? So, how come I've never met him before now?"

"That's because you were too busy hanging out with the nutty professor. Frankly I am glad your nutty buddy is gone. You know, you were too good for him, Mia, I never liked him."

"Sonny, I knew you disliked Randy, something you've never been shy about telling me. Now stop trying to change the subject," I replied as we came to a stop next to my car.

"By the way, take it as a compliment. Call Blair, I told him all about you." Sonny gave me a long hug followed by a quick kiss to my lips, and then he waited for me to start my car and drive away, before turning away to find his car.

"Sonny! You know I hate being fixed up," I called out as I drove by with a toot of my horn.

"Drive carefully," he replied with a wave of his hand, followed by a devious sounding laugh.

I never got around to calling Sonny's friend Blair that night, and it would be well over a month before I would even see him again. For, when I returned home from the basketball game there had been a message waiting from Sonya. Tameka was being kept overnight at the hospital for observation, and Sonya had decided to remain with her. Sonya needed me to stop by her place to pick up a change of clothing for her and her daughter. By the time I'd made it back home from the hospital, Maurice was already at home in the bed.

Saturday morning started off at a run. Anthony was supposed to stop by and take Maurice to the DMV for his drivers test, but one of his coworkers hadn't shown up at work and Anthony had to work his shift at the video store. Since Anthony was in competition for the assistant manager position, he couldn't refuse not to work and he wasn't able to leave work until after four. I would have postponed Maurice's driving test for another day but Maurice had just turned 16 and waiting another day would have driven us all mad. So I had ended up taking Maurice to the DMV and we had to stand in line for over two hours.

After the torment of hanging out at the DMV my morning was shot to hell. I ran my usual Saturday errands and was almost late for my hair appointment, pedicure and a fill. I decided to have an early dinner with Maurice and by the time we made it back to the condo, Anthony was home waiting for us, and he and Maurice decided to catch a movie as well. I barely had time to shower and freshen up before Claudia showed up for our movie date. Calling Blair was the last thing on my mind, and the business card Sonny had given me had descended deep into the depths of my purse. Out of sight and out of mind.

CHAPTER THREE

Shortly after exiting Interstate 8, I was looking for Black Walnut Drive which seemed to take me forever to find. I spotted the sign covered by long leafless branches, which looked like it read "B-ack al," I assumed it was Black Walnut. I was not about to exit my car in this dark place to get a closer inspection of the sign. As I turned onto the rough uneven dirt road, I could see the moon moving behind the clouds through the withered tree limbs overhead. The branches seemed to wave madly in the wind forming a cryptic arch against the sky. I slowed my car down to a crawl to maneuver down the narrowing road with only darkness ahead of me. It was during this time when my thoughts drifted to another point in time and I was sure this road was taking me to some mysterious area in the middle of nowhere where a UFO was waiting to beam me aboard and I could only hope to see my family and friends again. The road was now too narrow for me to even consider making a u-turn and flooring it back in the direction of Interstate 8 and the bright lights of the city. Shadows from the enraged trees danced above as the clouds covered the only familiar light from the moon. I looked behind me and I could barely catch a glimpse of the lights from Interstate 8. Now I was uncertain if I was on the right road or not.

I slowed my car to almost to a crawl, as I took the next turn, where the road dipped into a small gorge with a tiny stream running across it. I felt a sense of urgency as I pleaded for a place to turn around but the road began to climb upward. The few homes I'd seen earlier in the area were no longer visible through the dense trees. I was alone on the road, no street lights, no homes, and no people.

I guess this is what I get for not paying attention to the invitation which I should have opened and read on the day I received it in the mail. I shouldn't have assumed it was going to be at Sonny's or at

The Egg Roll. I had wasted so much time searching for my car keys and only after Maurice had decided to read glance at the invitation for me, was when it had been brought to my attention that the party was not at any of the two places I was familiar with, but at an address in Alpine of all places, which was a good hours' ride or so from downtown depending on traffic. I couldn't recall Sonny telling me he'd moved out to the Alpine area, way out here in the middle of nowhere. Maybe he wanted to surprise us all with one big housewarming party I told myself to ease the tension.

I slammed down hard on the brakes just as the road ahead of me appeared as if it were coming to a dead end, but instead, the road dipped downward again. As I drove further along I came to a large steel gate hung between two large stucco pillars. On the gate hung a sign which stated the road beyond was private and trespassers would be prosecuted to the fullest extent. Right now getting busted for trespassing seem like a pretty good idea to me, at least I wouldn't be out here alone. Then, seemingly out of the darkness, a man appeared in front of my car startling me. He was holding a flashlight over his shoulder and waving the light in front of my car. I let out an uneasy chuckle. After I'd come to a complete stop, he rapped on my window with the butt end of the flashlight. I was relieved to see another human being out here, but I was still a little uneasy about what he was doing out here on foot in the middle of the boonies. I could only come to the conclusion that I was lost in the sticks on this man's land.

As I rolled my window down a hair, I noticed he was carrying a clipboard in his other hand. I instinctively yelled out, "I-I think I'm lost" it was then I become aware of the white SUV sitting parallel to the fence. As he leaned over, the man illuminated the clipboard with his flashlight.

"Good evening, may I have your name please?" he asked

Now I was really confused. "Is this the Steward residence?" I asked with a bit of an attitude for I was beginning to become agitated about this whole thing.

"No, Miss. May I have your name please?"

"I'm sorry, I think I'm lost. I was searching for the Steward residence," I replied as I shifted the gear into reverse.

"The Steward party is being held here," he said with a nod.

Okay, so I was in the right place. I boldly rolled my window all the way down. "Mia Harris." When Sonny invited me to his party he never mentioned anything about his party being held way out here in an abandoned manor. Although I hadn't spoken to him in over three days, we normally spoke at least two to three times a day. I was surprised Sonny hadn't called to make sure I had the correct directions, or to make sure if I'd paid attention to the invitation, as he had informed me to do, or offer me a ride to the party. Oh, well, I guess that's what happens when your best friend gets married, and you become his second best friend. I really liked Macey, although in the beginning we did have our mistrust of one another. I thought she wasn't good enough for Sonny, and she thought Sonny and I had once been an item.

"Thank you, Ms. Harris," the man said stepping away from my car. With a shudder and a screech the gate swung open. I drove up the darken drive unsure of where the hell I was and what was Sonny thinking having his party out here in the middle of no man's land? I rounded a bend and the sight before me took my breath away. There were Japanese lanterns everywhere; they were hanging from the eaves of the large one story Mediterranean house, lining the long cobble stone driveway leading up to the arched covered entrance, and hanging in the two large trees flanking the front yard. The moon was also doing its part tonight as it dangled high over the house and the stars shone above the estate like a welcome beacon. I was sure I would see Don Quixote riding over the hill which was to the side of the house, sitting tall on his white horse, helmet high on his head and with his long staff in hand. I stop under the covered terrace behind several other cars, and my door was opened by a valet.

"Good evening, Ms. Harris."

"Good evening," I said a bit surprised that he knew my name. "How do you know my name?" I asked looking up into the face of a very attractive African American valet.

"Two-way radio," he said holding up a black oblong object in his hand. "Jeremy told me you were on your way to the house," he said with a smile. "This way please." He led me to the wide steps leading to the huge double front doors of the house, rang the bell and stepped away. "Have a pleasant evening."

Before I could answer, the door swung open and I was greeted by a Hispanic gentleman, with an even bigger smile on his face as he ushered me inside.

"Welcome, Ms. Harris, the other guests are expecting you out on the terrace. If you will follow me, please?" he nodded with an extravagant wave of his hand.

The house was beautiful. I took in the surroundings as I followed along behind the butler. The house was even more magnificent on the inside. On our way out to the terrace we passed a huge formal dining room where the caterers were setting up for dinner. I stopped and spared a brief second, watching as they dashed about the large round table laden with food. My stomach rumbled loudly, reminding me my last meal had been some time ago. The aroma of dinner was carried around the room on the breeze, drifting in through the opened French doors lining the wall leading out to the terrace. I followed along behind the butler, through the doors and onto a huge flagstone terrace. Out beyond the doors was a large kidney shaped swimming pool with a miniature water fountain and a hot tub to one side of it, and more Japanese lanterns lined the terrace. White paper lanterns sitting on green water lilies floated around in the huge pool, and the effect was breathtaking.

"Mia, you made it?"

"Sonny, how are you?" I asked as I turned to greet him, as we exchanged hugs and kisses.

"Excuse me, would you care for something to drink?" The butler asked.

"Yes, an Amaretto Sour, please," I said before turning my attention back to Sonny. I was full of questions. "Sonny, you could have warned me this place was out here in the middle of nowhere."

"I told you to read your invitation," he chastised.

"You know, this place looks fabulous. Did you and Macey buy a new home? No?" I asked as I received a reply of a brief head shake from Sonny. "Did you rent it for the night?" I asked as I looked around the huge yard as it rose upward before disappearing into the darkness. "You got me out here driving around in *no man's land*." But before Sonny had a chance to reply, Macey appeared at his elbow.

"Hi, Mia, isn't this place lovely?' Macey asked as she hung onto Sonny's arm as though to keep him from running away. Macey had the typical Asian look, dark hair cut into a shoulder length bob, and beautiful almond shaped brown eyes, but Macey was anything but typical. Raised by her mother and her aunt, Macey had been a rebellious teenager, giving her guardians ulcers and gray hair before their time. It wasn't until she had moved away to college had Macey learn to respect her Asian heritage and in the end she had went back to her cultural upbringing.

"Macey, how are you? It's stunning. Who lives here?" I asked again as I looked around at the other guests. It wasn't a large gathering, with only about 30 or so people and most of them I recognized as family and friends of Sonny's. There were also a few friends of Macey's whom I'd met before at their wedding, and there were a few new faces I did not recognize. But I did recognize the good-looking man from the restaurant as he made his way over to us. He wore a smile that could stop a clock, and I couldn't help but send one of my big smiles right back at him and I was hoping mine was just as radiant as his was.

"Mia, your drink," Sonny said as his eyes sought out what I was staring at. "Blair," Sonny said with a nod as he removed Macey's arm from his.

Blair was almost upon us and I could feel a tingle go up my back. I quickly ran my tongue over my teeth, just in case my magenta colored lipstick had found its way there. Upon closer inspection, he was even more handsome than I'd remembered. I lifted my head a bit, and stood a little straighter to make sure he had a good view of the *girls* as he stopped before us.

"Blair, I would like to introduce you to my good friend Mia Harris," Sonny said.

"Mia, it's a pleasure to meet you at last," Blair replied as he extended his hand to me. Oh the sound of his smooth deep voice was arousing to my ears.

"Hello, Blair." I slipped my hand into his. I wondered if he was always in the habit of looking so intensely at women. His eyes practically bored into my own, as if only the two of us existed and nothing else mattered. I could feel the scrutiny of his hazel eyes framed by thick crescent shaped eyebrows, looking right through me inquiring of my heart. I was staring so long at him without so much as a blink, which made the lights from the Japanese lanterns behind him appear distorted, turning the lanterns into a blazing fire. I blinked and realized his stare had transformed me to another place and my life before now was just a distant memory. A sea of hopeful desire washed over me as he moved closer. The way he tilted his head enhanced his commanding Roman warrior-like chin. His neatly trimmed mustache framed his sweet full lips, shadowed by his strong nose, which only a man could get away with. His skin tone was a dark mocha color and smooth as if a razor had never swept his cheeks. His hair was cut close to his head as if an outline had been drawn and the hair removed. His rugged chest could be made out from beneath the opening of his leather jacket, as if a Roman breast plate lay beneath his turtleneck sweater. His long arms and rugged hands looked as if they were meant for a knight's sword. His body resembled Sonny's, muscular, taut and very mannish. His stance was that of a proud and confident man. But behind those eyes all I could see was affection. He was *fine*. He was just right. Damn, every part of him screamed, *"Man-man-man!"* From his big hands to his broad chest, wide shoulders and arms bulging from under the black leather sports coat, giving him the appearance that he was made to pick you up and carry you off to his bed-

"Mia?"

I spared Macey a brief glance before answering her, not wanting to tear my eyes away from this fine specimen of a man. Under the leather jacket, Blair was wearing a tan turtleneck sweater, which clung to his chest, and a pair of form fitting black leather pants. Whew, it was a cool night but my temperature began to rise. I had to remind myself to breathe. It took every ounce of will power I could summon up to keep from fanning my face. "What did you say?" I asked, giving Macey a blank stare, and getting ready to question her as to why she was interrupting me.

"Blair was asking you a question," Macey replied with what I perceived to be a curious look on her face.

Good, I get to look at him again. Not even knowing what his question was I looked Blair straight into his beautiful eyes and replied, "Yes." I was ready for whatever it was he wanted of me.

"So your drink's okay?"

"Yes…yes, it's great, thank you," I replied as I took a quick sip from my glass to hide my embarrassment. I was behaving like I'd never seen a man before. I looked over at Sonny who was standing there with a smug grin on his face as well. "My friend Sonya, you remember Sonya, don't you, Macey? Well, her daughter was hospitalized again last night and I was on the phone with Sonya earlier and my mind was kind of preoccupied," I lied. It wasn't entirely a lie, only the part about being on the phone with Sonya. I hadn't spoken with Sonya since this morning but Tameka was back in the hospital again, but at the moment my mind was preoccupied with nothing else but this man standing here before me.

"No problem. I hope all is well with your friend's daughter?" Blair asked.

"It's asthma, really bad case of asthma," I said with a nod of my head as I turned to Sonny for a small piece of safe conversation. "So…Sonny, nice crowd you got here," I said as I shot him a quick smile and a wink as he gave me one of his arched eyebrow responses. It was one of our many wordless codes we sometimes use. My smile and wink was a plea for help and his arched eyebrow reply meant I was on my own.

"You've met everyone before, right?" Macey asked, missing the byplay between us.

I wanted to give Sonny a kick to his shin, but I just smiled sweetly and nodded. "Most." My eyes drifted back to Blair with his gorgeous kissable looking lips.

"Good, I'll be right back," Macey said as she excused herself. "Sonny, are you coming?" Macey grabbed his hand and with a slight jerk tugged Sonny's arm until he got the hint.

"Glad you could make it," Blair said showing off a set of even white teeth with his magnificent smile.

"So am I. So- I understand you and Sonny have known each other for a while?"

Blair nodded his head, taking a sip from his own glass as he glanced around the room. "I've known Sonny off and on for almost a year now. Missed his wedding though, I was out of town on business. That's the reason I decided to throw this little shindig for him tonight, you know, to make up for not attending his wedding. I hope the two of them will forgive me for missing their wedding. Do you think they will forgive me?" Blair asked as his eyes gazed into mine.

He was so smooth I could sip him from a straw. "I would," I replied a little too quickly. I took a long gulp from my glass trying to cover up my nervousness, as I watched him over the rim of my glass. Thoughts of being too old for this kind of behavior ran through my mind. Blair was staring at me attentively, and I begin to wonder if I had looked anything like he did now when I'd been scrutinizing him earlier. He smiled, and I lowered my glass as I returned his smile. He had a beautiful mouth, nice and full, and very kissable. I had to take a deep breath.

"Can I get you another one?" he asked with a nod toward my almost empty glass.

"No thanks. I'm driving and if I don't get some food inside of me soon I'm not going to be responsible for my actions."

"Dinner should be ready. Let me confirm with Macey what time dinner will be served, I'm hungry as well," Blair said as he turned away. Then he quickly did an about face, his eyes holding me in place. "Don't go away, I'll be right back," he said flashing me another one of his striking smiles.

Damn. "I promise I won't go, too far," I said coyly as I lowered my eyelids. I could feel myself blushing as he turned and walked away. "Stop it,' I said out loud as I made my rounds of the terrace, stopping to speak with those of whom I did know. I was still smiling, and at the same time chastising myself for behaving like a schoolgirl. I hadn't openly flirted like this in years. Shameless, and at the same time fun, I'll have to make it a point to flirt more often. It could've been no more than five or ten minutes before Macey popped up at my elbow.

"So, what do you think?" she asked with a huge grin on her face.

"I'm going to kill you, and Sonny. You two set me up." I said in a harsh tone and a teeth-clenching smile, as we made a beeline over to the other side of the pool in search of more privacy.

"But you like him right?" Macey asked as she reached for my hands, holding them and watching me while bending at the knees ready to burst with excitement. I could see Macey was trying to contain herself as we stood there whispering like two teenagers at a high school dance.

"I don't know," I lied, knowing with the whisper of two words my inhibitions would vanish and Blair and I would become one. It wouldn't be merely physical for Blair was the kind of man you could easily fall in love with. I nodded my head, making Macey wait before I spoke. "He's cute," I started as Macey gave me a quizzical look. "Okay, what am I saying? The man is fine, okay? But I don't know him; I mean what kind of a person is he, Macey? I know he owns his own business, but is he a good hearted man? Can he cook?" I asked as we broke into nervous giggles.

"Yes to both questions," Macey replied still holding onto my hands. "I mean on the rare occasions I've been around him, Blair seems to be a very nice man. He is always very pleasant and even tempered. Sonny spends more time with him than I do, so he can tell you more about Blair than I can."

"Okay, does he have children? Or maybe I should be asking if he wants children?" I silently prayed that the answer to my questions would be no. I definitely didn't want this to turn out to be another Randy ordeal. What if Blair already had kids? Although I had two sons of my own, I wasn't sure if I was prepared to share a man who had children of his own, talk about being selfish. Then there was the, what if he wanted children question. If things got serious between us, would I be willing to have another child for him, I mean after all, wasn't that one of the reasons Randy and I had split up? Okay, okay, so I'm getting a little bit ahead of myself, I'll just slow down and go with the flow, no matter where the flow took me.

"Sonny told me Blair doesn't have any children, and I'm not sure if he wants children or not," Macey said with a questioning look on her face.

"So what do you think, Macey?"

"I think Blair's a super guy, and you two make a really nice looking couple," Macey added with a giggle.

"Macey, you are so crazy. Okay, we'll see what happens next. He might not even like me."

"*He does!* Blair and Sonny are in the kitchen right now, talking about *you!* As a matter of fact, the two of them sent me out here to find out what you thought about Blair," Macey said as she started to jump up and down.

"Oh-good-God, Macey, this is so embarrassing. Now what will I say to him? I mean; I'm definitely attracted to him, but what about his personality? What if we're not compatible, what's his sign? Will you please stop it!" I said pulling on her arm, as Macey continued to bounce around on her toes.

"Okay, okay. Ask Blair the same questions you're asking me. You know, about kids, work, sign, that kind of stuff. Also ask him whether or not he can cook. Oh come on, Mia, you're smart, you'll think of something. Come on, let's go and eat. You two make the cutest couple. I wanted to take a picture while you two were standing there gawking at one another, but Sonny told me not to," Macey rambled as she steered me back toward the house.

CHAPTER FOUR

As the evening drew to a close I found a cozy oversized chair in one corner of the large living room. I was sipping on a cup of coffee as I waited for Sonny and Macey to return from seeing the last of their guests out. I'd discovered this gorgeous house belonged to Blair. The large living room was kind of bare but what little furniture it contained was quite expensive and very tasteful. I hadn't noticed how bare the room was earlier because of the crowd. I couldn't get pass the question as to why Sonny had never introduced me to Blair before now. I knew I was dating the professor but our relationship had dwindled up and died almost six months ago, but that has never kept Sonny from introducing me to his friends before. It was strange as well, especially since Sonny disliked Randy from the very first time he'd met him. I was pondering on the above when I was brought out of my reverie by someone clearing their throat.

"*Ahem.*"

Startled I looked up, and stared right into the gorgeous eyes of Mr. Blair J. Freemen. Who had slip in while my thoughts had been elsewhere.

"Hi." I said, flashing him my pearly whites. He smelled nice, too.

"Hi," Blair replied. "Did you have a good time?"

"Yes I did, it was—*entertaining*. What about you, did you have a good time?" I asked as Blair knelt down in front of me.

"Surprisingly, yes," he said with a nod. "I had a pretty good time. At first it was a little slow, but it picked up when you arrived."

Hello! I was thinking the exact same thing, for my night had certainly picked up at the sight of him. "Thank you," I replied with a demure smile and a slight nod.

"You're welcome," Blair said as he sat down on the floor, crossing his long legs in front of him. "It's always nice having Sonny around. I'm glad he's married, maybe Macey will be able to keep him out of trouble and on the right track."

Enough about Sonny and Macey, I wanted to stay with how the evening had picked up at the sight of me. "You sound like you didn't think you were going to have a good time? Why is that?" I asked.

"Well at the time I decided to give Sonny this party, I was trying to make up for missing his wedding. I'm not a partying kind of person and I didn't know what to do or how to even plan for one, so I was happy when Macey offered to plan the whole thing. I have to admit, I'm not exactly a people person so having a lot of strange folks in my home kind of freaked me out at first, but I got used to it and decided to enjoy the company."

He even blinked his eyes in a sexy way.

"You have a lovely home," I said as I looked around the room. "The man at the gate, the valet, and a butler?"

"No, no, they don't work for me. Well they do work for me but not here at the house. They were helping me out for the night," Blair said as I gave him a blank look. "Okay, the guy at the gate, Jeremy, he's the foreman of my business. The valet, Charles, and the butler, his name is Ernesto. They work for me, but not in the roles they had tonight. It was all Maceys' idea. It's so dark and secluded out here Macey thought it would be a nice touch to have someone at the gate and the other two guys. So instead of hiring strangers, I asked the guys if they wanted to make some extra cash and the rest you already know," Blair added with a shrug of his shoulders.

"Nice house." He appeared very relax as he spoke. He had scooted back some, leaning back on his hands, his long legs were now stretched out in front of him. This made a very nice profile of him.

"Thanks, I'm still working on furnishing it, but I'll get there, slowly but surely. Would you like to see the rest of the house?" he asked as he stood and offered his hand to me.

"Yes I would, thank you," I began, just as Sonny entered the room.

"Well, that's the last of them," Sonny called out as he rubbed his hands together. "The caterer has packed up and left, Jeremy dropped off the remote for the gate, and he and the other guys headed out about five minutes ago." Sonny lowered himself down onto the sofa into a half reclining half sitting position, looking up at me as he narrowed his eyes.

"What's Macey up to?" I asked as I reached down for my cup, but Blair beat me to it, and quickly scooped it up, and as I looked up, his eyes were level with mine, our gaze holding for an instant.

"I got that," Blair said as he straightened up, and headed off in the direction of the kitchen with my empty cup in his hand.

"She's in the powder room," Sonny replied with a grin on his face.

"Sonny, what time did Macey say the cleaning people were coming?" Blair called out over his shoulder.

"Around eight, I think," Sonny said as he yawned loudly behind his hand.

"What was that look?" I asked looking down at him as he reclined on the sofa.

Sonny sat up and looked around the room, feigning surprise. "What?"

"The way you were looking at me through the tiny slits in your eyes."

Sonny shook his head, as he raised his hand and rubbed the top of his head. "Nothing, it was nothing. Are you going to head out with us?"

"Sure, are you two ready to go?" I asked.

"As soon as Macey gets out of the powder room," Sonny replied giving me a queer look.

"Sonny, I know that look. Something is wrong, what is it?"

"What do you think about Mr. Freeman?" Sonny asked as his smile returned.

"Nice."

Sonny nodded, and then he stood up just as I moved forward, and gave me a long hard hug. "Good. I'm glad to see two of my favorite people finally get together."

"Thanks, Sonny," I said as I returned his hug.

"What's this? I turn my back for one minute and my husband of two months takes solace in the arms of another woman."

"I love this woman," Sonny replied giving my lips a quick kiss as he gave my waist a light squeeze. He held out one hand to Macey. "But you, Macey, are my wife," Sonny said as Macey stepped into our little circle.

"Hey, time out," Blair said holding his arms up high as he entered the room. "Man, how do you rank to get two pretty women in your puny little arms?"

"Man, you're just jealous. Don't hate the player. We're heading out," Sonny said as we all broke apart. "Thanks again for the party, Blair," he said as the two of them embraced.

"You the dawg," Blair said, thumping Sonny on the back.

"Thank you, Blair," Macey said, standing on her toes as Blair leaned down. "I love you."

"You're welcome, doll, and I love you too."

"Well we've got to go. Mia's going to follow us out of here," Sonny said, as he turned my way. "You ready to go?"

"Mia, I thought you wanted to take a tour of the house?" Blair asked with a look of disappointment upon his face.

"I was, but I don't think I can find my way of out of this maze, so I thought I'd leave now and follow Sonny and Macey back to Interstate 8," I said glancing from Blair to Sonny and back to Blair again.

"No problem. But if you want to stay and explore my house, I'd be more than happy to show you out, I mean it's still early." Blair said as we all stood around the room looking at one another.

"We could stay until after you've looked around- or maybe not," Sonny quickly stated as he received a poke in the side from one of Maceys' sharp pointy elbows.

"It is early," Macey quickly added. "I mean, just because the old married couple has to get home and let the dog out doesn't mean the two of you have to call it a night, right?"

"Macey, you don't have a dog." I started laughing first, and soon the others all joined in. I looked at Blair and we spoke at the same time. "This is a setup-"

"You know this is a setup-"

"Good night, we're out of here. Come on, Sonny; let's go let the *dog* out. Mia, I'll call you tomorrow for all of the details. Blair, thanks so much for the party, and don't forget the cleaning people will be here in the morning at eight o'clock sharp, goodnight!" Macey said her hand high in the air waving good-bye as she headed for the front door.

After seeing Sonny and Macey out, I was given the grand tour of the house. We checked out the four spare bedrooms of the split plan. A large king size bed dominated the largest of the spare rooms. Two stood empty except for a few boxes and each bedroom had its own bathroom. The fourth bedroom, which was closer to the front of the house, had been turned into an office and it was filled with a large desk and lots of computer equipment and monitors of every shape and size. On the way to the master suite we passed the powder room which had been painted to look like a small alcove with a view of the ocean.

Blair led me through the living room and into the master suite. Upon opening the double doors made of some kind of red looking wood, was it teak? My heart skipped a few beats as the doors swung inward. I was entering into his private domain, and all was missing was the sound of trumpets announcing our arrival. This room was the largest of all and it was also the most beautiful room in the house, beside the fact it only had a large platform bed and dresser in it. The room had high vaulted ceilings which made the room appear even larger and grander. Rugged beams ran up to an enormous center beam, which framed posts of the same wood the doors were made of, forming the supporting part of the roof. We entered the side of the room where the bed lay in the center. With a half wall behind it, forming a walkway to the bathroom and the large walk-in closet. I moved to the center of the room and turned away from the bed. There was a guitar propped in one corner of the room on its own little stand. Another wall was home to a large fireplace and the other wall was made entirely of glass sliding doors. I could see Blair's reflection in the glass as he reached out for the light switch which made a soft 'click' shutting off the lights in the room, and what I saw next was unbelievable; it was as if Blair had turned on the City. I hadn't realized in my travels here that it had been a mostly uphill trek and the lights from the nearest town could be seen in the distance. I stood staring out at the most gorgeous sight I'd ever seen.

After my tour of his home, Blair had me wait inside while he disappeared into the night and returned with two beautiful Dobermans. Blair had explained to me earlier how he had locked them away in the pool house until after the party. Orpheus was a black and tan male, and Eurydice, a red and tan female. I didn't get to close to them after Blair had explained to me they were guard dogs, so I admired their splendor from afar, real far, like from behind the French doors.

After extinguishing the Japanese lanterns, Blair made a pot of coffee and we settled down to chat. We hadn't had much of a chance to talk earlier, due to the constant interruptions from Sonny and Macey. We felt this would be the perfect opportunity for us to get to know one another further.

The only light left in the room was from the flickering light of the roaring fire Blair had made earlier. The raging flames appeared to slow time, transporting us back to an enchanted era. I was glad I had decided to attend the party; otherwise I would have missed the chance of getting to know this charming man. Settling down on row of large pillows that lined the sofa, I was getting lost in the excitement with the hope of many more intimate nights with Blair.

"Do you play the guitar well?" I asked, remembering the instrument standing in the corner of the room.

He smiled. "I don't like to brag, but I play very well, just like everything else I do."

Hmm, not only is he handsome, but conceited as well. "There's nothing wrong with you tooting your own horn." I replied as I returned his smile. "How long have you lived in the area?" I asked.

"About a year now, how long have you live in San Diego?"

"Thirteen years. I moved to San Diego when Maurice was three years old."

"And before San Diego?"

"Arizona."

"Really?" Blair asked, as he moved in closer to me. "What city?"

"Phoenix."

"I almost settled in Phoenix."

It truly was a small world. "Really? What changed your mind?"

"The heat," he replied with a shake of his head. "I'll never forget the day I visited there, it was so hot the rubber on my tires melted," Blair said with a laugh.

"What's this I'm hearing? I can't quite place your accent; originally, you are from...?" I asked after we'd laughed a bit.

"Up north, Washington State."

"Really, I thought I heard a bit of a southern accent. I heard Washington was very nice, even thought about moving up there myself once or twice, but the boys and I stopped off in San Diego and we fell in love with the beach as well as the city, so we decided to stay. What brought you to the San Diego area?" I wiggled my toes inside of my shoes, wishing I could take them off, but not wanting to be presumptuous about the depth of our relationship. I mean, after all, Blair was the host, and he was still wearing his shoes. The comfortable warm glow of the fire, and the comfort from the warmth of the body of this handsome man sitting beside me put me in a place where I hadn't been in a while. Blair was seducing me with a spell I hoped he would never lift.

"My, ah, pool and lawn business."

"On your card it states you've been in the area for seven years." There was magic on his lips, so kissable.

"Jeremy, my foreman, ran the company for me while I was away in Washington; of course, I handle the financial end of the business."

"Do you own another company in Washington?"

"No, I was attending school, finishing up with my education and attending to some other loose ends." Blair spoke hesitantly. For a moment, his eyes left me as he gazed into the fire and I felt his attention drift away to another place or a different time. Something had sparked a distant memory, taking Blair away from me for a few precious seconds. Then, as suddenly as he had drifted off, Blair snapped back from his reverie, his charismatic smile lighting up the room again. He jumped to his feet, pulling at the hem of his turtleneck. "I'm going to grab something to eat. Can I freshen up your coffee, or would you care for something else?"

"Another cup of coffee would be nice." Odd, the way Blair had suddenly drifted off in the middle of our conversation.

"Be right back," he said, dashing off toward the kitchen.

After returning with my coffee and a plate piled high with an assortment of leftover snacks the caterer had left, Blair was more talkative than before. We discussed my sons, my job, and every other interesting topic under the sun, while he finished off his plate of food. I tried bringing up our Washington discussion again, but Blair would always steer the conversation in a different direction. After he'd eaten, Blair fixed an Amaretto Sour for me and he decided to try one too. After making a run to the powder room, we settled down again and our new topic was Sonny.

"I know you and Sonny have known one another for a while now, but exactly how many years has it been?"

"Oh wow," I said containing my joy, I knew what he was really asking and why. The night could only get better from here I thought. "Sometimes it seems like Sonny and I have known each other all of our lives," I said as I thought about the number of years Sonny and I had actually known one another. "We met soon after I moved here."

"That's a long time. May I ask you another question?"

"Sure?"

"Has there ever been anything between the two of you?" Blair took a long sip from his glass while staring intently at me. The look on his face was now more inquisitive than sexual. I could tell he was interpreting my body language. "This stuff is too sweet," he said as he held up his glass containing the Amaretto Sour. "Hold that thought while I switch to cognac," he said as he jumped to his feet and left the room.

I was relieved when Blair left the room, because thinking about his question took longer than I thought to answer. In the beginning Sonny had hinted about us being more than *just* friends. And, once or twice Sonny and I had let our friendship flow into some pretty heavy petting, but apart from those few instances, there was nothing. One of those times had been right after my divorce had become final, but we'd felt it was too soon to start a relationship. Deciding instead to wait and make sure it was something we desired, and not just a rebound love affair. The affection between us had blossomed into a great friendship. By the time Blair had returned, I knew what my answer would be.

"No," I replied, as Blair rejoined me. I gazed deep into his mysterious eyes hoping to catch a glimpse of his affection. The flames reflected in his now smoky brown eyes made it seem as though I was looking into his soul and the flame was of his burning passion for me. "There has never been anything between us. We're just friends."

"Not *just* friends," Blair said in a cheery tune. "From what I understood, you two are the *best* of friends," he finished with a nod of his head.

"Yes, Sonny and I are close. Sonny has been there for me when I needed him the most, and I've supported him in his time of need as well. Why do you ask?" I tried to interpret Blair's body language, as he sat up from his reclining position before answering. He was a bit hesitant, taking a sip of his drink before answering.

"Because our mutual friend Sonny gave me a warning about doing right by you and not causing you any harm. My man threatened me with bodily harm if I hurt one hair of your lovely head," Blair replied, with a smile as he reached out and touched a lock of my hair. With the anticipation of his touch my eyes focused on the floor. He shook his head, before continuing. "Sonny is something else. We've been sparring partners many times, and even though our boy out weighs me by twenty pounds or so, we always end in an even match, but I know I can beat him. We've been practicing in martial arts for about the same length of time, but my skills are honed to kill. Then again, from the look on Sonny's face tonight after he warned me to treat you right, I knew if I should happen to cause you any grief, our boy would probably beat my black ass down," Blair said with a smile and a laugh as he looked me straight in my eyes.

41

I had no idea what Blair had meant by his statement, about how he was trained to kill, and I thought, isn't that what the sport is all about anyway, training to kill? But instead I just agreed with Blair about the sincerity of Sonny's statement. "I agree completely, Sonny is a character all right, and he probably meant every word he said too."

"That's just it; he did *mean* it, every single word. Even though he laughed about it afterwards, I could tell Sonny was very serious," Blair replied as he started to laugh. "Are you seeing anyone at this time?" Blair asked after we had quieted down from our laugh.

"No, I'm not. What about you, are you involved with anyone?"

"If I were I wouldn't be sitting here with you tonight."

"I've heard that line before."

"No. Mia, I'm serious," Blair replied, with a shake of his head and he seemed to be slightly annoyed by my reply. "I've been running around getting my life together and perfecting my business skills, and don't forget I was a full time student. To be honest with you, I haven't had time to date. As a matter of fact, it's been a while since I've even been on a date."

"What's a while?" I asked leaning toward him.

"If you're talking about a serious relationship, it's been about six years. If you're talking about a plain old booty call-"

"A booty call?" Is he serious?

"Yeah, a booty call, you know, straight up sex with no love attached to it, that's a booty call. It's been about two years since I've had one of those."

"Okay, I know what a booty call is," I said as I held up my hand to him, and thinking how I'd had one or two of those in my early years, but I wasn't going to confide in him, at least not on our first date. "I also find that hard to believe. I mean a vibrant handsome young man...how old are you anyway?"

"How old do you want me to be?" Blair asked with an unreadable expression upon his face, as he leaned in closer to me. We sat immersed in each others eyes; the dark windows in the center of his eyes concealed the hazel. His stare consumed all of me, and from then on I knew my affection for him was the same sensation he was feeling for me. As he spoke I could feel the warmth of his breath on my face, detecting no odor from the food he had consumed earlier, only that of the sweet cognac which he had sipped on earlier.

"Your birth age," I replied genteelly. Blair seemed to be on the edge of my personal space which was rapidly diminishing as he advanced even closer. My eyes drifted lower to the area around his nose and cheeks. His skin now the color of brown sugar after it had been wet. My eyes drifted to his lips- "What?" I asked. I had seen Blair's lips move, but I'd missed hearing his words. With him being so close to me, the hunger in my heart had sent my mind to another place. I took my eyes off of his lips and looked up into his eyes. I couldn't let the lust for his soft lips distract me from his words.

"Thirty-four." Blair spoke softly, as he stared into my eyes. He leaned in even closer to me, and just before our lips touched, Blair turned his head to the side. His lips mere inches from my right ear, his breath gently caressing my cheek. I shifted my gaze up, and then down as he moved closer and closer. Blair was almost sitting in my lap. "How old are you?" His warm breath sent chills all the way to my fingertips. And his voice reverberated throughout my body. His words in my ear seemed to be just as pleasurable as a kiss.

Oh Lord, this man could have given me an orgasm just by whispering in my ear. Suddenly the temperature in the room raced skyward. I hadn't felt this way in a while. The last time I'd been turned on by being this close to a man was with Sonny, right after I'd first met him. Now why would I remember something like- "Forty-one." Damn, I'd meant to say thirty-five. "You look older than thirty-four," I quickly blurted out to cover my mistake. It was hard to focus; for my mind was in a deluge of passion not conversation.

"You don't look forty-one," Blair said at the same time, and we laughed out loud. "Okay, but really you don't look forty-one," he said again as he leaned back, narrowing his eyes and tilting his head from side-to-side. He held his hands in the air, his fingers shaping a square, as he playfully watched me through the middle. "At first I thought we were around the same age until Sonny told me the ages of your sons. So I kind of figured you'd be a few years older than me, not that I mind. Do you?"

Blair was younger than I'd thought. For some reason I'd thought he was the same age as Sonny, who had turned thirty-eight on his last birthday. "Right," I replied with a shake of my head.

"Oh, you don't believe me, huh? I know exactly what you're thinking. You probably think I'm the type of man who will say anything to get into your panties, right?"

"You're certainly not one to mince words, are you?" But that was exactly what I was thinking; we were certainly on the same level.

"Games insecure people play," Blair said as he picked up his glass. "My motto is; if you see something you want; go for it because it might not be there tomorrow." Blair took a quick sip from of his drink, and I noticed him watching me over the top of his glass. "A while back I learned life was too damn short for games. Mia, we're both adults, why beat around the bush. Oh, don't get me wrong, I do want to get into your panties," he said with a nod toward my hips, "remember it's been two *long* years. But, I'm not going to lie to you and lay sweet nothings on you simply to get there," he finished with a nod of his head, as he chuckled.

"I'm being honest with you about the age thing too, because it ain't nothing but a number. It doesn't make you, nor does it make me the person who I am. When Sonny first pointed you out to me, I liked what I saw, and I wanted to get to know you. So, I ask you again, does it matter to you about our age difference because if it does then we may as well say our good-byes right now before we get in too deep."

"You are a very serious minded young man-" I began, before he cut my words off.

"Serious *man* period. You ain't got to be throwing in the word 'young' all the time. Before I told you my age you hadn't mentioned the word *young* once tonight."

"May I finish my sentence please?" Young man with an attitude, I thought. But I had to admit; I'd met a few fifty-year-olds who behaved less mature than Blair.

"I'm sorry, but don't get hung up on my age, okay?" Blair said as he reached out and touched my shoulder.

"You certainly use that word a lot."

"What word?"

"*Ain't.*"

"It *ain't* nothing but a word," he said, grinning at me, his brilliant smile making him look younger than his given age.

"As I was saying before, you are a vibrant, handsome, mature," I hesitated, "*man* who hasn't been in a serious relationship for over six years, and since we're being outright with one another, were you recently released from prison or something?" Again we were eye to eye; his look didn't waver as he answered my question. Oh yeah, there's definitely something about him.

"No, I've never been incarcerated before. I told you before, I've been trying to get my business and education together," he replied as another smile broke out on his face. "Why do Black women always assume just because a brother *isn't*," he said with a wink of an eye, "in a serious relationship, is because he's been incarcerated for ten, or twenty years or because he's gay? And before you ask," he started holding his finger to my lips. "I'm not gay," he said with a serious look as he moved his hand.

"Not on the *down low* are you?" I asked him, my own expression just as serious as his, but deep inside I wanted to laugh out loud at his seriousness.

Blair leaned in even closer than previously, and before answering my question, he hesitated to take in the air around me, closing his eyes as he took a couple of deep breaths. "No. I'm straight up heterosexual male, all man. "Want me to prove it to you?" Blair asked, his warm breath tickling my eyelashes.

Damn, he was good. Blair certainly knew how to seduce a woman. I wanted to reach up and fan my face afterward. "Which wouldn't prove that you're not on the '*DL*'," I replied as I leaned away from him. Yes, he was definitely all male, right down to his scent. "What's the name of the cologne you're wearing?" I asked, quickly changing the subject as I moved away from him a tad bit more. It was definitely getting warm in here.

"I'm not wearing any. You probably smell my shower gel or my body lotion by PS," he said with a sly look on his face.

45

"PS?"

"Paul Sebastian."

"I've heard of it before, smells nice on you."

"You smell outstanding as well, what's the name of the fragrance you're wearing?"

"Amber Romance from Victoria's Garden."

"I like it, and the *romance* part fits the occasion." With every second Blair seemed closer. "So," he began, as he reached out and ran the back of his hand along my cheek. I closed my eyes as I leaned closer to him. "What else are you wearing from...Victoria's Garden?"

His touch sent thrills though my body. "Is it getting chilly in here or is it just me?"

Blair threw back his head and laughed a long robust hearty laugh. It filled the room and warmed my heart. It made his otherwise serious expression, when he wasn't talking about jumping my bones, more relaxing, and carefree. I attempted to control my own laughter, but soon I was laughing right along with him. "What's so funny," I asked after we had finally quieted down.

"Okay," he said after a while. "I could do one of two things. One, I could throw another log on the fire or two, we could move closer. I'd be more than happy to keep you warm." Now it was my turn to start laughing. "I guess that means I'll be throwing another log on the fire," Blair said with a cheery smile, as he stood up. "Are you really cold or was that you way of telling me to move out of your space?"

"Both," I replied between giggles. Ooh yeah, this was going to be interesting. It wasn't the chill in the room but the heat from Blair that was giving me goose bumps. His closeness was making me uneasy, and if Blair got any closer to me, I would not be responsible for my actions. At first it had been a physical attraction, but the more we chatted the more connected I felt toward him. And from our conversation, and Blair's blithely sexual behavior toward me, I knew the feeling was mutual. There was definitely chemistry between us.

"Okay, you win," said Blair, flashing another one of his gorgeous smiles at me as he grabbed a log and placed it on the fire. "There," he said dusting off his hands. "Can I freshen up your drink or maybe you would like something to snack on?"

"No, I really should be leaving," I said glancing down at my wrist, before remembering that I was not wearing a watch. "Do you have the time?"

"The last time I was in the kitchen it was a little after three. Now, Mia, don't tell me you're ready to go home?"

"Well, it is late, and I don't want to keep you up-"

"Mia?"

"I know you offered to show me out of this maze you live in and-"

"Mia?"

"I told a friend that I'd try and attend his church tomorrow morning, and if I don't get at least six hours of sleep I am utterly worthless the next day." I finally finished. Blair was standing in front of the fireplace, his hands behind his back with a bemused look on his face. Earlier he had removed his jacket and his form fitting turtleneck sweater hugged his chest and arms like a he'd been poured into it.

"Are you finished?"

"Yes I am."

"You don't have to make up excuses you know, if you're ready to leave just tell me."

"I thought I just did."

"Okay, let's go then, I'll even take you home if you want me to."

"No thanks, Blair, I can drive myself home," I said as I stood and gathered my shawl and purse. "Thank you for allowing me to hang out with you, although I hadn't planned on staying this late. I had a marvelous time."

"Thanks for coming over, and I hope we can get together again real soon because I enjoyed our time together. Let me get my keys," Blair said as turned and walked away.

I wrapped my shawl around my shoulders, opened my purse and removed my car keys. What a night, I couldn't believe we had spent this much time together. I glanced around the room again thinking what a nice man Blair was, a funny, handsome, and sexy as hell man.

47

I closed my eyes and smiled, thinking I'll definitely be seeing him again. His presence filled the room, even when he wasn't in it. Where the hell had Sonny been hiding him?

"You have a nice smile, your whole face lights up when you smile, and right now, you're practically glowing. I bet if the light was out in this room you would stand out like a beacon." Blair said, startling me with his return. He stood across the room shaking his head. "I wish I'd put that smile on your face."

"What makes you think you didn't?" I asked, surprised to see him standing across from me. I'd been facing the kitchen area, away from the hallway where Blair had emerged with his car keys. Not the same hallway he had exited to retrieve his keys.

"Because I wasn't in the room."

"Where did you come from?"

"Secret entrance. You ready?" he asked with a wink of an eye.

"Waiting for you." Once outside, the dogs were on us in a flash, but after a one-word command from Blair, they disappeared back into the darkness. Blair held out his hand for my car keys, unlocked the door and held the door opened for me. Minus the bright lights from the Japanese lanterns, which had given the place a look of gaiety, now there was an eerie look about the place. A mist had covered the grounds and a slight breeze was drifting through the trees. If I looked long and hard enough, I could actually see the swirling mist as it drifted on the night air.

"Don't forget to lock your doors. In what part of San Diego do you live?"

"My condo is located downtown, off of Seventh and C Street."

"Downtown? You mean *downtown* San Diego? What the hell are you doing living downtown?" Blair asked with a shocked look upon his face.

"I work downtown. I got tired of the commute from El Cajon, so when I heard about this architectural firm converting an old office building into condos, I bought an upstairs unit, two bedrooms with a loft, so my son Maurice has his own space. It's really quite nice; you should drop by and visit sometimes."

"Is that an invitation?"

"It is."

"Alright, I accept. Follow me to Interstate 8, and then I'll follow you."

"Blair, the invitation wasn't for tonight."

"Mia, I know that. Is there any harm in wanting to make sure you get home okay?"

"Blair, you really don't have to follow me home," I protested.

"I know," he said as he stepped back and closed my door. He disappeared down the darken drive, the darkness and the mist swallowing him up within seconds.

I shivered at the sight of Blair disappearing into the swirling mist, making the black night seemingly even colder. I inserted my key into the ignition and started the car, turning the heater on full blast. I couldn't believe he was going to follow me all the way home. It was about an hour drive from Alpine to downtown San Diego, and it was well after three in the morning. The sun would be well up by the time Blair made it back home. I couldn't let him escort me all the way home. I turn on my headlights, and squinted through the darkness, trying to peer into the mist in the direction Blair had disappeared. I heard what sounded like thunder, and thought we were in for some rain, just as a dark car came barreling down the drive, the mist swirling on each side of the car as he drove up. The black Corvette pulled to a stop next to my six-year-old Volvo. Blair motioned with his hand for me to roll down my window.

The interior of my car was now pleasantly warm from the car heater, and as I rolled down the window a blast of cold air invaded the inside, and before I could stop myself I shivered from the chill of the night air. "Blair, you really don't have to see me home. It's way out of your way. You don't have to do this, you know. I can make it on my own just fine," I yelled out, trying to be heard over the noise of his roaring engine. Blair swung open his door and stepped out of his car.

"Mia, I don't believe your sons or Sonny would appreciate the fact that I let you head out of here alone, especially at this time of night. What about when you get there? You got all kinds of destitute people living on the streets of downtown San Diego. You have to park your car-"

"The building has an underground gated garage-"

"Which can be broken into. I will see you safely home to your son."

"Maurice is spending the weekend with Anthony."

"Out of the car," Blair said opening my door. He reached around me and turned off the lights and removed my keys. "If you must insist on going home tonight then I will drive you. Your car will be safe enough here and I'll bring you back tomorrow to pick it up."

"Blair, I am not going to put you out like that. I'll get home okay on my own."

"Why are you being so stubborn?"

"Why am I being so stubborn? What about you?"

"It's late or early, depending on the way you see it, and the thought of you driving home alone at this time of night does not sit well with me. Why don't you just stay? I have four bedrooms that aren't being used, two aren't furnished but you can have your choice of any room in the house. Hell, you can even have my room if you want it, I'll sleep in one of the other rooms."

"Blair?"

"Mia, nothing, I promise you nothing will happen, you have my word on that and my word is always good."

"I don't even have a change of clothing," I begin, as I ran my hand through my hair. "No toothbrush-"

"Stay the night or let me drive you home."

"Then you'll be driving back and falling asleep at the wheel-Okay, Okay. How's this, you can drive me home and spend the night at my place."

"Great, sounds like a plan to me. Come on back inside while I grab a few items."

Once back inside, I waited nervously for Blair as I thought about what I was doing. What was I doing? We're not sleeping together, so what was I worried about? God, I hope I'm doing the right thing. Not that I was worried about him seducing me, it was more likely that I would be the one doing the seducing. Blair definitely had a magnetic appeal about him, and it was pulling me straight to him. Maybe I should just sleep here and leave in the morning. I covered my mouth, yawning loudly, remembering that I had been up since six that morning.

"All ready," Blair said as he dropped a small tote bag on the floor and began to stir the logs in the fireplace.

"You know what, Blair, on second thought I could stay here, and that way neither of us would have to drive tonight. Besides, the cleaners will be arriving tomorrow morning at eight, remember?"

"Woman, let me show you to your room," Blair said in a loud burst of air. "I know it's a woman's prerogative to change her mind and all, but, Mia, you are too quick for me," Blair said as we headed toward the rear of the house. Blair led me to the last bedroom in the hallway, the largest of the four, and the only one with a bed in it. "By the way, thanks for reminding me about the cleaners coming in the morning. Okay, bathroom's over here," he said as he threw open a door. "I'll bring you some towels-"

"I'll need something to sleep in too, a pair of pajamas, or maybe a tee shirt?" I asked as he gave me a long sultry look.

Blair looked me up and down. "I'm afraid a tee shirt will have to do, I haven't slept in a pair of pajamas since I was sixteen. I'll be right back."

The way Blair had looked at me sent little fiery fingers dancing up and down my spine. I folded my arms across my chest, and decided to sneak a quick look at the large bathroom in Blair's absence. It contained a sunken spa tub surrounded by mirrors on three walls, with a large separate shower at the other end of the bathroom, and a toilet in its own separate area. There was also a large closet and it stood empty aside from an oak chest with several sets of brand new white cotton sheets, still wrapped in the original package, stacked on top of it. Lying on closet shelf were two large fluffy pillows, also still in their original package.

"Towels," Blair called out as I poked my head out of the closet. "I see you've found the sheets." He stepped in behind me and grabbed the pillows from the shelf. "Grab a set of sheets," he said with a nod of his head, before making his way back out to the king sized bed. "You're in luck; I found a new toothbrush for you in my gym bag." He dropped the pillows on the bed, then reached down and picked up a white tee shirt. "So, are you all set? Is there anything else I can get you?"

You, my mind shouted. "No, I think I'm all set. Thank you, Blair," I said as I picked up a large body towel and two smaller ones and headed for the bathroom.

"Ah, I knew I was forgetting something," Blair said as he gave his forehead a smack with the palm of hand. "I'll be right back," he said as he dashed from the room. "Soap, he said handing me a bar of blue soap, "and I thought you might need this," Blair said as he handed me a midnight blue silk bathrobe with a beautiful crane amongst a floral setting on the back.

I thanked him again, and stepped into the bathroom, closing and locking the door behind me, then laughed at my actions. "Okay Girl, you're out here in the middle of nowhere with a man you hardly know and you lock the bathroom door, like a locked door can keep him out if he *really* wanted to come in." I spoke out loud, wishfully thinking that he would knock on the bathroom and ask me if I needed anything else. Maybe a visit from Blair wouldn't be bad at all. I reached out and unlocked the door, thinking he probably had keys to all the doors anyway.

The hot shower was just what I needed. I could've stayed in the shower all night, the water temperature, and pressure was just right. I was certainly going to stop over at the Home Depot tomorrow afternoon and buy me a new showerhead for my shower just like this one. This showerhead put my puny little one to shame, and with Maurice living at home, there never seemed to be enough hot water at my place, but a new showerhead would certainly make up for the lack of hot water. Intent on keeping my hair dry, I had wrapped a smaller towel around my head or else I would have paid the price the next morning. There was no way I was going to let my hair get wet, especially stuck out here without my blow dryer and my curling iron. Before leaving the bathroom, I rinsed out my underwear using the liquid hand soap and toss them over the shower door to dry during the night, because

I was not about to ask Blair to toss my unmentionables into the wash for a tumble with his dirty clothes. After putting on the tee shirt, which hung down to my knees, I slipped into the soft silk robe and stepped out into the bedroom. I smiled as I looked around the room. Blair had made the bed, turned out all the lights and had even brought in a couple of scented candles which he had placed on the nightstand. Blair had even left a tube of toothpaste on the bed for me next to a lovely fresh orchid.

After brushing my teeth, I sat on the side of the bed with the orchid in my hand marveling at how Blair had gotten a fresh flower in the middle of the night, or shall I say morning. The glow from candlelight gave the room a soft sexy look, and I stared at the bedroom door for a few seconds. In my mind I pictured him entering the room wearing nothing but a smile. Right, I thought after a few seconds had gone by, what was it Blair had said earlier, oh yeah, his word is always good. I rose from the bed, and blew out the candles, covering my mouth as I let out another loud yawn. I placed the orchid on the pillow, and laid my head down next to it. I closed my eyes for just a few seconds to reflect on this divine evening, as the heady scent of the orchid filled my nostrils.

CHAPTER FIVE

I lay comfortably as I rested on the thick billowy mattress in nothing more than a thin white sheer negligee. Blair was lying beside me wearing nothing but a smile, and I could feel the warmth from his unclothed body as he pressed against me. He lay on his side supporting my neck with his firm arm, his large rock hard package thrust against my thigh. Beaming with pleasure I returned his gorgeous smile, as he trailed a single orchid up and down my exposed thigh. Its' light touch arousing me with delight, as he teasingly moved the flower to my belly with an extravagant swirl. I was overcome with lust for his touch, as he slowly moved the flower to my breasts. My nipples rose in anticipation of just the simplest touch of his hand. Clenching my quivering thighs together, I lay yearning for his body to be one with mine.

My erotic vision of Blair was shattered with an annoying persistent tapping from somewhere in the distance. I tried to keep my current position and my focus on this sumptuous man lying next to me. But the unrelenting noise continued on and with an inpatient smack of my lips my head snapped around in the direction of the loud noise, and then back to Blair, only to discover that his once warm body was no longer firmly pressed against me and he had begun to fade away from sight. Now thoroughly irritated at the sight of my lover disappearing into thin air, I quickly turned my head back toward the bedroom door, where the annoying sound was emitting from. It had now grown to a thumping sound and then I realized I had been dreaming and the constant loud booming noise was only light tapping at my bedroom door.

As my opulent dream was washed away by the morning sun I rolled onto my stomach, bringing the pillow up and over my head trying to regain my fantasy world. I buried my face into the pillow and I felt a cool soft crunch. With the perfume of the orchid filling my senses, I could feel myself drift off back into my dream. I envisioned a meadow full of sweet flowers as I began to doze off, only to be awakened again this time by the voice of Blair. I cocked opened one eye, then the other, and realized what I thought was the morning sun straining to get through the blinds on the windows, and the tapping sound was coming from the other side of the door. It was Blair knocking at the bedroom door, asking me if I was awake. I raised my head from the now crushed orchid and answered him in my sleep filled voice. "What is it?" I croaked. Disappointed that Blair had awakened me from my dream, but pleased to know he was not completely gone.

"Are you awake?"

"I am now," I said as I slowly rose to a sitting position, running my fingers through my wild mane, just as the door swung opened.

"Good morning, did you sleep well?" Blair asked as he entered the room and began opening the blinds. I blinked as sunshine radiated throughout white the room. The light was so blinding that I had to hold my hands up to my eyes to shield out the brightness.

"Yes I did." I was surprised at how quickly I had fallen asleep last night. I could have sworn I'd no more than rested my head for a few seconds. "What time is it?" I asked as I reached for the robe lying at the foot of the bed and slid an arm through the sleeve.

"Just a little after twelve."

"Twelve?" Oh, no. I hadn't meant to sleep so late. I was so embarrassed at what he must be thinking of me. Here I was a guest at his house and I was snoozing the day away like I was a weekend guest lounging my day away. "Why didn't you wake me before now?" I asked as I scrambled from bed.

"Because I barely woke up myself until a few minutes ago," Blair said as he stood examining me with his hands on his hips.

I cleared the haze from my eyes and he came into pleasant view. He stood before me in black cotton boxer briefs that were griping his body as if he'd been dipped in liquid silk. My mouth opened and my mind shouted 'oh my goodness' the man was packing some *heat*. Not missing any important details I slowly brought my eyes up his sculptured body to his massive chest. The dark man was bathed in the radiance of the sun that lit the white room, every muscle accented in shimmering light. He was magnificent as my eyes glossed over him with extreme pleasure. It was as if he had stepped down from the heavens, Gods' precious gift to me.

"Would you like something to eat?" He asked.

I quickly snapped from my stupor and closed my mouth. Looking up into his face and I was relieved to see that Blair was too busy rubbing the sleep from his own eyes to notice my fascination of him as I inspected his body. I was behaving as if I'd never seen a man before, well, maybe one not this handsome. I mean, after all, Randy *never* looked this good in the mornings or any time other time for that matter. Then again Randy had twenty years on Blair.

"I didn't mean to sleep this late." I escaped to the bathroom and almost screamed when I saw my reflection in the mirror. My vain attempt to tame my thick unruly hair hadn't worked for most of it was sticking out like I'd stuck my finger in an electrical outlet. My eyes were still swollen from sleep, with crusty crystals mixed with traces of mascara that I'd been unable to wash away without the help of my makeup remover. I was slightly relieved for I doubted if Blair could have seen much of my imperfections with the short time he was in the room. Wait, what was that on the side of my face? I leaned in closer to the mirror to get a better look. Was it was just orchid juice from the crush of the delicate flower? Damn, who was I trying to fool it was dried up drool. Kill me now.

I showered and dressed in my outfit from last night, which didn't seem quite appropriate in the afternoon sun as it had last night. Because of the soap I'd used to wash out my underwear, they were now slightly stiff and scratchy, but I couldn't complain because they were also fresh and clean which made me feel a lot better about wearing last night outfit. My black slacks were acceptable, but my black sandals with their three-inch heels and my magenta top with the deep v-neck and spaghetti straps, with the matching shawl was a bit too much for Sunday afternoon attire. I couldn't do much for my hair, not without my curling iron, so I combed my hair back and away from my face, and used my fingers to arrange the now loosen curls into a more acceptable style than the one I'd worn earlier. At least I had my compact and lipstick, which were the only two things, besides my keys, which were able to fit into my tiny evening bag. I put my red lipstick on nice and thick hoping that my beautiful red lips would draw Blair's eyes to my mouth and not my eyes. As I completed my toiletries, I made a mental note to myself to always carry a change of clothing and a makeup bag in my car. Realizing that there was not much else I could do about my appearance, I decided to throw caution to the wind and go out and face the music. I stripped the sheets from the bed, bundling them up along with the towels I'd used and left the room. I followed the delicious aroma of food which directed me to the large cheery sunlit kitchen. I entered the kitchen just as Blair was flipping an omelet onto a plate.

"Mia, would you care for a ham and cheese omelet?" Blair asked, as he placed the plate on the table. Sitting next to the omelet plate was a smaller plate with a couple of slices of toast in anticipation of my arrival, along with orange juice and a pot of coffee.

"I thought you said you'd only just gotten out of bed?"

"I did," Blair replied as he removed the bundle of linen from my arms.

"So who let the cleaning people in?" I'd noticed on my way to the kitchen that the living and dining areas were spotless.

"I did. They buzzed me early this morning. They had their instructions and they knew what they needed to do. I hung around, feed the dogs and afterward, I inspected the rooms and sent them on their way. Then I went back to bed to catch a few more winks."

"I didn't hear a thing."

"You shouldn't have, there was nothing to clean in that part of the house."

As Blair disappeared into the laundry room, I pulled out a chair, sat down and inhaled the mouth-watering scent from the plate in front of me.

"This smells good," I called out to him. He was back in a few seconds and sat down across from me with a enormous grin on his face. I was happy to return his smile; at least now my face was clean.

I picked up my fork and was just about to indulge myself, when Blair lowered his head. Keeping the fork in my hand, I lowered my eyes as Blair said grace. I hadn't said grace at the table since I'd left my childhood home. Now this gorgeous man, not only did he have his own business, but he could cook, and to top it all off, he says grace before his meal. Well I guess this was the second black mark against me. First, there was the age difference, and now the fact that I didn't say grace. The first was something I couldn't change. Well as far as the second one goes, I guess I could start thanking God for the food; after all I thanked him for all else in my life.

"Amen. Can I get you anything else? Let's see, we have hot sauce, Tabasco, and salsa."

"No, this is good," I said as I spooned some salsa over my perfect looking omelet. Besides ham and cheese, my omelet was also filled with black olives, bell peppers, mushrooms, and onions. As I cut into it, the warm melted cheese created a cheese bridge from the omelet to my fork as I lifted a forkful to my mouth. I never knew eggs could taste so good. The hash browns were prepackaged, but were tasty, and nice and crunchy on the outside and soft in the middle.

"Where did you get that lovely orchid from?" I asked, remembering the flower from last night.

"I have a greenhouse out back. Orchids were my grandmothers' favorite flower," Blair replied with a slight smile. "A friend of hers used to grow them, and would always bring my grandmother a bouquet of orchids once a month. Raising orchids has turned into a hobby for me."

Is there anything that he can't do? I thought as we ate our meal in silence.

"Didn't you have a church date today?" Blair suddenly asked.

"It wasn't a date," I begin, still sorting through the list in my head. "A friend of mine invited me to visit his church and I told him that I might stop by today."

"Do you have a regular church that you attend?"

"No," I said with a shake of my head. "I used to go every now and again with Sonny, but that was a long time ago. What about you?"

"Yeah," Blair said with a nod of his head. "Sonny told me how you used to attend services with him. I attend the same church as Sonny and Macey, started a couple of months ago. It's an alternative church, spiritual, but of course you already know that. You should think about joining us sometimes. Did you know Sonny and Macey met in church? Oops, sorry, here I go again. Of course you know how they met; after all, you and Sonny are best friends." Blair said as he stood and began to clear the table.

I nodded. "I know," I said as I picked up my plate and carried it to the sink.

"Leave it, I'll get it later. We now have evening services which starts at seven. Would you like to join us tonight?"

"I'd love to, but I've already made plans for tonight." Please don't let him make a big deal out of this. I hated when born again, righteous Christian folk try to force their religion on you. "What? What did you say?" I asked, not believing what I'd just heard.

"No problem. Maybe you can make it some other time."

Blair must have read something in my face, or maybe he was a mind reader as well, because what he said next kind of threw me for a loop.

"What? You thought I was going to preach at you or something?" he asked with a grin on his face.

"Something like that."

"So, when are we going to get together again?" He asked, abruptly changing the subject.

"Well my youngest son has a basketball game in two weeks if you care to come."

"You mean I have to wait two weeks to see you again? Well, I already have plans to attend church tonight with Sonny and Macey, but what about tomorrow night, are you free tomorrow night?"

"Yes I'm free tomorrow night," I replied with a chuckle. He was persistent, but I did want to see him again and I was trying to make him think I was not *desperate*.

"Okay, let's meet for dinner tomorrow night."

"Great. How about at my place? Then I can show you how safe it is in the downtown area," I said with a smirk.

"Can you cook?" he asked

"Is snow white?"

Blair laughed. "What time should I be there?"

After we had agreed on a time, I insisted on helping Blair clean up the kitchen before leaving and he did his best to talk me into spending the day with him. During the washing up, Blair kept making excuses for us to sit down and talk, but all I really wanted to do was to get home and get out of yesterday's clothes.

It was well after three by the time I left Blair's place. In the light of day the road didn't appear creepy at all, in fact it was a beautiful leaf covered country road. On my drive back to Interstate 8, I really enjoyed navigating the twisting, turning, and dipping roads and discovered the ride wasn't much of a maze after all once I got my bearings. I was right about one thing though, the surrounding area was just as I had suspected, virtually uninhabited. I didn't see many homes at all, until I was closer to the Interstate.

The few dwellings I did see were of various shape and sizes. Some were large sprawling California ranch style homes with long concrete drives, and tiled, terracotta, or thatched roofs. There were one and two story homes; some were Mediterranean styled homes similar to Blair's. A few sat on hills or rises, and others I could barely see because they lay hidden behind trees and I could only see flashes of colors from the rooftops, or the fancy metal or plain wooden gates guarding the driveways leading up to the house.

After many more twists and turns, I finally made it through the tree cover roads to Interstate 8 leading back into the city. My cell phone had been off all night, and as soon as I turned it on the message light flashed like crazy. The first call was from Macey, who had called at seven in the morning. She whispered for me to give her a call as soon as I was awake. I'm not sure why, but I was glad Macey thought I was still sleeping when she called, since I hadn't been at home in my own bed. I laughed when I heard the second message from Sonny. His call came at seven fifteen and Sonny sounded as though he was whispering into the phone as well; he wanted me to give him a call at the restaurant around nine.

There was another call from Sonya informing me she was home from the hospital and all was well with Tameka. Even Claudia had left a message. Claudia had called me the morning of the party to cancel and she wanted to know how *Sonny's* old lame ass party had turned out. My baby boys were in the message queue as well, calling to make sure our dinner and a movie date was still on for tonight. I was meeting them for dinner in Chula Vista off of Interstate 5 at a very popular seafood restaurant called Tony's Fish Grotto.

I placed my first return call to my sons. Activating my automated voice command, I called Anthony's cell phone. My oldest answered on the first ring. That boy would make a great administrative assistant. "Anthony?"

"Mom, where have you been? Are we still on for tonight?"

"Yes, we're on for tonight." I was a bit surprised to see how smoothly the traffic was moving. Even on Sunday afternoons the traffic was usually hectic at this time of day. "So what did you guys do last night?" I asked, hoping to hear something about their evening and to find out whether or not they had been on their best behavior which was more than I could say about myself. I knew my sons were good boys and they knew right from wrong, but no matter how well your child was raised, teenagers hanging out in a group with their peers always seem to have a habit of getting into trouble. Anthony had long ago stopped discussing his evenings out, but I could still persuade Maurice into divulging information as long as Anthony wasn't around.

"Now, Mom, you know you're not supposed to ask us that question."

"I just wanted to know if you two behaved yourselves last night or will the cops be knocking on my door searching for you?"

"Moms, you know you don't have to worry like that. We were just hanging out with our guys, checking out the honeys, and collecting digits, if you know what I mean."

"No, I don't know what you mean," I replied frowning at his language. "Speak *English*, please. Where's Maurice?" I asked with a sigh.

"Rice is changing clothes for the tenth time. Hurry up, man, get a move on!" Anthony called out to his brother, as I held the phone away from my ear. When Maurice was a baby, Anthony had taken to calling his brother Rice since he wasn't able to pronounce his full name the nickname had stuck to this day.

"We were about to bounce over to the mall to pick up a few things."

"Okay, I'll see you two at the restaurant. Love you."

"Okay, Mom, we'll catch up with you later, love you, too."

I shook my head; Anthony was just too much lately. Since he'd moved closer to his school, and started sharing an apartment with another student, my child had practically grown up overnight. He was still a momma's boy, but now he didn't come home as often as he used to when he'd first moved out.

I had the private number to the restaurant programmed into my cell phone.

"Egg Roll." Sonny also picked up on the first ring.

"Sonny, how's my favorite guy?" I asked with a smile on my face. I could just picture him right this minute, grinning from ear to ear. Once, I practically knew his every thought, and he knew mine as well. That's just how close we used to be.

"I'm doing good, sweetheart, now that I've heard your voice. Glad you could take the time from your busy schedule to call me back. Did you have a good time last night? Tell me the truth now and don't lie because, baby, I heard you spent the night," he said laughing loudly on the other end of the line.

"Who told you that lie?"

"Lie? Mia, Blair and I have an understanding when it comes to you. I just finished speaking with him not more than five minutes ago, and he told me all about last night."

"You men are worse then women, where's Macey?"

"Macey is hanging out at the mall with her mother. Mia, Blair likes you a lot, a *whole* lot," Sonny said.

"Um-hum, and I suppose he told you all the details?"

"That you two slept in separate rooms last night, he also pre-pared breakfast for you this morning, and after breakfast you helped him with the dishes. Blair also stated the two of you talked until almost four in the morning, and he wouldn't let you drive home alone so he invited you to stay the night. Blair said you turned him down at first, and then you accepted."

"*DAMN.*"

"Like I said, he squealed like a pig."

"Wow, I'm impressed. You don't have many male friends and now it sounds like you and Blair have become really close."

"Well, I wouldn't say we were close, but Blair's a good man, Mia, and I'm going to make certain that when it comes to you, Blair and I will have an understanding, know what I mean? And anyway, Blair's my dawg!"

"You're crazy, Sonny. You're even beginning to sound like him," I said as Sonny's words made me smile. "I like him too. You forgot to tell me he was younger than me."

"Yeah, I heard you were kind of stumped about the age thing, but Blair said he convinced you it didn't matter. So, does it?"

"I'm working on it."

"Mia, what is there to work on? You're a woman and he's a man and you're what three, four years older than Blair?"

"Something like that, but who's counting?" I asked as I rolled my eyes skyward. God, I hope I'm not making a mistake, because I really liked Blair. My only concern about dating a younger man was I didn't want us to be the couple everyone would be pointing at as we walked down the street with me looking like I was his older sister, or worse, his mother. But here I go getting ahead of myself again, after all, what were the odds of our relationship lasting that long?

"Good answer, my dear, so stop your worrying. Now, what do you want me to bring to dinner tomorrow night?"

"Damn, baby, what didn't Mr. Blair tell you? Speaking of Blair, I still can't believe you never told me about him."

"You were involved with the *Professor* all last year, and then the two of you started doing that off and on again shit, remember? Anyway, during the times Blair and I were hanging out, you weren't available; besides, Blair does quite a bit of traveling."

"Not to mention how you never brought up Blair in any of our conversations. It's like Blair just popped up for the first time last month at the restaurant."

"Mia, I'm sure I've mentioned Blair to you before, especially about how he volunteers down at the center. Anyway, I wanted to keep you all to myself, remember?"

"Sonny-"

"I know, I know. How do you put it, *let's not go there.*"

I smiled. "You're a happily married man, now remember?"

"So you say."

"Sonny, enough, okay?" I wasn't surprised by his remark, but I was surprise to hear it so soon. I thought with his recent marriage to Macey, Sonny had finally accepted the fact that we were never meant to be. In the beginning, I'd known about Sonny's feelings for me, for I had felt the same for him and I had believed his marriage had ended the *emotional bond* we had on each other, but it looks like I was wrong.

"Okay, whatever you say, my *dear*. What do you want me to bring for dinner tomorrow night?"

Sonny and I spoke for several more minutes, and by the time we ended our call, Sonny and Macey were coming for dinner the following night with dessert. The next call I made was to Claudia but she was out, so I left her a message. I thought about having her over tomorrow night as well. I called Sonya, and invited her, but she declined. Tameka had only been released from the hospital this afternoon, and Sonya decided it would be best if the two of them spent some quiet time together.

I was dying to get out of yesterday's clothing, not to mention my scratchy underwear, so I rushed into the building and up to my third floor condo as fast as I could. I still had a few hours to kill before my evening out with the boys so I would have plenty of time to shampoo and blow dry my hair while I tried to come up with a decent menu for dinner the following evening. I had no idea what Blair liked to eat, and I was thinking maybe I should give Sonny a call and get some ideas on what to prepare when the phone rang.

"Mia, what's up?"

"Claudia? Girl, I've been trying to reach your behind all day."

"*Shittt*, girl, I had to get my ass out of Dodge. I drove up to LA yesterday afternoon and hung out with Bryan. So how was Sonny's lame ass boring party?"

"You're wrong, Claudia! It was anything but boring. I had a great time."

"Girl, that's because your ass don't get out much."

"Listen, the reason I called you earlier was to invite you to dinner tomorrow night that is if you're free?" I asked as I went a little into detail about having Sonny, Macey and Blair over. I thought by inviting Claudia over for dinner, she would appreciate a quiet comfortable evening with friends without all the drama she was used to. I'd met Bryan before and thought he was a decent guy and I'd also noticed how Claudia seemed to behave more like a woman her age instead of a spoiled child who wanted everything her way when she was with Bryan, so I wanted to include Bryan to dinner as well. I was feeling really good about the upcoming evening and was confident our meal would be great.

"So, how did you meet this guy and does he have a job?"

"Excuse me, Missy, but you have me confused with yourself. The men I meet always have jobs. You're the one who likes to support your men."

"*Whatevah*. Who is he?" Claudia replied with a smack of her lips.

"He's a friend of Sonny's. I met him last night at the party."

"You mean Sonny had single men at his party?"

"Yes he did, and as a matter of fact, Blair was the host. The party was at his house."

"Really? So that was his home address on the invitation? What does he look like?"

I could tell by her voice, that Claudia had stopped whatever it was she was doing and was paying attention to my every word. "Claudia, the man is fine, and he owns his own business."

"Get the fuck out! What kind of business, street *pharmacist?*" Claudia said with a devious little giggle.

"There you go, Claudia. You know as well as I do that Sonny doesn't associate with dealers or users."

"Well this Blair guy sounds too good to be true, a nice caring Black man- is he Black?"

"Yes he is."

"I had to ask, 'cause I know how you like to mix it up every now and then," she replied with a laugh.

"Whatever, Claudia," I replied as I shook my head at her comment.

"Anyway, a decent Black man with his own business, this I've got to see. You better add me to your little dinner party. What time shall I be there?" Claudia asked laughing loudly on the other end of the line.

"Anytime after six will be fine!" I replied.

"What shall I bring?"

"Just yourself, and if Bryan is interested, bring him as well."

"Naww, Bryan's fucking history."

Oh *shit!* Was it too late to rescind my offer? I was counting on Bryan being there to keep Claudia in line. "What do you mean *history*; didn't you just see him last night?"

"Um-hum, and that's why his ass is h-i-s-t-o-r-y. I was giving him his walking papers, and one last fuck to show him what he'll be missing when I'm gone. He was always telling me how good my shit was, but he hasn't driven down to see me not once this month, and I've been up to LA twice. Fuck him. Every time I suggest he come down and visit me, he always brings up work, or some other lame ass excuse. Shit, I ain't about to put up with his shit no more." Claudia said.

"Well, you're the one who let him get away with it, Claudia."

"I know, but it's over, no more Ms. Nice Guy for me. Oh, I know what I can bring tomorrow night, I'll bring some tequila, and all the fixings for some margaritas."

Right, Claudia nice? "Claudia, you don't have to bring anything. And I'm sorry it didn't work out with you and Bryan, I thought he was a decent guy, you two seem like a prefect couple."

"Hell, you know I can't cook, so I'll just bring the booze," Claudia said as we said our goodbyes.

CHAPTER SIX

"Maurice? Baby, I need some help down here, please," I called out as I lifted a bag up onto the kitchen counter.

"Be right down."

I headed for my room on the first floor, dumping a shopping bag and my purse on the bed.

"Mom, I thought you had today off? What do you need help with?" Maurice asked as he entered my room, his eyes taking in the shopping bag on my bed.

I reached up and patted his smooth cheek. My boys seem to be getting taller every day. Lately I couldn't get away with calling them *baby* in public. They grow up so quickly. "Baby, would you get the rest of the bags from the car for me please?"

"So who's this guy that you're trying to impress? You buy a new outfit?" he asked pointing toward the Nordstrom bag.

"I have perishables in the car, Maurice," I replied quickly. I headed for my bathroom, closing the door behind me. I was hot, exhausted, and embarrassed about the fact that my son was questioning me about my *date*. It had been a while since the professor and I had dated, but I didn't think I was trying to impress Blair. If Maurice noticed something then maybe I was trying to make an impression on Blair. My intentions had been to take the whole week off and spend spring break in Phoenix while the boys hung out with their dad, but they had changed their minds and we all decided to hang out close to home. Fortunately for me, their change of plans meant I could drop in at work to take care of some unfinished business. I knew it would only take me a few hours to finish up my project, giving me ample time to leave the office early and to pick up a few last minute items from the market and then a quick trip to the mall. I purchased a sharp looking emerald green two piece number. The top was long sleeved and long enough for me to add a belt or scarf if needed, but I decided not to because it tapered slightly at the waist for a nice fitted look. The matching palazzo pants had a nice wide waistband with a side zipper for a nice flat front and the color of the outfit was perfect with my skin tone. I'd found a fabulous pair of 18k gold hoop earrings complimenting the outfit along with a pair of cream-colored mules with two-inch heels. I liked to be comfortable in the kitchen, so stripped out of my work clothes and threw on my robe and brushed my hair away from my face, pulling it into a ponytail before tackling my dinner preparations. It was already three and dinner was at six. I had less than three hours to prepare meal for seven people. I was glad I'd had the foresight to put the chicken in the oven this morning before I left for work, and was thrilled to see that Maurice had followed my orders and had removed the roasted chicken from the oven.

Maurice was back from bringing in the last of the bags, and I went to him and gave him a big hug. "Maurice, thanks for taking the roasted chicken out of the oven for me. What did you do today?" I asked, washing my hands at the sink.

"What was that for?"

"Because, Maurice, I'm very proud of you and your brother. Is Anthony here?"

"What did I do?"

"Well, for one thing this kitchen is so clean I can practically eat off the floor and my chicken is sitting here ready for me shred."

"You told me to watch the meat and clean up."

"I tell you to clean up every day and you've never done it this well before. Baby, you know I appreciate your help." I replied as I gave the kitchen a once over.

"Thanks, Mom. I didn't do anything special today. Hung out at the mall with some friends from school," Maurice replied as he started unloading the bags. "Dang, Mom, you bought enough food to feed an army." Bending over, Maurice started tackling the bags on the floor, inspecting their contents as he worked. "So, you're not going to tell me who this guy is?"

"I told you and Anthony all about Blair last night and that he is a friend of Sonny's. I take it your brother hasn't arrived yet?"

"He should've been here by now. He called about thirty minutes ago and said he was on his way. How long has Sonny known this guy anyway?" Maurice asked.

He was not going to let this rest. "Maurice?"

"Yes, Ma'am?"

"Don't even try it." Maurice always called me *ma'am* when he was trying to get on my good side.

"What?" he asked with a look of surprise.

"I told you and Anthony all about Blair last night," I repeated. "Blair will be here tonight and you can ask him anything you want to."

"I know, but Anthony and I got to talking and we just wanted to know more about this dude. Mom, you know we have to look out after you."

"Why thank you, Maurice, but I can look after myself. Anyway, think of this a good opportunity for you and your brother to break the ice and find out all about Blair when he gets here. Thanks for bringing in the rest of the bags for me. Are you sure you and Anthony don't want to spend spring break in Phoenix?"

"Nope, we're cool. Anthony's going to spend the week here and we're going to just hang out. Mom, that shopping bag you brought in was awfully big, did you buy me anything?" Maurice asked as he backed away preparing to leave the room.

"I sure did, honey, I bought you some dinner."

Although my home wasn't as spectacular as Blair's, it was mine and well furnished. The living area was one large reading room. The walls were painted a shade of blue, which I described as *ice blue*, and the crown molding was trimmed in white. The room was comfortably furnished with a large white sofa, and two large overstuffed chairs in a deep chocolate color. I had selected dark pieces for the coffee and end tables to match the wood of the bookshelves, which covered two of the walls and both, were filled with books ranging from fiction to non-fiction, poetry, and art. I had accent pieces of blue, white and chocolate throughout this room and the dining room. The living room was my favorite room, and it well used too. From this room you could see into the kitchen, and the formal dining room. I had put out fresh flowers and before my dinner guest arrived, I was going to light scented candles, and place them in every available niche in the living and dining rooms to give the rooms a soft glow. Beside a powder room, and a den, the first floor also included the master bedroom and master bath. The walls in my bedroom were painted white. The comforter on my bed was designed with colors of light shade of pink, white, and a smattering of brown. I had carried the chocolate theme to my room as well by bringing in throw pillows and a large chocolate area rug.

For dinner I'd prepared my own specialty dish, chicken enchilada casserole with green chili sauce. It had been while since I'd prepared the dish because it was so time consuming, but well worth it in the end because everyone who had ever eaten it raved about it, including Sonny. After Anthony had arrived, and with less than an hour to go before dinner, I'd put him to work preparing the salad. Maurice even pitched in and made a pitcher of ice tea. After finishing up with the tea, I had Maurice chop up some more green onions and tomatoes for the relish tray. I'd tidied up the condo last night after I'd returned home from my date with the boys, but I was still dusting and picking lint off of this and that as I prepared dinner.

I surveyed the room one last time before heading for my bedroom to finish getting dress. I had less than thirty minutes to shower and dress. After showering I put on my new outfit, and as I stood before my mirror pinning up my hair, there was a loud rap on my door and soon afterwards Anthony announced our first guest.

"Mom, Ms. Claudia is on her way up."

I glanced over at the alarm clock sitting on my nightstand, thinking it was early and noticed that it was six on the nose. Condescending Claudia was the first one here I thought. Shaking my head I put on my new earrings and stepped back from the mirror. Not bad, the outfit complimented my figure and the color worked well with my complexion. I pinned my shoulder length hair up equally on the side of my face and decided to leave the back loose. I fluffed my bangs, sprayed a generous amount of perfume between my *girls*, on my neck, shoulders, and behind my knees and stepped into my new mules and sashayed out the room, feeling like a million dollars and anxious to get this evening started. I was anxiously anticipating Blairs' arrival. Most of my thoughts today had revolved around him, and I kept picturing his handsome smile.

"Hey, Mia."

"Hello," I said, joining Claudia in the kitchen. Claudia was in the process of getting the blender down from the cupboard. Although I had told her not to bring anything, she had insisted on bringing the ingredients for my favorite frozen drink, margaritas.

"Damn, girl, look at you! I like that color on you. Now I see why you left work early. Wow, and look at this place, it looks great in here. Girl, what did you do to it?"

"Thank you," I said with a bow. "Just sat a few candles in all the right places and wham," I said with a clap of my hands, "instant ambience! You look nice," I commented. "Looks like I wasn't the only one out shopping for a new outfit."

Claudia, smacked her lips. "These old things? Honey, this is just something I pulled out of the back of my closet," Claudia replied as she busied herself with getting ice from the freezer. "Shit, this old sweater has been hanging in my closet for so long, I'm surprised the moths haven't eaten it up. Am I the first one here? The parking spots out front are getting kind of scarce. If the others don't get here soon they'll have to park a mile away."

"Blair's riding over with Sonny and Macey," I said scrutinizing Claudia's outfit. Noticing how she'd forgotten to cut the little plastic string that holds the price tag from her *old* sweater. It appears that in her haste Claudia had ripped off the price tag leaving the little plastic string behind. Claudia was wearing a little black leather mini skirt which also had the telltale signs of being new. The indention mark left from the antitheft device was still visible on the side of her skirt. The short-sleeved tight and probably 100% cashmere lavender sweater accented her slender midriff and she looked really nice in lavender. Claudia's smooth bare legs needed no nylons and were elevated three inches by her stilettos. Her long fingernails and toenails were polished in two colors, the top half was polished in a silver color and the bottom half was crimson red and her middle toe of her left foot was sporting a rather large toe ring. I stood looking at Claudia's immaculate body, her large breasts, skinny waist, and perfectly round butt and not to mention her outstanding facial features embraced in her dark lovely hair which she wore long and loose tonight. The elated feeling I'd had earlier which had kept me going all day melted into the realization that in a beauty contest next to Ms. Claudia, I could only hope to get best personality. Feelings of utter despair consumed me. After looking at her I looked down at myself and suddenly I was feeling old, frumpy, and dumpy! I stood beside Claudia in my now ugly green outfit feeling like her mother. While she wore her hip little outfit, with the body of a twenty-one year old, belying the two-year age difference that separated us.

"Hi, Ms, Claudia," Maurice said as he joined us in the kitchen. From the look on his face, I could tell Anthony had told Maurice about Claudia's skimpy little outfit. And knowing Maurice he had come down to check Claudia out, because his eyes were practically bugging out of his head.

"Hey, here's my favorite guy. How are you doing tonight, Maurice?" Claudia asked as she gave Maurice a kiss on his cheek, then she reached out and wiped away the cherry lipstick her kiss had left upon his cheek with the back of her hand. Claudia was wearing several bracelets on her left wrist, which jingled with her every move, and she was also sporting a ring on each finger. "Maurice, why don't you put some music on and jazz this place up. Put that Maxi Priest CD on for me, baby, you know the one I like."

The intercom buzzed and Anthony was downstairs in a flash moving with the speed of the wide receiver that he was. "Yeah?" he barked into the intercom.

"Blair."

I pulled the casserole from the oven and place it on the counter. Moving like a zombie, I slowly removed the oven mitt from my hand.

My throat began to constrict and my eyes filled with water, what the hell was I thinking? How could I think someone as charming and successful as Blair could ever be attracted to me? I could just picture Claudia hanging onto his every word tonight and giving him those *I'm all yours love eyes* and by the end of the night he won't even give me a second glance. I felt a dull pain in my stomach when I glanced over at Claudia and wished for the hundredth time that I were two sizes smaller. Not as small as Claudia, but if only I could be two-sizes smaller.

"I'll be right back," I said quietly to no one in particular. I turn away from everyone so no one would notice the single tear as it made its way slowly down my cheek as I headed for my bedroom. Once there, I closed the door behind me and leaned heavily against the door full of torment.

What the hell was I thinking? Blair was thirty-four years old, and childless, and here I was, a forty-one year old woman, with two grown sons, with my youthful childbearing days long behind me, it would never work. Especially with me dressing like an old woman, I thought as I headed for my closet, knowing full well it would be in vain, for there was no black mini skirt, or tight cashmere sweater hanging in my closet. In desperation I picked up the phone and called Sonya. She was the one whom I always went to for advice, or just to get things off my chest.

"Sonya?" I choked.

"Mia? I thought you were having folks over for dinner tonight?"

"Sonya, I sure wish you where here tonight, because I need somebody to slap me. I don't know what I was thinking; this man is thirty-four years old."

"So, what's your point?"

I let out a long sigh, in an attempt to steady the trembling of my voice. "The point is, Claudia is here and she is wearing a skirt so short and a sweater so tight, hell, even I want to sleep with her damn ass. Sonya you should have seen the look on my sons faces when they saw her."

"Girl, you're crazy." Sonya was laughing loudly on the other end of the phone as she said this. "Honey, that man don't want Claudia, I don't care what she's wearing. Remember, it was you that he was interested in, not Claudia. Blair knows class when he sees it. You know, he could've gone *White* like the rest of the successful *brothas'* do. Give a Black man his own business, and some cash, and ain't nothing right unless it's *White*. So right there, you know he's different, because he's still interested in *sistahs* instead of a *White woman*."

"Well, that may be true, but Blair hasn't had a chance to see Claudia at her best."

"Uh-huh, you mean her tackiest, honey, what are you wearing?" Sonya asked, as I proceeded to describe my outfit to her. I stood before the mirror doing a slow turn, trying to convince myself that all was not totally lost. "That sounds nice, so why are you still hiding out in the bedroom? Mia, if you don't get your butt back out there and join the party, and stop hiding in your room I'll come over there and slap you myself. Call me tomorrow and we'll do lunch or something."

"You know what, Sonya, you're right! I'm going to look through my closet one more time and see what else I can find to wear. Thanks for your ear. Next time we do lunch it's on me, bye-bye." I said quickly, as I headed back to my closet trying to see what else I could find to wear, simply to discover that all was exactly as it was before. I don't know what I was expecting. I guess I thought some small miracle would change everything in my closet while I'd been on the phone with chatting with Sonya. Or, maybe my fairy godmother would finally decide to come out of hiding and wave her magic wand, transforming the clothes in my closet into something fun and sassy. But, as I pushed and shoved my way through the racks of clothing, everything was exactly as it was before, geared toward business wear. Even my casual clothes were business casual, and I didn't own a short skirt to my name. All of my dresses and skirts were professional length, ending just above my knees.

I have a great flat stomach, but my midriff bearing days were long gone, thanks to the stretch marks of childbirth. I stood before the mirror in my green outfit and let out a loud sigh, it was this or nothing. Well, there was one thing I could do, I thought, as I rushed to my top dresser drawer and pulled out a large multicolored scarf. The bit of green in the scarf matched my outfit, and I used it like a belt, as I wound it around my waist. Yes, that was much better. Thank God my stomach was still flat enough for me to get away with this look. The scarf broke up the green, and helped me look more like a happy go lucky hostess ready to entertain an attractive man.

I was still a bit nervous but my little chat with Sonya had brought back some of my confidence, but not enough to stop my stomach from spinning. I'd hoped I was going to spend the dinner hour full of radiance and on the throne of contentment, because I really liked Blair and I wanted him to like me. But not now, I had to go and invite Claudia. Damn, why had I invited Claudia anyway? I realized that I couldn't afford to stay in my room any longer for it was time to leave my room to face the beauty that is the beast on the other side of my bedroom door. After touching up my makeup, I lifted my chin and practiced a couple of smiles.

I could hear laughter and Claudia's loud voice from the other room. I had to join my guests for it would be impolite of me to linger any longer, or in this instance hide out in my bedroom. And to top it all off, I was no longer excited about seeing Blair. My bubble of joy had been busted. I gave myself a little pep talk, my hands in the air. "Time to go; get your butt moving Ms. Thang!" I'd already hidden away much too long, and it was now or never. Taking a deep breath, I brought a funny memory to mind, smiled and left my room for the second time that evening.

There was a short hallway, barely the width of a small closet that separated my room from the living area. Stepping into the hallway I turned and saw Blair in the living room sitting on the sofa. Oh, he looked so fine in his gray slacks and a black v-neck sweater I thought. Staying true to her credo Claudia, stalked her prey from above as she sat on the arm of the sofa next to Blair. The margarita in her hand hid her wet crimson claws, as she cunningly laughed at his every word. Her legs poised to leap, her left hand behind his back, one little pounce and she would have him in her clutches. Anthony handed

Blair a bottle of beer, and as Blair looked up he saw me standing in the hall. I was so lost in my own uncertainty; I missed out on Blair's smiling eyes and later that night he informed me he was silently pleading for me to rescue him from Claudia.

I had invited Claudia over to share in my joy, but seeing her was like a punch in my unsuspecting stomach. As my delicate lashes held the water from overflowing down my cheeks, I fought back the urge to grab the revolting alley cat at the scruff of her neck and throw her out the door. In a last effort to salvage my dignity I brought an amusing story to mind, one that Sonya had shared with me a long time ago, before Sonya had owned a car and when she had worn wigs to save her time as she rushed from school to work. Sonya would get up early in the mornings to catch the trolley and a bus to get to school. One day, when the Santa Ana winds were wrecking havoc in the area and while Sonya stood waiting for the bus, unbeknownst to her, her wig had blown off her head. Sonya had snickered to herself as she watch what she thought was someone else's wig tumbling down the sidewalk, and thought how it was so windy that some poor woman's wig had blown right off her head. Sonya was confident that her own locks was snugly attached to her head and as she reached up to give her tussled curls a toss, to her amazement discovered that her wig was no longer covering her neatly corn rowed head. Sonya was mortified when she realized the wig she'd spotted tumbling down the gutter among the debris that lined the street was her own burgundy tinted newly purchased synthetic wig. With a yelp, Sonya dropped her books and sprinted down the street, only catching up with her wig after it had become entangled in a pile of refuse. But, before Sonya had time to give her disheveled wig a good shake before putting it back on her head, Sonya had to dash back to the bus stop for the number 22 bus, the one she'd been waiting for, was now pulling to a stop at the curb. My heart may have been broken over Claudia's actions but my smile was truly genuine.

"Mia, good evening," Blair said with a huge grin. "I brought you these," he said as he picked up a bouquet of orchids lying on the coffee table.

"Blair, I'm so glad you could come," I replied, finally noticing his excitement in seeing me.

"So am I. I met your sons, good looking *young* men you got here. Excuse me," Blair said as he stepped around Claudia's knobby knees, coming around the coffee table to greet me. He reached out for my hand and drew me to him. "You look lovely," he whispered into my ear before giving me a lingering kiss upon my cheek.

"Thank you," I replied not missing out on the emphasis of the word *young*.

"Sonny, get out of that kitchen," I called out as I spied him and Macey from the corner of my eye.

"Hi, Macey," I said with a wave of my hand.

"That man has cooking in his blood."

"Just putting away dessert and getting us a drink," Sonny called out.

"I like your place. This is a nice size, very roomy," Blair remarked as his eyes took in a photo of Sonny and the boys posing on the beach. There were other photos of the four of us throughout my home, with memories of the good times we had shared together. "Nice picture, how many bedrooms did you say you had?" Blair asked with a wave of his beer bottle.

"Just two and a den, would you like a tour?"

Blair took a long swig from his beer before answering, his eyes boldly staring me down.

"Maybe later, after dinner. That's definitely your color," he said, followed by a quick flick of his tongue wetting his luscious lips.

"Thank you," I said returning his bold look, as I stood a little straighter in my new shoes. Suddenly I wasn't feeling so old, frumpy, or dumpy anymore. I felt Blair's hazel eyes taking me in, so I turned to the side and pretended to admire the flowers he'd brought as I relished the thought of his eyes caressing my body. Turning my head to the side to smile at him and making sure his eyes were on me alone. We stood smiling at one another for a few seconds more, until Claudia realizing her prey was escaping jumped up and tugged on Blair's sleeve.

"So, Blair, what kind of business did you say you owned?" Claudia asked as she leaned on his shoulder, in a vain attempt to change the focus of Blair's attention.

"Nothing special," he replied in a distant voice, as his eyes held mine for a second longer, then with a smile on his lips he turned to Claudia.

"Excuse me. I want get these into some water," I said as I left them to join Macey and Sonny in the kitchen, now confident that I still had the power, and chastising myself for ever doubting myself.

"What is *she* doing here?" Macey hissed the moment I joined them.

"Now, Macey, be nice," I said as we hugged. It was easy for me to say that, because now I was positive everything was going to be okay.

"Nice," Sonny said as he planted a quick kiss to my lips. "I've never seen you in this color before and it's very becoming on you. Nice," Sonny said again with a nod of his head.

"Why is *she* dressed like that?" Macey hissed.

"Don't worry about it, Macey, Blair is smitten with our girl Mia," Sonny said as he placed his arm around my waist, and gave me a squeeze. "Claudia could be naked as a jaybird, and she wouldn't get a peep out of Blair, hell I'd look, after all a naked body is a naked-" Sonny never got a chance to finish his sentence, because Maceys' sharp little elbow caught Sonny in his side. I smiled at the two of them, as Macey glared at Sonny.

"I see, so what else did the three of you talk about on your drive over here?" I asked, quickly changing the subject.

"Actually, Blair drove himself," Sonny explained as he released me from his grip.

"Oh? I thought he was riding over with you two of you?"

"So did we. The plan was for Blair to meet us at our place, but he called me this afternoon, said he'd decided to drive out alone. He was just walking up to the door when we drove up," whispered Macey.

I looked across the room where Blair and Claudia stood, now joined by Anthony. Claudia was going on about something, being very animated, as she used her hands to make her point, holding Anthony's attention, but Blair was aimlessly looking around the room as Claudia spoke. As soon as he spotted me, he excused himself and turned toward the opened kitchen and our eyes locked. The smile on his face seemed to beckon me.

I returned his smiled "Dinner's ready," was all I could say once Blair had stopped before me.

"Something sure smells good, need some help?"

"Sure, could you grab the pitcher of tea from the fridge?" I carried the casserole dish over to the dining room table and carefully sat the hot dish down.

"Girl, he is a looker," Claudia whispered in my ear as she joined me at the table.

You slut, I thought, as I smiled sweetly and replied, "You think so?"

"Damn straight."

"Claudia, he's the same man that paid for our lunch at The Egg Roll last month."

"Get the fuck out of here, are you serious? Damn! What did he do to himself? He was not that fine, *damn.*"

Drama queen. "Claudia, you are too much," I said just as Blair joined us at the table, as I greeted him with my best smile. I took the pitcher from him, our hands touching for a brief second.

"Thank you. You can sit anywhere," I said with a nod as I set the pitcher down on the table. Anthony brought out the salad before calling Maurice down to the table.

"Where are you sitting?" Blair asked as he leaned in close to me.

"Here," I said pointing to the chair closest to the kitchen. "In case I have to get up for something, and since I'll be sitting on the end, I won't disturb anyone with my comings and goings."

"Then I'll sit here." Blair pulled out the chair at the head of the table, the chair Anthony called Sonny's chair, and the one to the right of me.

Sonny and Macey followed along with the bowls of chopped tomatoes, cilantro, green onions, black olives, salsa, chips and gua-camole as they joined the rest of us at the table. Sonny sat to my left, and Macey sat on Blair's right. Maurice was on Sonny's left. Anthony, following along behind Sonny, brought the salad to the table. He grabbed the chair at the other end of the table and that left the set-ting to the right of Macey for Claudia. Claudia had gone back into the kitchen to pick up the pitcher of margaritas and upon her return, had just stood in one spot, stumped for a second on where to sit until Anthony stood and pulled out the vacant chair.

"Thank you, Anthony. Looks like we have at least one gentle-man at this table," Claudia grumbled.

"May I say grace?" Macey asked.

I lowered my head saying my own prayer and hoping it wouldn't be one of those long lengthy sermons Macey usually delivered at meal-time. I gave thanks as well after Macey had delivered grace. Thankful it had been short and sweet, as well as a little devious. She'd blessed the food then blessed the fact the Blair and I had finally met.

Claudia hardly spoke two words throughout the meal, and she left shortly after dinner. She passed on dessert, proclaiming loudly enough for everyone's benefit, how one little bite of the rich cheese-cake, and she would probably burst out of her leather skirt.

I was all prepared to walk Claudia out to her car, like I usually did whenever she visited with me, but her next sentence stopped me in my tracks.

"If I'd known everyone was going to be paired off I would have brought my own date," she said in a huff as she stormed out the door and headed for the elevator.

I turned and walked back into my condo, and now I was in a huff. After all, I had told her to bring Bryan. It wasn't my fault that she had dumped him. I called Anthony over to my side and asked him to do me a favor and see Ms. Claudia out to her car.

Later, Maurice and Anthony volunteered to clean the kitchen and afterward the two of them went up to Maurice's room. An hour later, Blair and I walked Sonny and Macey out to their car. After we'd said our goodnights, Blair and I did a slow walk around the block talking about the advantages and disadvantages of living downtown.

"Thanks again for having me over for dinner, Mia. That casserole was the delicious."

"Thank you, it was my pleasure," I said as we found ourselves back in front of my building. I hadn't noticed Blair's black Corvette parked on the street and I questioned him about this.

"In the garage at The Grand Hotel. I got a room there for a couple of days, thought I'd hang out downtown for while."

"Oh," I said pulling out my keys to unlock the double glass doors that led into the lobby of my building. "What about your business?"

"My business will be fine; anyway, that's why I have a manager. If I can trust him to run the place while I was away in Washington, I can definitely trust him to handle it for a day or two. And it certainly isn't like I'm not reachable, thanks to email, cell phones and the phone in my hotel room."

Anthony was sitting at the kitchen counter on one of the three rattan barstools that lined the counter, sipping on a Pepsi when Blair and I reentered the condo. "Now I remember you, you're the guy that teaches at the Community Center with Uncle Sonny. You look different. The last time I saw you, you were minus the facial hair and your head was shaved clean."

"Guilty," Blair said, holding his hands in the air. "When was the last time you visited the center?" Blair asked, as he grabbed the stool next to Anthony and sat down.

"It's been about three months now. Uncle Sonny's always on me about joining the staff at the dojo and to volunteer at the center. I haven't had much time to do either, especially with my curriculum. In addition to school, I have a part-time job on campus, and my mom is always on me about my grades, so I don't have a lot of spare time this year to get down to the dojo."

"You're that good, huh?"

"Uncle Sonny seems to think so," Anthony said as he rose from his seat. "Well, goodnight, Mom. Blair, it was nice seeing you again." After exchanging a hug and a kiss from me, Anthony disappeared upstairs to the loft. The loft had three solid walls with the open side facing the den just below it. Sometimes when Anthony stayed over he slept in the den, but tonight it looked as though he was going to share the loft with Maurice. There was plenty of privacy for us all. With the den door closed, they wouldn't be able to hear our conversation and we wouldn't be able to hear theirs.

I turned out the kitchen lights, and the room was filled with warmth created by the tender glow of the candles about the room. Blair and I sat in the living room on the sofa looking out at the lights from the city below.

"Nice view," Blair said after a while. We had been sitting quietly, each lost in our own thoughts.

"I like it."

"You're quiet tonight," he said turning around to face me, as he reached out and touched me on the shoulder.

"So are you," I replied as I leaned back, gazing into his eyes and what a lovely pair of eyes he had.

"I was being polite and waiting for you to start the conversation," Blair said as he positioned himself in his seat to face me. He crossed his legs, placing his arm over the back of the sofa.

"Okay I'll start. My friend Claudia is interested in you."

"I know. While you where in the kitchen your friend asked me if she could have my phone number. I asked if she needed her lawn mowed or her pool cleaned, and she said neither. Then she told me she lived in a condo in La Jolla." Blair uncrossed his long legs and leaned forward. "Mia, why did you tell me Claudia was interested in me? Am I missing something here? Is this your way of telling me you're not interested?"

"No. I just wanted you to be aware."

"Thanks, but I'm not interested in Claudia. I am interested in seeing more of you, and I was hoping you were interested in seeing more of me."

"Blair, I'm not going to lie to you, I am attracted to you. But, I want you to know that I'm searching for *forever*. I'm looking for more than just a weekend sex partner. I want don't want to be someone's *booty call* and I'm not into musical beds, so if all you want is a warm body then I'm not the woman for you. I want more; a *lifemate*. I want a man who is going to be there for me, to support me and I'm not just talking about financially, but emotionally as well. I want a partner who has my back, Blair. Someone who is going to encourage me, and to help me achieve my goals. A man who is not afraid to be with me because I might do better than him, make more money than him. Someone who is going to help me be all that I can be at whatever it is I want to do. A partner who is going to respect, and appreciate me, and to value whatever contributions I make to the relationship. It won't be one-sided either, for I would do the same for him. I would help my partner pursue his goals and his dreams, encourage him, and support him in any way that I can. Because to me, a relationship is like a partnership, two people striving for the same goals, dedicated to the other. That's what makes it all work," I said studying his face.

"Damn, Baby, forever is a long time."

"You're right it is a long time, if you're comparing it to a *booty call*."

"Who said anything about a *booty call*? You remember what I said the other night, don't you? I want the exact same thing, a serious relationship and I like that word, *lifemates*. I've already played the field, Mia, and it's not what I'm looking forward to at this time. I'm at the age were I want to settle down with just one woman. I've done it all, played all the games, and I've been played as well. I'm ready for a serious commitment, and if it's with the right woman, then marriage is a big possibility. If I'm talking marriage, then I want someone in my life that has the same values I have and I believe that person is you."

Blair and I studied each other in silence for a few seconds. We slowly began to move forward, I had not noticed until my eyes began to close how much I was anticipating a kiss from him. Oh, and what a kiss. His kiss was like candy to my lips, soft and firm and I swear his lips were sweet too. Reaching around my back Blair gently encircled me with his strong arms, drawing my body to his. At first I couldn't get into it, as I was busy keeping one ear opened just in case Maurice or Anthony should enter the room. It would have really been embarrassing, necking in front of my sons. The thought quickly faded when my chest came to rest tightly against his.

I threw my arms around Blair's shoulders, as he slowly leaned backward, resting his back against the arm of the sofa. It was ecstasy, as Blair brought his hands to the back of my head, his fingers entangled in my hair. It was only a few seconds when we broke apart, but we were breathing like we'd just finished running a marathon. I slowly opened my eyes not wanting these feelings to end and found Blair staring at me with a pleasant smile upon his face.

"I can't believe you didn't let me taste those lips last night," he spoke in a low voice as he nibbled my chin, and placed light kisses on my neck. "Stay the night with me." He said his breath hot on my neck as his hands caressed my back.

"I can't-"

"I promise I'll have you back in time to go to work on Wednesday."

"Wednesday? What about Tuesday," I asked as I lean away from him.

"I'm talking about Wednesday of next week, 'cause, baby it's going to take us that long just to get out of bed once we've had each other."

"That bad?"

"No, that good," he said as we laughed. I pushed away from him and sat up. Blair stood and turned his back to me. "No balcony?"

"The loft has one," I said adjusting my clothing.

Blair turned to face me. "I didn't mean to turn my back on you, but I didn't want your sons to come running down here at the sound of your screams," He said this as he continued to adjust his own clothing.

"Say no more," I said, knowing exactly what he was referring to. Our kissing and his caressing had also affected me in more ways than I cared to admit.

"You feel good," Blair said as he drew me close. "I can't believe ain't nobody hitting this," he said as his hands slid down my backside.

Not yet, I thought, as I leaned into him. "No, as I said before, I am not seeing anyone. My last relationship ended about six months ago."

"Really, he must have been a fool," Blair replied as he brought his hands back up to my waist.

I wanted to reply, you're right. But of course my answer was; "We had irreconcilable differences." I reached up and stroked his strong chin, and when my hand strayed close to his mouth, Blair kissed the palm of my hand.

"Well I guess it depends on how hard you want to work at keeping your relationship. Some men give up on the romance once they get what they want. Me, I'm a true believer that whatever it took for me to get you, then you can guarantee I'll keep right on doing it to keep you."

Spoken like a man. "Is that so?" I asked.

"Yes, or my name isn't Blair J. Freeman," he replied as we kissed again. "I'd better go," Blair said as he gave me one of his beautiful smiles.

I didn't want to let go of him, and I silently pleaded for him to stay, and from the passionate way Blair was holding me, he didn't seem like he wanted to let go either.

"Would you like to meet me for coffee tomorrow morning? Wait, what time do you go to work?"

"Not until Monday, and coffee tomorrow morning sounds wonderful."

"Monday?" Blair took a step backwards and gave me a long hard look. "You mean you're on vacation or something and you weren't even going to tell me?"

"Spring break. I took off because the boys and I had plans to drive to Phoenix. They were supposed to spend spring break with their dad, and I was going to stay and visit with some friends, but Anthony and Maurice changed their minds last night. They decided to hang around town instead. Go to the beach and maybe pop down to Tijuana for a couple of days. So," I said with a shrug of my shoulders, "I have the rest of the week off."

"What about you, now that Phoenix is off your agenda what are your plans for the rest of the week?"

"Nothing concrete. I was thinking about maybe taking a trip to Vegas, or just hang out in Tijuana with my sons," again I shrugged my shoulders, "I really haven't decided on anything yet, because until last night I thought I was going to be in Phoenix."

"I have an idea. Why don't you let me treat you and the fellows to a week in Las Vegas?"

"I can't let you do that."

"Why not?" Blair asked with a wild look in his eyes.

"Because, it wouldn't be right."

"Says who? Do you think the guys are still up?" Blair asked as he turned and headed toward the stairs. "Anthony? Maurice?" Blair called out from the foot of the stairs, and as if on cue, they stuck their heads out over the banister. "You two want to hang out in Vegas with your mom and me the rest of this week?"

"Sure!" they eagerly replied as they bounded down the stairs like two six year olds. "When are we leaving?" Maurice asked.

"As soon as I can get us a flight out of here and find rooms," Blair replied, his eyes on me.

"We can verify departures on the Internet," Anthony said as he rushed into the den to turn on the computer. Maurice was right on his heels, as they discussed which site to log onto.

"So, I take that as a yes from the guys, now, what about you Ms. Harris?" Blair asked with a guarded look on his face.

"Let's see if we can find a flight out and a hotel with some available rooms first, before we decide, after all this is spring break."

"There'll be plenty of rooms in Vegas," Blair said as he took my arm and we strolled into the den.

Of course Blair had been right, as he had predicted, there were plenty of rooms in Las Vegas, for anyone willing to dish out $400 a night and up. Money didn't seem to be an object to Blair as he rattled out a credit card number from memory, and booked us a large suite at Caesars Palace. Getting a flight out of San Diego to Vegas wasn't a problem either. Since Blair only flew first class he flew all of us first class as well. I guess with a little luck and a lot of cash you can get just about anything in this world, even last minute. I voiced my concern about this but Blair just shrugged his shoulders. Played it down, stating it was only money and when you die, you couldn't take it with you.

"Okay, I'll go on one condition, that you allow me to reimburse you for either our airline tickets or I could pay half of the hotel bill," I challenged him. Brave words for a broke women, I thought. Even if I cut back on my household account, this would be a stretch for me.

"Forget it," Blair replied, with a casual wave of his hand. "Consider this my treat."

I tried to compromise with him, but Blair insisted that it was no big deal. Blair was very adamant about treating us to this trip. "All right, but I must insist that we not stay for the entire week."

"What difference would that make? If we stay two days or the rest of the week, it will cost the same, especially since I've already made the flight reservations and we're scheduled to return on Thursday. If you're so concerned about cost, then altering our flight to return home a day or two earlier will cost another hundred dollars each."

"So much for that," I replied with a wave of my hand. "I was simply trying to save you some money."

"Mia, did I ask you to save me money? Don't worry about it, okay? I got this."

With that said and done, our trip to Las Vegas was sealed. We left for Las Vegas Tuesday morning, right after Blair returned home to drop off his car, and to pack some essentials. Blair contacted his office informing his manager he was going to be out of town for the rest of the week. Anthony and Maurice followed Blair home and they all rode back together in Anthony's Blazer. We took a shuttle to the airport, landing in Las Vegas just a little after ten in the morning. A limo picked us up from the airport and drove us straight to our hotel. Our suite was fabulous, it was huge and decorated with beautiful pieces. The suite included a sitting room and three bedrooms with their own bath, and later on I discovered the suite had cost Blair more than $400 a night, but he never told me exactly how much he had paid for our little last minute trip.

Anthony and Maurice were sharing one bedroom with double beds, I had a bedroom, and Blair was in the third room. Depending on my cash flow, I usually visited Las Vegas about three times a year. But this was the first time I'd ever had the luxury of staying at a classy hotel. Living on the West Coast and with Vegas being no more than a six-hour car ride away, or less than an hour by air, Las Vegas was the place to go for a fun trip, especially if there was a three-day weekend involved. Sonya, Claudia and I would drive or fly to Vegas for our birthday celebrations, or like the time we flew out to catch Celine Dion's show for my birthday, I loved me some *Celine*. If we were lucky, we sometimes hung out at Claudia's parents' timeshare which was about a mile from the strip. And on some occasions we would stay at another popular hotel in Las Vegas and split the cost of the room three ways. Now I'd have a story to tell the girls upon my return. Me high rolling in Vegas and the best thing about it was I didn't have to share a bathroom with two mirror-hogging women.

This would be the boys' fourth trip to Vegas, and like always, Maurice and Anthony had dropped off their luggage, changed into swimming trunks and had disappeared, only pausing long enough to promise to meet us for dinner later on. Since Maurice was too young to gamble, as on previous trips to Vegas, the boys usually spent the majority of their time hanging out by the pool during the day, and meeting people their own age. Some of the casinos had designated rooms away from the gambling areas for those under 21 which contained video games and other amusements underage visitors could enjoy. There was something for everyone in Las Vegas, some of the larger hotels even had roller coasters and water slides.

Since we hadn't decided on a meeting place yet, I'd given Anthony my cellular phone because his phone was limited to the San Diego area only. Blair and I decided to unpack first and get settled a bit before we headed out. As I was reading the in-house menu, Blair disappeared into his room to make a couple of phone calls.

Despite my guilt for letting Blair spend all this money on our little getaway, I was determined to have a good time. Not to worry Blair had said, and not worry was exactly what I was going to do. Still I couldn't believe that twice in one week I'd done something out of the ordinary. My extreme attraction to Blair was my only explanation for my spontaneity. Here I was in Las Vegas with a man I'd only known for two days. In my younger days I would have never done anything this out of the ordinary, but I had let my emotions go and they had taken me to Vegas! I stopped in mid-thought and shook my head in disbelief. I couldn't believe what I'd just said. I sounded like a seventy-year-old woman, *in my younger days?* Where the hell had that come from? I still had plenty of good years ahead of me, so why not enjoy them instead of behaving like I was an old maid. I was in the party capital of the world, *Sin City* and with a fabulous man. *Damn*, it was time for *me* to celebrate; I slipped out of my clothes and pulled out one of the few outfits I owned that looked like it was fun. It had been a while since I'd had any kind of fun.

"Mia, are you ready to go down to the casino?" Blair called out from the other side of my door.

By the time Blair had tapped on my door, my little pep talk had worked and kicked me into top gear. I was eager to get this party started. I was ready for all that Las Vegas had to offer. I quickly stepped out into the sitting room grinning from ear to ear. "Did you finish with all of our calls?"

"It was only a couple, and yes I'm all yours." Blair said absorbing my radiant spirit with a smile. I'd changed out of my work slacks into a pair of navy blue cropped pants, a matching short jacket with three quarter inch sleeves and a pale silk yellow sleeveless shell beneath the jacket. Hoping we wouldn't be doing too much walking today, since I was sporting my new mules from the night before. Blair smiled as I threw a small purse with a long strap over my head then pulled my arm through the strap. "You look like you're ready for anything."

"I am." I replied as headed for the door. Blair was wearing a pair of sage colored Dockers with a black short-sleeved pullover, which stretched around his large muscular shoulders. Blair was still smiling as he held the door open for me and we headed out to the elevators. He put his arms around me as we waited for the elevator.

"We're going to have a terrific time! I'm glad you're here with me."

"So am I," I replied as I gave him a quick kiss. We held hands on the ride down and continued to hold hands as we strolled into the casino area. I let go of Blair's hand, and was ready to try my luck at the slot machines. Then I noticed that Blair had turned in the opposite direction toward the gaming tables.

"Mia, come give me luck, watch me play."

Two hours later we were at another popular hotel watching the white tigers. Blair didn't need me around for luck, but he sure treated me as if he did. My man walked away with more than twenty thousand dollars in winnings. He told me in order to win big you had to play big. I cringed every time he put down a five hundred dollar chip. I'd stood awestruck as Blair played with the same somber expression regardless of if he won or loss. I spent the time thinking what Blair had played with today, was my household budget for months. The hotel upgraded our status to high rollers and even offered us free meals for the rest of our stay.

At Blair's insistence, I played the dollar slot machines, instead of my usual quarter slots, big spender that I was. After hitting a jackpot of five hundred dollars I'd called it quits. Blair laughed when I took my winnings and walked away exclaiming that this would pay for Maurice's basketball camp this year. Blair had given me a guarded look at my comment, but didn't say a word as we left hotel.

I'd forgotten all about my earlier comment as we stood watching the white tigers, so I was taken by surprise when Blair suddenly grabbed me by my elbow and guided me through the crowd of onlookers and out the door of the hotel, stopping only when we'd reached the huge bronze statue of Siegfried and Roy and their white tiger that stood out front of the hotel.

"Does your ex-husband help you out, I mean financially?"

"Excuse me?" I asked at his question.

"Your ex-husband, does he help you out financially with his sons?"

"Yes he does. Why do you ask?"

"Well, when you hit that jackpot earlier, you said the money was going to go toward Maurice's basketball camp tuition."

"Yes, it is. Maurice's dad paid his tuition last year, and it's my turn to pay the tuition this year."

"Oh. So he is a part of their lives?"

"For the most part, yes," I replied not knowing were Blair was going with this series of questions.

"How often does he see his sons?"

"You know what, Blair, they're not babies. They can pick up the phone and call their dad anytime they want to see him. Maurice visits his dad from time to time. Last year after camp he stayed with his father for two weeks. Anthony, on the other hand, hasn't seen his father since his graduation from high school, but that's between Anthony and his dad."

"How long have you been divorced from their father?"

"Fourteen years," I said as my eyes searched the sky. Blair was questioning me as if he had some deep rooted anger in his past. I was having a great time being here with Blair in Las Vegas that is until Blair put a damper on it by bringing up my ex. I was not going to let this bother me. I was in Las Vegas with money to spend and I was going to have fun. "How did we get on this subject anyway?"

"I'm sorry, does it bother you?"

"Yes it does, because I was having a great time until you brought up my ex-husband."

"So what do you want to do now?" Blair asked as he caressed my hand.

"Up to you," I replied, in a somber mood.

"Okay, let me ask you this. What would you be doing right now if I wasn't here with you?"

"Easy question, taking in the sights or my favorite thing to do in any city, shopping!" I exclaimed suddenly in a better mood.

"Okay then, let's go shopping," Blair said as he stepped to the curb and hailed a cab.

After we had settled into the cab, I used Blair's cell phone to call Maurice and Anthony, who had returned to the suite and was await-ing my call. On the way out to the outlet stores, we swung by the hotel to pick them up.

Again Blair insisted on paying for all of our purchases, and once Anthony and Maurice discovered this, there was no stopping them. Of course, I was the bad guy of the hour, and made them return some of the items they had brought up to the register. Blair was all smiles, and kept insisting that it was okay since he had won big at the tables, but I held firm. I did let Blair buy them a few needless items like one of every *Michael Jordan* item the store had.

After we'd finished our shopping, we dropped off our purchases at the hotel and then we hit the Strip, deciding to visit the fabulous Bellagio. We strolled through the beautiful Botanical Gardens and around the man-made Lake Como watching the spectacular water show orchestrated to classical music.

By the time we made it back to our rooms it was well after ten, and by then I was dragging my feet. I was thankful I'd purchased a pair of comfortable sandals at the outlet store and had the foresight to replace my mules, but still, we had done quite a bit of walking. At the Bellagio we'd chosen an Italian restaurant to eat dinner, and I discovered Italian food was Blair's favorite cuisine. I'd eaten too much and my clothes were practically bursting at the seams, but what I'd eaten didn't rival Blair's healthy appetite. He was either really crazy about Italian food or he hadn't eaten in a week. The food was deli-cious and if I wasn't careful more dinners like this with Blair would cause my waistline and butt-. I stopped in mid-thought refusing to complete that line of thought because I was beginning to sound like someone else.

During their earlier haunts, Anthony and Maurice had discov-ered one of the many 21 and under dance clubs and they headed out to party the night away decked out in their new clothes from head to toe. I was beat and all I wanted to do was take a long soak in the large Jacuzzi bathtub in my room. I shared this with Blair as I made my way to my room.

"Mia?"

I turned and looked back into the sitting room. Blair was standing at the bar making himself a drink. "Yes?"

"Let me know if you need some help with that," he said with a smile.

We'd held hands all day and even though we weren't touching now he was able to give me shivers just by the way he looked at me. "I'll keep that in mind," I said as I turned one of my sexy smiles on him before I turned away and entered my room. Once in the bathroom, I turned on the jets in the tub, adjusted the temperature, added some scented bath salts and let the tub fill as I undressed. Just right, I thought as I finally slipped into the bubble-filled tub. I made sure the quick jets of water made impact with every inch of my body to deter the many aches and pains I would have from walking around town in 2-inch heels trying to be cute. As I enjoyed my soak, my thoughts drifted to Mr. Blair J. Freeman. I giggled like a sixteen year old as I remembered our day. We had behaved like newlyweds, the way we'd held hands and touched one another throughout the day. We even snuck in a few kisses every chance we got. I soaked in the tub for about fifteen minutes, aroused the entire time by the thoughts of Blair's sexy hands stroking my body. My overwhelming urge for Blair's sexy body pressing against mine was so intense that it was time for this bath to end. One more second and I would have called him in and we would be together.

I stepped out of the tub flushed with desire. I dried off and rubbed on scented body lotion. I kept reminding myself that he as just a few steps away in the other room, but I wasn't ready to bring our relationship to the next level. I slipped into my panties and bra and donned my long sateen robe, courtesy of the hotel, and hurried off to Blair. As I pulled the door to my room close I noticed that Blair was no longer in the sitting room and the lights had been turned low, but the light from his room shone brightly through the crack under the door.

I hesitated and then went to his door and rapped lightly before losing what little courage I had summoned up to do something this daring.

"Come in," Blair called out.

I cautiously opened the door to his room, not sure of what I would find on the other side. I peeked in to find Blair wrapped in a towel from the waist down, with the phone up to his ear. His body glistened with droplets of water. He wore a single gold chain around his neck with what looked like small medallion or locket hanging from it. I would never tire of looking at this beautiful man. The towel was tucked in below his navel; his midsection was a mirror of his chest, firm and just as wet. Just as that day in his guest room, my eyes took in the sight of him and it was as before, he was a stunning piece of work.

"Just a second, I was about to listen to my messages," he said holding up one finger, his eyes embracing my body. "On second thought, my messages can wait," he said hanging up the phone. "Feeling better?"

"Much better, thank you. Getting ready to take a shower?" I asked, knowing full well he had just stepped from the shower seeing the water glisten off of his well sculpted chest. This had to stop. I was behaving like I'd never seen a man before. I don't know what had gotten into me, lusting over this man like he was the last man on this earth.

"Just finished," he replied as he brushed a few droplets of water from his arm.

I crossed my arms feeling shy and almost losing my nerve; until seeing his pouting lips. "You said if I needed anything to let you know."

"That's right. So, what can I help you with, Mia?" he asked as he came forward.

"Umm, I really shouldn't be asking you this but..."

A deluge of passionate thoughts surged through my head, but was it too early? How could I ask him to do this with me, I thought as I looked down at my feet.

"Mia, you can ask me anything." Blair said pulling me closer to him, into his bare damp chest.

I rested my head on his damp shoulders, the sweet aroma of Blair's clean body, urged erotic thoughts. I wanted to grip him with my legs and press his body against mine, but the sensible side of me blurted out, "My feet are killing me, do you know how to give foot massages?"

Blair laughed, as he reached for my hand and lead me to the bed. He lifted my foot into his lap and began massaging it. I wanted to scream! His manipulations sent me to heaven! I closed my eyes as his magic hands massaged away the pain from my feet, then his hands found their way to my calves, sending me beyond heaven. I lay back letting his strong hands work the ache right out of me. Blair lifted my other foot, working the same delight as before, feet, ankles, calves, and thighs. Blair worked and stroked my muscles while I moaned with pleasure. It was pure bliss the way his strong hands massaged my worn-out and aching muscles. I wished his hands to go higher, as my body turned to putty in his hands. But instead, I did the unthinkable and drifted off to sleep.

I awoke to the sound of someone else breathing in the room and the warmth of a body lying beside. I turned to find Blair sleeping as close as possible without touching me. His eyes were closed and his mouth was slightly opened, with one arm behind his head and the other lying across his stomach. His chest was still bare but he had changed into a pair of white boxers and I was able to get a closer look at the gold chain around his neck and discovered it was a locket not a medallion as I had thought before. I felt a tad bit guilty as I stroked his body with my eyes as he slept.

I was a little disappointed but at the same time relieved upon discovering that I was dressed exactly as before. My underwear was still intact and the sash to my robe was still tied snugly around my waist. My stirrings awoke Blair and he stretched his long arms high over his head.

"You should have awakened me?" I said as I sat up, feeling as though I'd been caught with my hand in the cookie jar for watching Blair as he slept.

"I was not going to wake you. You looked so beautiful laying there, sleeping like a baby." Blair swung his legs out of bed and stood.

Thinking only few minutes had gone since I'd came in for my foot massage; I got out of bed and headed for the door. "I'd better get back to my room before the boys get back."

Blair was still standing next to the bed. "They're already here."

"What?" I pulled my robe around my knees and brushed my hand absently through my hair.

"They returned a couple of hours ago. I was in the sitting room watching TV when they came in. They sat around for a few minutes with me and we talked about their evening."

I turned and looked toward the door leading back into my suite.

"Don't worry, they thought you were asleep in your room," Blair said, apparently interpreting the look of worry on my face.

"What time is it?" I asked.

"Just a little after two," Blair replied as he walked up behind me and slid his arms around my waist. "Stay with me tonight."

I leaned into him, my back against him, and wrapped my arms around his, my hands covering his. He felt so good. I turned around, in his arms. If only he knew. I wished for nothing else but to stay in his arms through the night. "Blair-" I began.

"I promise I'll be on my best behavior," he said as we moved our lips together. My knees turned to jelly as a soft moan escaped me when Blair pressed his moist lips firmly onto mine. He gently caressed my lips with the tip of his tongue until they parted, allowing his tongue to explore mine.

"If this is an example of your best behavior then we're both in trouble," I said as his kiss sent a charge of excitement through me.

"No we're not. I don't have any condoms and I would never insult you by suggesting we make love without one."

"Make love?" Was all I heard as I kissed him until he let out a long low throaty groan.

"Yes, make love," Blair replied. He slid the robe down over my shoulders and down my arms pushing it to the floor. He then began to softly kiss my neck, shoulders, and arms and gradually we drifted backwards to the bed. Kissing me deeply, Blair moved his hands downward as he slowly caressed my body, his large hands sliding up and down, touching every inch of me. He gently stroked my breasts as his eyes took in the sight of me. "You are so beautiful." His voice cracked as he said this, and his breath tickled my ear sending me into a spin. He kissed my chin and my neck continuing down and stopping at my nipple gently giving it a nip through my bra. It was erotic as hell, and with each touch of his lips I throbbed in anticipation. One minute I wanted him to stop, and the next I wanted him to take me right then and there. He stopped just long enough to say, "I want you so badly," in between kisses.

I placed my hand on his head moving his lips lower to meet my own hungry kiss. Sitting on the edge of the bed, Blair lowered himself down on his knees, his lips against my abdomen. He slid his hands under the waistband of my panties giving them a light tug. I started to protest, but just as quickly his mouth came down on mine, pushing me back down onto the bed with his electrifying kisses.

"Tell me what you like," Blair whispered in my ear.

I sighed loudly, as he trailed his tongue down the side of my neck. I moaned. "Don't stop." Placing my hands against the side of his head, I gently guided his lips back to mine for a long sensuous kiss. After many long minutes of kissing and fondling, I finally came to my senses. I pushed away from him and looked into his eyes. "Blair, I can't do this. My sons are in the next room, and I don't feel comfortable doing this knowing they are just a few feet away."

"We're not doing anything-" he begin.

"Not yet, but we will be if we keep this up," I said as I glanced down, feeling his large erection against my thigh. I looked up, and our eyes locked in an unbreakable stare. Could he feel the desire in my eyes, because I wanted him so very badly.

"So you think that little of me?"

"No. Baby," I begin as I rubbed his arm. "It's just the opposite. I mean, once we get started who says I'll want to stop?"

"I'll stop."

"What if I won't let you?" My body was on fire, if I didn't get back to my room soon, we were going to be rolling in the sheets, on the floor, in the bathroom, on the dresser. "Oh somebody stop me please," my mind screamed.

Blair smiled and lowered his eyes, "I'll stop," he said again, as he kissed me softly, then again. He cupped one breast in his hand, and gently kissed it.

My lips were saying *no* but my body was screaming *yes, oh hell yes* "Blair."

"Trust me," he said as his hand entered beneath the waistband of my panties, "I'll stop."

In spite of the warmth of the room, Blair's touch made me inhale and then sent shivers up my spine. "They will hear me."

"Who? Who will hear us? Don't tell me you're one of those loud screaming mommas?" He asked as he raised his head to look at me with an amused look upon his face.

"I do not scream," I replied with a slight attitude knowing a little humor was just the water I needed to douse out the flame of passion.

"Okay. If you don't scream then what makes you think we'll be heard?" Blair looked as though he was enjoying my discomfort.

"Forget it, okay. It isn't right for me, a mother, being intimate a few feet away from her children. How can I set a good example for my sons if I can't practice what I preach? I'm sorry but this just isn't right." I pushed his hand away, stood up, adjusted my panties and bra and quickly headed for the door. I picked up my robe threw my arms in the sleeves and knotted the sash around my waist. Safe.

Thankfully Blair hadn't followed me to the door because I don't know what I would have done if he'd protested me leaving the room. But Blair was a gentleman, as he stood next to the bed with his arms folded across his chest. Oh what the hell. I rushed back over to him and gave him an unforgettable kiss, a kiss that would definitely keep me up for the rest of the night. "Good night."

CHAPTER SEVEN

I didn't rise from my slumber until around ten the next morning. I had slept later than normal because usually when in Las Vegas I slept very little not wanting to waste any time sleeping away the hours. Las Vegas was a twenty-four seven city and when we visited we tried to cram in as much time as possible into our days to enjoy every minute of our stay here. But since Blair had kept me up all hours of the night, my inner clock was running a little behind this morning. But our late night hadn't seemed to bother Blair at all for he had left a note informing me he was at the gym working out. Maurice and Anthony and slept in as well and now they were up, dressed, and on their way out to meet a few people they'd met the night before. They had all arranged to meet for breakfast and afterward they had decided to visit a couple of the larger hotels to ride the roller coasters. They were in a hurry to get their day started and were impatient to get out.

After getting dress and ordering a pot of coffee from room service, I was surprised to see them still hanging about, until Maurice approached me for a loan.

"Mom, can I hit you up for a loan until I get my allowance?" Maurice asked.

I looked at my sons who were now young men and who would one day soon have lives of their own and I would lose them to their wives and families. I smiled at Maurice, with his handsome boyish face, and a hint of fuzz over his top lip. He was trying to grow a mustache for his eighteenth birthday which was in two years and at the rate it was growing he would need the full two years to grow it out.

"I'll give you some money Maurice, but don't forget you're sixteen, and you'd better behave like the smart boy I know you are. Get my purse, please. I guess you want a little extra something too, huh?" I asked Anthony as he sat next to me, and reached out for my hand.

101

Anthony was clean shaven, no facial hair for him. They each wore their hair short and even a stranger could tell they were brothers. Both sported the same long nose, light brown eyes and of the same height. Their skin tone was lighter than my own, and having spent most of their early teens at the dentist office, they had beautiful even white smiles.

"Only if you can spare it, Mom," Anthony said as he flashed his pearly whites at me.

"Trying to butter me up, huh?"

"Mom, you know you're the best," Anthony said as he pulled me into his arms, giving me a big kiss upon the cheek.

"Here you go," Maurice said as he handed me my handbag.

I counted out one hundred each from my jackpot winnings. "Easy come, easy go," I said just as Blair entered the setting room.

"Good morning, all," he said enthusiastically looking around the room rubbing his hands together. "So what's on the agenda for today?"

"Morning, Blair, we've already made plans for today, but we could meet you guys for dinner," Anthony said as he and Maurice headed for the door.

"Anthony, you still have my cell phone?"

"Right here," he replied patting his pocket.

"Watch out for your brother-" I began

"Mom, come on! I can watch out for myself. I am old enough to know the difference between right and wrong, you know? I'm not a *baby*," Maurice said giving me one of his stubborn looks.

I placed my purse on the small dining table. "You two just make sure that you stay together and if it doesn't feel right, then don't do it. Maurice Harris, if you roll your eyes my way one more time you will be spending the rest of the day right here in this room." With this last statement I got a quick kiss on the cheek and *"I'm sorry"* from Maurice before they bolted out of the room.

Blair was sitting on the arm of the sofa slowly shaking his head, and grinning at me.

"What are you grinning at?" I asked as I sat down on the other end of the sofa.

"You know, you're one bad *Momma* keeping those two young men in check the way you do. I can tell they respect you."

I returned his smile, as I looked him over. Blair looked fine in his tight jeans, white polo shirt, and new sandals he had purchased last night. "Don't you love and respect your Mother?"

Slowly Blair's happiness seemed to melt away. His shoulders slumped and he lowered his eyes. I wished I could take back the seemingly harmless words but it was too late. "My Mother is dead." The words were a cold knife to my heart.

"Oh, Blair, I'm so sorry." I moved over to him, noticing an unreadable expression on his face. He turned away to hide what I thought was his pain. Hesitantly, I reached out, laying my hand on his shoulder.

"Don't worry about it; she died a long time ago. So what's on our agenda for today?" he asked turning around to face me and his whole persona had changed, Blair seemed guarded, even his eyes appeared darker.

I gave him a long hug and a quick kiss to his lips. Blair responded to me by tightly wrapping his arms around me, turning my quick kiss into a deeper one. I melted into him all cocoon-like wrapped up in his strong embrace. I nuzzled his neck, as the warmth from his breath on my neck brought back memories from the night before. I was ready to be carried away in his arms. Who knows what would have happened if his cellular phone hadn't ringed.

Leaving one arm around my waist, Blair removed his phone from his belt. "Sonny, what's up man?" Blair rolled his eyes skyward as he said this.

I took this opportunity to leave his embrace, and headed for my room to repair the damage to my makeup. Ten minutes later I emerged to find Blair back in his room and he had left his door open. Grabbing my purse I joined him in his room. Blair was still on the phone when I entered the room.

"We're leaving Thursday afternoon. Okay, we'll see you then, bye. That Sonny is like a police dog, my man's always sniffing." Blair looked at me as though it was the first time he'd seen me this morning. "You look nice," he said after a while.

I looked better yesterday; I thought but thanked him anyway. Today I was also in a pair of jeans, a short sleeved pink cotton blouse and a pair of Nikes on my feet. I was ready for a day of walking. "So, what are our plans for today?"

"We could stay here and continue were we left off last night," Blair said with a mischievous look on his face. "Anthony and Maurice will be out all day, I can put a do not disturb sign on the door and you can scream all you want," he said with a wink.

I smiled at his statement. "I do not scream. And anyway, what if something happens and they return back to the room early?"

"Mia, either you want to do this or not. You know I *can* wait until you run out of excuses."

"Blair, I am not making excuses. You know as well as I do that all the best made plans are made to be broken."

"They are not coming back to this suite, this is Las Vegas. Trust me on this one, Anthony and Maurice will find plenty to do in this city, and keep out of trouble as well," Blair quickly added.

"No," I said with a shake of my head. "It's too close for comfort. I'm sorry, Blair, I can't do it." It was true; I really didn't feel comfortable. I had no qualms about having sex with Blair, he was like a magnet, but not with my boys around, I wasn't ready for that, not yet.

"Okay, let's get out of here and find something to eat, I'm starving," Blair said as he rubbed his hands together. We left the room, but as we were waiting for the elevator Blair ran back to his room to pick up something he'd forgotten.

After breakfast, Blair felt lucky again so we headed for a different hotel for some more gambling. Blair made a beeline straight for the gaming tables, and I headed for the dollar slot machines. I wanted to see if my luck from yesterday was still holding. I'd been playing for about an hour or so before I was joined by Blair. We kissed like we hadn't seen each other for days.

"Let's go for a walk," he said after releasing me.

"Okay, this machine has gotten cold anyway. What about you, did you get lucky again?"

"I sure did," he replied steering me out the door. We stepped outside and hailed a cab to the MGM.

After the *MGM*, we crossed the street to visit the *Luxor*, and *Excalibur*. Last on our list of casinos on that end of the strip we wanted to visit was *New York New York*. But after only ten minutes or so inside, Blair and I became separated. *Paris Las Vegas* was supposed to be next on our list. I hung around the area were Blair had last seen me and waited for him to come back this way, as I played a couple of more machines and an hour later Blair finally showed up. We didn't make it to *Paris Las Vegas*, for Blair insisted we visit the *Bellagio* again. Blair seemed to be in a hurry as he reached for my hand and steered me out the door and into a cab. By the time we made it into the hotel we were practically running. Everything was in fast forward, but I just followed his lead. Although I made sure we stopped to take a picture at the entrance of that grand hotel.

This was one of the most exclusive hotels in Las Vegas, but the way Blair was dragging me through it you would have never guessed it. Blair seemed to be ignoring everything I thought we'd came to see. "Baby, we visited this hotel last night, and we saw everything that there was to see."

"Where are restrooms?" I asked as I scanned the walls for the familiar sign. Even though we had visited here the night before, I still couldn't remember how to get to the ladies room because the hotel was enormous and it easy to lose your way.

"Come on," Blair said, with a smile giving my hand a tug as we weaved through the crowded casino. I thought we were on our way to the ladies room until we came to a large foyer filled with elevators.

"Blair, we can't use those elevators. You have to be a guest at the hotel to use these elevators," I said, pointing at the large sign hanging from high above just at the entrance to the foyer. Blair winked at me as he pulled out a key card and stuck it into a slot near the elevator. The elevator doors slid open and Blair whisked me inside. Seconds later, when the doors opened again, we stepped out onto an exquisite carpeted hallway. Blair grabbed my hand and pulled me along behind him as he read the numbers on the doors. He stopped before a room and stuck in his key card on the slot on the door.

I was still speechless as we entered the lovely suite. And here I thought our suite at *Caesars Palace* was grand. This room was beyond anything that I could have ever imagined. I roamed around the large sitting room, and then into the bedroom, after remembering I had to use the bathroom. When I returned back to the sitting room Blair was still standing in the same spot as before, with his back leaning against the door and a sly look on his face. He started to smile as I slowly advanced toward him.

"So this is where you disappeared to for over an hour. Blair, what are we doing here?" I asked, returning his smile which grew even bigger upon discovering he'd been busted.

"I'm sorry I had to leave you alone but I wanted to go some-place where we would have some privacy," he said drawing me close, while he slid his hands down my curves, stopping just below my hips, forcing my body against his. He started caressing my lips with his, moving slowly down my neck as he placed small kisses following the curve of my neck.

"Blair?"

"Hmmm?" he raised his head as I return his kisses.

"What made you think we'd need this much privacy?" I asked, as I waved my hand out toward the room.

"Well," he begins, as I stopped him from speaking by kissing him full on his gorgeous mouth. He was a great kisser and I could do this all day. I pulled away, his eyes holding me with a smoldering look. "Well," he begin again, "I thought perhaps the space would come in handy just by chance I want to chase you around the suite without any clothes on," he finished and before he could take another breath, I took another kiss from him.

"And may I ask what you're going to do with me after you've caught me?" I followed this up with another, even longer French kiss. This time Blair ended the kiss, and my body temperature shoot sky-ward as his tongue made a warm moist trail down the side of my neck, and then back up to my lips. I slipped my hands between our bodies and sought out the zipper on his pants. I could feel his body stiffen in anticipation of my touch.

"Well…I, if you don't drive me mad before hand, I thought I'd throw you down on the floor and have my way with you." Blair was groaning and moaning by the time he completed his statement. For now, my hands were in position inside of his pants. I'd found the pot of gold at the end of the rainbow.

I kissed him again, as he throbbed in my hands. He was hard and warm to my touch. I opened my eyes, my lips breaking contact with his, but we were still very close as my hands tighten their grip on my prize. His eyes popped opened, his breathing became slightly more rushed. I was impressed at how well he was keeping his…cool. "Umm, that sounds like a plan," I said as I rubbed my cheek against his. "But, I have an even better idea," I said and flicked his earlobe with the tip of my tongue. I released him from my grip and reached up and slowly opened the first of the three buttons on his polo shirt. After undoing the next two buttons, I slipped my hands under his shirt, pushing it up and over his flat stomach, his broad chest, and his wide shoulders. Blair pulled his long arms from the sleeves and whisked the shirt over his head, depositing it on the floor. Next I placed both hands flat against his stomach and slowly moved my hands upward until I came into contact with his nipples. The smell of him was intoxicating and his hard body felt good beneath my hands. I rubbed each nipple between my thumb and index finger, making slow little circles, around and around as I lowered my head first to the right nipple and then to the left nipple. Giving my full attention to both, first with my tongue and then with my teeth.

"*Ahh*," Blair groaned. His large hot hands were up the back of my blouse, as he groped for the hook on my bra. He lowered his head, his lips searching for mine and I raised my head as my lips ended his search. At last Blair was able to undo my bra, freeing my breasts from their enclosure. One hand immediately slipped between us and captured my left breast, while his other hand strayed to the small of my back. With our lips locked in their own heated embrace, Blair moved forward, guiding me to the bedroom as I busied myself with the opening of his belt buckle and the unsnapping his jeans. We didn't stop moving or unlock our lips until the mattress hit me in the back of my knees. Still planting kisses on my face, Blair quickly unbuttoned my blouse, removing it and my bra.

I wasn't prepared for what came next, as Blair stood back and took in the sight of me. His eyes grew wide with excitement and the sound that emerged from his mouth was more like a yelp than a yell or like a painful cry with some other undistinguishable sound thrown in and then "Oh my God," as he drew me in close to him and his hands as well as his mouth were all over my breasts. Blair muttered something else unintelligent as he stepped back and dropped his pants. And there he stood with the body of an Ebony Greek God. Oh yes! I could almost picture him naked and chiseled in chocolate colored stone standing on a pedestal being worshipped by adoring women. I smiled at the sight of him, my breasts still tingling from his earlier assault. Blair reached out and grasped the top of my jeans and reeled me into him. With one hand, Blair worked the snap and lowered the zipper of my jeans. He dropped to his knees as he pushed my jeans down and over my hips and onto the floor followed by my underwear. Blair pressed his face against my abdomen, moving his face slowly across my waist and stomach while his hands cradled my breasts. Earlier I had been so aroused I was quivering and longing with desire. Now, it was as though my abdomen was the canvas and his face the paintbrush, as Blair moved his face up, down, and across my middle. His touch was gentle and sweet and erotic as hell, adding flames to the smoldering embers within. I touch his head, and Blair looked up at me. His eyes were laced with desire like molten pools of hot cocoa. He stood and gently gathered me in his arms and our lips locked in a long deep sensuous kiss.

It only took us two steps to get back to the bed. I threw back the comforter and the top sheet, and turn around to wrap my legs around this delicious man, only to discover that he was no longer in the room. "Blair?" I called out with disappointment because he was no longer by my side.

"I'm here," he replied as he entered the room with a pack of condoms in his hand. "They fell out of my pocket," he said waving the packet in the air. Apparently he noticed the look of disappointment on my face, for he tossed the packet on the bed and pulled me to him. "Here, let me heat you up a bit."

A few minutes later, Blair was retrieving a condom from the pack. His eyes fixed on mine as he ripped the packet open with his teeth, and with a little help from me, we rolled the cold wet piece of plastic into place. Blair spiced the moment, grimacing as he wiped his mouth with the back of his hand, as though his mind finally registered the bitter taste of the condom packet.

By the time Blair slipped inside of me, a part of me died right there on the bed and floated up to the heavens. That's how amazingly breathtaking our union was. Blair stilled any movement on my part, with only our lips moving as we tasted one another. Blair began to move, as he slowly slipped in and out of me. My muscles were working overtime constricting around his hardness, gripping and pulling him deeper and deeper inside of me each time he entered. It didn't take long for me to reach my peak as my insides throbbed, clutched and pulled him in as my orgasm rocked through me, wave after wave. It was the big one that California had been waiting on, at least a 10 on my Richter scale, only I was in Las Vegas and the earth shaker was Blair. It was nonstop, raw hot wild sex and the bed was alive with our hot sweating bodies. Our arms and legs raised high in the air, and the room loud with moaning and groaning. I could hear the blood rushing in my ears. Blair's heavy breathing about the room; pushing, shoving, slipping, and sliding, in and out. *"Blair."* Blair rolled over and now I was on top and I rode him like the black stallion that he was and this time he called out my name. *"Mia."*

"Woman, I can't believe you made me wait this long," Blair said with a shake of his head.

"Well, was it worth the wait?" I asked.

His smile melted into a pucker as he lowered his head for another one of our passionate kisses. "Every damn minute," he whispered in a husky voice. We rolled over and lay on our sides, face-to-face, and no longer joined at the hips. "You know you're a very attractive woman. Tell me, where have you been all of my life, beautiful lady?"

"Well for the first seven years of my life you weren't even born yet."

"Don't start," Blair said as he planted a wet sloppy kiss to my nose.

"You asked," I said with a kiss to his lips and before I could pull back, his arms tighten around me and we went into another wave of sensuous kissing. Blair was a great kisser and I couldn't get enough of his hot sexy kisses. Blair stopped and pulled back, but not to far, for we were still nose-to-nose, chest-to-chest, stomach-to-stomach, hip-to-hip.

"You taste just like I thought you would, sweet."

I rubbed his arm, marveling at the strength in them. "Uh-hum, I bet you tell that to all your women."

"Only the ones who are sweet," Blair said with a smile as he traced an outline of my lips with his finger. "You know what?" he asked as he gave me a gentle kiss, "I could stay like this forever."

"So could I. So Blair, now that you've had me, I hope you're not going to stop trying to get me into your bed?"

"Are you kidding? Hell no."

"You are such a smooth talker." I replied sarcastically.

"And you're a sweetheart. I know what you're doing." He replied.

"What?"

"That's okay. I still think you're a sweetheart."

"I have no idea what you are talking about, but you're a sweetheart too," I said as I sat up in bed.

"Damn, baby, your *twins* are *banging!*" Blair said as he raised his head admiring my breasts.

"I take it you like my *girls*? Is that what all that commotion was about earlier? For a minute there I thought you'd lost your mind, the way you were calling out to God, Mary, and Joseph. And you laughed at me because you thought I was going to be the loud one?"

"I wasn't laughing *at* you, I was laughing *with* you. Your breasts are beautiful. I like them a lot, very, very much," he said with a couple nods. "Makes me want to reach out and touch and feel and kiss and touch some more," he said as he reached out and did just that.

I laughed. "Thank you." And then I thought, should I tell him? Oh what the hell. "This is what twelve thousand dollars will get you. A little something my plastic surgeon hooked me up with."

"What are you talking about? You're not telling me the *twins* are implants are you? Because I know implants when I feel them, and the *twins* are not implants," Blair said as he reached out again, as though to convince himself that they were not implants.

"You are funny. No they're not implants. I had the 'twins' over-hauled last year."

"Overhauled? Now who's funny? Listen to you, talking like they're a car or something."

"Yeah, well you know, we're just like mechanical devices. We all need a little maintenance every now and again. A little nip and tuck in all the right places, and the 'twins' are sitting pretty again," I said picking up the term Blair used, even though I liked calling my breasts my *girls*.

"You got that right. They are definitely sitting pretty. Sitting right up and saluting me!" Blair said as he leaned in grabbed and nipped me with his teeth. "You look like you've been in a fight." He said as he gently touched my shoulder were a welt had formed.

"You look like you ran into a wall yourself." I had banged my head on Blair's chest and he was also sporting a few marks on his back as well.

"I was just thinking," he started as he pulled me back down onto the bed, "If I'm really gentle, is it to soon to have you again?"

Around six that night Blair and I were jarred out of a sound sleep by the chiming of Blair's cell phone. The air conditioner was blowing out a steady stream of cold air, but we lay wrapped in a body-heated cocoon of each other's arms. Blair cleared his throat as he fumbled around the nightstand for his cellular phone.

"Hello? Anthony?" Blair said as he cleared his throat again. "Are you two back in the room? I'll tell you what, why don't you guys go ahead and, ah- hum," Blair cleared his throat. "Go ahead and order some room service and we'll see you guys first thing in the morning, okay?" He asked as he looked my way, and I nodded my head. "What?

Tell Maurice he can order whatever he wants. Okay, I'll tell her, bye," Blair finished with a smile. "Anthony wanted you to know they were on their best behavior today." Blair wrapped his arm around my waist as he said this, brushing his lips against my forehead; as he let out a loud sigh. "You tried to kill me today, you know that?"

"Me? What about you?"

Blair laughed, as he tightened his hold on me. "You're too much."

"Too much is better than not enough, right?" I closed my eyes, my head resting comfortably against Blair's chest, feeling the vibration deep in his chest as he chuckled. Definitely all man, I thought, and what a man. We had made love for most of the afternoon, only stopping to order room service and to eat. Blair was insatiable, and I'm not simply speaking of his appetite. We had pigged out on fried shrimp, Buffalo wings, coleslaw, and French fries, followed by large slices of carrot cake and a bowl of fruit for dessert. Blair seemed to be munching on food throughout the day, claiming he had to keep his strength up. We washed our meal down with bottles of sparkling wine. I wasn't sure if I'd fallen into an exhausted sleep from our love-making, or if I'd just simply passed out from all of the wine I'd drank, but whatever the reason, my mouth was terribly dry.

"Is there any more water left?" Earlier, we had raided the mini bar of all the bottled water it held, along with a couple of bottles of rum, during our vigorous lovemaking.

"Hold on a sec," Blair said unwinding himself from the entanglement of my legs and arms. On one side of the bed we had an assortment of trays, glasses, and bottles' littering the floor next to the bed, and this was the side Blair leaned over as he reached down producing a small bottle half filled with water.

I sat up and reached for the bottle of water, as Blair twisted off the cap and handed it to me. "Oh, just what the doctor ordered," I said after a couple of sips. I closed my eyes, taking several more quick gulps, finishing the bottle off. I opened my eyes to find Blair staring at me. I looked at the empty bottle in my hand then back at Blair. "I'm sorry. Was this the last one?" I asked, thinking maybe he'd wanted to share a drink of water. Blair slowly shook his head, a slight smile upon his face, his eyes drifting down to the *twins*, and as I looked down at his naked body, I noticed how he had *rose* for the occasion. My body tingled with desire, and anticipation from the way Blair's eyes bathed over me, as well as from the memory of our earlier sessions of love-making. When Blair leaned toward me and took the empty bottle from my hand, my breath came out in short little gasps and when he began to caress *twins*, I was ready and looking forward to what was to come next.

CHAPTER EIGHT

"See you Sunday night," Maurice said as we hugged. "Blair, thanks for the trip, I had a great time."

"Yeah, Blair, thanks for the trip, it was a blast," Anthony said as he thumped Blair on the back. "See you Sunday, Mom, love you-Peace out!"

"I love you too. No later than ten Sunday night, okay?" I shook my head at his theatrics.

"I know the routine," Anthony said, pointing a finger at me as he headed for the elevator. "Come on, little Bro, let's roll!" Anthony called out to Maurice as he swung his bag over his shoulder, and stepped into the elevator.

Anthony and Maurice were off to Long Beach for the rest of their break to visit their cousins Chris and James. We'd just gotten back into town an hour ago; just long enough for Maurice to unpack his dirty clothes, and to repack fresh clothing. I wasn't concerned about them driving out to Long Beach, for Anthony had proven on numerous occasions how skilled a driver he was. Keeping a clean driving record was one of the conditions I had encouraged him to keep simply for the privilege of having me pay his monthly car insurance premiums for him. Of course I could trust Anthony to keep a clean driving record because he was such a good driver, which was one of the reasons I had decided to purchase him the Chevy Blazer in the first place. I was equally impressed by the way he kept the Blazer in such excellent condition.

I was in the process of repacking when Blair entered my bedroom, yakking away on his cellular phone. Blair stopped just long enough to give me a hug, followed by a quick kiss to my lips. He'd been on the phone with his office nonstop the minute we'd arrived from Las Vegas. Before we'd left our suite at the *Bellagio*, Blair had asked me if I would like to spend the rest of the week with him in Alpine. So, with very little convincing from Blair and with no plans for the remainder of the week I couldn't say no and now here I was packing a fresh bag for my trip to Blair's place up in Alpine.

I bent over to pick up a pair of sandals and my body screamed in protest. Every inch of my body ached. How could this be, how could I possibly ache in places that I didn't even use? What the hell had I been doing? Well I knew what I was doing, but that didn't explain why the back of my neck hurt as well. Now I had some inkling of what it must feel like to participate in one of those *triathlon* competitions. My body was anticipating a nice relaxing soak in the Jacuzzi and some more of Blair, to help melt away my aches and pains.

Blair placed his hand over the mouthpiece of the phone, "Mia? Are you ready? Our ride is here, okay Jeremy we'll be right down."

"What? I thought I was driving us out?" I quickly threw the pair of sandals into my bag and zipped it shut.

"Let's go." Blair said picking up my bag.

"I thought I was driving us to your place?" I repeated.

"Jeremy is taking us. You didn't honestly think I would let you drive home alone on Sunday night did you?"

"Blair, let's not go through that again," I said with a shake of my head as I followed him out the door.

"We're not. Don't forget to lock up." With my bag in his hand and his bag slung over his shoulder, we headed out the door for the elevator.

"Jeremy, this is Mia Harris, Mia, my manager, Jeremy." Blair said as we stepped up to a big white Ford Expedition parked at the curb with Blair's company logo on the side.

"Hi, Jeremy," I said reaching out to shake his hand. Remembering him from the night of Sonny's party, he'd been the man at the gate. Blair held the back door for me, and gave me a hand up into the tall SUV. The minute the doors closed the two of them started talking business as we headed down the street to the freeway. Tuning them out, I turned to watch the view from the window. After about fifteen minutes of nonstop talking, Blair reached around between the seats and placed his hand on my knee apologizing for ignoring me. I told him not to worry about me; I'd been thinking now would be a good time to take a quick catnap, since neither of us had gotten much sleep last night.

It was mid-afternoon on a Thursday and traffic wasn't all that bad as we made the forty-five minute trip to Alpine without any serious traffic delays. I woke up from my little cat nap once we'd reached the area with the dips in the road. The jerking, rocking, and swaying motion of the SUV caused from the unevenness of the road jerked me from my slumber. At the entrance to the gated drive, Blair jumped out and pushed a series of buttons on a keypad mounted onto a white pole mounted next to the gate. Within seconds of the gate swinging inward, Orpheus and Eurydice ran up to the gate, their little tails wagging in glee, excited about seeing their master back home as Blair reached out and gave them each a brisk rub on their broad chests. I was curious as to who had cared for the dogs while Blair had been away, thinking perhaps it had been Jeremy. I looked his way and was about to question him on this until I saw his fearful expression as he watched Blair interact with the two large dogs. Jeremy seemed quite shaken from the sight of the dogs. Blair checked his mailbox before hopping back into the SUV, and we drove the additional half-mile or so up to the house with the dogs following in close pursuit. Of course Blair was the first to exit, calling his pets to his side, and the three of them disappeared around the side of the house and out of view.

"We can get out now," Jeremy, said as he stepped out, opening the rear door and removing our bags from the back seat, along with his own briefcase. He seemed to know the routine well enough, I thought as he helped me down from the big truck. "I hate dogs," he said in a flat voice. We were standing by the front door when it swung open. Blair reached down and picked up both bags, dropping them off in the foyer.

"Jeremy, can I get you something cold to drink?"

"I wish, but my boss doesn't allow me to drink on the job," Jeremy replied with a smirk.

"Mia, make yourself comfortable. I promise I'll be right with you. I just want to check out a few figures with Jeremy and sign off on the payroll checks," Blair said with a smile.

I made a beeline straight for the kitchen. I was starving. I'd skipped breakfast and had passed on the limited snacks they now offered on the plane, opting to try and catch up on my sleep instead, and now it was well past three. I had to admit, that for a bachelor's pad, Blair's kitchen was well stocked as I searched through the cupboards for something to nibble on. Opening the fridge, I discovered a tray containing steak kabobs marinating in a reddish looking sauce. There was also a Caesars salad and a tray of miniature egg rolls, along with a couple of bottles of white wine. Well, that answered my question about who had taken care of the dogs. This was definitely one of Sonny's signature meals. I pulled out the steak kabobs and sat them on the counter just as Blair entered the kitchen.

"Jeremy said good-bye," Blair said, walking up behind me and slipping his arms around me and giving me one of his great bear hugs. "Hmm, I see Sonny's been playing chef again. I suspected he was up to something when he asked me what time our flight was getting into San Diego. Look's good. I'll start the grill."

I couldn't have agreed more with Blair. Especially about starting the grill and I was even happier upon discovering that it was a gas grill, which meant no waiting for the charcoals to heat up, so our dinner was ready in practically no time at all. An hour later, as we sat out on the patio enjoying our dinner, Blair and I discussed our recent trip, and our mutual friend, Sonny Steward. "When I saw those steak kabobs I had a hunch that Sonny had been here," I said as I stabbed at a piece of lettuce with my fork. "He took care of the dogs for you too?"

Blair nodded. "Actually, he and Macey hung out here at the house."

"Jeremy doesn't seem to be much a dog person," I said.

Blair shook his head. "You'd think someone as big as he was wouldn't be afraid of dogs, but he is. The man is deathly afraid of dogs, no matter what size or breed. Long story," Blair replied at my questioning look.

"Things okay at the office?"

"Jeremy's a good business man, I trust him completely. "By the way, did I mention Sonny and Macey would be spending the weekend with us? Sonny's been working long hours, staying late and closing down all week and then making the drive out here. He wanted to get things taken care of so he could have the weekend off. I told him he should have a little more faith in his managers; give them more responsibility to his staff, that way he can have more time off."

"It isn't that Sonny doesn't trust his managers, Sonny is a workaholic and he loves to cook. And no, you didn't mention anything about Sonny and Macey hanging out with us. Sounds like we're in for a fun weekend," I replied as I rolled my eyes.

"What?"

"Nothing."

"Do you usually roll your eyes at nothing?"

"Well, I thought I was going to have you all to myself this weekend," I replied as I reached out and touched his hand.

"That can be arranged," Blair replied as he gave my hand a squeeze. "When Sonny asked if he and Macey could come out and spend the weekend with us I assumed it would be okay with you. That's what I get for assuming, right?" he asked as I nodded my head. "You know, it isn't too late to call Sonny up and uninvited them."

"No, really it's okay. I was being selfish. I'm sure the four of us will have great fun."

"I like you being selfish," Blair replied, raising my hand to his lips. "We'll have a good time, you'll see. There will be plenty of times when it'll just be the two of us, *Ms. Selfish*, because I like where your thoughts are going, so keep that thought, okay. By the way, I've been meaning to ask, how long have you been with your company?"

"I've been there just a little over five years now."

"Ever thought about going into business?"

"All the time," I begin remembering my business proposal. I lived and breathed that proposal for a year. "As a matter of fact, Claudia, Sonya and I were thinking of opening up our own recruiting agency. Claudia's dad was going to back us, but then I decided I didn't want Claudia to have that much control."

Blair nodded his head. "Don't trust her, uh?"

"No, it isn't that, I mean, Claudia can be a bit much at times. And God forbid for Claudia's name to be link to anything with my name. I know her, and she'll just…oh, I don't know. Something's just not right about her lately, but I can't quite put my finger on it. Know what I mean?"

"Then don't do it. Always go with your first instinct. Did you tell them why you changed your mind?"

"No, I just told them the time wasn't right."

"You still want to do it."

"Definitely," I replied as I picked up my fork. "There's money to be made in the temporary business, the industry is booming."

"Let me back you."

"What?" I asked, setting my fork aside.

"Let me back you," Blair repeated.

It had nothing to do with me not understanding his question, but it had come as such a surprise. "Blair, you're sweet, but I can't let you do that."

"Why not? What kind of business does Claudia's dad have?"

"He's a physician. The whole thing started one day when I just happen to share with Claudia my plans for opening my own agency and she talked her dad into applying for the loan for me, but, Blair, I can't let you do that. What if the business is a flop and you lose your money?"

"Wait a minute; you were going to let Claudia's father secure a loan for you, right?"

"I know, but that was Claudia's idea, not mine."

"So why didn't she go ahead and do it without you?"

"She doesn't have my passion, or the smarts for that matter." It was true, Claudia was a daddy's girl who drove fancy sport cars and spent her entire paycheck on shoes and clothing. I'd started with my current company a year after Claudia and she was still an administrative assistant, and I had been promoted three times in five years. I loved the recruiting business and had learned as much as I could, and I advanced with the company as it had grown.

Blair threw his head back and laughed. "Check out my baby. Seriously, did you do an analysis? Did you research other temporary agencies in the area and find out what the pros and cons were on owning this type of business? Are you going to go with direct hire only, or will you be pay rolling temporary assignments? What about stock, did you do a comparison of stock of the other companies?"

"Sounds like you know a little bit about the business as well. Of course I did it all. I didn't go as far as checking out the stock of other companies, I just let it all go and decided not to pursue it. The timing wasn't right."

"You still have your research?"

I nodded my head.

"May I review it?"

"Blair-"

"Yes or no?"

"Okay, I'll let you review it. But that doesn't mean I'll let you back me."

"Stubborn lady."

"Stubborn man."

"Spell it."

"What?"

"Stubborn man," he said with a wink. I just loved the way Blair wetted his lips, and now I knew how his luscious lips felt and tasted. I had to look away from him, busying myself with the folding of my napkin and placing it on the table, as memories of our times together flooded my thoughts. Blair was driving me crazy. I wanted him over and over again. He was so alive and full of vivacity; rarely did he sit still, barely long enough to eat a meal. He was full of get-up-and-go, his presence lighting up the room whenever he entered. Blair just seemed to shine and sparkle, and he was constantly on the move, bringing cheerfulness with him wherever he went, and to whatever he was doing. His drive and enthusiasm even followed him into the bedroom. I was drawn to him like a fish to cool clear waters, like a moth to the amber dancing flame, like a mosquito to warm flesh. He was exactly what I needed at this time in my life, my strong black knight.

I was unable to remember were I had heard that poem before, had it been in a novel I'd read, or in a romantic movie I'd seen. There was more to the poem but I couldn't remember the rest of the words, but I felt it truly showed how I felt about Blair. I was out of control and in love with this man and it was frightening. Whenever I closed my eyes I could see myself spiraling into a dark hole. The bottom was not in sight, but I've always known that there was someone at the bottom waiting to catch me, and I assumed that person was Blair. I glance back, not being able to take my eyes away from his sweet sexy mouth, knowing I was hooked and not able to get enough of him. Blair looked up and smiled, his piercing stare holding me in place.

Blair raised his napkin and dabbed delicately at the corners of his mouth, his eyes never leaving my eyes. "Are you enjoying your view, pretty lady?"

I smiled and nodded my head. Blair was adorable and he was aware of the hold he had over me. "Yes," I replied. The man was turning me on just by running his tongue slowly over his lips. "Are you?"

He smiled that all knowing smile still holding me with is gaze. "Absolutely, without a doubt."

I laughed. "What ever happened to a simple yes?"

"Mia, there is nothing simple about you. The way you talk, laugh, walk, and when you throw your head back when you laugh just turns me on. Your hair in the sunlight, your stunning smile, your womanhood, your touch, your scent, the way you moan and wiggle when you're beneath me. Baby, there is nothing simple about you. I'm going to enjoy spoiling you, you know that?" Blair asked as he leaned over and kissed me." Blair pushed his chair back and stood up, holding his hand out to me.

I didn't know what to say to his charming words, so I simply held out my hand to his. I was blushing as I returned his smile, and my desire for him seemed to burn a hole in my soul as I replied to his charming words. "Blair, no one has ever said anything closely resembling to what you've just said to me before. That was beautiful."

"From my heart," he replied, as he pulled me to my feet.

I felt like a young blushing bride at the thought of some of things we had done. I amazed myself by how brazen I was with Blair. I could feel adoration in his eyes when we undressed each other with the lights on. Blair made me feel like the most beautiful star *Venus* burning brightly in the sky, I hadn't felt this alluring in a long time. The way Blair had desired me in Las Vegas, the way he yearned for me now vanquished all doubts and insecurities I'd harbored about myself. I was like a teenager and he was like my first love. He bathed me in his love and I wanted to rejoice in his love forever. This was it, I was certain Blair was my *lifemate*. It was so right, it felt so perfect, and how in sync we were, in heaven and on earth. Blair's aura was radiant; his outstretched hand seemed to shine through me, and in me, touching my heart. I could feel the passion of his soul as waves of his love consumed me.

"You know what?" I asked as I rubbed my cheek over his cheek, feeling the roughness of his five o'clock shadow against my face.

"What?" He spoke softly, as though not to stir the air around us, his breath warm against my cheek.

"I want you right now, drop your swim shorts." Blair shocked me by taking a step back and dropping his shorts. I hadn't expected him to obey my command, and I couldn't help but laugh.

"What? You wanted me to drop my shorts just so you could laugh at me?" he asked, as he began to chuckle.

"You caught me by surprise," I said between giggles. "You pulled those shorts off so fast, I hardly saw you move." My laughter quickly turned to a scream, when with lightning speed; Blair reached out and pulled the straps of my one-piece suit down off my shoulders, and my suit was halfway down my waist by the time I had a chance to react. Then, Blair scooped me up into his arms and carried me into the house.

"Hello *girls*," Blair said as he laid me down into bed, before stretching along beside me.

CHAPTER NINE

"So, what have you two been up to?" Macey asked the next night, as we lounged out on the terrace in comfortable reclining chairs while Blair and Sonny stood at the grill grilling chicken for our dinner.

"Macey, if you have to ask, then I'm not telling," I replied with a chuckle. If only she knew, I thought dreamily as I did a slow stretch remembering our lovemaking sessions from last night, and this morning. I looked over at Blair just as he turned to me and we smiled that all knowing smile.

"You've changed," Macey said and when I pulled my eyes from Blair and looked over at Macey she was giving me a long hard look, studying me as she waited for my reply.

"What do you mean?" I asked as I leaned forward and took a sip from my glass of lemonade. I had added a splash of tequila to spice it up.

"I don't know, but there's definitely something different about you. You've loosened up, yes, that's it. You used to be so stiff and proper. When Sonny first introduced me to you I thought you were stuck up, but then I discovered that was just your way. I like you better this way, though."

"Well, thanks, Macey."

Macey waved her hand in the air as she continued. "Sonny's glad you and Blair finally got together. I don't know why it took Sonny so long to introduce the two of you. He's known Blair for almost a year now. Sonny says it makes him happy to see you happy. I wish I had what you have," Macey said with a loud sigh.

"Like what?"

"Like your friendship with Sonny."

"Macey, haven't you ever heard of the old saying be careful of what you wish for? Anyway, you have something more than his friendship, you're his wife."

"I know that, but you're his best friend, and best friends are a lot closer than husband and wife."

"Okay, maybe the two of you should get a divorce, and then you could become his friend." I was aware of the direction our conversation was heading, for we'd had this conversation plenty of times before and I knew exactly how it would end. For the longest Macey had been jealous of my friendship with Sonny. I wasn't the stiff and proper person Macey made me to be. As a matter of fact, I was just the opposite. In the beginning, Macey had been the one who had made it difficult for us to be friends and it took some time for her to warm up to me.

When I'd first met her, Macey had confided in me at how shocked she had been upon discovering I was African American. Macy had informed me how often Sonny would speak of me with nothing but kind things to say about my sons and me. Then there had been the time when Macey had inquired if Sonny was the father of one of my sons, and I remembered how I'd laughed at her question, and then I'd felt sorry for her because the look on Macey's face was as though she had just finished eating a bad egg. In the beginning stages of Sonny and Macey's relationship, Macey had walked out on Sonny one night threatening never to return. That had been the night Sonny had finally invited Macey to his place, and Macey had seen the many pictures of our strange little family. Sonny had confided in me how Macey had demanded that he end his friendship with me that very night, and how Macey had threatened to leave Sonny if he didn't do as she said and remove all the photos of me from his home. Sonny then explained how he had held the door opened and had bid Macey a goodnight.

Long after the two of them had gotten back together, Macey had shared the story of that night with me, and I'll never forget the look on her face when Macey had made clear to me how hurt she'd been when Sonny had held the door opened for her, bidding her a good night. I can still remember the look of hurt in her eyes as Macey had explained that particular scene to me. Macey had looked away from my scrutiny as she went on to explain to me how difficult it had been for her to swallow her pride and call Sonny up the following week, apologizing to him. Macey had sworn she was not the jealous type, but just watching the interaction between Sonny and I always made her envious, that is until she got to know me. Now we merely behaved as friends, if only for the sake of Sonny.

That had all taken place over three years ago, and Macey still didn't know Sonny as well as she thought she did, for if she did she would not have put so much demand on him about starting a family. Macey wanted children badly, but Sonny did not. I brought my attention back to our current conversation, leaning in closer, as Macey had lowered her voice. Macey was speaking of a friend, who had recently had a child, a little boy, and Macey was curious to know which would be easier to raise, boys or girls.

"What do you think, Mia? You have two sons, are they easier to raise than girls, or would you have rather had a girl? I prefer a daughter, at least I would be able to relate to her, I mean, after all, I'm a female and I believe I would be able to understand her wants more so than a male," Macey was saying as she twirled a lock of hair around her middle finger. I was just about to answer when Sonny interrupted.

"Hey, what are you two up to?" Sonny called out in his deep baritone voice. "No whispering over there."

"Mind your business, Sonny," I called back to him.

"Excuse me, but you have two thirsty cooks over here," he said, and to prove it, he held up his empty beer bottle, turning it upside down.

"Honey, don't you think you've had enough to drink?" Macey asked as she stood and walked over to stand next to Sonny, reaching out to rub his back.

"Macey, I've only had two beers, and anyway, I'm not driving, we're staying the night remember?"

"Man, I'll grab you another one," Blair said as he walked away, and as Blair passed my way, he reached out for my hand, pulling me up and out of the recliner.

"All you had to do was ask," I said as we walked side by side into the house, his arm around my waist and my arm around his waist.

Blair looked over his shoulder before speaking. "Sonny says Macey is in a foul mood."

"He's right about that. Macey's ready to start a family," I said as we entered the kitchen.

"Oh, I see. She told you this?"

"Yes she did, in a round about way. Macey was going into her how *two friends are closer than husband and wife* routine, and discussing raising children. So, I kind of guessed the direction she was heading. That's how she always starts the *baby* conversation."

Blair opened the door to the fridge and took out two bottles of beer. "Ah, and I take it she was referring to you and Sonny's friendship? Now don't tell me Macey is jealous of you and Sonny?"

"Macey used to be jealous of our *friendship*, but I think she's past that stage now. I may as well tell you now because I'm sure you'll hear about it sooner or later, if you haven't already heard it before. Sonny paid half the cost of Anthony's Blazer. I'd planned on buying Anthony a car for his graduation with the help of his dad, but at the last minute his father bowed out, so Sonny pitched in and helped me with the cost. Macey was so furious that she threatened to leave Sonny for good, this time. She'd left Sonny before, you know? But she came back to him. I offered to make payments to repay Sonny, but he wouldn't hear of it. He really cares for my sons, and they have a lot of love and respect for him too. Sonny is like an uncle to my sons."

"Sonny told me about that incident. So, that was you, huh?" Blair asked as he turned to me. For a second or two he didn't say a word and then he stepped right up in my face, so close, that at first I thought he was going to kiss me. But instead, Blair peered deeply into my eyes, as if in search for something. "You would tell me right?" Blair asked.

"Tell you what?" I asked, not sure of what he meant.

"If you ever gave my man Sonny some booty, if you two have ever slept together?"

"Blair! How crude-"

"Man, don't you know you're not supposed to ask a woman a man's question. Ask me, I'll tell you." Sonny had come into the kitchen carrying a tray of cooked chicken. He sat the tray on the kitchen table with a loud bang, and boldly stepped between us.

"Actually, Sonny, this conversation is between Mia and me," Blair said with a wave of his hand as though to dismiss Sonny. "We've already discussed this issue the first night we met and I was just asking now to-"

I didn't allow Blair to finish his statement. "To what, Blair? To catch me off my guard, to see if I gave you the same answer as before?" I had taken a step back, but my eyes never left Blair's face as I stared over Sonny's shoulder at Blair, for I wanted him to see my eyes as Sonny told him the truth.

"Okay, I'll ask the *man*. Sonny, have you and Mia ever sleep together?" Blair asked, ignoring my question, but keeping his eyes on me.

"Of course not! Our relationship was never like that. Mia's my friend and I love her like a sister, no more, no less!" With this said Sonny picked up his beer and stormed out of the kitchen.

"You still had doubts? After all we've done and said you still have doubts about my relationship with Sonny?" I asked, as I pointed at him.

"Not until now, not until I found out it was with *you* that Sonny had defied his fiancée, and had given *you* the money for Anthony's wheels. The two of you may have never slept together, but *that* man loves you more than like a *sister*."

"Oh, shit, Blair, *please*, and to think I was falling in love with you." I turned to walk away, but Blair grabbed me by my arm and led me though the back door. "What are you doing?" I asked as I struggled with him.

"I want to talk with you," he said as we stopped near a tree in the back yard.

I snatched my arm away from him and folded my arms across my chest. "Say what you've got to say," I said, angry at the audacity of this man, I was just too through with him at this moment. How did he have the gall to ask me that question? I couldn't believe him. I'd practically given him my heart on a silver platter, and here he was behaving as I'd done something wrong, like he was my father or something!

"First of all, I want to tell you that you weren't there the time Sonny talked about helping out a friend to buy her son a car. You weren't there, Mia, to see the look on my man's face as he described what a truly wonderful person you were, and at the time I didn't know he was referring to you." Blair said as he threw his arms into the air. "You weren't *there* to hear the catch in his voice when he talked about how rough the first year of your divorce had been for you, and how for a long time he wanted to make things right for you. Mia, you weren't there, but I *was* when Sonny told me about the first time he'd ever kissed you; yeah he told me that," Blair said with a nod of his head. "Sonny asked me if I'd ever kissed an angel before, and at first I didn't know what he was talking about, but now I know. You weren't there, to witness the hurt look on his face when he told me how the two of you had decided not to pursue a romantic relationship because you were on the rebound from your ex-husband. I believe you both, when you say you've never had sex with one another other before, but I know the two of you have slept in the same bed before. Am I right or wrong about this?"

God make him stop! "Blair, I don't understand why this is so damn important to you." I said angrily. I was so upset I was on the verge of tears, but Blair couldn't see them because I had turned my back on him.

"Because, Mia, I don't like being lied to. Because when I ask you something I want the truth from you. Why? Because that's what love is made of; truth and honesty in a relationship makes for a stronger bond, and love is stronger than anything else in this world. My grandmother instilled that in me at a young age, Mia. Truthfulness is what love is all about," Blair said, in an aggravated fashion.

"What do you want from me, Blair? First you give and then you take away," I said finally turning to face him.

"No," he said in a voice much softer than before, his hands gesturing in the air. "Baby, that's not what I'm doing," Blair said as he lowered his voice. "When Sonny said all those things to me about this person, I didn't know it was you he was speaking of. I thought it was someone else that he spoke of. Then after seeing the pictures of you and your sons, that Sonny kept at his place, and upon seeing how delightful you are and what a doting mother you were, and your smile. I- I just fell in love with that person, even before I'd met you," Blair said reaching out to me, then letting his hand drop down to his side before actually making contact with me. He bought his hands to his face; folding them as if in prayer and then letting them drop back down to his sides. "I didn't know that the woman in the photos was the same person that Sonny had kissed and called an angel. I had no idea it was you he spoke of. At the time I believed it was two different women. Mia, now that I've met you, and seeing how well we click as a couple, it feels exactly what I've been waiting for all my life. And I don't want to lose you," he said with a shake of his head.

Blair didn't touch me and I didn't touch him. I leaned up against a tree, my back resting upon the mighty trunk. I folded my arms across my chest, and lowered my head. With my eyes closed I could actually visualize that night all over again as the time slowly ticked away. The only sounds were those of the woods out behind Blair's backyard. I could hear the faint flurry of the treetops as a light wind played among branches. A sweet melody from the birds high in the tree above me made this otherwise dark moment light. The bark of a dog from far in the distance, and the loudest sound of all, which only I could hear was the racing of my heart, for I did not want to share what I had deemed to be my cherished time with Sonny. I spoke softly, but quickly. For I feared if I didn't tell Blair the truth now, I never would or worse, I'd run away from him and his piercing eyes, never to look back again.

"One night Sonny and I were sitting around talking and it had grown late. I lived in a one bedroom apartment at the time. My sons shared the bedroom and I slept in the living room on a sofa sleeper. It was right after I'd left my husband, and things were pretty rough for the three of us." I stopped and took a deep breath, vividly remembering that night. Blair stepped forward and gathered me into his arms, and as he did this he turned me around, my back was now facing the back door leading into the kitchen. I held on to him, breathing deeply of his scent and marveling at the notion of how quickly I'd fallen in love with this man. After a few seconds, I continued with my tale, holding tightly onto Blair, his strength encouraging me. "That was the *first* time Sonny and I had kissed, but we decided not to take it any further. We talked some more and we felt it was too soon, that I was too vulnerable at the time." I smiled at the memory. "Sonny was a perfect gentleman that night, for we talked well into the night, and then we fell asleep, you know, right there on the sofa, fully clothed. That night we had snuggled, and kissed because I suppose that was what we needed at the time. Sonny promised- tha- that he would always be there for me- for us. I promised him that I would always be there for him as well, and we've kept our promises to each other. Sonny has been there for me, through thick and thin and I've been there for him as well. I love him; I really do, but not the way you think. What Sonny said today was the truth; he is a brother to me and an uncle to my sons. If all I've said today makes what I said to you earlier a lie, then I'm sorry, because what Sonny and I have is just between the two of us. I believe if circumstances had been different at the time, maybe he and I most likely would be together today as man and woman. But, Blair, I'm not ashamed, nor am I embarrassed, and I will not feel guilty about what happened that night. Because that was our time and it was before you, and before Macey." I looked around at the sound of a throat being cleared behind my back, and spotted Sonny and Macey standing just a few feet behind us.

"I feel the same as Mia does about this. We did nothing wrong. This happened long before either one of you came into our lives," Sonny said as he joined us under the tree with Macey at his side.

"I just wish someone would have told me the truth sooner," Macey wailed. "All this time I thought something was still going on between the two of you," Macey said, but I could hear the skepticism in her voice.

"I told you there was nothing between us," Sonny said, with a trace of harshness in his voice, as he looked down at her as though she was his enemy.

Macey lowered her head from Sonny's scrutiny, as she spoke. "But, Sonny, I wish you would have trusted me enough to tell me the whole story about your relationship."

Sonny opened his mouth to reply, but seemed to change his mind as he turned to me. I gave a slight nod, but all I wanted to hear was what Blair had to say. Throughout my tale his body language hadn't changed. He'd continued to hold me tightly, his head resting on top of mine, his left hand stroking my back, his right hand in mine, but- he had said nothing the whole time.

"Hey, dawg, if you're standing here with me, who's watching the chicken?" Blair asked in a gruff manner.

Sonny threw one arm around Blair's shoulder and one around my waist and next Macey squeezed in, joining our group hug.

Blair blew me a kiss over the top of Maceys' head just before we broke apart and the four of us headed back into the house. As we reached the back door, Blair reached out for my hand, and we entered the house hand in hand, but something had changed in Blair. After all was said and done I had a feeling that Blair still had some doubt about Sonny and I, and it was if a dark cloud had made it's way into our otherwise cheerful day even though in reality, the sky above was still perfect as ever.

I'd decided that the night couldn't have gotten any worse, but then I've been wrong before. Macey and I got drunk off of margaritas laced with Grand Marnier, and Sonny was flying high off of cognac. Blair was the only sober one amongst us. The three of us were intoxicated and jovial, along with being loud and boisterous, as we sang old Motown hits. Around midnight Blair herded Macey and Sonny off to the spare bedroom, and after placing clean towels in the bathroom he left them to their own devices.

I was still out back on the terrace, sitting beside the pool, all bundled up in a big towel and drunker than I'd cared to admit. After seeing to his guests, Blair returned outside and spotting me in the same spot he knelt down before me. He placed his hand on my knee as he peered up into my face.

"Sweetheart, are you ready for bed?" he asked and I could make out a trace of a smile on his face.

"I'll be in, when I'm in." I was still harboring a grudge about his earlier behavior, questioning me the way he had. I'd had an attitude for most of the night after our conversation under the tree. The more I thought about it, the more it had irked me. The nerve of him acting as though nothing was wrong, I thought as I pushed his hand away from my knee. "I maybe have drunk to you but I'm not stupid," I spat out and in my condition, what I'd just said had made perfect sense to me.

Blair turned his head away, hiding his face from me, but I could hear what sounded like a snicker of laughter just before he lowered his head, and his shoulders started to shake. "Baby, no one mentioned anything about you being stupid," Blair said as he stood up and held out his hand to me. "I have to let the dogs out. Why don't you go inside and wait for me in the living room."

I refused the offer of his hand, and quickly stood up, merely to fall down again. Blair caught me just before I hit the ground. No doubt about it, I was stone drunk. "I walk on my own feet," I said, my voice sounding slurred even to my own drunken ears. I removed my arm from his hand and took a step forward.

"Mia, wait, here let me help you. I haven't seen this many drunks in one night since I lived in the Bronx," Blair mumbled.

After safely depositing me in the living room on the sofa, Blair returned outside to let the dogs out. By the time he'd gotten back from his task, I was back outside again, this time with my hands on my hips, swaying from side to side. The bigger of the two dogs, Orpheus, dashed ahead of Blair, but Blair called him back to his side. "Mia, what are you doing out here?"

"Looking for bubbles."

This time Blair laughed so hard he almost fell to his knees. He couldn't keep a straight face as he peered up at me with mirth in his eyes. "What bubbles, Mia?" He asked, as the grin on his face grew larger.

"Bubbles, my bubbles. Blow bubbles so puppies can chase," I replied, looking at him with disgust, thinking was he dim-witted or what? I could understand me, how come he couldn't, and why was he laughing?

"There won't be any bubble blowing tonight, sweetheart," Blair replied as he led me back into the house. "Come on, baby, let's get you into bed."

I stumbled along beside him, staring back over my shoulder at the dogs. "Puppies coming with us?"

"No, sweetheart, the puppies are not coming with us," Blair replied with a snicker.

In the wee hours of the night I awoke and stumbled into the bathroom. I didn't turn on the lights, preferring instead to keep my eyes shut the whole time I was on the toilet, and thankful that Blair had the decency to put the toilet seat down. I tried to keep as still as possible, because it seemed that any movement, no matter how slight, sent my head into a rapid spin. It was spinning in so many different directions that I couldn't even keep up. My mouth felt as though it was full of cotton balls and my throat was dry and raspy. Finally, after what seemed like a thirty-minute peeing session, I stumbled back into the bedroom with my eyes still tightly shut and climbed back into bed. Actually, what I'd done was crawled over Blair, not once, but twice, the first time when I'd exited the bed, and again as I crawled back into bed. For some reason Blair was sleeping on my side of the bed, the side nearest to the bathroom. I heard him grunt as my knee came into contact with his thigh, and as I settled back into bed he turned toward me.

"You okay?" he asked.

"No," I replied as I snuggled up to him.

Blair wrapped his arms around me, as he rubbed my back. "No? What's wrong?" he asked with concern in his.

"I could use something to drink," I said with a smack of my lips.

"Ooh, I don't know about that, baby. What did you have in mind?" he asked peering at me though the semidarkness, and with the outside lights shining though the un-curtain windows, I could just make out the skeptical look on his face.

"Water," I said after a few seconds of letting him sweat. "Just plain water."

"Oh, okay, I can handle that," Blair said, with obvious relief in his voice. "I'll be right back." Blair rolled out of bed, and pulled on a pair of sweats before leaving the room.

A few seconds later, I heard the sound of a bang, followed by yelling and a very colorful string of swearing. I popped up in bed like a jack-in-the box, and boy was that a big mistake. My head let me know that it was still attached to the rest of body by throbbing and spinning so violently I could now tell you what being inside of a tornado probably felt like. Then my head went into so many different spinning variations, for a minute or two I didn't know where I was. Breathing deeply through my mouth, I was ultimately able to calm my traitorous head, as I gradually put one leg at a time, over the side of the bed and then stood. Taking baby steps and keeping my eyes closed, with my hands stretched out in front of me, I felt my way along the hall in the direction of the kitchen. After a few steps, I cracked opened one eye, thankful for the darkness of the hallway, and once I'd made my way to the kitchen, I reached out and turned on the kitchen light. Talk about an unintelligent move. The light from the kitchen was so harsh I had to use my hands to shield my eyes against the brightness. Peeking through the cracks of my fingers, I scanned the room, spotting Blair sprawled out on the kitchen floor, an overturned chair, and a naked Sonny was lying flat on his stomach right across the kitchen entrance. One more step, and I too would have tripped over Sonny, joining Blair on the floor.

Blair sat up and began to knead his injured foot as he swore under his breath. "Man, what the hell are you doing in here?"

"Macey got sick and threw up in the bed," Sonny replied, without raising his head.

"So you're sleeping in here on the kitchen floor?" Blair asked as he got up and limped for the fridge. "Ouch, shit! What the hell did I hit?" Blair asked, leaning on the refrigerator for support.

"My head. This is the kitchen? I thought I was in the bathroom." Sonny raised his head from the curve in his arms, and looked around the room with his eyes half closed.

"Sonny, you're not wearing any clothes?" I said as I looked down at his bare backside.

"Mia, will you go back to bed, please?" Blair growled, as he removed a bottle of water from the fridge.

Sonny turned his head, and looked over his shoulder at me. "Hmmm, nice underwear, Mia."

I looked down and let out a quick scream, and then instantly regretted it, for the noise was like a knife slicing into my brain. The fact that I was wearing simply panties and my bra, no longer mattered to me as the pain in my head outweigh everything else at the moment.

"Mia, please go back to bed, and here, take your water," Blair said as he passed the bottle of water over to me. "Come on, Sonny! Get your drunken ass out of my kitchen. Come on, man, get up," Blair said, reaching out and helping Sonny to his feet. "Let's go see what kind of mess Macey has made."

I headed back to bed taking tiny sips of water. Blair and Sonny went the opposite direction, with Sonny bumping into the wall or worse, bumping into Blair who would let out a stream of obscenities. I walked into the bedroom and climbed into bed taking another sip of water before placing the bottle down on the nightstand. Then I heard a loud

"Damn, Macey, what the hell did you eat?"

I slowly got out of bed and closed the bedroom door, drowning out the rest of the voices and confusion vibrating through the house. I was sleeping my butt off by the time Blair made it back to our room, but the slamming of the door brought me abruptly awake, causing me bolt straight up in bed. I had to grit my teeth from the pain searing through my head, as I gingerly return my protesting head back down to the pillow.

"Dear God, will this night ever end?" Blair shouted out into the room. "Sorry," he said, stripping out of his sweats as he limped into the bathroom, and seconds later I heard the water from the shower running. I was dozing again by the time a naked Blair, smelling fresh from his shower was sliding under the covers beside me and waking me from my slumber.

"Come here my drunken beauty, let me ravish you."

"Hmm, not tonight, Blair," I said, pushing him away, "I have a headache."

CHAPTER TEN

"Stop it. Go away," I said, pushing away at the hand on my arm. "It's too early. I have a headache. My mouth is dry. And, if you don't have a large caramel mocha in your hand with an extra shot, then go away and leave me the hell alone," I muttered as I pushed at the hand that was now tugging at the covers.

"Good morning to you too, doll. I have something better than coffee."

I struggled up onto my elbows and slowly cracked an eye open. "Who are you," I croaked, my voice full of sleep making my words sound more like a croaking frog than a *doll*. I opened my other eye and was damn near blinded. I blinked as I tried to focus in on Blair, but there was just too much light in the room. Blair laughed, as he stood before me like a black Adonis dressed all in white and he was holding a tray, hmmm, breakfast? My eyes roamed up to the top of his head and back down the length of his body, down to his bare feet and then back up again. Blair looked like he was the second coming or something. He was so bright my eyes hurt just from the sight of him. "Why are you so bright? What time is it? Awww, my head," I groaned as I rubbed my temples. "What did you put in my water?"

"Here, sweetheart, this will make you feel better," Blair said as he handed me a glass.

"What is it?" I asked as I peered into a glass of brown liquid.

"Just drink it and when you've finish that, there's coffee and it's just the way you like it; strong, extra sweet with a touch of cream," he said sitting a coffee mug down on the nightstand.

Blair stood watching me like a proud papa sending his first born off to communion as I took a sniff of the horrible looking stuff in the glass and almost gagged. It smelled horrible. I put my hand up to my mouth, covering my nose as well. "Blair, I'm not drinking this stuff, it stinks, and oh dear God, Blair, its *moving!*" I said as I peered at the swirling brown liquid. I took several deep breaths of good air, as I held the glass at arms length. "Take it, *take it!* What are you trying to do, poison me?" I asked; my voice rising to a fevered pitch as the glass began to slip from my unsteady grasp. With one swift move, Blair reached out and removed the glass from my hand, just as I was letting go of it and not one drop of that horrible looking liquid was spilled. "Blair, that's nasty. I'm not drinking that," I said with a slow shake of my head. I looked up at Blair, who stood before me with the proffered glass between us. A shiver went through me as I looked at the glass in his hand.

"It isn't poison, and after what the three of you put me through last night, you will drink every last drop of the contents of this glass, even if I have to put my knee on your chest and pour every drop of it down your pretty little throat," Blair said, in a voice laced with so much sugar I had to take two quick looks up at him, not believing what I'd just heard coming from his mouth. He was holding out the glass to me, with a *"woman, don't try me,"* look on his face, which didn't exactly match the sweetness of his voice. His eyebrows were practically touching one another, giving him a satanic look. Okay, so I was wrong, he wasn't the second coming.

It was a struggle trying to stare him down, for my head begin to throb, and my eyes started to tear up. As much as I hated to, I admitted defeat by rolling my eyes at him and turning away to look over his shoulders and out the window, anywhere besides the rolling liquid stench in the glass which he continued to hold out to me. I thought now would have been a good time for me to have ESP or some other unearthly power so I could float that stinky stuff right out the window and into the dumpster behind the house. I folded my arms across my chest, thinking of ways on how to avoid drinking that horrible smelling concoction Blair was still holding out to me, as though it was the nectar of life. He stood there with a frozen smile on his face, watching me through his long eyelashes. I wasn't sure whether or not if Blair was bluffing about holding me down and pouring the stuff down my throat or not. I looked back into his face, and I swear his eyebrows had fused together and I thought I saw horns spouting out of his head. I quickly closed my eyes, and silently counted to ten before opening them again.

"Blair," I said, trying my best to achieve a normal tone to my voice, to soothe this savage beast who stood before me, in an vain attempt to talk him into pouring that liquid garbage down the drain, but, I my voice still had it's early morning gravelly pitch, which at the moment was sounding more like a croak to my ears, so I stopped and cleared my throat. It was indeed a vain attempt, which I now know would not work, for no matter how sweet I sounded, Blair was not bluffing. This whole situation would have been laughable, if the contents of the glass he was holding in his hand didn't smell and wasn't moving. Hell, whatever he had in the glass it was *alive*. Damn, the aroma from the coffee sitting on the bedside table was calling my name, its scent luring me toward the steaming mug. Boy, I could certainly use a sip of coffee right about now.

Okay, time to try tactic number two. "Blair, you're not going to pour anything down my throat, and secondly, I didn't ask you to prepare anything for me. So what if I have a hangover, I can always sleep it off," I said, in my, don't mess with *momma* tone, the one I normally used when disciplining my sons. Head down, I ran a trembling hand though my hair, thinking it was too early in the morning for this kind shit and how this little ordeal was beginning to take it's toll on me. I needed caffeine and quick. But I was definitely not drinking that mess Blair was holding in his hand. The room was quiet, so quiet, you could actually hear a pin drop on the floor, and the floor was carpeted. Maybe he'd given up and left the room, I thought as I slowly raised my head and looked up to find Blair not only still in the room but still standing over me, except now he was wearing a warmer, kinder, gentler smile upon his face. Okay, this is better, I cheered silently, and sat up a little straighter in bed, adjusted the sheet that was high on my chest, and just as I was about to return his smile, my body froze, for upon closer inspection I suddenly realized that the smile Blair was wearing wasn't his usual, *"baby I adore you"* kind of smile, but more like a Mr. Hyde. Then I realized Blair was standing closer to the bed than he'd been earlier, a little too close for comfort, with the glass of swirling liquid still in his clutches.

Okay, new scheme, maybe I could show Blair the *twin girls,* making him forget all about the stuff in the glass, I thought, as I prepared to slip the sheet down a bit to put the *girls* on display. I couldn't just drop the sheet; it had to look like an accident. It had to be a quick sudden move that would allow the sheet to slip down just enough or Blair would look right through my little ploy.

I was ready to act on my plan, and I looked up at him, confident that my plan would work. But as our eyes met, something in Blair's eyes halted me from making my move, making me realize that whatever was going through his mind was even bigger than the *twins* and I had a sinking feeling my little tactic wouldn't work so I tried the next best thing. "Blair, I'm warning you, if you touch me I'll scream. Hmph," I said as I folded my arms across my chest, my legs jiggling nervously under the covers. That will show him. I'm sure my screams will draw Sonny and Macey to our room to stop this madness. It didn't work. An unmoving, and unspeaking Blair stood his ground, standing there holding the glass out to me. He had one eyebrow raised in an arc, with a silly little smile on his face. Defeat. Damn. With a trembling hand I reached out and took the proffered glass from him. I held it up in the air, peering at it from all angles. At least it wasn't moving anymore. I looked back up at Blair; still wearing that stupid ass grin on his face. I'll him, it would serve him right if I puke it all right back up all over his bed. I took several deep breaths, actually I was stalling and Blair was aware of my tactics as he took a seat on the edge of the bed directly in front of me in anticipation of watching me slurp down this- whatever it was. We sat eye-to-eye. He'll pay for this, and I think I'll aim my vomit right into his lap. I thought about holding my breath, then deciding against it. I wanted Blair to live what I was about to drink. I took a tiny sip from the glass. Ummm, not bad, was that honey? It didn't taste bad at all, that is if you could get past the smell. With a smack of my lips I finished off the rest of the contents of the glass in four gulps, with Blair, AKA, *"Sir Evil"* watching my every move, but now he really was wearing his *"baby I adore you"* smile on his face.

"Now, that wasn't so bad was it?" Blair asked in his school teacher voice.

"I tasted honey, was that honey I tasted? And what else was in it, and why does it smell so bad?"

"Ah-hah, now we're trying to analyze the contents." Blair plucked the empty glass from my hand and rushed out of the room; probably to give Sonny and Macey the same hell he'd just given me.

I scrambled out of bed, and let out the loudest belch I'd ever done in my life. The belch seem to come from the very tips of my toes, rolling through my body and out of my mouth, long and loud for what felt like five minutes or so. The noise of it even frightened me, and I was the culprit. Hand up to my mouth, I glanced around the room to make sure I was alone. Yep, it was confirmed, that disgusting sound really had come from me. I put on my robe before plucking my coffee cup up from the nightstand and took a sip, and oh, it was *so* delicious, just as Blair had promised. I took a couple of more sips, and then headed out to watch the show realizing how much better my head was feeling already. I was feeling so much better I was actually humming by the time I made it to the hallway.

I hasten my step, quickly making my way toward the sounds of moans and groans floating down the hallway before me. Finger combing my hair, which was all over my head, I reached the guest bedroom and stopped just inside the door. Although the bedding had been changed last night, the room still reeked of vomit. Remembering my own reaction from the stench of Blair's hangover brew, I quickly took a step back into the safety of the hallway and away from the smell of vomit.

Blair had been a busy little beaver since he'd entered the room. He had raised the blinds and the two windows in the room had been thrown wide opened. Blair was now in the process of using his arms to fan fresh air into the room, while he threw verbal insults at the occupants in the bed. I couldn't see Macey, but I could hear her. She was hidden beneath the covers, and I could have sworn she was cussing Blair out, Chinese style. Sonny was laying flat on his back on top of the covers, with one arm flung over his face, and I was happy to see that he was wearing his underwear this morning.

"Blair, don't make me get up and kick your ass," Sonny said with no enthusiasm at all in his voice.

"Man, your funky ass can't even walk, how you gonna kick a brother's ass? Drink this," Blair demanded. He pulled Sonny's arm away from his face and pulled him into a sitting position forcing the glass into his hand.

"It's not as bad as it smells, Sonny," I said from my post in the hallway.

"You're in on this too, huh? I should have known," Sonny said without opening his eyes. He downed the contents of the glass in one gulp, which was immediately followed by a loud belch, much louder than the one I'd let out earlier in my room. The loudness of it seemed to vibrate throughout the room. Sonny handed the glass back to Blair and fell back onto the bed. "Now, get out."

"Come on, Sonny, get out of bed, man. Macey? Are you decent under there?"

"Stop shouting," Macey moaned from beneath the covers. She didn't get a chance to say any more before Blair reached out and ripped the covers off of her. Luckily for all us, Macey was wearing a large tee shirt.

This was too funny. I smiled as Blair grabbed Macey by her thin arm and pulled her little body into a sitting position. Blair let go of Macey as he turned around and plucked the last glass of the reeking drink from the nightstand, as Macey's slight frame rocked from side to side. At one point she came perilously close to falling off the bed. From instinct, I started to rush forward as Macey tilted toward the side of the bed, but Blair reached out just in time, and stopped her tilt by placing the flat of his hand to her forehead pushing her backwards. While Sonny, who was still on his back, reached out and grabbed Macey by the arm, helping to steady her, or else she would have tumbled to the floor.

Blair was relentless, as he held the glass under Macey's nose. As tiny as she was, Macey was not going down without a fight. She threw out a few more verbal insults in Cantonese which I doubted even Sonny could understand as she snatched the glass from Blair's grasp, spilling half the contents onto the bed covers and finishing off the rest in two swift gulps, followed by a loud burp as well.

"Now, was that so difficult?" Blair asked, as he looked around at the three of us. He was wearing that stupid, Jekyll and Hyde smile again; as he clapped his hands together like he was *Gandhi* and we were his followers. Then Blair waved his hands high over his head and with a big smile on his face proclaimed; "Now let's all hop into the shower and then get dressed. It's a magnificent day outside and I have a busy schedule planned for us." Blair said, his speech animated, as he stepped into the bathroom and seconds later we heard water running from the shower.

"Man, why are you so bright?" Sonny asked, swinging his long legs out of bed and heading for the bathroom, waving for Macey and me to follow him.

"Because I am the *only* sober person in this house, and I'm wearing white to signify purity, and to separate myself from the three of you- *HEY!*"

It took the three of us to get Blair into the shower, and thank goodness it was one of those big walk-in ones, for we all ended up in there together. Later, dripping wet, Blair and I headed back to our room. His all white cotton outfit was still white, but very wet.

"I guess you could say, *Sir Evil*, we put a damper on your purity shit. Or better yet, it rained on your parade." I laughed, happy to be able to pay Blair back for making us drink his hangover brew, even if it had helped with our hangovers. I was still reveling in our payback, and before I could finished my statement to Blair, I realized I may have said too much judging from the glare in his eyes as he slowly came toward me, peeling off his wet clothing and backing me up against the bathroom sink. "Come on now, Blair, I mean, you got what you deserved, right?"

Blair threw back his head and laugh in an evil way, making me laugh as well as he said; "Now, Madam, *Sir Evil* will see that you get what you deserved," Blair said as he dropped down to his knees before me.

"I don't like this," Macey said just before she came to a halt in mid-stride. Macey bent over and began brushing something away from her pant leg.

"That's two of us," I replied, my eyes searching the area for any tell-tale sign of creepy crawlers. I had a phobia about creepy crawlers. I probably had the biggest case of arachnophobia in medical history and every other type of creepy crawler phobia and taking strolls in wooded areas was just not my idea of *fun*. I collided into Macey, nearly knocking her to the ground just as I was thinking about how much I dreaded bug bushes. "Macey, what are you doing?" I asked, suddenly agitated with her for almost making me fall into one of those very bushes, probably full of every type of insect imaginable, and Lord knows, my imagination was in full swing right at this time. I finally realized what Macey was doing and took a tentative step backwards. If something had gotten on her I certainly didn't want it on me.

"I think there's something crawling on me."

Now why did she have to go and say that? It was all I needed to start screaming. "What is it?" I asked as I retreated further away from her, brushing away at what I imagine to be thousands of little crawling critters off of me jumping up and down in what my sons call my *creepy crawler dance*. Macey screamed, and begin to jump up and down as well, hands waving wildly in the air. I was jumping about and doing my own dance, as I searched the area around me, screaming just as loudly as Macey.

"What! What's wrong? What is it?" Blair and Sonny asked, as they raced back to us, followed by a barking Eurydice.

"Something's on Macey," I replied rushing to stand between Blair and Sonny as I continued to brush away at the unseen vermin on my clothes. I reached out and grabbed Blair's arm pulling him close.

"Nothing's on me. Mia, you screamed first, I thought something bit you," Macey said.

"Then why did you scream?"

"Because you did." We stood there like the Marx's Brothers, each pointing the finger at the other before breaking out into a fit of laughter. We ended up leaning against each other, holding ourselves up as we laughed so hard we had tears running down our faces.

"Uh, excuse me ladies, I hate to break up this funny little moment, but do you think we can move along now?" Blair held out his hand to me, but I just brushed past him still chuckling.

"Who died and left you head of this safari?" I asked under my breath.

"Can we go back now?" Macey whined, "I'm tired."

"We've only been out here for twenty minutes," said Blair.

"By whose watch?" Sonny asked with what looked like a snarl on his face.

"Come on, Sonny, we've done this hike before, I know you can't be beat from walking."

"Wait, what was that noise?" I asked, stopping in my tracks. We where hiking in the wooded hills behind Blair's house. This had been the plan he'd made for us, to die by exhaustion and fright.

"Mia, for the last time, there are no snakes out here."

"For your information, Blair, I've watch those nature shows on PBS before and there are always snakes and big spiders in places like this!" I said as I timidly stepped over a small bush.

"Baby, the dogs have been all over this area, and there's nothing out here," said Blair as he whistled. Immediately the brushes rustled and Eurydice ran up to him. Out of the two dogs, Eurydice was the friendlier of the two. She had more of a personality than Orpheus, whom Blair had to leave behind. Although Orpheus tolerated Sonny, he didn't seem to care too much for Macey.

"You know how it is in the movies," Blair said as he made his way to the head of our little line, "it's always the person in the back of the line that disappears first." We all laughed as Macey ran past me and jumped up on Sonny's back.

"Now that's what I like to hear, everyone having a great time," said Blair.

"*Oh shut up, Blair!*" the three of replied in unison.

"Now tell me that wasn't fun," said Blair as we entered our bedroom.

"Blair, that was not fun," I said heading for the bathroom. I kicked off my Puma's and pulled my tee shirt over my head, leaving a trail of clothing behind me.

Blair was in the process of removing his clothing as well. "Come on, Mia, admit it, you had a great time, didn't you? As a matter of fact we should hike the area two, or three times a week. It will allow you to get to know the surroundings, and the hiking will also help build muscles in your calves and it gives you stamina too. Just think about it this way, if you had to run for cover out back, the trees and the bushes would provide great coverage and you'll also have the advantage over the assailant because you'll know the area."

"Blair, what are you talking about?" I was stepping into the shower as he babbled on. I turned to face him, as he stepped in behind me. I placed my arms around his waist. "Why would anyone be chasing me? What are you anyway, some kind of undercover agent or something?" I kissed him on his chin but not before noticing the strange look on his face, and as I lean away he was back to his normal self again, smiling as though nothing was out of the ordinary.

"Of course not, what makes you say that?"

"The reference you just made about me being chased, and how the area provides great coverage, and so on."

"Just a typical scenario, baby. You know, like knowing all the exits of a place in case of a fire. Just being prepared that's all."

"That's all?"

"Admit it; you had fun today, right?"

Saturday evening proved to be much calmer than Friday had been. No tearful confessions or drunken bodies on the kitchen floor. Just four friends sitting around watching rented movies, eating microwave popcorn and pistachio ice cream, which Blair had picked up on an ice cream run, with an occasional beer or two thrown in. Later, after we'd finish watching movies, the four of us sat around the fireplace listening to jazz music as we discussed our weekend and made plans to hike into Cleveland National Forest next month. Blair even played a couple of songs for us on his guitar.

I was sitting on the floor; my back up against the sofa with my head resting on Blair's knee, when the Temptations CD started to play and a soulful tune with a cha-cha tempo caught Blair's ear. Blair threw his hands up in the air and stood up, pulling me to my feet.

We started to cha-cha with Macey and Sonny cheering us on. After dancing apart for a few seconds, Blair pulled me into his arms and we danced the remainder of the song cheek-to-cheek. As the song ended we continued to dance, dancing our way right into our bedroom and into bed, and we didn't stop dancing until well into the night.

I was in love with Blair J. Freeman, and there was no doubt in my mind whatsoever that he was the one for me. I was trying to figure out the exact moment when I'd realized I was in love with him, for this weekend had been a whirlwind of passion and fun. Spending this time with Blair was the best thing I could've done. It brought so much joy to me, and I couldn't remember having a better time than this week that I'd spent with Blair. It was late Sunday morning and we'd just finished saying our good-byes to Sonny and Macey. I think I may have been imagining things, but Macey and Blair seem to freeze in their tracks, as Sonny and I hugged and said our good-byes. Sonny whispered into my ear, and I smiled, as tears stung at my eyes. I kissed him upon the cheek, as he placed his right hand to his heart, and stepped away from my embrace.

The four of us had promised to meet later that evening at church, and after services it was off to The Egg Roll for a late dinner prepared by Sonny. As Sonny's car disappeared around the bend, Blair reached out for my hand and we entered the house together, hand in hand.

"So what was that all about?" Blair asked.

"What?"

"You and Sonny," he said with a fake smile planted on his face.

I shook my head. I didn't know if I should laugh or be angry with him. "This is unbelievable. Man, you are just too much. Is it always going to be this way, Blair? Every time Sonny I share a laugh, a hug, or even to kiss one another on the cheek, are you going to ask what it was about?" I asked in disbelief.

"Yes, when I'm around, and when I'm not around I expect you to tell me on your own."

I shook my head; as much as I loved him, this man was beginning to tire me. "Don't you trust me, Blair?"

"Yes, Mia, I do."

I looked away from him as I smiled at the thought of Sonny's sweet words. "Sonny said; look at my little sister, glowing like a firefly in the night. The two of us are truly blessed to have found happiness in someone else's arms. Wasn't that a charming thing for him to say?" I asked as I turned and looked back to Blair, who had stopped in his tracks. He stood there, staring at me with his arms folded across his chest and a dour expression upon his face, and it was obvious he hadn't thought Sonny's words charming at all.

"See? That's what I mean! Why would Sonny say some shit like that?" Blair asked.

"Blair, that's how Sonny is. You've known him for a while yourself and you know how he is about family."

"But you're not his family, Mia."

"Not in that sense. But we do have a bond similar to blood relatives. Do you have sisters or brothers?"

"No, I do not," he said. "When I first moved here Sonny was the first guy I met who was real with me. When I walked into his business and volunteered to work with him teaching martial arts classes, Sonny was straight up front with me right from the beginning. All this time I've listened to him talk about his friend Mia and I've always thought there was something more to what he was saying. Sonny denied it just like you're denying it now, but I know he loves you, and you love him."

"Of course we love each other."

"I'm not talking about that brotherly, sisterly crap! I'm talking about *real love*, Mia and you know what I'm talking about too. I'm talking about the kind of love that is shared between a man and a woman."

"Blair, I don't know what else to tell you, I'm trying to explain this to you the best way I know how. The time Sonny and I kissed was over ten years ago, not yesterday. Blair, I will not alter my friendship with Sonny just to appease you. I respect Sonny and his friendship means more to me than you will ever know."

"I'm not asking you to change-"

"Yes you are."

"No, I mean- what is this bond between you two? It's like you two have a hold on each other."

"After my divorce Sonny was there for me; he kept me going after I'd given up."

"He kept you going? Mia, lots of women get divorced every single day."

"Yes, and everyone *copes* with it differently."

"Then tell me what I'm missing here, Mia. Explain to me what made your divorce so different from any other of the millions of people who get divorced everyday? Don't tell me you were still in love with your ex-husband? Why did Sonny feel it was up to him to care for you and to help you get through your divorce? Why did *you* feel it was necessary to have his aid in getting you through your divorce?"

This was frustrating as hell. I didn't know what else to say to Blair without dredging up old memories. Memories that had been buried long ago and it didn't look as if Blair was going to let it rest until he knew every little intricate detail of my relationship with Sonny. I'd never told anyone about this part of my life before. Sonny was aware of my secret, and I knew my secret would always be safe with him. How would Blair feel about me after he'd heard my story? Angry tears welled up in my eyes as I raised my head and looked into his eyes. I wasn't ready to share this part of my life with him. This was one part of my life that I didn't want Blair to know about, at least not yet, not now, maybe not ever. But, I wanted his trust as well as his love. I was afraid I would lose Blair if he knew the truth. God give me strength for I would have to tell Blair of the night I almost died. I didn't know what else to do and I felt as though my back was up against a wall. I reached out to him, and then I pulled away, suddenly afraid of his touch, of what he would think of me. Hesitantly I moved away from him. "Blair, why are you doing this?"

Blair moved forward, closing the gap between us. With his hands on my shoulders, he halted the progress of my retreat as he looked down at me with gentle loving eyes. "Because, Mia, I love you. I realized we've only know each other for a precious few days, but we have to start this out right, no secrets, no guessing, and no doubts. Was it because you still cared for your ex-husband? "

"It had nothing to do with love. I'd fallen out of love with him after the birth of my first son, long before the divorce." I had to look away from his prying eyes, still not sure if I could go on for consciously, it was hard for me to relive the horror of that night.

"Baby, please don't look away from me," Blair said as he gently placed a couple of fingers under my chin, forcing me to raise my head and look him in his eyes. "So tell me, why didn't you leave ex-husband after the birth of Anthony if you no longer cared him?"

"Because I was afraid to…if you really must know I was afraid of the unknown. I was terrified of being out there in the world alone, and afraid of raising a child on my own. It was a feeling of desperation, of not knowing if I had what it took to survive out there on my own. I'd left my parents' home at age eighteen and dove right into marriage. Then after my divorce, suddenly I was alone for the first time in my adult life and with two small children. I was facing the unknown on my own. I don't know how to explain all this to you, Blair, but it was as though I was suddenly thrown off balance, falling into a dark bottomless pit with no safety net and no one to catch me or help me out once I'd fallen in. I was in a new city with a new job that barely paid my rent. The money I received for child support was so minimal that paying for childcare, feeding my sons, and keeping them clothed was a joke. They grew like weeds and without Sonny's aid I don't know what we would've done. Sonny was such a big help to me, even though he was struggling himself, but with what little he had he was always willing to share with us. Blair, you just don't understand," I said with a shake of my head, "Sonny did so much for us," I said sighing loudly as I moved away from his touch, even though I wanted to remain close and to keep Blair near I stood firm, determined to get the sorry details out in the open before I lost my courage.

"Without Sonny I wouldn't be here today." Blair started to wave me away, snorting loudly, but he suddenly stopped, as I stood before him shaking in my shoes. I ran a trembling hand through my hair, as fresh tears rushed down my face.

Blair pulled me into his arms. "Mia-"

I looked up into his eyes and I let the words just tumble out. "Sonny saved my life, and the lives of my children, okay? He kept me breathing until the paramedics arrived." I covered my face with my hands, shaking my head as I relived that night. "It had been a horrendous time for me. You'll never know how bad it had become. Things had gotten so awful, and I was so frantic all I wanted to do was die. Just *die* and I would have if it hadn't been for Sonny." Blair had his arms around me now, gently caressing me.

Blair led me to the sofa before disappearing from the room. He returned seconds later with a glass of water and a box of tissues as he joined me on the sofa. I was now gripping a tissue in one hand and a glass of water in the other. "It was a stupid, *stupid* thing for me to do, but, that night, I don't know what had gotten into me." I closed my eyes, as the misery and loneliness I'd been feeling then crept over me like a blanket, and I felt dreadful. I shuddered as I placed the glass down on the floor. "I was feeling sorry for myself, and all I wanted to do was to drop off the face of this earth. No matter how hard I strived to get ahead, no matter what I did, it never seemed to be enough! I'd grown weary of the day to day struggle trying to survive, trying to keep food on the table, and trying to keep my children clothed, healthy, and strong. Oh, I was strong at the start and very ambitious; seeking out a good job, and finding the best day care, and struggling to keep it all together. I knew what my goals were, and I did not want my children to suffer from my lack of ambition." I said as I banged my right fist into my left hand punctuating my words. "I was pushing and pushing until I couldn't push anymore. I kept telling myself the next day would be better, but the next day would be just as bad as the day before or worse. It was a constant uphill battle every single day and I couldn't take it anymore! I would ask God over and over again, why me? Dear God, why me? Why me? *Why?*" I paused, as I tried to regain control of my emotions. The memories were painful for me to endure, both physically and mentally. My stomach felt as though it was in knots, and my head ached, but I continued on with my story. "I grew so sick and tired of it all. I didn't care anymore," I panted. "I was done, finished, through with it all. That night after I'd put my sons to bed, I turned on the gas and to make sure I wouldn't get cold feet I took a bottle of sleeping pills." I couldn't look at Blair's face. I didn't want to see the look of disgust I knew he would be wearing. I rushed on with my tale, speaking faster and faster.

"I thought that was it. I thought I had put an end to my so called suffering. Not knowing that a force inside of me wasn't ready to give up, not yet. For you see, during that time Sonny and I lived in the same apartment complex, right next door to one another. Sometimes Sonny would watch the boys for me on his days off while I went to work, so he had a key to my apartment. But that night, for some reason I'd left my car headlights on, so when Sonny returned home from work, he stopped by to tell me this." I looked upward, searching the ceiling, trying to will away the tears that threatened to fall. "Sonny said he knocked and when I didn't answer his knock, he just let himself in and when he came in-" I paused, my voice cracked because these next words were the hardest for me to say. "Sonny said all he could smell was gas...*gas*. The room reeked of it, nothing else, nothing but gas." I sobbed, and I began to shake, as I was overcome with emotion and the memories from that night took hold of me causing me to drop down to my knees. "Sonny said he turned off the stove, and since I was nearest to the kitchen, he pulled me outside before going back inside for the boys. While he was moving my sons next door to his place, Sonny had dialed 9-1-1, and had the operator on the line. Thank God my babies had been kept safe and with no ill affects from my madness. The same force that had made me leave my car headlights on, also had made me close the door leading into my sons bedroom, and with the kitchen being right off of the living room I'd gotten the worse of the gas, and the sleeping pills had done their job as well. After he had rushed back to me, Sonny realized that he couldn't wake me and he just assumed that I'd taken something. He told me afterward that he been so frightened, because he thought I was dead, and that he'd arrived too late to save me." He was my knight, and he had saved me. I looked around room as the revelation hit me full in the face. Sonny had been my knight in shining armor. I looked over at Blair, as though

I was seeing him for the first time. I had to finish my story. Oh good God, I'm losing my mind.

"Th- the- the only thing Sonny could do- the only *thing* that Sonny could think to do was to stick his fingers down my throat… and- and after I'd gagged and threw up, Sonny said he had no doubt in his mind that I was still alive." I couldn't go on as the tears rushed down my face. I was bawling like a baby and I couldn't stop the tears because, oh my God, it was Sonny. Talking about this was releasing so many memories for me. I shook my head to clear my thoughts. Then I remembered why I hadn't spoken of this for so long, it was too difficult and emotionally draining. Even after so many years it still brought horrible memories. All this time, I had stored the memory of that night away inside of me for such a long time. Outside of my therapist, only Sonny knew about that night. We'd only spoken of it a few times, and then we had locked it away like it was an old skeleton, hiding it in the back of the closet, never to mention it again and I'd stopped seeing my therapist a few years ago. I'd never mentioned that night to my sons, and I thank God that they were too young to understand what had really happened.

Blair came to me as my thoughts took me back to that night. "Mia, stop. Please stop, don't do this to yourself. Baby, I'm so sorry. I'm truly sorry. Shhh, you don't have to say any more, you don't have to speak of it any more. Please, don't cry. Don't cry," Blair said as we rocked from side to side.

I shook my head, pulling away from him, but he wouldn't let me leave his side. I had to finish this. I had to share this horrible secret with Blair. "By telling you this- if- if this is the only way for me to prove my love to you, and to make you understand how- what- when I say-" I stopped to catch my breath. "To make you understand what I mean when I say- when I speak of how deeply my love for Sonny is! You see, in telling you this, if this is the only way for me to prove to you what Sonny means to me then I have to finish, Blair, I have to tell you about that night." Blair gently cupped my face in his hands, staring down at me with a look of concern. I closed my eyes and took another deep breath before continuing, when Lord knows all I really wanted to do was to curl up and hide from his scrutiny.

"Sonny said after I'd thrown up I stopped- breathing." My voice was barely audible, just a whisper now, as I pulled away from Blair. "I don't care what you think about us anymore, Blair, and regardless of what you say to me I owe Sonny my life. Because as I lay there on the ground in my own vomit, that man," I said, with my hands high in the air, "That courageous beautiful man breathed life back into my body. Sonny stayed with me until help arrived! Do you hear me, Blair? Sonny breathed for me- can you *understand* what I am saying!" I was on my knees, in front of Blair as I rocked back and forth from the pain of the memories. Blair reached out to me and I waved him away, as I tried to resist his touch. But Blair was able to pull me into his arms, holding onto me. I was too confined, too close to him. I couldn't see his face so I wiggled out of his grip backing away from him as I continued my tale of woe.

"Let me go. Sonny didn't tell anyone about my sons being in the gas filled apartment that night. Blair, do you know why Sonny did not tell the authorities? Because- Blair, because, they would have taken my children away from me. Do you hear what I am saying to you!" I was shouting to the room, my hands constantly in motion as I continued to back away from him. "My sons would have been taken away from me that night. If it had not been for Sonny my children would not be with me today! He told the police my sons had been with him at the time and that he was my boyfriend. Sonny had to lie in order for him to keep my sons with him so they wouldn't have to be placed into a foster home while I was away in the hospital. I was committed for ninety days for a mental breakdown!"

Blair made another attempt to hold me, console me, but I shook my head, holding out my hand as I kept him at bay. My tears were endless as I was carried away back to that hateful time. I tried to compose myself as best as I knew how, and after I'd dried away a few tears and blew my nose I continued on with my story. "To this day- to this *DAY*! I still cannot explain what happened to me, what it was that drove me to do such an awful thing to my *children*. My life just blew up, and I couldn't take it anymore and at that time I didn't care what happened to me. It was like my life was over, and I...I just couldn't take it anymore. Since I was hospitalized, I lost my job, it was a new job, you see, less than a few months old, I don't actually remember how long I'd had the job," I said with a shake of my head, "all I remember is I didn't have any health insurance at the time, and no sick leave to speak of, so I lost my apartment too," I said with a chuckle, and I had no idea why I was laughing. I felt like I was going insane.

"See I told you. My life went from bad to *worse*. Sonny moved all of my things into his place and after I'd been discharged from the hospital, the boys and I continued to stay with him until I could get back on my feet. Sonny had a one bedroom, so, the boys and I shared the bedroom and Sonny slept on the sofa." I was calmer now as I rose from my spot on the floor, and begin to pace about the room, taking deep calming breaths. "There is nothing, nothing in this world as horrible as what I attempted to do to my babies," I shouted out pounding my chest, "after that night I vowed I would be the best mother ever." I stopped pacing as I came face to face with Blair. "You know, Blair, people say that sometimes things are always darkest just before the light, and I want you to know, that, Sonny Steward, is the light in my life. I love him, Blair!" I shouted, raising my hands in the air as I shouted at him. "I love him dearly and he loves me! What we have is so much deeper than *anyone* could possibly imagine! What Sonny and I share is- is different. It's not the same as what I feel for you. My love for you is so, so- my love for you is the kind that gives me goose bumps whenever you enter the room. Blair, only you can take my breath away when you touch me. The kind of love that all you have to do is to look at me, and, I'm yours, mine, body, and soul. You make me want to drop down before you and spread my legs and let you inside of me and hold on to you for dear life. The kind of love that makes me want to spend the rest of my life with you. Give myself to you one hundred percent. That's the kind love I'm feeling for you. And, Blair, I wouldn't blame you one bit, after hearing this shit, if you didn't want to return my love." It had been difficult for me to share with Blair my tale of woe, but I had to get my feelings out there, at least now Blair was aware of my feelings for him. What happens to us now would be all up to him. This time when Blair came to me I allowed him to gather me into his arms and hold me close as he rubbed my back.

"I know. I know," Blair spoke calmly. "Come on, baby, let's get you to bed so you can rest," he said. Once I'd lain down, Blair disappeared, and as emotionally distraught as I was, I was amazed that I could fall asleep.

Blair came to me some time later to lie down beside me. I was awake then, but too afraid to move, frozen in one spot. I was amazed at how quickly Blair had captured my heart, now I was scared as hell, because I didn't know what to expect next. I didn't know if he was going to take me home and drop me off at my door with the old lineage, "I'll call you," or what? As I lay there, I wanted to be brave about this whole predicament. To prepare myself for what was to come next, to be prepared for the worse possibility of all; of having to live the rest of my life- without him. There's nothing like baring your soul to someone you love and not knowing what's around the corner. I was no longer sure of what our situation was. At the moment, the one sure thing I knew was that I loved him, but how did he feel about me? Especially now, and then I thought, how would I feel about me if the shoe were on the other foot? Blair probably thinks I'm a mad woman; after all, I'd tried to kill my children, my own flesh and blood. How could anyone love me, knowing this ugliness about me? God only knew that the last thing I wanted was Blair's sympathy. All I wanted him to know was how deep my gratitude was for all Sonny had done for me. I didn't want Blair to think of me as less of a woman, or worse, a weak person, and for him to hate me for my actions of that night so long ago. We hadn't known each other long, but even knowing him this short length of time, my love for Blair was like no other love and in my eyes, Blair was my lifemate and I was his and I felt in my heart that Blair was the piece, that missing piece of the puzzle that had been missing from my life all this time.

I could feel his body next to mine, but neither of us touched the other. I was lying on my side facing the opposite direction, and Blair had lain down behind me. So what next, I thought? Should I wait for him to make the first move or should I just throw caution to the wind and- I turned to Blair, my lips hungrily searching for his, smothering him in a kiss which took our breath away. I didn't know what would happen to us now, but I did know I wanted to spend one more night in his arms.

At first Blair was very gentle with me, and I put all of my heart and soul into what I thought would be our last time together. My whole body was tingling with a heighten sensation; the special feelings only his touch seem to bring to me. Everywhere Blair touched me seemed to generate heat, a quickening, a burning desire. I was hot; Blair was hotter. What had started out slow and tender soon turned wild, with my head banging against his chest, as we rolled over, and over, our bodies almost crashing down onto the floor. My orgasm was hard and long, washing over me with a blinding force. I bit down on Blair's shoulder as he shuddered and released inside of me, with my name upon his lips.

Afterward, I begin to drift off to sleep, with Blair still throbbing deep inside of me, amid a tangle of his arms and legs, and bed linens. Blair spoke softly in my ear, apologizing if he'd hurt me, whispering his love, and how sorry he was for making me open up old wounds. I don't know how long we stayed that way, but his words and his actions told me I could count on him. Emotionally exhausted, Blair and I spent the rest of the afternoon in bed, talking and cuddling, neither of us not wanting to let go of the other. Occasionally Blair would exit the room only to reappear again with a glass of juice, or a glass of wine. Once he brought in a steaming bowl of chicken soup, and on his next visit to the kitchen Blair returned with a tray containing a pack of crackers, along with a tin of sardines smothered in hot sauce. Blair was so sweet and I smiled as I saw this, because once I'd told him that one of my favorite things to do after sex was to eat sardines smothered in hot sauce with crackers and Blair had remembered this.

Another time Blair woke me and in his arms he was carrying a tray loaded with food; green seedless grapes, several different types of cheeses, crackers, salami, ham, and a bottle of white wine, ice cold. After we'd eaten, we dozed again. Blair woke me later by throwing back the covers, and helping me from the bed. He led me to the bathroom and when we entered, I cried out in delight, releasing tears of joy as he held me in his arms, and I believe Blair cried as well. The bathroom was filled with orchids, of every shape, type, and size, and later I'd found out that Blair had emptied his greenhouse to carry out this accomplishment. The sunken tub was filled to the brim with scented bubbles mingling with more orchids.

After floating among the bubbles and orchids, we made love again, but this time at a much slower pace and it was fantastic. I was so emotionally distraught that I was almost in tears from this tender show of affection. It was then that I knew, in my mind as well as in my heart that Blair would not abandon me. Later, as I lay in bed, I could hear Blair on the phone as he stood just outside the bedroom door, and from the sound of Blair's end of the conversation I became mindful of whom he was speaking to.

"Mia is strong, she'll be all right. She has you, and now she's got me."

CHAPTER ELEVEN

"What about him?" Sonya asked as a man with an exaggerated swagger walked by. We where downtown, sitting outside a local coffee shop sipping on frozen coffees. The table we sat at had a large blue umbrella, and a small wind chime hanging from it which made a light tinkling sound whenever a light breeze chance to stir the air around us. I had taken Blair's advice and his financial assistance to start my own temporary agency. The Harris & Freeman Agency would officially open for business just as soon as I could find the personnel to help me run the place. Sonya was definitely a score. The woman knew the recruiting business about as well as I did, and I knew my business. I'd just recruited Sonya to work with me, and we were celebrating her acceptance as we gaze out at the busy downtown street as we sipped our frozen coffees.

Sonya and I went back a long way. We'd met in college, and at the time both of us worked full-time jobs during the day and attended classes at night. Claudia and Sonya were like day and night. Sonya and I were more alike in lifestyles and goals than Claudia. Sonya had a great attitude and a generous heart. She was always ready to help you out in any way she could. Sonya was tall, around five feet ten, a big woman in height and weight, but I never noticed her weight stopping her from achieving the things she wanted in life. Lately Sonya had taken to wearing her hair in a crazy big afro with the tips of her hair colored red, and her hairstyle went well with her personality. I loved it when Sonya pulled her wild locks back and away from her face. Her coffee colored skin was flawless. Sonya had a beautiful heart shaped face, and when she wore her hair tied back and away from her face with one of her many colorful scarves framing her face, her profile was equal of the Greek goddess Aphrodite. Her clothing style was bohemian, loud colors and crazy designs. And depending upon the weather, Sonya wore boots with fringes, and sandals with two and three inch heels with lots of straps winding around her long shapely legs. Sonya owned regular pumps and mules that she would wear to work, but she would change out of these if we met after work for a drink or dinner. Sonya wore multiple gold or silver bracelets on both wrists, colorful scarves that she would wrap around her head or sometimes Sonya would twist a scarf into an elaborate design in her hair or she would tie long scarves around her thick waist. Sonya owned as many belts as she did shoes, big thick belts made of leather and chain belts of silver and gold, or belts made of leftover scraps of material which she would add a large heavy elaborate belt buckle, and necklaces and earrings to match her every outfit and her mood. You could hear Sonya coming before you saw her, for her belts, and jewelry would make music as she walked. At work Sonya would tame her look down by wearing a nice conservative blazer to cover her colorful outfit and her tops were less revealing at work, but on the weekends and when we would hang out after work, Sonya would let it all hang out. Claudia liked to tease Sonya by calling her *"gypsy"* woman, but the look worked for Sonya and it fit her personality to boot.

"Gay," I said as I sucked on my cold frozen drink from my straw. After removing the paper from the straw, I had stuck it into the tall mound of caramel and whipped cream, then I'd given it a quick stir before getting down to slurping on the gooey goodness. "He walks better than I do. Damn, I wish I could move my hips like that," I said with a low chuckle.

"Girl, you're crazy. Okay, okay, what about him?" Sonya asked with a nod of her head.

I looked across the street at a tall good looking well-dressed Black man, who was running to catch the trolley as it pulled into the 5th Street station. His shoes were clean and shiny, and his beige suit coat hung neatly on his tall frame, and the colors in his tie complimented his suit and his brown shirt. The man stopped to allow a woman to board ahead of him and from the angle of his head you could tell he was checking her out. "Married," I replied as I took a long sip from my straw. The drink was cold and frothy as it went down my throat as smooth as silk, giving me an instant brain freeze.

"Really, and what makes you say that?"

"Too well dressed to be single, and too all up in that woman's business to be gay. Which means he's married and his wife shops for his clothes and lays them out the night before," I said with a snap of my fingers.

Sonya laughed, as she reached out to high five me. "Mia, you are too much and you're probably right too. Oh my goodness, look at this joker coming across the street," Sonya said with a nod of her head.

"Oh no," I said as we turned away from the approaching figure. It was hard trying to contain our mirth, for the man was wearing a color coordinated jogging suit, with one leg of his matching pants rolled up to his knee. He sported several gold chains around his neck, in a layer effect, with the thicker chains on the outside, and the thinner ones inside. He was also wearing several bracelets on each wrist, and a ring on each of his ten fingers.

"Too much jewelry!" We spoke at the same time, and then we broke out into laughter as Sonya held up her arms and rattled her bracelets.

I shook my head. "Rapper *wannabe*," I whispered to Sonya, as the man passed by us, flashing a gold tooth smile at us.

"Wait a minute; he might be a rapper with a big fat contact. Let me give him my phone number," Sonya said as she smacked the table with her hand, in a pretense to follow after him, after the man had walked out of hearing distance. "Honey, it's been a dry season for me. The only thing that's been between my legs lately runs on triple *"A"* batteries and I'm not talking about my battery operated razor." Sonya laughed.

I laughed along with her, damn near choking on my drink. "Sonya, you need to stop!"

"I'm serious. What is wrong with the men today? Honey, you have to be either white, a Halle Berry look-a-like, or on welfare with ten kids to get a man's attention these days."

I laugh even harder at her newest comment, and decided to give up trying to drink my iced coffee. "Ten kids? Damn, Sonya, why does the woman have to have so many kids?"

"To guarantee a government check big enough for the woman to support his behind," Sonya proclaimed loudly.

I chuckled as I tried to take another sip from my straw, letting Sonya continue her ranting.

"Girl, I'm serious. I don't understand it. You know, it's like the African American men are afraid of a hard working woman who can pay their own way. It seems the more money I make the lonelier I become. One weekend my cousin Jeff invited me to a party in LA. He told me there would be a lot of men there for me to meet. Jeff was right, the party was jumping with all kinds of men, tall ones, short ones, black ones, white ones, Puerto Rican, ugly, handsome, you name it, they where at this party. There was so much meat at this party I could have started my own delicatessen," Sonya said with a laugh. "I finally got up the nerve to talk to this one guy who had been following along behind me like a puppy. Well we found a quiet corner and got down to some serious conversation, and you know what he told me? He said I looked like I made thirty-thousand plus a year, and he didn't date women who made more money than he did. Hell, I didn't have the heart to tell him I made that much when I was in my twenties," Sonya said with a shake of her head. "Girl, what is wrong with this world? Remember, Lenny? Well I saw him last week over at my brothers' place. You know my youngest brother, Raj?" Sonya barely waited for my acknowledgement as she continued on, "and do you know what that fool had the nerve to say to me? *'Oh, you to high and mighty to pick up the phone and call a brother these days, huh?'* I wanted to say, 'You goofy fool, you slept with my cousin, I don't want your black ass anymore.'"

"Are Jeanette and Lenny still together?"

"Not anymore," Sonya replied with a shake of her head. "Jeanette hasn't said anything to me about it, but I heard it through grapevine that Lenny is now shacked up with Jeanette's so called best *friend*, Dottie. Lenny lost his job, and after six months of unemployment Jeanette finally saw the light and kicked his behind out. Now get this; Raj told me that Lenny wanted Jeanette to support him. My brother said Lenny told Jeanette he was trying to find himself. Raj said, Jeanette told him she got fed up hearing the same old line every time she mention the word *job* to Lenny, so the next day when Lenny told Jeanette he was trying to find himself, she opened up her front door and told Lenny she saw a likeness of him down the street and if he hurried he'd be able to find himself. I'm still trying to figure out if the fool caught up with himself yet." We laughed as Sonya finished speaking.

I shook my head. "Well, at least Jeanette wised up to him before it was too late. So, are you and Jeanette speaking to each other again?"

"Once in awhile, but it will never be like it was before, you know what I mean? I still drop Tameka off over there; I can't interfere with her relation with her cousins. She's known Vanessa and Troy since she was a baby and they all love each other. Sometimes when I drop Tameka off I go in and sit a minute, but Jeanette killed our whole relationship for me. I can't trust her anymore. You know what the funniest thing is, Mia? I never thought Jeanette would stab me in the back like that. I mean, if anybody knows how much I loved me some Lenny...was Jeanette." Sonya reached out and picked up her drink, her eyes staring out into the distance, the spark that was always there in her eyes suddenly dim.

"Sonya, did you ever ask Jeanette why she did it?" Sonya rarely spoke of what happened between her and Jeanette, but on the rare occasions when she did open up the door to her life, Sonya would let more and more out each time. Sonya once told me she felt good getting it out, and I understood exactly what she meant.

"No, I've never spoken to Jeanette about it and she has never mentioned it either. It's like it never happened, you know? Anyway, that's enough about my pathetic life. How are the boys and how's that good looking Blair doing?" Sonya asked as she sparked back to life again. "You are so lucky to have hooked up with someone like Blair, he is the best. You two make a great couple. Are you sure he doesn't have a brother tucked away somewhere?"

"Thank you, Sonya," I replied as I reached across the table and patted her hand, "and remember this, there is nothing *pathetic* about your life. You are a career woman raising a daughter on your own and by the way, you're doing a hell of a good job raising Tameka. Today young girls Tameka's age are getting pregnant or worse into drugs and shit. I know how hard it is, because I'm raising two young men as well and believe me, if not for Sonny, I don't know what kind of shape I would be in today. Right now, I am grateful to have Blair in my life, but he's the lucky one to have caught me!"

"I hear you," Sonya giggled.

"But, I'm sorry to have to tell you Blair is one of a kind and I'm keeping him all to myself," I replied with a grin. "The boys are doing great and Anthony is excited about graduating soon. Now, back to business, I'll see you in the office in two weeks, and I'm delighted to welcome you aboard as a new employee of Harris & Freeman," I said as I reached out and shook her hand.

"Mia, you don't know how much this means to me. I am so proud you finally got off your butt and got your business started, and happy as hell you want me to come and work for you too. You know I'll never let you down."

"I know, Sonya," I said as I peeped out over the top of my sunglasses laughing at her words. "I know you won't let me down, that's why I'm bringing you in on my side."

"You go Ms. Black Business Woman. I thought this was a celebration," Sonya said as she took a sip of her iced coffee. "Shouldn't we be drinking something stronger than this?"

"I wish, but Blair and I have to meet with the property-owner of the office building in a couple of hours. Maybe we can meet for dinner tonight, at The Egg Roll. I'll give Claudia a call and see if she's free tonight as well. Hell, it' Friday, right? Can you get a sitter?"

"Not a problem. I'll drop Tameka off at her grandmother's. She's always complaining about how she doesn't see enough of her granddaughter, so this will give them some time to bond."

"You're taking Tameka to Tijuana?" Sonya had met Tameka's father one night while a group of us had taken a week long cruise to the Mexican Riviera. Sonya had a seven day fling with Tameka's father, Rafael, who had worked on the ship, and on his days off the relationship continued with Rafael spending time with Sonya, that is until Sonya had gotten pregnant, and then Rafael's visits had ceased.

Sonya had met Rafael's mother, Victoria, who lived in Tijuana, after the birth of Tameka, and Victoria had stayed with Sonya for a couple of months after the birth of her only grandchild to spend some time with her granddaughter. Now it was a monthly ritual for Sonya and Tameka to take a bus to TJ for the weekend so that Tameka could visit with Victoria.

"Hell no. I didn't tell you? Honey, Ms. Victoria has set up residence in San Ysidro, you know, the American version of Tijuana. It's been about three months now. She lives next door to Sylvie, her sister. Victoria called me last night, asking if Tameka could spend the weekend with her so this will work out just fine for me. It will be nice for Tameka too, now she can spend more time with her grandmother."

"And Rafael, what has become of him?"

"That fool is somewhere in Florida."

"Florida? Really? How long has he been there?" I'd been so caught up with opening my own business and dividing my time between Blair and my sons that Sonya and I hadn't had a chance to really sit down and talk about what was going on in our lives.

"He ran down south the end of last year, right after I hit his ass up for child support. Ms. Victoria said she got a postcard from him a few weeks ago. She wrote him back asking him why he wasn't sending money for his daughter. Rafael wrote back telling her he was working on a big deal to make some quick money. He told her he wanted to buy her a big house so Tameka and I could stay with her," Sonya replied with a shake of her head.

"Working on a *big deal*? What kind of deal?"

"Drugs, of course. What else signifies a '*big deal*'? Ms. Victoria thinks he's trying to get into the business."

"That man's going to mess around and get himself killed one of these days."

"Same old Rafael."

"Sad."

"A waste," Sonya said with a shake of her head.

"Claudia, glad you could make." Sonny and I stood just inside the door of The Egg Roll discussing the layout of my new office when Claudia arrived that night to join us in celebration of me opening my own business.

"Sonny, how's life treating you these days, man?" Claudia asked as she thumped Sonny on his back. "And look, here's the woman of the hour, Mia!" Claudia said as we hugged. Where's the man of the hour, oh- there he is now, hello, Blair!" Claudia called out to Blair as she waved at him.

"Funny," I replied. "Can you believe what Sonny did to this place?" I asked as I looked around the room. Sonny had hung a big white banner across the room with "Congratulations, Mia" in large red letters. After meeting with Sonya, and before my meeting with Blair, I had called Sonny informing him I was bringing a group of people over to The Egg Roll for dinner, not suspecting that Sonny would exactly close the place down after lunch. By the time Blair, Maurice, Anthony, and I had arrived at the restaurant there was a big "Closed" sign on the door, with "Private Party" posted in one of the windows. There was food everywhere and even Sonny's parents had made an appearance. It was always a pleasure to visit with them for they loved seeing the boys for they were like the grandparents my sons never had.

"Sonny, you are too much," I'd said as I gave him a big hug.

"Anything for you, babe," Sonny replied giving me a squeeze and a quick kiss to my lips.

"Uncle Sonny, did you make my special egg rolls?" Anthony asked.

"When your mom told me you were coming, I made an extra batch just for you," Sonny replied as he gave Anthony a slap on the back, as Anthony headed off in the direction of the food.

I shook my head as Anthony made a beeline for the buffet table. During the time when we had all lived together, Sonny would allow Anthony and Maurice to help him prepare our meals. And as they'd gotten older, and once Sonny had acquired The Egg Roll, he would take them to restaurant to help out in the kitchen, or to help bust tables during the summer. Once, while Anthony was helping Sonny prepare a batch of egg rolls, Sonny had asked Anthony what would he like in his egg rolls, and Anthony had replied shrimp and coconuts, so ever since that one time, the shrimp and coconut egg rolls have kind of stuck. Sonny had even put them on his menu, calling them "Anthony's Egg Rolls" and they didn't taste bad either.

It was a nice little gathering, and everyone got plenty to eat and drink, and I was thankful it was a Friday night; for it was well after midnight by the time we finally left for home.

"Your place or mine?" Blair whispered into my ear.

"It all depends, or are you to worn-out to drive back to your place? How about if tonight we stay at my place, and head out to your place in the morning," I suggested.

"Sounds like a plan to me," Blair replied as he hid a yawn behind his hand. "Your place it is. Maybe we can invite everyone out tomorrow," Blair said as he looked around the room, and upon spotting Sonny, Blair raced off in his direction. "Hold on, let me find out if Sonny's free tomorrow."

"Thanks for coming, Claudia," I said as I looked around the room. "What happened to Raymond?" I asked, speaking of Claudia's latest conquest.

"Raymond got pissed off about something and took his old stale ass home. Look, I got to go," Claudia said as she dug around in her purse searching for her car keys.

"Well, give call me tomorrow. Blair wants everyone to come out to his place for a bar-b-que."

"Okay, I'll give you a call. Good night," Claudia said as she glanced around the room as though in search of someone.

"Are you okay," I asked. Claudia had seemed preoccupied about something all night.

"It's nothing. I'll catch you tomorrow."

"Bring Raymond," I called out to her departing back.

It was the next day and I was in the kitchen busy putting the finishing touches on the potato salad when Blair came tearing into the room. I looked up as he banged his fist on the table. I could tell by his face that he was in a mood to vent about something.

"You need to check your *girl*."

"What?" I asked as Blair entered the kitchen. "What are you talking about?" Not again, I thought to myself. Claudia had a way about getting on Blairs' last nerve. No matter how often Blair would tell Claudia off, she just kept on coming, like the damn energizer bunny. Even after I had brought it up to her attention, Claudia would just laugh and say she was only teasing Blair, having some fun. Well, from the look on his face, her teasing was anything but fun to Blair.

"Claudia. She's tripping big time. Every time I turn around she's all up in my face. I'm telling you, baby, it's pretty damn frustrating when I have to keep asking her to step back every time I turn around. And her man Raymond is hanging out in the corner, sulking and shit."

"*Claudia?*" I couldn't believe Claudia was still hanging onto Blair's every word, especially since we were a couple now. I had even asked Claudia to cease with *teasing* as she called it.

Blair nodded his head, as he picked up the platter holding the marinating steaks and a second one with chicken, both ready for the grill. "*Claudia*," he replied with another nod of his head.

"I don't believe that. I've never noticed her anywhere near you." Which was true, for each time I was with Blair Claudia was no where to be seen. I wonder what kind of game she was playing this time.

"That's because she does this shit when you ain't around."

"Blair, why would Claudia disrespect me like that?" Why indeed, I thought as I gave Blair long look?

"I don't know. Why don't you go and ask her."

I shook my head as I left the kitchen, with Blair on my heels. It was time for me to have another conversation with Claudia, hopefully for the last time. I was not interested in being the mediator for them; they were both adults and should be able to handle this on their own. But why was Claudia still playing games after I had approached her about how uncomfortable it made Blair feel? As we stepped out onto the terrace, all we could hear was Claudia shouting like a banshee, and cursing like a sailor. She was wearing a yellow thong bikini and a pair of yellow mules, her long hair flowing down her back, one hand on her hip, her other hand waving back and forth in Raymond's face, her head swiveling on her long neck, and an ugly sneer on her face as she cussed him out.

"You son-of-a-bitch, who the hell you calling a slut, you poor ass mother-"

"Whoa- whoa-" Sonny said as he ran forward and stepped between the two. "This is a *family* outing," he said nodding in the direction to where a group of young children were splashing in the pool. Blair had invited three of his employees over along with families to enjoy the day as well.

"Claudia, what is going on here?" I asked as Blair and I approached them.

"Nothing, ain't shit going on 'cause this fool is leaving, right now. Adios, sucker. Get to stepping!" Claudia said as she pointed a long ruby tipped finger toward the front of the house.

"Come on, Raymond, let's talk," Blair said as he guided Ray toward the house, with Sonny in tow.

I grabbed Claudia by the arm, forcing her to face me. "Claudia, what the hell," I begin, and then lowered my voice. "What the hell are you doing? Claudia, take a good look around you, you're not at *home*. You're a guest here, show some respect, okay? Some of these people work for Blair, and you're out here acting all stupid and shit. What the hell is wrong with you?"

"Oh please, Ms. Prim and Proper, put a fucking sock in it," Claudia replied loudly as she snatched her arm from my hand.

Oh no she didn't! I moved in closer, and calmly gathered her in my arms, turning her to face me. "Claudia, please do not mistake my kindness for stupidity," I said as I lowered my voice. "Blair was in the kitchen a few minutes ago telling me you where all up in his face, *again* and now you're out here in front of his employees and my family and friends acting like a damn *termite!*" I could tell from her face that Claudia was shocked by my words, but at this point I was beyond caring what she thought. I took a step back, releasing my grip on her. "Claudia, I suggest you catch up with Raymond, because you're going to need a ride back to La Jolla." Claudia sputtered as she tried to get her bearings, before she staggered backward, her eyes focusing on me, like it was her first time noticing me. "Are you drunk?" I asked, as Claudia shook her head as she stomped passed me and headed for the house.

Macey walked up next to me as we stood and watched Claudia snatch her towel up from a chaise lounge, and push her way past Blair and Sonny who where retuning back to the terrace. "That woman got problems," Macey said with a nod of her head. "What did you say to her?"

"Something I should have said a long time ago." I nodded, agreeing with Macey. There was definitely something bugging Claudia and I was going to find out what it was.

CHAPTER TWELVE

"Hey, baby, here you are," Blair said as he slid into the empty seat next to me.

"Hi," I replied as I laid my head on his shoulder.

"How's Maurice?" Blair asked, gently rubbing my back.

My hands shook noticeably, as I reached for Blair's hand. "You didn't get my messages? I left one on your cell phone and my number on your pager."

"Left my pager and my cell phone in Jeremy's truck. I'm stopping back at the office later on to pick them up. What about Maurice?" Blair repeated, as he gently squeezed my hand.

"They don't know yet. He has a knot in the palm of his left hand the size of an egg. I've already signed the release forms for surgery tomorrow morning." I was scared, and I'm sure I had a far away look in my eyes, because I definitely didn't want to be here. I just wanted to take my son home, not wanting to believe this was happening to Maurice. I looked down at Blair's hand in mine, trying to distract my thoughts as I traced the lines inside his hand.

Blair gripped my hand, stilling my fingers. "Surgery? Is it that bad? What about the doctor, do you have a good surgeon?"

"Maurice's doctor is on his way, but he's just a pediatrician not a surgeon. I called his father, that *fucker*! He said he'd try and make it out this way by the end of next week. He didn't think he could make it before then because he and his *wife* had plans to drive *her* son back to school, and to spend some time with *her* parents. *His* son is here about to be operated on for God knows what, and he can't even come out to check on his own son!" I was definitely upset, for during my time with Blair, I don't ever remember speaking negatively about my ex-husband, and now here I was giving him all four barrels.

"Baby, Maurice is going to be just fine," Blair said as he gave me a long hug. "You look worn-out from all of this. I know you're upset, and, baby, when it comes to your children; you're an abominable force to go up against, because you're one fierce momma. Don't do that. You have nothing to feel guilty about, and stop beating yourself up, Mia. You do everything for your sons; you give them your all. That is what I admire and love the most about you. You would never send your sons out into the world of crime just to get your high on."

"What? Blair, what did you say?"

"It's going to be all right."

"I don't understand what happened. I don't know why Milton didn't notice anything wrong with Maurice's hand while he was there visiting with him. I mean, after all he was with him for two whole weeks. Blair, you should have seen him. Maurice was in so much pain that he was in tears when I picked him up from the airport. Maurice had to have been in pain when his dad put him on the plane. How could he have not known something was wrong with his *own* son?"

"Let me call my doctor and see if he knows a good surgeon affiliated with this hospital."

"They're preparing a room for Maurice now. They gave him something for the pain and he's out like a light right now. I called Anthony; he's on his way here. Oh, Blair, I feel so damn helpless!" I said as tears clouded my sight.

"It'll be all right. I'm here, and I'll take care of everything. It's going to be all right," Blair said as he hugged me close to him.

It was not long after my conversation with Blair that Maurice was transferred to his own room. Blair and I, along with Anthony sat quietly in the room, each of us with our own thoughts. I thought I had composed myself until Sonny stepped into the room. The moment I saw him, my whole demeanor changed. I'm not sure what came over me, but it was like Sonny came into the room in a flash of white light. He stopped just inside of the doorway, his eyes searching the room and when our eyes met, the next thing I knew I was in his arms bawling my eyes out. This was all so normal for me, to be holding onto him for what seemed like dear life, as my son lay helpless in the bed next to us. Sonny was my Rock of Gibraltar, steadfast, the lighthouse in my stormy life, the surrogate father my sons could count on. For Sonny to come to the hospital to give us his moral support almost brought me to my knees. Sonny had never failed me, and he was always there anytime there had been an illness or sickness with the boys. Sonny knew the names of the boys' doctors as well as I did. I could always depend on him and he was the emergency contact for the family. I felt another arm around me as Anthony joined our little huddle. We stood that way for a long time, as Sonny's soothing words comforted us. When we finally broke apart, Blair was no longer in the room.

"Dr. Moon is here," Sonny said, referring to Maurice's pediatrician. "He's at the nurses' station going over Maurice's charts. Dr. Moon has already conferred with the admitting physician and they decided to bring in an entomologist as well as an infectious disease doctor to take a look at Maurice's hand." Sonny and I stood at the foot of the bed staring down at Maurice. Anthony had disappeared into the bathroom.

"Why an entomologist?" Blair asked as he rejoined us.

"Because the admitting physician seems to think that the knot on Maurice's hand may be from an insect bite so they want a specialist to look at it. Even though the admitting physician saw no puncture wounds, they want to play it safe and cover all of their bases."

"When I had questioned Maurice earlier, he didn't know how he had injured his hand. At first Maurice thought he may have injured his hand playing ball, but he couldn't remember falling or anything," I said with a shrug.

After our conference with Dr. Moon, Sonny stayed for a bit longer, but he had to return back to the restaurant to close up, promising to return early the next day. As we were preparing to leave, Anthony got permission to stay the night with Maurice. I tried to dissuade Anthony from staying, since Maurice would be in a drugged sleep for the rest of the night, but Anthony was very persistent and a cot was placed in Maurice's room for him.

Blair followed me home and decided to stay the night with me. It was well after eleven by the time we made it back to my place, and I was practically dragging my feet by then.

"Baby, I know you're wiped out. Why don't you change out of your clothes, and I'll run a nice hot bubble bath for you, and while you bathe I'll make us a couple of omelets," Blair said as he steered me into the bedroom.

By the time I'd joined Blair in the kitchen, he was preparing a tray for me. I felt and looked a little better after my bath, but Blair commented on how my shoulders seem to be sagging a bit.

"I was planning on serving you dinner in bed."

"Oh, Blair, how sweet of you, thank you," I said as I gave him a hug and a light kiss. "I'm really not hungry, so why don't we just have our omelets here in the kitchen? Anyway, I'm afraid if I eat in bed I'll fall asleep while eating."

"How are you feeling?" he asked holding me his arms.

"I don't know yet. It's all so surreal. I'm concerned about Maurice and, Blair, I'm really frightened, about what's going on with him," I choked up as tears filled my eyes. Our life was going so well now. I finally had someone in my life and my sons were on the right track and everything felt so right, and now this.

"Don't worry, Maurice is a strong kid, he'll be okay." We stood there holding onto each other for a few seconds more, before I pulled away, but Blair quickly reached for my hand before I could move away. "Mia?"

"Yes?"

"Will you marry me?"

"What?" I asked, as I raked a hand through my hair, my mind still at the hospital with Maurice. Blair gave my hand a squeeze and repeated his question.

"Will you marry me?"

"Blair, think about what you're asking. I mean y- y-your offer couldn't have come at a worse time. I don't know what's going on with Maurice right now. I don't know what's going to happen next. It could be something critical," I said as I broke down again. I was feeling so helpless and I didn't want to feel this way. I just wanted my son back, whole and healthy again.

"It isn't anything critical. Baby, please don't cry."

"But what if it is? Don't you see, Blair, I can't marry you. I won't be able to give our marriage the time and attention it will need because I'll be busy taking care of my son," I said sobbing on Blair's shoulder, as he gently patted my shoulder.

"I won't mind. I just want you and your sons in my life, Mia. I don't want you, Maurice or Anthony to ever want for anything ever again," Blair said as he raised my hand up to his lips.

"Blair, I love you, have loved you since the second day I've known you. But I just can't ask you to give up your freedom to marry me, and what about children of your own? I have all I want and I have no intention of having more."

"I've told you before I don't want children. Mia, I just want you in my life and I want to be a part of yours."

"I can't let you make that sacrifice of not having a child of your own, and for you to become tied down to me with two grown men. You should have your own family, Blair."

"You, Anthony, and Maurice are my family."

"Blair-"

"Love conquers all, remember? I want to be able to share your burden. Help you to lighten your load. Since I've helped you with your business loan you haven't taken one red cent from me, and I of all people know what a struggle it can be during your first year in business. I want to be with you every single day and night, and know that when we leave each other in the morning we'll be back in each other's arms again in a few hours. I want to see my clothes hanging in the closet next to yours. I want to see your head on the pillow- next to my mine, every night." And at this, Blair dropped down to his knees with my hand still clutched in his and he looked up into my face. "Mia Harris, will you marry me? And before you answer, I just want to say it doesn't have to be right away. We can wait until Maurice is better if you want to, it doesn't matter to me. But until we do marry I want you and Maurice to move into the house with me."

I couldn't think, as every emotion I could feel, and think, played about on my face. My hands shook noticeably, as I looked down at Blair, shaking my head from side to side. I was in such a dilemma.

How could I marry Blair? I didn't know what was going to happen with Maurice. How could I drag Blair into the unknown? He was being such a dear to offer to marry me. What if Maurice's illness suddenly becomes life threatening, or if Maurice should loose his hand or his arm. And then there was Anthony. Anthony would be graduating at the end of the year and he'd probably move back into the condo with us. It was too much to think about right now. "Blair, I don't know. Anthony graduates soon and until he finds a job he'll probably have to move in with me."

"No problem, as matter of fact your condo will be empty after you and Maurice move in with me, Anthony can stay with us, or here at the condo, it doesn't matter. Whatever he decides to do we'll give him our support. I understand from Sonny that Anthony will be teaching at the dojo this summer, and if he chooses to stay in the condo we can handle everything. He even has a job as assistant manager of the pool and lawn service if he wants it."

"Well, Blair, it sounds to me like you have it all figured out," I said as I looked around the room before my eyes drifted back to Blair. "I'm flattered you would want to marry me, but-"

"I haven't figured it all out yet, but given time I will. So was that a yes?"

"Blair-"

"Mia, my knees are beginning to hurt on this tiled floor."

A smile broke out on my face. "Yes, Blair, I'll marry you."

"Baby, that one word is sweet music to my ears. You don't know how much this means to me to be spending the rest of my life with you," Blair said as he jumped up, grabbing me about my waist and started spinning me around in his arms.

"But let's not tell the boys until after Maurice's surgery and we know what's happening with him, okay?"

"Baby, whatever you say, because you see standing before you the happiest man alive."

"Blair, seeing you happy makes me happy as well," I said as we sat down to our now cold dinner.

It was Valley Fever, which was also known as *coccidioidomycosis*. We found out the Valley Fever fungus lives in the soil, and is spread through the air once the soil is disturbed. Once the fungus enters the body, and without proper treatment, Valley Fever can lead to severe pneumonia, meningitis, and in some cases even death. We all learned a lot about Valley Fever that year, because the disease not only affected Maurice, but all of us. We found out that the Valley Fever fungus grows naturally in the soil in the southwestern part of the United States, as well as Central and South America. Once airborne, the organism is inhaled, and once infected you will experience no symptoms at all. A small percentage of the infected population develops flu-like symptoms along with fatigue, which can sometimes last for up to a month. Sometimes the disease can even spread outside the lungs, to the brain, skin, or like in Maurice's case the bone in his left hand. Then the disease is called *disseminated* Valley Fever.

I was breathing a whole lot easier once we discovered that the disease was treatable, and not contagious. And, in most cases once you've had Valley Fever your body creates immunity to it.

After talking with specialists, and doing our own research, we found out Valley Fever usually attacks African Americans and other minorities more aggressively than non-minorities. The organism had infected the bone in Maurice's hand, which had damaged the bone. During surgery the abscesses had been drained and the infectious tissue removed. Maurice spent an additional week in the hospital on intravenous anti-fungal medication. Before his release from the hospital, Maurice was inserted with an intravenous line, called a *pic-line*, which would remain in his arm until after his out patient therapy was over. Maurice still receives his treatment on an outpatient basis, once a day for up to four hours a day. We were told that after four months of this type of aggressive treatment, Maurice would then be placed on oral medication for the duration of his therapy. There was even the possibility that Maurice would have to continue to take his oral medication for two, maybe three years until all traces of the fungus in his blood was gone.

Maurice's hand was healing quite nicely, but he was pretty bummed out about not being able to play on the basketball team this season. In a way, I was glad he was no longer playing basketball, for I wanted Maurice to stay home and get his strength back and to take it easy until next year. The last thing I wanted was for him to re-injure his hand.

CHAPTER THIRTEEN

It had been raining all day as I came home from work mentally exhausted, and irritable as hell. Twice this week Claudia had taken off work during our busiest time, and without any kind of advanced notice. Claudia would leave for lunch and then call back an hour later stating she would not be returning for the rest of the day, and she had pulled this same trick today. Claudia was aware that Mondays and Fridays were our busiest days, and because of Claudia's inconsideration, Sonya had to work through her lunch again today, and I had to cancel a couple of appointments with perspective clients to help Sonya with running the office. The same thing happened last month, and the month before that. Five times last month and now here it was December and Claudia was doing it again.

It was well after seven by the time I pulled into my parking stall. I left my car and headed for the elevators thinking about my upcoming physical. Damn, I needed some vitamins or something, for keeping up with Blair and working twelve hours a day was starting to wear me out. I could hear music blasting from my unit as I stepped out of the elevator, and I knew for a fact that Anthony was in residence; since he was the one person I knew who had to listen to his music at that volume. It was a week before Christmas and Maurice and Anthony were on winter break. Maurice had been back at school for a few days now, after spending some time at home recuperating from his surgery. I'd tried to convince him to stay home until after the Christmas holiday, but he was missing his friends and had grown tired of lying around so Maurice had been adamant about returning to school as soon as possible.

Blair and I had announced our engagement to my sons one night at dinner, shortly after Maurice had been released from the hospital. Blair had taken the three of us out to an upscale restaurant downtown, and it was there that we shared the news of our upcoming marriage. Maurice had taken the news rather calmly, but with Anthony it had been a whole different story. After Blair had informed them of the news, Anthony had stood up from the table so abruptly that he had almost knocked his plate onto the floor. Then he had looked from me, and then to Blair before turning and leaving the restaurant without saying a word to anyone. I hadn't seen or spoken with Anthony since that night.

Later that same evening, I'd called Anthony's apartment and his roommate had informed me that Anthony was not in. I called several other times, but Anthony always seemed to be out, so I gave up knowing he would call me when he was ready to talk, and from the sound of the music blaring from the other side of the door, tonight was the night.

I shrugged out of my wet trench coat shaking the wetness from it before unlocking the door and entered my condo for the last time as an occupant, for this weekend, Maurice and I would be moving in with Blair. As I stepped inside, I assumed Blair had been by judging from the stack of cardboard boxes piled high in the small foyer. Blair had promised earlier to stop by with more boxes, and to lend a hand with the remainder of the packing. Maurice and I, with the help of Blair, whenever he was available, had been packing boxes off and on throughout the week. The den was the only room left which we hadn't finished packing up. Maurice and Blair started tackling the den the night before and with any luck they would be able to finish up tonight. I was leaving most of the kitchen utensils for Anthony's use, except for my favorite set of crystal glasses.

"Hello," I called out loudly, as I tossed my coat over the pile of boxes. Instantly the music was turned down.

"Mom's home!" Maurice called out.

"Hi, Maurice, how's your hand?" I asked as I headed for my room. My eight-hour pantyhose and bra were working overtime and I was ready to ditch them both.

"Still here," Maurice replied as he came downstairs, following along behind me to my room.

I'd expected to find Blair in my room on the phone but he was nowhere to be seen. "Where's Blair?" I asked as I reached for Maurice's hand. I wanted to make sure his dressing wasn't soiled or needed to be changed, which it did.

"He was here earlier but Jeremy called a couple of hours ago and he took off. Blair said not to cook because he would pick up something on his way back," Maurice grimaced as I flipped his hand over and applied a light pressure to it. The outer sutures had finally been removed, and the surgeon had left a small unstitched hole for excess drainage, stating the opening would eventually close up on its own.

"I had no intention of cooking," I said, as I rubbed his arm. Even though the *pic-line* was taped to his arm, every now and again the dressing holding it in place would become lose and I had to reapply fresh tape to it as well. I couldn't wait until my baby had completed his therapy, and I'm sure Maurice felt the same. As I was kicking off my shoes a movement caught my eye and I looked up to see Anthony lingering in the doorway to my bedroom. "Anthony, what have I told you about playing your music that loudly? I'm surprised the neighbors haven't called the police and complained."

"I just turned it up fifteen minutes ago."

"You know if you're going to be staying here you cannot be playing loud music. The people in this building are not going to stand for it, especially old Mrs. Jamison on the second floor. She *will* call the police on your behind."

"Dag, not even a hello to your first born son, just jumped right down my throat like I was a stranger or something." Anthony grumbled.

"What? Boy! Anthony, it's been a long week and secondly I've been calling your behind for two whole weeks now. Last weekend Maurice and I even drove out to see you and you pretended you weren't home, and I know you where there because your Blazer was sitting in your parking stall. Later on at the mall we ran into AJ, and he told us he'd left you at home studying, so don't lie."

"What do you know about this *dude* anyway?"

"What *dude*?"

"This dude, *Blair*." Then Anthony did something I hadn't seem him do in years; at least not to my face, which was rolling his eyes.

"Oh, now he's a '*dude*'? What happened to '*you're the man, Blair?*' Or is that only when he's spending money on your behind? What's going on here, Anthony? Why did you get up and walk out of the restaurant like that? And why haven't you returned any of my phone calls? I thought you liked Blair?"

"Mom, I never said I didn't like him, I just don't think the two of you should get married that's all!" Anthony had his hands shoved deep inside the pockets of his jeans as he stood there glaring at me.

I was standing in the door of my bathroom, my hands on my hips. It had been a while since I'd seen Anthony behave so insolent before and I was shocked. "Why not?" I asked as I tried to shake off the fatigue that was pulling at me. I sat down on the edge of the bed. It was apparent Anthony was having difficulties about my upcoming nuptials to Blair. For me, this conversation should have taken place two weeks ago. But leave it to Anthony to pick tonight of all nights. "Sit down," I said as I patted the spot beside me.

"Mom, I just don't think you should marry him," his voice was a bit subdued as he said this.

"Anthony, what is this all about?" I asked, looking at the man sitting next to me who was not my little boy anymore. He had grown up so quickly and it still amazed me because I still saw him as my little boy.

"Anthony said you should've married Uncle Sonny," Maurice intervened.

"What?" I asked jerking my head around to Maurice who was sprawled flat on my bed with his good hand beneath his chin. "Me marry Sonny?" Maurice shrugged his shoulders and I turned to face Anthony again, noticing the tears in his eyes.

"Rice, you got a big mouth. Mom, you've got to admit Uncle Sonny has always been there for us. I mean he was more of a dad to us than our real dad. I have more happy memories of him than I have of any other man in my life-"

"Anthony-"

"Uncle Sonny has always treated me like his son, and you know he'll do anything for us and I'll do anything for him."

"Anthony, listen to me-"

"I know you two love each other, because I used to listen to the two of you talking late at night when you thought Rice and I were asleep. When I was younger I used to dream of the two of you marrying and having Sonny for my dad. I believe if you hadn't starting seeing the professor, Uncle Sonny would have asked you to marry him instead of Macey."

My son was openly crying now; bringing tears to my eyes. Anthony's big hands wiped away at the tears running freely down his face. I even heard a few sniffles coming from Maurice as I snatched up a handful of tissues from the box on my dresser, and handed them each a couple. I drew Anthony into my arms and held him close until we had all composed ourselves. "Anthony, I wish you would have shared these feelings with me a long time ago because I would have explained to you then the different type of love your Uncle Sonny and I have for one another," I said as I reached out for Maurice's hand, holding one hand of each in mine. "Anthony, I never knew you felt like this about Sonny. I know you and your brother care for Sonny, but I never dreamed it was like this. I love Sonny, I won't deny that, but not how you think." I smiled as Anthony reached over and gave me a hug. "Boy, your Uncle Sonny would probably fall down laughing if he could have heard you."

"He didn't laugh."

"What? You mean you told him the same thing?"

Anthony nodded, as he continued on. "Uncle Sonny drove out to see me the other day and he told me to stop behaving like a baby and to give you a call. I told him how I felt, and how I thought it should be the two of you marrying. I asked him if he loved you and he said he did. And you know what, Mom, Uncle Sonny didn't laugh."

"What else did your Uncle Sonny have to say?"

"He told me to call you and tell you how I felt about you marrying Blair, and how you would explain it all to me."

I smiled and raised Anthony's hand to my lips. "Did I explain everything to you, Anthony? Do you understand now why I cannot marry Sonny?"

"Yeah, you explained it okay. I just thought you and Uncle Sonny were…you know, in love for real. But I still don't know why you and Uncle Sonny shouldn't get married."

"I don't know what to say, Anthony. The timing was never right for us. I wish you would have told me how you felt a lot sooner. How long have you been feeling this way?"

"Shoot," Anthony said with a shake of his head. "Since I was old enough to know that Uncle Sonny was doing everything for Rice and me that our real dad should have been doing. I realized how every time you and Uncle Sonny are together how much the two of you laugh and smile, and you know what, Mom?"

"What."

"You still laugh and smile a lot when Uncle Sonny is around. But, this marriage, something doesn't feel right about Blair, Mom and I don't want you to get hurt."

"Oh, Anthony, you're so sweet." I reached out, hugging him close. "Baby, I'm not going to get hurt," I replied just as the downstairs buzzer went off announcing a visitor.

"Food's here," Maurice said as he jumped up and raced into the living room and out the door.

As Anthony started to leave the room, I reached out for his arm as he started to follow his brother out the room. "Anthony, you don't have to worry about me, okay? Everything's going to be fine. I'm in love with Blair and it would mean so much to me if you would give him a chance and try to get to know him."

"Okay," he replied curtly as he left the bedroom. By the time Blair was in the house, Anthony had the tape gun out and was taping up the bottom of a few of the cardboard boxes.

"Mmmm, something smells good," I said as I joined Blair and Maurice in the kitchen. "Smells like Italian to me." Blair gave me a quick kiss and a hug before turning his attention back to his conversation with Maurice.

"Well don't worry about it, Maurice, you'll be playing like a pro again this time next year and the surgery, the pain, and all else will be just a distant memory. You're young, you'll bounce back," he said giving Maurice a pat on the back. "Anthony, you content on making boxes all night, or will you be joining us for dinner?" Blair called out as he searched the cabinets for something. "Hey, Mia, you got any balsamic vinegar? Where do you keep the olive oil?"

"Behind you, Blair, it's in the cupboard on your left. No, the one next to the stove." I had no intention of sharing Anthony's feelings with Blair. I had a feeling Blair would not be too happy to hear that my oldest son would rather I marry our mutual friend. I had no fear of Anthony ever speaking with Blair about what we had discussed, but then it suddenly dawn on me, that Maurice didn't have any qualms about discussing his feelings out in the open.

"Maurice, let's change your bandages before we eat," I said, hoping to get him alone. I wanted to make sure he wouldn't mention our earlier conversation to Blair. The night was too short to get into a heated debate with Blair about Anthony's dislike for him.

"It's okay, I'll change it later." He was in the process of taking plates down from the cupboard.

"Right now, Maurice," I said as I headed for my bedroom. Maurice mumbled something under his breath, but he followed me to my room regardless. I stood facing my bedroom door as I removed the wrappings from his hand. "Maurice, the conversation we had earlier is not to be repeated to anyone. Do you understand me?"

Maurice made a smacking sound with his lips, giving me a look of aghast. "Mom, I'm not a dummy you know? I won't tell *Blair* if that's who you're talking about. Is this the reason you wanted to check my bandages, so you could warn me to keep my mouth shut?"

"You're right, Maurice. You're not a dummy, and I'm sorry if I made you feel that way," I said as I wrapped fresh gauze around his hand. "There," I said patting him on arm. "Go eat." Blair entered the room just as Maurice was leaving.

"Work late today?" He asked, on his way to the bathroom. I followed along behind him as he headed over to the sink.

"I was there until seven. Claudia didn't return to the office after lunch today."

"Baby, why don't you just fire her ass? She wouldn't be pulling that stunt if she was working for anyone else." Blair said as he began to wash his hands and then his face.

"I know what you mean," I said shaking my head. "Sonya and I talked about this very subject tonight. We placed an ad in the local paper for a senior executive recruiter."

"What?"

"Yes, I've decided to make Sonya the new office manager of Harris & Freeman. I should have made Sonya manager in the first place. You know what's really funny?" I asked handing Blair a towel.

"What?"

"I thought Sonya would be the one with the attendance problem, especially with her dealing with her daughter's illness. That's why I gave her the sales position instead of Claudia, to give Sonya more flexibility with her time. But ever since Sonya moved out of her old apartment building and into her new home, her daughter's health has been much better. Apparently it had to be something in that apartment triggering Tameka's asthma attacks."

"Probably filled with mold," Blair replied as he hung the towel over the shower door. I smiled as he rolled his shirt sleeves back down and smooth his hands over his head, before he did a quick glance of himself in the mirror. Blair finally looked up and spotted me admiring him. Blair wet his lips as he folded his arms across his chest. "I love it when you smile at me like that."

"I love it when you wet your lips while you're looking at me. It's such a turn on," I replied seductively.

Blair stepped forward and placed an arm around my waist. With his other hand, Blair pushed my hair back and away from my face and traced my ear with his thumb. "Have I told you lately how much it means to me that you want to marry me?" I barely had time to nod my head as Blair's lips crushed down onto mine. After a few seconds he raised his head, and stared straight into my eyes. "Have I told you lately how much it means to me that you want to spend the rest of your life with me?" Again, a quick nod, before his lips claimed mine, leaving me breathless. "Have I told you lately, how much I love Italian food and how my plate is in the kitchen, right now getting cold? Let's go eat," Blair said as he grabbed my hand and pulled me along after him. "I haven't had anything to eat since breakfast and it's been one hell of a busy day."

Anthony and Maurice were sitting around the breakfast bar when Blair and I entered the kitchen, and as I passed by Anthony, I smiled, and gave him a pat on the back.

"Anthony, so glad to see you could join us," Blair said as he picked up a plate and handed it to me.

Anthony nodded his head as he slowly chewed on a piece of garlic bread, and as he did this he look up at Blair and they stared at each another, neither looking away.

I could feel the tension in the air. "Anthony and I had a talk tonight," I said, as I headed over to the small wine rack on the counter and removed a bottle of wine, praying Anthony wouldn't get upset and walk out again. I placed the bottle of wine, along with the corkscrew on the counter next to Blair then headed back to the cabinet for a couple of glasses.

"So, Anthony, what was it? You finally came to the conclusion that I'm not such a jerk after all, huh?"

"I never said you were a *jerk*, Blair. I just don't think my mom should marry *you*."

I almost dropped the glass I was holding in my hand when Anthony said that, and I was thankful my back was to the room.

"Oh really, and just who do you think your mom should marry, Anthony?" Blair asked as he sat down across from Anthony.

I froze, with the two wine glasses in mid-air as I slowly turned to face the room. Blair's back was to me and Anthony was facing me as he slowly picked up his napkin and wiped his mouth before answering. His eyes were hard, emotionless, as he stared at Blair. It was so quiet in the room you could've heard a mouse pee, as Maurice was fond of saying, and speaking of Maurice, even he had stopped chewing his food. His head cocked to the side, his mouth hanging open as he stared at his brother.

"Who do I think she should marry?" Anthony asked, as he looked us all in our faces, nodding his head, as a smile broke out on his face. "Arnold Schwarzenegger."

I hadn't realized I had been holding my breath until it all gushed out at once. I moved to stand behind Blair placing a glass in front of him, behaving as normal as possible. Maurice was laughing so hard that he almost choked on a piece of garlic bread.

"Man, that was stupid," Maurice finally spat out.

"Not as stupid as you. Look at you; you can't even eat without spitting food out all over the place." Anthony said as he rose and headed for the sink. "Mom, what time will the movers be here tomorrow?"

I had now joined Blair at the bar as he fiddled with opening the bottle of wine. "They're supposed to be here by nine."

"Hurry up and eat, Rice, and I'll help you finish packing up the den. Hey, mom, can I keep your CD player?"

"Arnold Schwarzenegger?" Maurice huffed as he rose from the rattan barstool. "Mom doesn't even like him anymore, and no, you can't have the CD player, she gave it to me." They left the kitchen throwing insults at the other.

"*What, he's joking right?*" Blair asked, as he turned to me with one eyebrow raised. He held the pose for a couple of seconds, before reaching out and pouring us each a glass of wine.

I smiled, as I slowly dipped a finger into my wine glass. I placed my finger in my mouth seductively. "I used to love me some Arnold."

"It that right?" Blair asked.

"That's right. I've seen all of his movies, and have collected them as well," I said as Blair rose from his seat and stood before me. He took the finger I'd dipped into the wine glass and placed it into his mouth, slowly sucking on my finger, his eyes never leaving mine. After a few seconds, he removed my finger from his mouth, and with a quick flick of his tongue, wetted his lips. "You are so damn sexy," I said, wanting to take him right there in the kitchen. But I settled for a kiss instead.

"Spell it," Blair said afterward.

I had no idea what he wanted me to spell, for my mind was still on our kiss. "Spell what?" I asked.

"*Schwarzenegger.*"

CHAPTER FOURTEEN

"Don't do that."

"Why not?" Blair asked as he gently trailed the tip of his index finger up and down my right thigh. His caress, as brief as it was, sent chills down my leg. Blair dipped his head lower, his lips hovering just above the valley between my thighs. Oh no, I thought, to myself, he's going to go down on me. Although I enjoyed oral sex, I was a bit apprehensive because this would be a first for us and I wasn't sure if Blair was good at oral sex. Was he a biter, or a slurpper, or just plain not good at it? I thought as I shivered from his touch.

"Oh I don't know, it- maybe I'm not fresh enough down there." I tried to wiggle away as I gently gave his head a push. I mean, what else could I say? I was finding it hard to be honest with him on this subject.

Blair chuckled as he removed my hand from his head, bringing my hand to his lips instead. "Mia, we just had a shower and you smell," he begins as he dipped his head again. Blair looked up, glancing up at me with a wide grin on his face, "Good enough to eat," he said as he lowered his head again.

"B l a i r!" I cried out as he brought me to the edge of an orgasm. Well Blair definitely knew what he was doing.

"Did you enjoy yourself?" He asked as he kissed the inside of my thighs, making his way up my body. Stopping only long enough to dip his tongue into the well of my navel, and as he did this, Blair paused, tilting his head to one side as he spoke, "I like that.".

I rubbed the back of his head as he shifted on the bed, straddling me. "Like what?" I drew in a quick breath as Blair flicked his tongue over one of my nipples.

"The way you called out my name," Blair said as he lowered his head bringing his lips close to mine. I'm going to have to do that more often just to hear call out my name."

"You always make me call out your name."

"Not like that. I don't know, baby, but I think I hit the right key or something that time." He said as he laughed.

"Oh is that right?" I asked as I laughed along with him.

"Well did I?" Blair asked as we quieted down.

We were lying on our sides facing each other and I was rubbing his chest and luxuriating in the feel of him. I took my time answering him, because Blair knew exactly what he was doing in the oral sex department, and he had hit the right key alright. As a matter of fact, he hit several right *keys* and it gave him the right to gloat, so I had to give him that. "Yes, Blair, you absolutely, positively hit the right keys, baby," I said with a smile as I leaned into him and kissed him.

"That's what I'm talking about," Blair replied as he rolled over on top of me.

"You know what you are?" Blair asked me some time later that same night as he gave one of the *twins* a gentle squeeze.

"No, what?"

"You're *multi-orgasmic.*"

"Blair," I said as slapped his hand away. "You made that up. That isn't even a word."

"I did not make it up, and it is so a word."

"Okay, what does it mean?"

"It means, that, you my dear," he said punctuating each word with a kiss to each of the *girls*, "have multiple orgasms back to back."

"Uh-huh, and how do you know I'm not faking it?"

"Because you can't fake this," he said as he placed a finger inside of me, making me squirm. "Ohh, nice and wet."

"Okay," I said after a few breathless seconds. "Or I could just be a nymphomaniac."

"I don't have a problem with that either, but you are definitely *multi-orgasmic.*"

"Umm-huh. Spell it."

"I can do better than that, I'll show you."

I smiled and groan, as I stretched like a cat as memories of my first night in my new home made me blush. Blair was lying next to me, on his back, and as usual his head was raised slightly by a couple of pillows beneath his head. I became aware that when we first got into bed, we would always start the night wrapped up in one another's arms, but as the night progressed Blair would always assume the position he was in now, and I also discovered that he was also a very light sleeper as well. I could tell from the smile on his face that he was watching me, watching him.

"Morning."

"Good morning."

"Did you sleep well?"

"Like a rock."

"Well I certainly won't disagree with you on that. I have never known anyone to sleep as soundly as you do. If someone were to break into this house you'd never know it."

"That's why I have you here to protect me," I said coyly as I slipped out of bed. "It's after ten, Maurice is probably dying to get outside and explore the area."

"Maurice is already up and out." Blair slid from the bed; naked as the day he was born, moving like a big cat on the prowl for his meal.

"Don't tell me you let my son go outside by himself with those killer dogs?" I was already slipping on my robe and strolling for the bedroom door.

"Baby, they're guard dogs not killer dogs. I introduced Maurice to the Eurydice and Orpheus months ago, and again this morning. They will not attack him unless they are instructed to." Blair headed for the bathroom, giving me a nice view of his backside. He had an incredible body, the body of a fighter. I've watched Blair and Sonny spar a couple of times and it frightened me to see them trying to out do the other. Blair just shrugged it off, saying it was all part of keeping fit.

I was tempted to follow along behind him, but chose to go outside to see what Maurice was up to instead. I found Maurice out back in the process of positioning himself for a dive off the diving board into the heated pool, with his left arm all wrapped up in plastic. My sons were excellent swimmers and to watch them was like watching underwater ballet. They both loved the water.

"Hi Mom," Maurice waved, as he dove into the pool.

Eurydice, who had been lying by the pool, had now made her way over to my side. Eurydice came to a stop in front of me, giving my hand a little lick. This was her way of acknowledging me, and after I'd scratched the area between her ears, Eurydice returned to her spot by the pool. Orpheus, the male was nowhere in sight and I assumed Blair had shut him away in the barn-like building in the back of the house. I walked to the edge of the pool and dipped my foot into the water, amazed at the warmth of it for the morning was still chilly.

Maurice swam up to me and pulled himself out of the pool. "What's for breakfast?"

I stepped back before he could splatter me with water. "Maurice, how long have you been up?"

"Oh, for a couple of hours now," he replied as he grabbed his towel.

"So why didn't you prepare breakfast for everyone?"

"I didn't know if I was allowed to."

"Maurice, don't even try it. You know this is your new home as well as it is ours. Why would you say something like that anyway?"

"I don't know. So I can just go in and cook like I used to do when I was at home?"

We turned and headed for the house and I rubbed his arm as I spoke. "This is your home now, Maurice, and of course you can go in and cook, and just like at our old place, you clean up after yourself when you're done as well." As we entered the house we ran into Anthony who was yakking away on the phone, and judging from his expression it was probably a female on the other end of the line. I continued on into the kitchen and found Blair, with his cell phone up to his ear, as he poked around in the fridge.

"I'll ask Mia and get back with you. Give my love to Macey. Baby," he said as he sat his phone down on the counter, "Sonny wants to know if we'd like to come by their place for dinner tonight?"

"I don't have a problem with that as long as we can leave early. I would really like to finish unpacking this weekend if I can." The thought of coming home after a long day at the office and dealing with unpacking boxes of stuff, really didn't appeal to me right now.

"Well we could work on it right after breakfast and do a little more tonight. If we all work together we'll be finished in no time."

"I was thinking maybe we could buy a Christmas tree today or tomorrow?" I asked hesitantly. I guess Blair and I didn't know enough about each other after all, because I wasn't sure on his views regarding Christmas. I knew Sonny and Macey celebrated Christmas and they attended the same church as Blair, but I wasn't sure how Blair felt about having Christmas decorations in the home. I was into all of the holidays and enjoyed decorating my home for the seasons.

"Sure, no problem. There's this place not far from here that sells live trees. They're so full and green they look like they never left the earth." Blair pulled out a carton of eggs and other items that went into his ham and cheese omelets. "Is everyone okay with omelets this morning?"

"Blair, you don't have to fix breakfast for us."

"Mia, you know I like to start my day off with a large breakfast, so how would it look if I fixed me something but nothing for the rest of you? Cause you know I don't mind."

"Blair, what's cooking?" Maurice asked as he entered the kitchen wearing a pair of sweatpants and a tee shirt.

"Ham and cheese omelets. Go ask your brother if he's interested in one? Mia, you want to give Macey a call and let her know we'll see them tonight around seven?"

My breakfast was ready and sitting on the table by the time I'd finished my conversation with Macey, who for some reason had been overly long winded this morning. As I sat down at the table with Blair, Maurice and Anthony had already finished their breakfast, and all eyes were on me as I reached for my fork. Maurice actually giggled as I reached for the peppershaker. "What's so funny?" I asked, as I looked around the table at them as I proceeded to sprinkle pepper on my omelet. My hand stopped in mid air as I watched the flakes of pepper float down onto my plate. My mouth flew opened, for sitting right on top of my omelet, snuggled between two pieces of parsley was the biggest marquise diamond ring I'd ever seen. On either side of the marquise were five baguette diamonds, which created a frame for the larger diamond, all set on a sterling silver band. I looked over at Blair, my mouth hanging opened, mesmerized by this beautiful piece of jewelry. "It's beautiful."

"I was going to put it in your pasta the other night but I thought that would've been a little too messy," Blair said as he reached over and plucked the ring out of the parsley. Blair blew on it, and then used his napkin to gently dust away the last few remaining specks of pepper before he lowered himself before me.

"Oh, Blair, it's so beautiful, thank you," I said as Blair slipped the ring on my finger, with Maurice and Anthony in the background, clapping their hands.

"Mom, I can't believe you didn't see that big old ring sitting there," Maurice said as he came around the table and gave me a hug. "Man, Blair, we should've had the video camera set up in the corner of the room."

"Yeah, Blair, this was definitely a Kodak moment," Anthony pitched in sarcastically as he left the room with a wave of his hand.

"What's with him?" Blair asked and I just shrugged my shoulders. Anthony was like a light switch when it came to Blair, on one minute off the next. I was thankful there had been no confrontations between the two, at least not yet.

"He'll come around. Our marriage is a lot for him to comprehend; things are going to change for him as well."

"I know, but I thought we were getting along okay, that is, until we announced our engagement and then it was like he just turned cold on me."

"Well, you have to admit you've spent more time with Maurice than you have with Anthony. It's easier for the two of you to be together than is it with Anthony, I mean, with Maurice still at home and all. Maybe you should plan some time alone with Anthony, you know, just the two of you."

"You're right. Maybe I should plan a little get together with just us guys, Maurice, Sonny, and Anthony."

I smiled, seeing through his little ploy. "Oh, I see, you want Maurice and Sonny around as buffers?"

"No, I can do something alone with Anthony, but I don't think he'll want to come if it's just the two of us. This way I'll have a better chance of him not turning down my invitation."

"Yeah, right," I replied jokingly.

"Seriously," Blair replied with a serious look. "If I approached Anthony right now and invited him to a weekend in Santa Monica he would turn me down flat without even a blink."

"Okay, I believe you. Not," I replied, rushing from the room as I made up an excuse about being in a hurry to finish unpacking.

"Just for that, you're coming along as well," Blair shouted.

Before heading to my bedroom, I decided to check in on Maurice. I found him busy setting out his personal items and was pleased that he had taken an interest to his new surroundings.

"This room is much larger then my other room at the condo." Maurice explained as he dusted off the CD player I had given him. Maurice had chosen the room farthest away from the rest of the house as his own. It had been his decision to keep his old bedroom furniture from the condo, and the room was large enough to hold the desk and computer that used to occupy the den at the condo.

Blair and I had chosen to keep the bedroom where I had spent my first night and the other bedroom as guest rooms. The fourth room, which was the first room you encountered in that part of the house, had been designated as our office space. Blair still hadn't done much on decorating so we were going to make decorating the rest of the house a joint project, except for Maurice's room. Maurice would be free to do whatever he wanted to do to his room.

After making sure Maurice was settling in, I headed off to do some serious unpacking of my own. Blair was already there and in the process of removing some of his things from the master bedroom closet and into the closet space in the office. There was plenty of closet space but since Blair was equally as guilty as I was about being a clotheshorse, the closet space was filling up rather quickly as my things filled the vacated space. There was also an armoire in our bedroom for our use, and Blair had ordered a matching dresser as well. I had purchased rugs for room, and the next items on my list would be a nice comforter set, and maybe a set of vertical blinds or curtains for the French doors facing the rear of the house, because at the moment the glass doors were uncovered. Blair had suggested maybe we could just have the windows tinted. There was a lot to do, but we had plenty of time to settle in as a family.

By the time I made it back to the master bedroom, Blair was in the process of unpacking a box containing all of my black shoes and he made a remark on how amazed he was at the number of shoes I owned, wanting to know why anyone would need twelve pairs of black shoes. I reminded him of the many shoes he owned, but I didn't mention the other four boxes that needed to be unpacked containing the rest of my footwear in various colors of red, brown, tan, and grey. Then there was the box containing my many pairs of boots. It was going to be a long day of unpacking for me. Blair was already talking about adding an addition to the already large walk-in closet to accommodate all of my things and to move the rest of his clothing back into our bedroom. I was surprised at how helpful he was with the unpacking. Blair was so thoughtful, creating space for me if I needed more room to add one more pair of shoes, or to hang another blouse or whatever the need, Blair was there sorting it all out.

"You got that pretty smile again," Blair said as he turned around and caught me smiling at his back. We'd been surveying our progress in the closet when all of a sudden I just stopped to admire him.

"Just admiring the view," I said as I gave him a long hug and planted a soft kiss on his beautiful lips, before stepping away. "You know what I love about you, Blair? You are the most caring and thoughtful man I've ever known. I'm so lucky to have you in my life. I'd just about given up on falling in love again and when I did fall in love with you, I was surprised at how quickly it happened, but then you made it easy for me to love you, Blair. No matter what it is that you do, your words and your actions show me in so many ways how much you care about me, I mean, me as a person, not merely as a piece of meat," I chuckled as Blair shook his head at my words. "I love it when you take into consideration my needs and wants, sometimes before I can even anticipate them. And the way you handle things, no matter what it is, you always put your heart into. You do so much for me, and in doing so, you satisfy all of me, no matter what it is." I touched my heart and my head as I spoke, "Emotionally, physically, spiritually, and mentally. Listen to me babbling," I said lowering my head, feeling slightly embarrassed. "Blair, you make me complete." Blair placed his finger under my chin and lifted my head, then leaned forward and kissed me gently upon the lips.

"Oh Blair...I want you to know that having you in my life has made me the happiest woman on earth and it has been such a long time since I've been happy, truly happy." I could see the question in his eyes, the question his mouth didn't have to speak, and I answered his look. "Yes, Blair, even more so than Sonny."

"What made you say that?" he asked pulling me back into his arms, his voice hoarse with emotion.

"That was the answer to your unasked question, the question I saw in your eyes." He didn't have to admit to it, because his smile told me I'd been right. "Tell me, Blair, is this what you're trying to do, top whatever Sonny has done for me? Are you trying to take over were Sonny left off?"

"Babe," Blair begins with a shake of his head, "that's not my style. I love you and I can honestly say I've never loved a woman as much as I love you, not since my grandmother. As a matter of fact my grandmother was the only other woman I've ever told I loved her. You see, Mia, I love who you are, the person that makes you, *you*. Mia, you bring out the best in me too, and having you in my life makes me whole. I know how sometimes you get frustrated with yourself about losing weight. No. No, baby, don't turn away," Blair said reaching out for my hand as I started to walk away. "You just don't see yourself the way I do. Mia, you're *beautiful* to me just as you are. I don't know what your hang-up about your weight is, and I don't know what's been said to you before by other men. Baby, you need to look within yourself as well as out, because one is nothing without the other, and when you put them both together, lady, you are beautiful, and don't you ever, ever let anyone tell you differently. *Love* isn't all about looks, height, or weight, it's about *heart*. It's how you feel in your heart for that special someone."

His tender words almost brought tears to my eyes. I held onto him. "God, thank you for bringing this man into my life," I said to the ceiling. "Beauty is in the eye of the beholder," I said to Blair.

"Then I'm beholding you," he replied as we kissed.

Well that completed our unpacking for the day, because three hours later the four of us, along with Sonny and Macey were on a flight for Las Vegas. Blair and I were married the next day in the little White Chapel on the Strip. It had taken a lot of convincing from Sonny and Maurice to get Anthony to join us in Vegas. Because even though Anthony had promised me that he would try and get along with Blair, Anthony was still in a funk about our marriage.

CHAPTER FIFTEEN

Our little family spent Christmas Eve at The Egg Roll along with fifty other people we had invited. Sonny normally closed the restaurant for Christmas day but this time he had closed it on Christmas Eve as well. Blair had invited all of his employees and I had invited Sonya and our new assistant from the temp agency, and we dined on a meal fit for a king and his royal court.

Don't ask me why, but I wanted Claudia there as well to share in my joy, so her name was added to the list of invitees, and I was surprised she had accepted the invite because Claudia was still very angry with me for firing her. Claudia and I hadn't had any contact since the day I let her go, but not because I hadn't tried. After several voice mail messages, emails, text messages, and a couple of trips over to her place, I had finally given up on chasing her down. Hell, I'd even forgiven her for going after my man. I'd buried the hatchet and was ready to let all ill feelings go down the drain, after all life was too short to dwell in misery and I was speaking from experience. After we'd gone through the motions of wishing each other a Merry Christmas, Claudia had moved to one side of the restaurant and I had remained on the other. I don't know what I had expected, but I didn't think Claudia would accept an invitation and then behave as though I didn't exist. And to my surprise, Claudia was even avoiding Sonya who had nothing to do with anything.

Later, after a great dinner prepared entirely by Sonny, Claudia retreated to the other side of the room, keeping her distance from me. Claudia was now speaking loudly about the room and I could tell she was drunk.

"I'm going over there and tell her if she doesn't quiet down she will have to leave," Macey said as she joined me at the bar.

"She's just trying to get attention, that's all," I replied as I ordered another margarita. "Claudia's hurting, Macey. She's all alone."

"That's because besides her parents, you are the only person who tolerates her ass," Macey said with a toss her hair over her shoulder. "You know when Sonny comes out of the kitchen he's going to put her out of the restaurant."

"I'm not sure what has gotten into her. I know she can be pain at times, but lately, her behavior has gotten weird even for Claudia. She won't talk to me, I've been trying to reach for a while, but she's been avoiding me and then she turns around and accepts my invitation for tonight and has barely said five words to me," I said with a sigh. I felt badly for Claudia, for she didn't have many friends and all of her so-called male friends were with her solely to get what they could out of her. And once well meaning folks got to know Claudia, they usually avoided her once they got to know her because of her coarseness and she could be very vulgar. Claudia always seemed to be angry at the world and she had a difficult time letting go of a grudge. Macey was right; besides Claudia's parents, I was the only other person who tolerated her theatrics, simply because I knew when to ignore her. Claudia reminded me of when my sons were young, acting out for attention, which was what she was doing now. The few people, who had been speaking with her earlier, had walked away leaving Claudia alone. Even Sonya, who had stopped by for a brief chat, had left Claudia alone.

"Claudia," I called out as I approached her. "What's going on, girl? What have you been up to lately? I haven't heard from you in a while and you never replied to any of my messages. Don't you think you should slow down on the alcohol a bit?" From the look Claudia gave me I thought she was going to jump up from her seat and try and hit me, but after a few seconds a smile spread across her lips, turning her back into the beautiful woman that she was.

Claudia picked up her glass and took a sip from it before speaking, her eyes never breaking contact with mine. "Oh, now you're playing the faithful friend, watching out for me," Claudia said as she sat the glass down on the table with a loud bang. "Don't you think it's a little too late for that, Mia? I mean I must have been out when you stop by to check on me, last week or was it two weeks ago, *girlfriend*? When I was having problems you never once came to me and asked if

I needed any help. *Noo*, not you. I guess it was because you had your hands full fucking your stud- well, well, speak of the fucking devil, and he has his little side kick with him too," Claudia said with a nod, as she looked beyond my shoulder.

I turned around as Blair and Sonny made their way over to join me. Blair reached out for my hand and he placed his other hand on the back of my neck as he leaned in and gave me a kiss upon my cheek.

Sonny sat down at the table next to Claudia, reaching out to rub her back but she leaned away from him before he could touch her. He smiled as his eyes lingered on the glass on the table. "Enjoying yourself, Claudia?"

"Who wants to know?" Claudia asked.

"I thought you were bringing a date?" Sonny asked her, ignoring her earlier question.

"Fuck you, Sonny." Claudia rose and came around the table to stand before us. Claudia was a little unsteady on her feet as she swayed from side to side. "So, Mia, my *sistah*, my *girlfriend*, how is it having a young stud to fuck every night? I know he can keep it up for you all night long 'cause he's young, big, and so damn healthy." Claudia reached out and touched Blair on his arm, drawing her hand up and down the length of his arm.

Neither of us said a word, but I could feel the pressure from Blair's hand as his grip tighten on the back of my neck, before he pulled his arm away from Claudia's touch. "Yeah, motherfucker, you pretend to be all caught up in *Momma Mia* and her two kids and shit, but I know you just playing along with this bitch until you get what you want from her, just like she got her business all started up and shit from you, you're waiting on something from her too. I can't see what the hell you could possibly want with Mia; after all she ain't got nothing on me. So you go right ahead and keep on playing her until your eyes open, but by then it will be too late."

"Claudia, let me call you a cab." Sonny said as he rose from the table. His hand went up in the air as he signaled for one of the waiters.

"Mia, used to be my friend, she used to be there for me until your black ass came into the picture." Claudia nodded her head at Blair as she spoke.

"Claudia, whatever friendship we had just few out the door with your statement. I guess we were both fooled into believing we were friends. And as far as work, what happened between us on the job was purely business, and it had nothing to do with our friendship or our *pretend* friendship. You know as well as I, that any other company would have fired you long before I did. I gave you every opportunity to get yourself together and you just ignored my warnings completely. I offered to sit down and speak with you about what was bothering you but you repeatedly turned down my offers, or you would say you were coming simply to cancel again. Claudia, you know this has nothing to do with Blair or anyone else; this is between you and *me*."

"It ain't that, and you know it," Claudia spat out. "You just got too high in the head and forgot *where* you came from, that's all. We *sistahs* gotta stick together. Especially black women, cause we get the *shaft* from every fucking body!" Claudia said waving her arms high in the air, as she pointed around the room. "We get it from the brothas, we get it from the white man, and the white women. Hell, even the fucking Chinese are fucking us," she said, pointing a finger at Sonny. "If we don't watch each other's back then we're fucked, and that's what I am right now, Mia, I'm FUCKED!" Claudia spat out as she pounded her chest, as tears streamed down her face. "You call yourself a friend? A true friend would have never turned her back on me in the first place. This *damn termite* pops up, and all of a sudden you just forget all about me. Claudia who?" she cackled. "Yeah, right, some fucking friend you are. You think you're something but you ain't shit, *bitch*. You're a fucking *termite* just like he is," Claudia spat as she made stabbing motions in the air.

I cringed at her words, for partly what Claudia was saying was true. There was so much *newness* in my life that I'd run out of time to do what I used to do for fun, like spending time with my girlfriends. I had become so caught up with the day to day operations of my business, Maurice's illness, my relationship with Blair, and trying to figure out how to improve Anthony's relationship with Blair, that it didn't leave much room in my life to spend time with friends. The wheels of my life had become a bit bumpy, but of course this wouldn't be permanent. My business would soon be operating error free, and Maurice was getting better every day, and my relationship with Blair was great, and Anthony, well that was a whole different story. Then there was this new disclosure about how Claudia felt about Blair.

The waiter stepped up and glanced over at Claudia, before giving Sonny a nod.

"So what the fuck you gonna do mother-fucker, throw me out?" Claudia asked as she caught the by-play between Sonny and his waiter.

"He's going to call you a cab, Claudia," Sonny replied as Macey joined our little group.

"I don't need a damn cab; I can drive wherever I wanna go."

As the waiter turned to walk away, Blair held up his hand to him and instructed him to call a cab.

"Making me quit my job to come and work for your ass, and then you up and fire me like I was nothing to you!"

"Claudia, I am not going to discuss this with you tonight. I can stop by and see you next week, or you're welcome to come by the office." I didn't think this was the time or place for this discussion. Not to mention that Claudia had left her job on her own accord, inviting herself to come and work for me and I couldn't exactly tell her not to come, but in the end it hadn't matter because I ending up firing Claudia anyway. I had no other choice, for Claudia was not doing her job. On the rare occasions Claudia actually graced us with her presence; she was still not getting her work done. I was not going to stand here and argue with her on what was supposed to be *my* night. Claudia had every opportunity to confront me the day I fired her, and as far as sisters watching each other's back, well Claudia had let me down as well. "How dare you stand there and point the finger at me, trying to put me in my place when you don't even know your own place. All this time you've been trying to get my husband in bed with you, and now you want sympathy from me?" I asked with a shake of my head. "You won't get any sympathy from me, Claudia, you made your own bed, now lay in it." With that said and done, I turned and walked away. Even though the music was still playing, the few people who had been dancing had practically stopped and stood gawking at our little group. Drama, who the fuck needs it!

"You, *bitch*! You only married this *termite* because he set you up in that business."

I didn't stop as I held up my hand and continued on into the kitchen. I didn't know that Claudia had so much animosity toward me. What had I done wrong to make her hate me?

"Mom, you okay?" Anthony asked as he joined me.

"I'm fine, baby, I just had to leave before I slapped Claudia silly." I looked up to see Blair enter the kitchen.

"Anthony, you want to ride with me to take Claudia home?"

"I thought she was taking a cab."

"She doesn't want to leave her car here."

"So why are you taking her home?"

"Because she won't let Sonny drive her."

"Then let her ass walk," I said as I headed back into the restaurant. Claudia was sitting in the waiting area trembling and crying what I thought to be phony crocodile tears. "Anthony, take Ms. Claudia home, Maurice you drive Anthony's Blazer and follow him," I said as I turned and headed back into the restaurant area.

"That works," Blair said as he came up behind me, grabbing my hand and leading me out onto the dance floor. The DJ was spinning a nice smooth slow song, and Blair ease us out onto the dance floor among the other couples.

"It works very well." I took a deep breath as Blair wrapped me in his arms. Drama, I thought as I rested my head upon his shoulder. Claudia's words had cut like a knife. "Blair, I want to apologize to you for all those times you told me Claudia was flirting with you. I didn't realize how bad it must have been for you, and here I thought I was being a good friend to Claudia. I mean, what was I supposed to do? She wasn't doing her job and any other company would have fired her long before I had. I'd given her way too many chances to redeem herself, more than she would have been given if she had been with another company. I knew Claudia had been hurt, but she shut down on me, wouldn't talk to me so what was I supposed to do?"

"Don't worry about it, baby." Blair gently rubbed my back; rubbing the knots out, as the music soothed my soul. "Claudia has some real serious issues."

"Like alcohol and a captive audience," I replied.

"She can be rather dramatic."

"You poor, baby, I'm so sorry I ever doubted you."

"How long have you known her?"

"About six years now, and this was her best performance yet."

"Has she been out searching for work?"

"Claudia gets a monthly stipend from a trust fund her grandfather set up for her. She is an only child and she has always gotten what she wants. Her condo and car are paid for. Ms. Claudia doesn't have to work if she doesn't want to." The record had ended and I was sharing this information with Blair as we headed over to the bar to join Sonny and Macey.

"Then I must be missing something. I don't understand what the hell that was all about?" Macey said, as Blair took the barstool next to her and pulled me in to rest between his legs.

"It's about drugs," Blair said as he picked up the beer Sonny had placed before him.

"What?" we all asked in unison.

"Your girl's doing *crack*." Blair took a sip of beer as we all stared at him. I had to turn around and face him for I was completely shocked at his comment.

"What makes you say that?" I asked him.

"I can smell it on her, and besides she has the look of a *crack* head, a junkie."

"How do you know this?"

Blair looked over at Sonny before he answered my question. "I've been around a few junkies before and I can tell you, she wasn't shaking because she was cold- Claudia needs a hit."

"Blair," I begin as I raised my hand in the air. "You let me send my son out there to drive her home, driving her car, with Lord knows what Claudia has in her car, and you didn't say a word to me about this before?" I had taken a step back from him, my voice full of rage. "My son is driving her car. Mind you, a twenty-one year-old black man driving a top of the line BMW out there on the streets with a *crack* head who just so happens to look *white*. What if Anthony should get pulled over, Blair? What do you think is going to happen-"

"I offered to drive her home-"

Sonny jumped in, his eyes hard as ice. "You should have said something, Blair. I would have never allowed Anthony to drive Claudia home if I'd known that. I would have sent Jimmy here instead," Sonny said as he rose from his seat.

"Man, who are you to *allow* or disallow Anthony to do anything?" Blair stood up and took a step forward.

"Shit, Blair, cut the crap! This ain't even about you. Did you hear what Mia just said?"

"You damn right I did. I heard every damn word *my* wife said, man!"

"But you still allowed Anthony to leave with Claudia."

"Claudia might not have anything in her car or on her person for all we know," Macey quickly added as she looked from Sonny to Blair, as they stood toe to toe. Sonny walked passed Blair, their shoulders brushing, as he headed for the kitchen while the three of us stood in silence. I was concerned for Anthony and angry with Blair, but at the moment I didn't know what to do about the situation. Macey touched my arm and I gave her a weak smile. It was a good forty-five minute drive to La Jolla so all we could do was wait until they returned.

"I'm sorry about all of this, Mia. This was supposed to be a happy time for you," Macey said as she gave me a hug and left to join Sonny in the kitchen.

All this time Blair had just stood there staring at me with an unreadable expression on his face. "I wouldn't worry about it, Anthony's a good driver, he'll be okay," Blair said as he too walked away from me.

I turned to face the bar, picked up my drink and downed it before returning the glass back to the bar. I was mentally estimating how much time had elapsed since Anthony and Maurice had left, when I realized I didn't know what time they'd left. Then it hit me, damn, Claudia's on drugs. She's a junkie. Now that Blair had mentioned it, everything about what was happening with Claudia's behavior this past year made perfect sense to me now. Claudia had always been thin, but now she looked emaciated, and it made me think back on her appearance and behavior when she had worked for me. Her lunchtime disappearances, her edginess, all of this I had labeled as stress. We'd all been stressed during the first few months of getting the business up and running, but thinking about now, what difference would it have mattered to Claudia if my business folded? I'd been far too occupied and hadn't noticed anything strange about her behavior at the time. Of course, I tried talking to Claudia on several occasions, but she had also played it off, and like a dummy I had believed her, but all I had done was to let her continue with her destructive behavior. In a way, Claudia had been right, I should have been there for her, I should have been more insistent, but I was so wrapped up in my own little world I'd been blind to Claudia's needs. I really cared about her well being, and tonight was Claudia's way of asking for help. Now the million dollar question was; what was I going to do about it? This night had turned into something a whole lot different than I had planned it to be. The night had gone from a celebratory one to a night of drunken confessions and blame.

CHAPTER SIXTEEN

"Mia, what is wrong with you. All I did was look at the woman. Damn, you act like I slept with her, and even if I wanted to, we where in a public place and that, my dear, is against the law."

"Men, you make me sick. Every time you see a woman you conveniently forget that you're with one. Looking is one thing Blair, ogling is another especially with your wife sitting right there beside you." Blair and I had just returned from a celebratory luncheon at an exclusive downtown restaurant in honor of Claudia, which had been given by her parents.

I had finally confronted Claudia about her drug problem threatening to tell her parents if she didn't seek help for her problem. Claudia had promised me she would quit, but when I confronted her again two weeks later, she still had not followed through on her promise, so I had called her parents and informed them their daughter had a drug problem. After hearing about her involvement with drugs, Claudia's grandfather threatened to cut off her allowance, and the day after her grandfather's threat, Claudia had signed herself into a drug rehabilitation center. So when May came around we had two things to celebrate, Anthony's graduation and Claudia's clean and sober day.

Blair and I had started arguing on our drive home from the restaurant. While at the restaurant, an attractive woman had walked by our table and all the men had practically drooled on themselves, and on the way home Blair and I had argued about his behavior.

"Mia, if I didn't want to be with you, I wouldn't be here. What is it going to take to make you realize that I am with the woman I love? You're the one who's always eating salads and dieting and shit, like I want a skinny woman. I like you just the way you are, and you're not *fat*. I like being able to feel my baby when I hold her, and check out your ass when you walk in front of me. I don't want my woman to look like

213

an ironing board. Hell, I was just looking, and comparing, and liking what I had a whole lot better, that's all. Would it make you any happier if I checked out the men instead? What about that brotha who served us back at the restaurant, did you think he had a big dick?"

"Blair, now you're just being crude. Why are you behaving like this? All I said was, you could hardly keep your eyes in your head when that woman walked by." As I entered the house I threw my purse down on the table in the foyer and continued on into the living room. It was warm outside and even warmer inside as I reached out and turned the thermostat down to sixty. Instantly the refrigeration came on, sending a blast of cold air out of the vents.

"I got your *crude* right here," Blair said, hands cupping his private parts. "I asked you if it would make you happy if I checked out the men instead. Oops! My bad, you don't know how to be happy. I believe if you weighed ninety-eight pounds you'd still be unhappy about it. Being unhappy to you is what sleeping and eating is to normal people."

"Is that why you were all in Claudia's face? Smiling like a school-boy? Is that how you want me to look?"

"Claudia is *anorexic* and a *junkie* as well, there is no such word as *ex-junkie*, because once a junkie always a junkie. And, sweetheart, for your information I was all in her damn face because she was in mine. Claudia ain't nothing but a bitch in heat. I had to tell her to *fuck* off. If she was a true *friend* to you, she wouldn't have been all up in my face all the time trying to get me to screw her. I told you about her advances a while back, when Maurice was in the hospital."

"*Arghh!*" I gave him a look of disgust as I threw my hands high into the air. "Claudia and I had a talk and she blamed the drugs on her behavior. She informed me that was all in the past. And you can stop being so damn vulgar," I replied with a shake of my head.

"You can't change a person like Claudia, baby, she will always be the way she is. She's a *taker*, and more you give of yourself to her the more she will take. You want to hit me? Is that what you want to do, Mia? You want to hit me, don't you?" Blair asked as he tilted his head to one side, and looked at me like I'd just spurted wings.

"No, I do not want to hit you, Blair." God I wanted to knock him out.

"Yes you do, I can see it in your eyes."

"Blair-"

"Go ahead and hit me, if it'll make you feel any better, then hit me, Mia."

"Blair, stop it!" He was beginning to annoy me, big time.

"I know you're mad, look at you. Don't hold it in, go ahead and hit me, or scream, yell, cuss me out, do something. Get mad, go on, I want you to get it out of our system."

"Blair, get out of my face. Go away and leave me alone. Please go away and leave-me-alone."

"I know you want to hit me, I can see it in your eyes," Blair said as he peered into my face.

Now he had gone beyond annoying me. I hated his guts. He was right; I did want to hit him, right in his big fat mouth.

Blair threw his arms up in the air. "Yell! Do something! You're too cool and too calm. Come on, Mia, get mad. Throw something!"

Who would have believed, that just this morning that same mouth had been gentling nibbling on my- "What? What did you say?"

"I said do you want me to call your boy, Sonny for you?"

I shook my head. "Blair, you need to be quiet."

"Okay, now you see how it feels, huh? Now you know how I felt when you stood there and accused me of wrong doings with Claudia-"

"Blair, do us all a favor and stop acting your age!" I yelled at him.

"Oh, now we're getting somewhere. So, now I'm acting my age, am I? And what age was I behaving this morning when I had my face between your thighs?"

"This conversation is over!"

"No, it's not, because for once and for all we're going to get this age business over and done with."

"This conversation is over! OVER! OVER!" I shouted as I spun around and stormed out of the room, down the hall and into our bedroom. I slammed the door shut behind me. I was kicking off my shoes, when the bedroom door was thrown opened, and Blair stormed into the room slamming the door behind him.

"Don't you ever, ever; as long as I'm *Black*, slam a damn door in face again when I'm speaking to you!"

"Blair, what's gotten into you? Get out of my face and cut this mess out!"

"Me? What's gotten into me? I should be asking you the same question. What is it going to take to make you believe me when I say I love you? You! For whom you are, not for who you want to be! Here take this," Blair said taking out his wallet, pulling out money and credit cards and throwing it all at me. I stepped back and watched it all fall to the floor. "Take this and go out and join one of those damn health spas, and eat nothing but fucking seaweed all fucking day and sit in fucking saunas and sweat all fucking night! Go! Will that make you happy, Mia? Will it! Because I'm sick of this bullshit! I'm sick of your moaning and groaning about your weight, hell you were bigger than this when we first met, and did I complain then? But the question of the day is am I complaining *now*? Either you stop your bitching, or you do something about! I don't know what else to do. I've tried my best to make you happy and I'm at the end of my rope here, Mia. I don't know what else to do for you- for us! If it's not your weight then it's our age difference. You just won't let it rest. I'm through," Blair said holding up a hand to my face. "I'm just sick of hearing it."

Why was he doing this? "Why are you being so evil, Blair? So tell me, is this were you storm out of the house and into the arms of one of my best friends. Hmmm, let me see, would that be Macey or Sonya. Which one will it be, Blair?"

"You left somebody out, Mia. You said *best* friend, what's the matter you don't think I'm good enough to fuck Sonny? Or is it in Sonny's bed you're planning on jumping in?"

I slapped him, as hard as I could. I reached back and grabbed all the force I could muster up and I slapped Blair so damn hard, that if Blair had been a smaller man he would have fallen to the floor from the force of the impact. The sound of the palm of my hand smacking against his bare skin sounded like a crack of a whip as it echoed through the room. I would have slapped him a second time if Blair hadn't reached out and grabbed me by both wrists, pulling me up against him.

"You feel better now? Did you get it all out of your system, Mia?" Blair asked through clenched teeth. I don't know who was shaking more, him or me as we stood face to face. His grip on my right wrist tightened until I yelled out in pain, then he released me and left the room, the door banging shut behind him, making me jump at the loudness of it. Tears stung at my eyes as I rubbed my aching wrist.

Oh my God, what just happened? What had that been all about? What did I just do? I hit my husband, I hit Blair! Damn, I hit him. Why had I let it get blown all out of proportion? When? What happened? It wasn't even that serious of an argument. It was over nothing, nothing at all!

Shaking my head from side to side, with my hands on my head, I turned and paced about the room. I stopped in front of the mirror and gazed at my image. I was still wearing the new outfit I'd bought for Claudia's luncheon. It was a gorgeous sky blue two-piece suit, the short tapered jacket stopping just at my waist. Blair had been right about my weight too, I did weigh less now than when we'd first met, I was down two dress sizes. So why was I still obsessing about my weight, and I never looked my age, as a matter of fact, Blair looked older than me. So what the hell *was* my problem? He'd been right, lately I had been depressed and moody as hell, and Blair did everything in his power to please me and to make me happy, now this. God, I was happier now than I'd ever been, and still I didn't appreciate Blair and all the things he'd done for me. When had I stopped appreciating Blair? What was my problem? Blair was the best thing that *ever* happened to me and I couldn't even remember the last time I'd told him I loved him.

I folded my arms across my chest and started pacing around the room again. He'll come back and when he does I'll apologize for being such a horrible person. Maybe I should go to him, or maybe I should wait for him. Dear God, what did I do? I hit Blair. I slapped my baby. This was our first major argument and it had been about nothing. It must have had something to do with my birthday, which had just passed a week ago. I usually spent my birthdays in bed stuffing my face with ice cream and microwave popcorn and being all out lazy, but this year I didn't have a chance to be depressed about getting older because thanks to Blair, I had a business to run. I also had Blair to thank for my birthday present which had been a new car, a black Mercedes. But I think he bought the car more for himself than me because he drove it more than I did. Me, I'd grown partial to his Corvette. But, whatever the reason I was behaving this way was beyond me. Perhaps I should see my doctor. Maybe it was a chemical imbalance, or menopause. Oh dear God, I hoped not. Oh, poor Blair, how could I explain all of this to him when I didn't know what the problem was? "Drama, oh Lord, don't give me any more drama in my life, cause all I'm looking for is happily ever after."

As I lay waiting for Blair, I dozed off and on as I waited for him to return. Shaking off the vestiges of sleep, I glanced over at the clock on the night stand and noticed it had been over two hours since Blair had left the room. I'd changed out of my clothing and had slipped into a pair of jeans and was wearing one of Blair's tee shirts with his business logo on the back. My wrist was throbbing like crazy, so I decided to head to the kitchen and search the freezer for an icepack. Eurydice was lying out in the hallway across the bedroom door when I opened the door. Blair had taken to leaving Eurydice in the house instead of outside with Orpheus when I was home alone. Her short stubby tail began to wag at the sight of me. I liked having her around since I was alone in the house most of the time, especially now that Maurice was spending the summer with Anthony and with Blair traveling out of state as much as two to three days a week.

I lucked out; there was an icepack in the freezer. One thing you could always count on living in a household full of men, who were constantly pulling a muscle, spraining an ankle while playing ball, lifting weights, or sparing, there would always be icepacks in the freezer, of various shapes and sizes.

I stood gazing out of the kitchen window as I held the icepack to my wrist, which looked a lot worse than it felt. There was a vase of orchids sitting on the kitchen counter looking a lot like I was feeling, sad. The time had come for them to be tossed out, but I wasn't anything like those orchids, I wasn't finished yet. Blair was my *lifemate*, and he and I were destined to spend the rest of our lives together. I plucked the dead flowers from the vase, and was turning toward the garbage to throw them out, just as the buzzer went off, announcing a visitor at the gate. The house was so quiet I had jumped at the sound of the noise, before reaching out and pushing the talk button on the intercom.

"Mia, I'm at the gate," Sonny said in an anxious sounding voice.

I pushed the code for the front gate, asking myself why Sonny was here. We'd just spent the afternoon with the two of them at the Claudia's celebratory luncheon and Macey hadn't mentioned anything about coming over. I picked up the icepack, holding it against my wrist and on my way to open the front door, I stopped and did quick glance at my appearance in the mirror hanging in the foyer before opening the door and what I saw made me cringe. Mascara smudges ringed my eyes, and my hair was a mess, going in a hundred different directions all over my head. Too late to do anything about it now for I could hear the sound of car doors closing in the front drive. I would pop into the powder room and make repairs after I'd let Sonny inside.

As soon as I the door opened, Macey rushed in followed closely by Sonny. They brought with them a sense of urgency, as Macey took one look at my appearance and burst out into tears. Sonny reached for my hand and gently examined my bruised wrist. "Blair?" he asked in a soft voice, and I noticed hardness about his eyes as he did a swift check of my face.

"I don't know," I replied still not sure why they where here. "What's up? Macey, now I know I don't look that bad. Is something wrong?" Now I was really confused, for after each question Macey seemed to cry a little bit harder and louder.

"His car's out front," Sonny said as he rushed into the living room and then out onto the terrace calling out Blair's name, with

Eurydice trailing after him, her little stubby tail wagging away at the sight of Sonny.

"Sonny, what's going on here?" I asked as I started to follow after him, but Macey reached out and grabbed my arm. "Macey, what is wrong with you?" I asked again as I pulled her into my arms and held her while she cried on my shoulders.

"Blair called Sonny and told him he'd messed up," Macey finally said between sniffles.

I looked up and out into the backyard and across the pool, and that's when I saw him. A barefoot Blair was casually strolling toward the house, as though he had not a care in the world, and at his side was his faithful companion, Orpheus. The big dog had somehow matched his pace to Blair's or Blair had matched his pace with Orpheus, for they moved in unison. I noticed that Blair had also changed out of his suit and he was now wearing a pair of white baggy sweats and a tight white tee shirt emphasizing his chest and arms, and perched upon his nose was pair of dark shades. There was something about his posture, but at the same time my heart swelled with love as I watched him saunter toward us.

It was as though time had come to a stop. The weather was ideal, a bit warm, and the sky was clear, not a cloud in sight. The crystal blue of the sky made a perfect backdrop to the greenness of the lawn. Macey continued to cry, her head resting upon my shoulder. I looked over to my right and noticed Sonny standing just at the edge of the terrace looking out into the distance at Blair. I started to call out to Sonny, to come and help me in comforting Macey, just as he took off running towards Blair, and it was then that the words Macey had spoken to me earlier finally sunk in and I knew what was about to happen. A feeling of dread came over me, and a cold hand reached out and gripped my spine, turning my blood ice cold as the revelation of what was about to transpire temporarily shocked me into silence. I was frantic as I stood there shaking my head, trying to get my vocal cords to catch up with my mouth to form one lousy word, no-no-No-No- "NO!" I shouted as I shook Macey off and ran out the door and out onto the terrace.

Funny what goes through your thoughts at a time like this, all hell was about to break loose right in front of me, and all I could think of was an article I'd read once, about dogs. The article was about how sensitive animals were and how they were able to sense fear as well as other emotions in human beings. I was sure Orpheus sensed Sonny's intent to harm Blair because his head popped up and he dashed a few feet ahead of Blair, coming to a halt, placing himself between the two.

"No! Mia, wait!" Macey called out from behind me.

But I was beyond turning back, as I raced ahead of Macey. "Blair, stop his nonsense!" I called out, and as I started to pass Sonny, he reached out and seized me by the arm, pulling me to his side. Eurydice growled and leaped at Sonny.

"EURYDICE, NO!" I screamed. The Doberman dropped to the ground just mere inches from us. "Sonny, she thinks you're going trying to harm me, let go of my arm. Blair! Blair, stop this nonsense!" I pleaded as my heart pounded in my chest. I could not believe this was happening. Why was Blair doing this?

"I thought you were a man, Blair, but then a real man wouldn't hit a woman, would he?" Sonny said in a voice as hard as steel.

Upon hearing his statement, a wave of fear enveloped me. For as long as I'd known him, I had never heard Sonny speak in this tone before. I knew then what was to come and I had to stop them before it was too late. I looked up at Sonny silently pleading for him to look at me, but he kept his hard stare forward, ignoring me as I tugged at his arm. "Sonny, Blair didn't hit me. Who said he hit me? I hit him. Sonny, don't do this. Please stop!" It didn't matter what I said, for Sonny continued to ignore me.

"Man, I ain't got nothing against your dogs, and you know I can kill them with my bare hands," Sonny said in an icy tone.

I screamed at Blair to stop, my free hand waving in the air at Sonny's words, and as I looked up into Sonny's face, I had to look away, because the look on his face frighten the hell out of me. Sonny's eyes never left Blair's face, his jaws constantly clenching and unclenching, and his one free hand was balled into a tight fist. "Sonny, please stop. Blair did not hit me. Do you hear me? Macey! Macey, make him stop!" I shouted into the air, afraid to turn around and let the two of them out of my sight for fear of what they would do to each other.

"I can't," said a soft pleading voice from behind me.

Blair snapped his fingers and both dogs returned to his side. He turned and jogged back to the barn to lock them away. I knew what he was planning to do and I started to follow after him but Sonny still had a grip on my arm. "Sonny, please let go of me!"

"Mia, go into the house with Macey."

"No! I will not go into the fucking house with Macey; you go into the house, Sonny. If you do this...I- I swear I will never, *ever* speak to you again. Do you hear me, Sonny? I'll never speak to you again." I was finally able to snatch my arm away from him, as his grip loosened at the impact of my words.

"I told Blair what I'd do if he ever hurt you, Mia."

"Sonny, Blair didn't do-"

"Come on, man, what's it gonna to be?" Blair called out as he came forward.

I ran to him, fighting the uphill grade of the lawn. "Blair, what the hell do you think you doing? Whatever it is, I want you to stop. I want you to stop right now. Do you hear me? Don't do this, Blair, please don't do this." I flew into his arms practically knocking him over. "Blair, don't. Listen to me! You've got to stop this *shit*. This is childish and stupid."

"I have to do this. I hurt you, and I promised your guard dog, I would never hurt you," Blair said with a nod in Sonny's direction. "Now I have to take my punishment like a man. I love you, Mia," he said as he kissed me. I clung to him as he attempted to free himself from my grip.

"Don't do this, Blair. Please, stop. Blair, if you love me you wouldn't do this to me." Blair stopped and stared at me, removing my arms from around his waist.

"To you? What am I doing to you, Mia?" Blair started moving forward again. I looked around to see Sonny looming behind us and I place my body between them, with my back to Sonny and my arms around Blair's neck.

"Blair, I'm begging you to stop, please, please don't do this." I could feel his heart beating against my chest, just as quickly as my own heartbeat. His breathing coming out in quick little puffs against my face, I clung to him, my feet practically off the ground. Blair smiled, and hugged me close then reached out and removed my arms from around his neck. "NO!"

Things happened so quickly afterward, that I didn't even get the chance to see who threw the first blow. I yelled and cursed at them at the top of my lungs trying to get them to stop, as feet, arms, and their bodies flew through the air, amid the sound of grunts and skin hitting skin. I dropped to my knees and buried my face in my arms, for it nearly killed me to see the two men in my life, that I loved the most, more than life itself, trying to kill one another. I felt every kick and punch they dealt each other and it made me sick to my stomach. I covered my ears and screamed for them to stop. All of a sudden, I felt something wet splash on my arm and looked up to see Macey with the high-pressured water hose that Blair used on the pool deck, drenching Blair and Sonny with it.

I rose, and stood stunned, and in shock, as Macey handled the high-pressured hose like a pro. I moved back and away, making my way around the pool and back to the terrace. They had to stop, stop or risk getting an eye put out for Macey was aiming the stinging stream of water right at their faces. Both were sputtering, cursing, and yelling, with their arms covering their faces, shouting at Macey, telling her to stop, but Macey was relentless as she aim the hose at one and then the other, making sure that each had they share from the high-pressured hose. Blair finally went down and rolled over on his stomach, his face cradled in the circle of his arms, protecting his face. Sonny landed on his side, his back taking the force of the water. They continued to yell at Macey, yelling at her to back off as she continued her assault with the hose.

Macey started to cry again, as she dropped the hose and ran for the house. I followed her inside, closing the door behind me, and just in time too, for the hose was wiggling like a giant snake spraying water everywhere. Macey stood trembling in my arms. We turned at the sound of the door opening and Macey's tears turned to laughter as Blair and Sonny stood dripping wet just inside the door. They looked like victims from the *Titanic* movie.

"I need to get away," I said after a while. "Would you like to come with me, Macey?"

"Yes," she replied softly with a nod of her head. Macey turned and looked once over her shoulder at Sonny, before picking up her purse and heading for the front door.

Blair stood in the background staring at me with wild questioning eyes. I picked up my purse and was digging inside for my keys because I needed to leave the house as quickly as possible. I'd forgotten Blair had driven earlier so I searched the hall table for car keys and at the moment it didn't matter which set of keys I found first, for any keys would do. Right now all I wanted was to get behind the steering wheel of a car with power and speed and both cars fit the bill. At last I spotted the keys to the Corvette, which I snatched up and hit the front door at a trot behind Macey. Macey and I had done all we could do, if they wanted to kill one another then so be it, but we did not have to be around to watch them. I eased out of the valley, taking the hilly roads at slow speeds, but once I hit Interstate 8, I was driving at speeds of about ninety miles or more and we didn't stop until we'd reached Yuma, Arizona, 140 miles later. We decided Yuma would be a good place to spend the night, so we found a nice clean hotel off of the Interstate. We were physically and mentally drained after a day like today. We talked a bit, but after an early dinner, which neither of us had much of an appetite, Macey and I decided to call it a night.

At breakfast the next day, I scanned my caller ID on my cell phone, and it was just as Macey and I had suspected. We each had received numerous calls from Blair and Sonny, and my sons had called me as well. I returned the call to Anthony and Maurice to let them know that I was okay, but Macey and I decided not to call our so-called significant others. I was still much too angry with Blair and Sonny, and if asked by anyone if I knew either of the two, I would have lied and denied knowing them. I didn't tell Anthony of our whereabouts, nor did I go into details about my flight out of Alpine and I didn't mention the reason either. I merely informed Anthony if he needed to reach me for anything to call me on my cell. I had Anthony call Blair to tell him I would see him on Monday. I knew Blair would call my sons and try to pump information from them, so the less they knew of my whereabouts the better. I knew I could depend on Anthony to say as little as possible to Blair, but I also knew that Anthony would have no misgivings about informing Sonny of my location. I called Sonya as well, informing her that I would be in to work on Tuesday morning and for Sonya to cancel any appointments I had on Monday.

After a long lingering breakfast Macey and I headed to the mall and purchased new outfits and other essential items including bathing suits, and then it was back to hotel to lounge around the pool as we sipped on frozen margaritas discussing our husbands and to remember our wedding vows, especially the "for better or worse" part. After a couple of hours of animated speech, and after downing a couple of pitchers of margaritas, Macey began to cry. She wouldn't stop blubbering about how much she was missing Sonny, and how she couldn't stand to spend another night away from him without speaking to him. After several minutes of this, Macey jumped up and out of her chair like she'd been electrocuted and left the pool area. Ten minutes later she returned informing me she'd just gotten off of the phone with Sonny and he and Blair were driving up to Yuma today. I proceeded to call Macey several not so nice names; and if I remembered correctly they all consisted of four letters. I reminded Macey the reason why we where here in the first place, and how this was supposed to be our little excursion away from our childish husbands. With a lot of help from the tequila, I was on a roll. I even went as far as to accuse Macey of being a wimp. Well Macey had also had her share of tequila induced courage, because she raised herself to her full height of five-feet-one and proceeded to tell me off as well. After she had ran out of steam, or she probably just grew weary of holding herself up, Macey then promptly informed me that I would thank her later, and with a toss of her head, which almost landed her in the pool, Macey left in a huff informing me she was off to reserve another room for herself and Sonny.

Emotionally spent and reeling from the affects of the hot Yuma sun and the tequila, I retired to my own room. Once I'd reached my room, I set the air conditioner as low as it would go, to help counteract the heat from the sun, and fell into a margarita-induced sleep, not waking up until well after sunset.

I could feel his body lying next to me even before I'd opened my eyes. I didn't move a muscle as I cast my eyes sideways. I'd been right; Blair was lying next to me, sleeping soundly. He was sleeping in his normal position, propped slightly up in a sitting position. Holding my breath, I slowly turned my head and looked closely at his face, and then my eyes drifted downward, the length of his body and back up again. Blair was still dressed, wearing a pair of black shorts and a tan short-sleeved polo shirt. His feet were bare; no socks, which meant he'd probably been wearing a pair of sandals. I discovered a bruise on his forehead, but I couldn't see more without moving, and with Blair being such a light sleeper any movement or sound, no matter how slight would awaken him, and I wasn't ready to speak with him at the moment.

I slowly released my breath, and suddenly Blair sat straight up in bed and looked around the room. He tilted his head backward and stretched his neck as though to remove a cramp and then stretched his arms upward, before turning to face me. Neither of us said a word; as Blair slowly laid back down again, his head just inches from mine as our eyes locked in a stare. He was also sporting a nice bruise just below his left ear, near his jawbone. I couldn't see any more bruises on his face and couldn't tell if he had any beneath his clothing, but I wanted to add a bruise of my own, right to his mouth, but I resisted the urge because I was still much too angry with him to kiss those beautiful lips of his.

"I love you, and I'm sorry I hurt you."

I didn't answer him; I just continued to stare at him.

"No yelling, no screaming, no name calling?"

I remained silent.

"Okay, I'll say it for you; I was a total ass-hole, a dickhead-"

"Let's not forget immature-"

"Okay, I agree. I'm all those things and more." Blair placed his hand on my arm, rubbing it gently. "I am truly sorry, Mia, I didn't mean to hurt you and I promise you it will never happen again. I love you, baby, please forgive me." His hand moved steadily up my arm, to my shoulder and continued up to my face, resting gently on my cheek. "I thought I'd never see you again. When Macey called and told us you where in Yuma, I was ecstatic. When I didn't see you downstairs with Macey I wasn't sure if I should get my own room or not. It was a good thing for me Macey still had the key to this room. I knocked, and when I didn't get an answer I used the key."

I wanted to kiss him so badly it hurt, but I held back, hoping my face was not expressing my true feelings. "What happens next, Blair?"

"About what?"

"About us. Are you and Sonny going to go though this bullshit every time you and I argue? Every time you hold my wrist too tightly, or yell at me too loudly, or every time I slam a door, am I going to see more of this behavior from you? Or are we going to handle it ourselves, Blair?"

"You know I didn't mean to hurt you, Mia. I'm just trying to love you the best way I know how and it doesn't matter how many times I tell you, or how many ways I show you, it gets real complicated when I have to compete with *Sonny*."

I closed my eyes and let out a loud sigh. "Blair. Blair. Blair, you don't have to compete with Sonny for me, you already have me, heart, body, and soul. You're doing this to yourself, blowing it all out of proportion." I sat up, my back resting against the headboard. I pulled my robe closed and crossed my legs at the ankles. I was still wearing my bathing suit and earlier, before lying down I had slipped on the matching rust colored silk robe. I looked up and found Blair's eyes glued to my chest like it was his first time seeing the *girls*.

"Hold out your hand."

"What?"

"Hold out your hand," he repeated. I did as he asked, and held my hand out to him. "To prove my love for you, I want you to have my heart, but since it's humanly impossible for me to physically give you my heart, I want you to have this, in lieu of my heart," Blair said as he placed a small black velvet box in my hand. "It's kind of like an IOU," he said, as he flashed me a quick smile.

I shook my head as I opened the box. It was a beautiful heart shaped diamond pendant on a delicate sterling silver chain. "So, now you're trying to buy my love?"

"Whatever it takes, Mia. I'm giving you my heart to keep close, forever and always, because I know you'll keep it safe for me." Blair said as he searched my face.

"Thank you, it's beautiful," I said as I lowered my eyes. "Blair, I want to apologize for the things I said to you yesterday and for hitting you. That whole argument was just so unnecessary. You're right, you know. You've done so much for me and I don't know what was wrong with me yesterday. Blair, I don't even remember the last time I told you that I loved you, and I do love you, Blair, with all my heart. I still can't figure out what came over me, but, what you and Sonny did was uncalled for."

"You're right, I agree, it was uncalled for and I'm sorry for my actions as well. I didn't mean to hurt you, baby, and I apologize for causing you any distress. But, Mia, you have to realize that I fell in love with *you* and not your dress size. I fell in love with *you*, Mia. Now, don't get me wrong, I like the entire package. And when I say package, I mean *everything*. Baby, I love everything about you, right down to that tiny patch of gray hair on your-".

"Okay, Blair, I get it," I said as I held up my hand. Blair was beaming as he spoke, with a mischievous look in his eyes.

"Look at you blushing. You know you like it when I kiss that spot. But, seriously, Mia," he said, his face and voice taking on a serious demeanor as he reached out for my hand, "you are the best thing that has ever happened to me and losing you right now is not an *option*." And as he said this, Blair leaned toward me and before I could stop him his lips met mine, as his hand dipped deep inside the top of my bathing suit. That's all it took, just one kiss and I was his again, all my anger and hurt feelings melted away, as I allowed Blair to work his magic on me.

After a night like last night, I was surprised either of us even had the energy to rise as early as we had and found ourselves back in one another's arms again for another session of wild love making. As Blair and I headed out to the parking garage the next morning, we ran into Sonny and Macey. I guess Blair and Sonny had arranged for us to all leave at the same time. I hadn't spoken to Sonny since the incident back in Alpine, and at first it was awkward for us, but I couldn't stay angry with him no more than he could stay angry with me. But that didn't mean I was ready to speak with him today. I smiled at Macey, but ignored Sonny as our little group came to a stop. Macey and Blair exchanged greetings, and I could feel Sonny's eyes upon me, as I proceeded to stepped around him. I didn't get far, for Sonny reached out halted my advancement.

"Mia, we need to talk. Mia and I will meet you two back at the cars." Not waiting for a response from Blair, Macey, or myself, Sonny started off in the opposite direction of the parking garage with me in tow. "What's the word, Mia? Are we still best friends or what? I know you said you would never speak to me again, but I know you really didn't mean it. Did you?" He asked when I didn't reply.

"Sonny, Blair is as much to blame as you are. I cannot believe the two of you actually fought. It was a sickening sight to watch-"

"Mia, Blair hit you and I told that son-of-a-bitch I was going to kick his fucking ass-"

"Sonny, please don't say another word! Just listen to me! Blair didn't hit me, okay! I told you, I slapped him and when I reached out to hit him a second time Blair grabbed me by my wrists. We struggled a bit, and yes, I admit his hold was a bit too tight, but it wasn't intentional, it was an accident, Sonny."

"Yeah, right, that's what they all say. Blair could've just walked away from you! He didn't have to touch you, period!"

"Sonny-"

"Mia, Blair's a friend, but you," Sonny begins, his finger pointing in my face, "I feel responsible for you, Mia. What do you think the boys would say if they knew Blair beat you?"

"You keep my sons out of this! Blair did not *beat* me, and anyway, Macey is your responsibility now, not me. Actually, I'm no one's responsibility, not yours and not Blair's. I don't need you to take care of me or watch over me," I said with a sigh. I turned and started to walk away, only to stop after a couple of steps. I retraced my steps back to Sonny. "Do you know how badly you hurt Macey? Do you have any idea how it feels to watch your husband fighting over another *woman*?" I was all in his face, as I said this.

"I was not fighting over you; I was fighting for your honor!" Sonny yelled. "Macey understands this, if she does not, then she should. Macey was raised to respect her husband's wishes and I am her husband!" Sonny shouted as he pounded his chest like he was King Kong or something.

"Listen to yourself, you're so full of shit, Sonny, and you know it! You've never bought into that bullshit before and now all of a sudden when it's convenient you're a good Korean son and husband." I was practically shouting at him now. "That is still not justification for what you and Blair did. Blair told me the two of you talked, and "I hope, no I pray the two of you resolved this mess because-"

"*I love you*. I love you, Mia."

For some reason his words hit me right in the middle of my stomach. It was like a swift blow to the gut, and I had to stop myself from placing my hand to my stomach. "I love you too, Sonny, and so does Macey who is your *wife*." I wanted to back away, but I couldn't quite make myself pull away from his stare. It was if his eyes were willing me to stay put. I lowered my eyes, looking instead at the black asphalt driveway.

"Mia?" Sonny placed one hand on my shoulder, and with two fingers, he gently raised my chin, forcing me to look at him.

I looked up into his eyes and what I saw almost made me drop to my knees. "Oh, Sonny, don't. Please don't say it, let's leave it the way it is," I said placing my hand on his arm. "That was a long time ago, let it be. It's dead and buried, *please* let it go."

"I've always loved you, and no one, as long as I live, will ever hurt you."

"Maybe we should just end our friendship."

"We've tried that before, remember?"

"Sonny, we can't continue this way. Your friendship means a lot to me and to *Blair*-"

"I love you, Mia, and I'm not talking about as my sister, but as a man, who loves a woman."

I didn't want to hear this. I raised my hands to my ears. "Sonny-" I begin, and then I turned and walked away. But I stopped again and turned to him. "I'm in love with my husband, okay? I love Blair, and you love Macey."

"I love Macey, but I'm in love with you, Mia Harris, always have and always will be. Remember the day you asked me why I had never introduced you to Blair before? I'll tell you why, but I'm sure you already know answer. I wanted to keep you all to myself," Sonny said with a shake of his head. "I refuse to let life keep us apart."

I shook my head as I walked away.

"Mia?"

I turned to him.

"Next time I won't stop," Sonny said as his eyes drilled into mine, giving me chills on this otherwise warm morning.

I tried to run, but I couldn't because my feet had turned to lead. I tried to quicken my pace, stumbling a couple of times, as I hurried along. I felt like I was standing still, but I knew I was moving because the entrance to the parking garage was closer than before. It was an awful feeling, like trying to wade through water in lead boots. I was afraid to look back, fearing that Sonny might be right behind me and somehow he might try and stop me from returning to the garage. I knew I had to get back to the parking garage as quickly as possible least Blair become suspicious of my lengthy absence, and I didn't want any more altercations between Blair and Sonny. My mind was clouded with doubts. Next time he won't stop. What had Sonny meant by that? Did it mean he wouldn't stop fighting until one of them was seriously hurt, or- I almost turned around, but I resisted. I mustered up every ounce of will power I could draw up on and I kept moving forward. Although the weather was warm, I was sweating for a whole different reason. Sonny would always be dear to me, but I loved Blair, I'd made the right choice. I loved my husband.

Just before I reached the entrance of the parking garage the Corvette came roaring out of the darkness, the engine of the car intruding upon the stillness of the morning. The passenger door swung opened as the car came to a stop in front of me. I let out a sigh as I slid into the cool comfort of the black leather seats. Blair had the air conditioner blasting cold air, and the sound of jazz music was blasting from the car speakers. I was still sweating, and I could feel his stare, as he glanced at me once or twice, before maneuvering the Corvette out onto the highway. I knew Blair was waiting for me to speak first, but I was having difficulty assembling my thoughts to come up with something to say to him.

"All done?" Blair asked, nonchalantly, as he fiddled with the stereo volume.

My first attempt at a reply proved futile, for I was unable to control my tongue which felt thick and too long, crowding my mouth. I nodded my head, as I placed my purse on the floor between my feet, stalling for time. "Yes," I finally got out, "all done." I still couldn't look at him, for I was afraid of what Blair might see in my face. Earlier in our relationship Blair had made a statement about how trust and honesty played a crucial part in a good relationship, and I did not want Blair to see the dishonesty in my eyes for I felt I had betrayed him because of my feelings for Sonny, and Sonny's words to me.

"Did you chew him out like you did me?"

"Yes I did, and then some." We headed for Interstate 8 in silence; I was lost in a jumble of thoughts about Sonny's declaration to me. After a time Blair finally spoke again, apparently he was trying to engage me in conversation.

"So did you have Sonny groveling and sweating?"

"He sweated, but I think he's saving the groveling for is wife," I replied. "I hope the two of you have learned a lesson from all of this. Your actions, no matter how sound they may have seemed to you at the time will always have an effect on the ones you love." I reached out and changed the CD, and when I couldn't find the CD I was searching for, I turned on the radio and found a station playing loud rock music.

"Are you proud of me?" Blair asked.

"For what?"

"I didn't say a word when you and Sonny disappeared to have your little *talk*," Blair replied sounding all smug.

Blair was right, he hadn't made a fuss when Sonny and I had disappeared for our little chat, but I don't think *proud* was the word I would have used. I finally turned to look at him. I stared at him for over a minute, but Blair kept his eyes on the road and after a few seconds had gone by I repeated my question. "For what?"

CHAPTER SEVENTEEN

"Mom, look what I found," Maurice cried out as he hurried toward me carrying a shoebox.

"Maurice, what's in that box?" I asked taking a step back. If it came out of the barn it was bound to have something with six legs or more in residence.

"Don't worry, Mom," Maurice said, smiling at me. "I already dumped the box out while I was inside the barn and checked it out for bugs. There's nothing in it except for some old pictures and stuff," he exclaimed, dropping the box on the patio table. He reached into the box and removed a couple of photographs. "Look at this one, I think this is Blair," Maurice said as he held up a picture of a man with shoulder length dreadlocks. "Check out that hair," he laughed.

I took the picture from Maurice's hand, my eyes not believing what I saw. It was Blair all right, but a much younger Blair. He was wearing a three-piece black suit and carrying a cane with a bored expression upon his face. Standing next to Blair was a very unattractive woman and next to her was a tall bearded man wearing a dashiki with his hair also in dreads, but much longer than Blair's. I flipped the picture over and saw an inscription made out to a "Smithy" and it was signed from your big sis and hubby, dated around twelve years ago. I pulled a chair out and sat down. I removed my sunglasses, taking a longer look at the photograph. This was definitely Blair, but I was confused. Although Blair had spoken often of his grandmother, he'd never mentioned a sister. Blair had mentioned his mother once before but that was only to say she had died when he was young.

Maurice had now lost interest in the box and was heading for the diving board with Eurydice in tow. I continued to search through the box and found more photos of Blair as a chubby little baby, and one photo of him when he was around five or six sitting in the lap of a very attractive elderly woman; grandmother? Or another relative, I speculated, flipping the picture over. Aha, it was his grandmother; it was signed grandmother Betty and her little joy. There was also one of Blair around the age of nine or ten, a very skinny and serious looking Blair. Then, it suddenly dawn on me; I hadn't seen any pictures of Blair in the house when I first visited his home. We'd taken photos since we'd been together and those where now on display throughout the house. I asked myself why Blair would kept his photos out in the barn instead of inside the house, and why he'd never shared the contents of this box with me before? I dumped the rest of the contents of the box out on the table before me, and a small black leather address book fell out among the group of photos. I picked up the address book and begin to thumb through it, noticing that it was rather bare. Only a couple of names and numbers, but one did catch my attention. It was Lawanda Goodbyte and next to it in parentheses, the words "big sis."

I stared at the phone number for a long time, deciding whether or not I should call his sister. There had to be a reason why Blair had never mentioned her to me before. If I did decide to call how would I start the conversation? Hello Lawanda, how are you, and oh, by the way, your brother never mentioned he had an older sister. Well, I certainly didn't feel comfortable reaching out and touching her, at least not without speaking to Blair about it first. Maybe he and his sister had a serious falling out about something; serious enough to keep Blair from discussing it with me. Why else would he keep his photos out in the barn, and keep him alienated from his sister. I deliberated on how to bring the subject up in conversation. It had to be sensitive in nature, otherwise why would Blair not tell me about his sister?

"Have you ever known me to snoop around in your things, Mia?" Blair asked me later that evening as we were preparing for bed. We'd started this discussion calmly enough at dinner, but now Blair was throwing a fit about me invading his privacy. "No you haven't, why, because if I wanted to know anything about you and your past I've always ask, right? Right?" he asked again, his face just mere inches from mine.

"What's going on in here?" A voice from behind me asked. I turned to find Maurice standing in the bedroom doorway. I'd forgotten we had left Maurice sprawled out on the sofa watching TV in the living room and Blair probably woke him with his shouting.

"This is none of your concern, Maurice. Go to bed," Blair snarled.

"Mom?" Maurice looked from Blair to me, his seventeen-year-old body straightening to his full height of six-feet-four inches tall.

"What are you looking at? Dammit, I said go back to bed," Blair said with a wave of his hand.

"Blair, there's no need for you to talk to my baby like that," I said stepping in between the two of them. "I'm sorry if we woke you Maurice, go to bed, everything's okay." I placed my hand on his shoulder and gave him a gentle push out the door. Just before he left room, Maurice turned and gave Blair a long hard stare.

"He's not a baby, Mia."

"He's my baby, and I'm sorry about going through your things, but Blair, you didn't have to jump down Maurice's throat like that," I said as I closed the bedroom door.

"I didn't mean to yell at him…it's just that, I don't care for people going through my private things."

"People? Blair, I'm your wife, and if it was so private why was it laying around out in the barn?"

"I'm sorry, that didn't come out right-"

"I thought we were supposed to be equals in this marriage fifty-fifty? You don't even trust me enough to talk to me about your sister. What other secrets are you keeping from me?"

"It wasn't lying around. The box was on a shelf in a bigger box. I removed it to get something out and forgot to put it away. I'm not keeping any secrets from you, babe, it's just that- well, she's my half sister and we didn't exactly get along. I didn't meet her until I was eleven years old, and she was already in her twenties. Lawanda and I weren't close. She was a part of my life that I've long forgotten." Blair closed his eyes, rubbing them with the back of his hand as he plopped down on the bed. He eyes popped open just as quickly as they had closed, as he rose from bed and headed for the bedroom door. "I'll be back I'm going to apologize to Maurice."

I just stood there; arms folded across my chest, thinking what the hell was going on here? What was all the secrecy about? After being married to his man for over a year, I still didn't know anything about his family, and the box of pictures proved that. I was still standing in the same spot when Blair returned to our bedroom.

Blair wrapped his arms tightly around me, the scent of his cologne filling my nose. "Let's talk about this tomorrow morning okay, babe. I'm wiped out right now. It's been one long day."

"Blair, I don't understand; tell me how long will we have to be married before I meet your family? I remember you telling me your Mother had died, but you've never once mentioned a sister to me. I know you lived with your grandmother until age ten, so when did you meet your Mother for the first time?"

Blair released me from his arms and stepped around me, as he headed for the bathroom, throwing the same old lame words at me as before. "Good God! Baby, you're going to drive me crazy with this shit. I don't want to talk about it right now, Mia, all right!" The bathroom door closed with a bang.

"OH," I yelled as I reached out for a pillow and threw it at the bathroom door just as it opened.

With a calm look on his face Blair looked down at the pillow and then back up at me. With a shake of his head he began to speak. "That mess happened long before I met you and it doesn't matter anymore. Trust me, Mia; you don't want to know, okay?"

"What do you mean, I don't want to know? I love you, Blair, and I want to know all about you, the good as well as the bad. I've shared some pretty horrible things with you about my past, and you've stuck by my side; you didn't run away from me and I'm not going to run away from you either. We are in this marriage together, through thick and thin, until death do we part!" I cupped his face in my hands, staring fiercely into his eyes, "Blair, we are *lifemates*."

"Woman, you're going to drive me crazy. Okay, okay," he started, as I took a step back, and away from him. Blair threw his hands up in the air, and then brought them down again, placing his hands on the top of his head as he walked back and forth about the room.

"My family invented the word '*dys*' in *dysfunctional*. We were the cream of the crop as far as dysfunctional families go, and I washed my hands of them a long time ago.

"Brenda, my so call mother really is dead, and trust me, Mia, there was no love between us; none at all. Brenda was a junkie! She died of an overdose of heroin when I was seventeen years old. They found her body in an alley, a block from our old neighborhood. And Lawanda, well she was no sister to me. She was a hooker, and in my eyes she will always be just that, a hooker. I didn't meet her until a year after I'd moved in with Brenda. Lawanda had been incarcerated for soliciting. She had been in and out of juvenile detentions and prison for soliciting, dealing and using drugs since she was twelve years old. I guess you can say like mother like daughter," Blair said with a bitter laugh.

I winced from the hurt look upon his face. "Oh, Blair, I'm so sorry," I said as I reached out for his hand.

"For what? Death was the best thing that could've happened to Brenda. Doing the whole time I lived with her, Brenda said less than a 100 words to me, or should I say '*at*' me? Brenda would always yell at me to stop looking at her. I was her son, Mia. Her ten year old son and I'm positive Brenda had no love for me either." Blair said with a shake of his head. "Brenda and Lawanda," Blair snorted, "uneducated, and coarse, you name it and they would fit the bill. Brenda never understood that her lifestyle was foreign to me. Living with her was like living in another world. A God loving, caring, grandmother, with a college education raised me. My grandmother taught junior high school and raised me to say 'yes sir' and 'yes ma'am' and to respect my elders. Living with my grandmother, I got my butt beaten for misbehaving, living with Brenda, I got the shit beaten out of me just because I looked at her the wrong way."

"Oh, Blair, I'm so sorry. But, all these years have gone by and you've only get one family; maybe it's time for you and your sister to reconcile."

"Out of the question," Blair said with a shake of his head, as he raised one hand high in the air. "Lawanda has her life and I have mine. There hasn't been any room in my life for her since I was sixteen."

"Maybe she doesn't feel the same way as you do-"

"Mia, give it a rest okay? I'm going to bed."

"When was the last time the two of you talked?"

"Did you not hear what I just *said?* I have not spoken to Lawanda since I was seventeen. When Brenda died I got a phone call from Lawanda asking for cash to bury her and that was the end of our relationship. So, if you do not mind; *please* do not bring this up again."

His words stung me, for I was hurt that he hadn't shared any of this with me before tonight. Blair let out a loud sigh and reached for me.

"Having you in my life has made me happy and fulfilled. The last time I was this happy was when my grandmother was alive," Blair proclaimed in a voice gentler than before. He brushed my lips with his. "I'm going to bed, good night."

"Blair?"

"Mia, no more," Blair said holding his hands high in the air, "I've had enough of this topic. Enough talk, this discussion is over."

We finished undressing in silence, as my thoughts dwelled on our earlier discussion. I'd been an only child and my parents had passed away years ago. So it was unimaginable to me why Blair, who had a sibling, wanted nothing to do with her. I entered the bathroom my mind still working overtime on how to bring Blair and his sister together again, and prayed that my own sons would never alienated themselves from one another.

By the time I returned back to the bedroom, Blair was already in bed, head covered up, pretending to be asleep. I knew he was pretending because he was on his stomach and not his back. I crawled into bed, scooting under the covers and over to his side, wrapping my arms around his waist. I placed my face next to his; his eyes popped opened. I moved in closer still and place a light kiss upon his lips.

"You know I would do anything in the world for you, baby, anything except that. One of these days I will tell you the whole sorry story, but not tonight," Blair said, turning over onto his side, and away from me.

Our anniversary was just around the corner. In a few weeks, I was planning a party here at the house, and after tonight's conservation I was seriously considering inviting Blair's sister Lawanda, and her family to the party. I wasn't even sure if Blair had any nieces or nephews. Maybe, somehow I could convince Blair to place the call to his sister.

CHAPTER EIGHTEEN

"Maurice, let's go- we're going to be late," I called out. Maurice had been accepted to Morehouse College on a basketball scholarship and it was time for us to head out to the airport. I would have rather Maurice attend a college closer to home like Anthony, but after a long discussion with Blair, Maurice had chosen Morehouse over the University of San Diego. I'd been moping about all morning, already missing my baby. Anthony was going to meet us at the airport, as well as Sonny to see Maurice off. Against my better judgment, Blair had given Maurice a Chevy Tahoe for his graduation gift. I'd preferred to get Maurice something similar to Anthony's Blazer, not the huge SUV that Blair had chosen. But as usual, Blair had gotten his way and had arranged for a representative from a local Chevy dealership to meet Maurice at the airport in Atlanta with his new SUV. Maurice would be spending some time with a friend who lived in the area before school officially started.

My heart dropped at the sight of Maurice coming down the hall lugging the last of his luggage. Maurice had been adamant about me not traveling with him, wanting to do it all on his own. Tears stung at my eyes as he passed me in the foyer making his way out the large black SUV Blair had purchased shortly after our marriage. During the rare times when Maurice and Anthony spent time with us, it was the one vehicle large enough to transport the four of us at one time. So today we would be using the Lincoln Navigator because in addition to Maurice, we also had his luggage. It looked as if Maurice was taking all of his belongings with him. Watching Maurice prepare for his departure was harder than I'd thought. I still couldn't believe my youngest was leaving me. I stood and watched as Maurice walked out of the door, and as he exited, Blair entered. As Blair bent to retrieve a small duffle bag, he caught me staring out the door at Maurice. Instead of picking up the suitcase, Blair reached out for me instead.

"He's a big boy, Mia, he'll be okay. He'll do great in school," Blair said as he released me. Blair retrieved the duffle bag and headed back outside.

I did my best to hold back my tears, for I had refused to cry in front of Maurice. I busied myself with arming the house alarm, and took a stab at putting on a brave face before I joined Blair and Maurice outside. Once outside, I stood for a second watching Maurice as he tossed a ball out into the yard for the dogs to chase. I slowly made my way over to the back of the SUV, as Blair stuffed the last of the bags into the back. Orpheus caught the ball, and brought it over to Blair, and I stood back and watched as Blair and Maurice horsed around with the dogs. I was happy to see them get along so well together, but still sadden about the fact that Maurice was leaving home.

On the drive to the airport we discussed Maurice's career of choice. Of course his first choice was to be picked up by one of the professional basketball teams after college, but if that failed then he would fall back on his next love, sports medicine. Maurice would be entering premed and then off to med school. Maurice wanted to become a doctor specializing in Infectious Disease or orthopedics, which he became interested in after his bout with Valley Fever. Maurice had convinced me he was ready to undertake the trails and tribulations of becoming a doctor. Although I was extremely proud of my sons, I wasn't ready to let either of them go, not just yet.

Anthony was really excited for his brother's college of choice, and was even thinking of relocating to Atlanta himself, to give Maurice moral support. After helping out at the center with Sonny over the summer break, Anthony had secured a permanent position as a graphic artist with a very large and prominent company. Anthony discovered the company had a sister company in Georgia and after six months, he would be eligible to transfer to that office. Blair had been disappointed when Anthony had turned down his offer to work at his pool and landscaping company, even at the level of assistant manager. I doubted that Blair and Anthony would ever become close, but I was happy because one out of two wasn't bad and Blair and Maurice had an excellent relationship. I let out a loud sigh, realizing that soon I would be losing both my sons to their wives and a family of their own, and the prospect of an empty nest didn't appeal to me. Of course Blair was upbeat and terrific by being there for me whenever I was hit with the crying mood.

Maurice would be flying back for Thanksgiving and Christmas break, and of course I would visit with him. Being that Maurice was on the basketball team, there was always the possibility of me attending his games played on the west coast.

It was a sad day at the airport, I tried to be strong but in the end, the tears won out. By the time Maurice walked through the security check line, and when Maurice had turn and waved good-by, we all had tears in our eyes. Blair and I turned down Sonny's invitation to join him and Macey for lunch. For all I really wanted to do was to go home and drown in my misery. Anthony accepted Sonny's invitation, and he and Sonny headed out for The Egg Roll. Blair held my hand as we made our way back to the parking garage. Blair was his usual talkative self as we left the garage and headed out for home. I was feeling so miserable, that I hadn't even noticed that we where on Interstate 15 instead of the eight until almost an hour later.

"Blair, this isn't the way home."

"Ah, you finally climbed out of that fog, huh?"

"What are you doing?" I asked.

"I thought it was time for a trip," Blair replied, as he reached out and took my hand. "We're going to Palm Springs for few days."

"Palm Springs? Blair, what are you thinking? You know I was off work for most of last week and I have to be at work early Monday morning."

Blair gave me a brief look and a smile as he gave my hand a squeeze. "You need to get away. The office will be there when you get back. I called Sonya last night, told her you'd be back on Tuesday."

"Oh you did, huh?"

"Yes, I did."

"But, Blair-"

"But nothing, we are going to Palm Springs and that's the end of that," Blair replied with a grin.

"What about a change of clothing?"

He was grinning like the *Cheshire cat* from the *Alice in Wonderland* book as he brought my hand up to his lips for a quick kiss, before turning his attention back to the road. "I packed us a bag last night."

"You packed a bag for me?"

"Everything we need is in that bag."

"Oh really?"

"Trust me."

"Trust you?"

"Yes."

"Uh-huh."

Once we reached the hotel in Palm Springs, Blair removed one small overnight bag, which supposedly contained all we would need for the next three days. Upon inspecting the contents of the bag, I found it contained one negligee, a tube of toothpaste, two toothbrushes, a bottle of bubble bath, and an assortment of candles lying at the bottom of the bag. "You do have another bag hidden somewhere in the SUV, right?" I asked as I made another search of the bag, checking the outside pockets just in case I'd missed something.

"No, that's all we'll need," Blair said, as he leisurely stretched out on the bed.

I walked over to the bed holding up the sheer negligee, looking though it, and down at Blair. "What about clothes? Am I supposed to wear this out to dinner?"

"Who says we're going out?" Blair asked as he sat up and pulled a small bottle from his shirt pocket. "I thought we'd start with dessert first."

I laughed. "What is that?" I asked, knowing full well what it was. It was flavored body oil, the kind that heated up when it came into contact with your skin. And judging from the label, it was my favorite kind too, chocolate flavored. Blair smiled as I laid down on top of him. Our kissing was endless; they went from long sensuous kisses to short quick ones, ear and neck nipping, lip bruising, and tongue sucking kisses that made me want to keel over. Blair began to remove my clothing, and as he unbuttoned my blouse, he punctuated each button with a kiss to my mouth. We were giggling like teenagers by the time Blair got around to removing my blouse. I gave in to the moment, forgetting all of my worries as I fell in love with my husband all over again.

CHAPTER NINETEEN

I was humming *Rudolph the Red-Nosed Reindeer* as I brought out the Christmas decorations from the closet of our home office. Blair had brought the decorations in from the barn last week, after going through them and making sure the containers where void of any creepy crawlers.

Maurice was coming home today. Anthony was at the airport right this minute picking him up. Maurice had chosen to stay with Anthony at the condo during Christmas break, but they would be spending Christmas day here at the house. Although I'd been a little bummed out about the fact that Maurice wasn't spending his two weeks here at the house with me, I was appeased because San Diego was a lot closer than Atlanta, and I could always stop by and visit with him after work.

Anthony and Maurice had promised to stop by for dinner later on, and staying over afterwards to help me with the Christmas decorations. Tomorrow night Blair and I would be celebrating our second wedding anniversary.

Although Blair wasn't aware of it, after numerous tries, I was finally able to contact his sister Lawanda, inviting her and her family to our anniversary party. At first she had been blatantly rude with me and didn't seem to know whom I was referring to when I mentioned 'Blair' by name, and then I remembered the writing on the back of the picture was signed to *Smithy*. I didn't get a chance to call until this morning because Blair had taken the little black book from me and had hidden it someplace or he had destroyed it, and I couldn't recall the phone number but I did remember her last name. Although I knew it would be too late for Lawanda and her husband to attend the party, Lawanda had promised to call back to speak with Blair later on tonight, and she had insisted I keep our conversation a secret from Blair until then. So I was in a good mood today for a couple of reasons. My sons would be home for Christmas, and I had begun the healing process between Blair and his sister.

Blair smiled at the good looking woman standing in front of him, that is, if you liked blondes. I knew she was flirting with him, but I behaved as if I didn't notice. Blair finally walked away from her, looked around, spotted me, and blew a kiss in my direction. I turned and made my way across the terrace toward the caterer and his crew as they sat out plates of hors d'oeuvres. I had gone all out for this party. Maurice and Anthony and helped me decorate the whole house with Christmas decorations, as well as red and green Japanese lanterns floating in the pool, giving the place a festive air. There was holly, and mistletoe throughout the house, as well as large pots of red and white poinsettias, and chrysanthemums. Blair had purchased the largest Christmas tree he could find and it stood in the center of the living room beautifully decorated by me with a little help from Blair. The whole house smelled of Christmas, and good food, and I was ready to get down to the business of eating and I was certain Blair was as hungry as I was. I'd had Blair running errands for most of the day. I wasn't sure if he'd eaten anything besides breakfast this morning, and I was thinking I should prepare a plate of food for him. Blair was wearing a bored expression, and that was as good as sign as ever that it was time to eat.

All of our friends had graced us with their presence on this day of celebration, as well as Blair's employees and their spouses, and my staff from the staffing agency. It wasn't a large gathering, because I knew how Blair felt about large gatherings. I had purposely kept the guest list short, that way Blair knew or recognized just about everyone here, which was the way he preferred it. The party wasn't going to be a long one either; I'd promised Blair to have everyone out of the house by midnight. The two of us were leaving for Hawaii in two days, for the honeymoon we'd never had. Blair wanted to leave the next morning, but I wanted to spend some time with my sons so Blair and I had compromised and put our trip off for a couple of days. I wasn't sure what was going on with Blair, but he seemed on edge for most of the day. As Blair turned and headed back toward the house, I caught his eye, and nodding politely to the person before him, he walked over to join our little group.

"Baby, are you having a good time?" I asked Blair, as I gave him a gentle kiss upon his lips.

"I'm having a terrific time, sweetheart," Blair replied as he reached out for my hand and gave it a light squeeze. I was wearing a long black dress with a low cowl neck in the front and a very low back, stopping just at the top of my butt. My hair was piled high on top of my head, with a few ringlets hanging on the side, and earlier, before the guests had arrived, Blair had commented on how radiant I looked in my new dress. The dress had two side splits, and when I moved Blair caught a glimpse of what he called my sexy legs, long and glittering. My feet were encased in a pair of black high-heeled sandals, and Blair couldn't keep hands or his eyes off of me. Throughout the evening, every time he was near me, Blair would whisper how marvelous I looked and smelled. Of course, Blair was looking good enough to eat in his black Armani suit. Earlier, before the arrival of our guests, we almost didn't make it out of the bedroom in time, with Blair trying his best to talk me into having sex with him while fully clothed, but I wouldn't do it, so we got undressed again, and shower again, but it was well worth it in the end.

"Did the phone ring?" I asked as I returned his squeeze, casting a soft smile on him.

"Haven't heard it ring all night."

"Where's Anthony? I bet he's on the phone tying up both lines."

"Uh, Anthony's over there," Sonny said, pointing out into the yard where Anthony stood speaking with an attractive woman.

"Who is that woman talking to my baby?" I asked, as I started moving in their direction.

"Mia, leave it alone," Sonny said pulling me back into our little circle.

"Who is that woman?" I asked again.

"She came with Sonya's group," Sonny informed me.

I kept my eyes on Anthony. Now I recognized her, Sonya had brought along a date and the woman was his sister or cousin, I forget which, whom I'd never met before tonight.

"I think her name is Mary or Maryanne or something like that," Sonny finished.

"Oh right, that's her date's cousin from LA," Macey said as we all stood watching Anthony and the mystery woman.

"Don't you think she's a little to old for Anthony?" I asked as I folded my arms across my chest.

Blair chuckled, as he reached for my arm. "Come on, baby, let's go inside and get us a glass of champagne and something to eat," he said steering me back into the house before I could get a chance to intrude on Anthony and the woman.

"Mia? Baby, wake up."

"Huh? What is it? What's wrong?"

Blair took advantage of the fact that I was not the easiest person in the world to wake up. I was a slow riser and it took me a good while to get oriented in the mornings. While I sat there in a daze, Blair took this opportunity to pull a big bulky long sleeved sweater over my head.

"Blair, what are you doing?"

"Shhh, here put these on," he whispered, as he handed me a pair of sweatpants.

I was a little unsteady on my feet as I stood and stepped into the sweats before plopping back down onto the bed. "Why am I getting dressed in the middle of the night?" Blair had knelt down in front of me and was slipping socks and a pair of Nikes on my feet. "Why are you whispering and where've you been?" I asked taking in his attire. Blair was wearing a black turtleneck sweater with a pair of black pants and a pair of black boots. "Blair, what are you doing?" I asked as I reached down to still his movements.

"Mia, listen to me, I want you to do exactly as I say. Someone has broken into the house and they've started a fire." My eyes were wide in the dark room as I instantly came awake at Blair's words, my hands gripping his arm.

"Blair, what's going on? Eurydice, the dogs, where are they?" I asked, glancing about the room.

"Eurydice is here with us, Orpheus is just outside the room." he spoke in a low voice, and quickly, as he handed me a small flashlight and begin to lead me toward the fireplace. "Don't turn it on yet, wait until you get inside the walkway."

"Walkway? Blair, wait," I said, coming to a halt.

"Baby, we don't have much time," Blair said as he pulled me to him and kissed me, before he started moving forward again. Blair knelt down inside the fireplace and reached up to the opposite side of the handle that operated the flue, and pulled down a lever. He stepped back as the entire bottom half of the fireplace popped opened with a loud groaning sound, revealing a dark hole in the wall bringing a musty smell to my nose. Even though the room was dark, the hold in front of me was even darker. I stepped back in astonishment as this secret place was revealed to me, as Eurydice moved forward and took a guard dog stance in the opened section. Blair hooked a leash onto Eurydice's choke collar and handed it to me. "Mia, I want you to follow Eurydice. Go where she goes and do not let go of her leash. Do not try to guide her, she will guide you."

My eyes were wide with fright as I clung to him. "Blair, what's happening? What is this?" I asked nodding to the opening in the fireplace.

"Baby, listen to me, I need you to be strong for me. Will you do that for, Mia? Will you be strong for me? Please, just this once, don't ask me any questions and go with Eurydice and do not look back. I'll explain everything to you later on. Will you trust me?"

I was full of questions, but before I could open my mouth, Blair kissed me again, long and hard, and then held me close for a few precious seconds.

"You're so soft and warm, and the scent from our lovemaking still clings to you. I love you so much, Mia, so much. You are my heart."

I felt Blair tremble, and I was afraid, because he was always the brave one. I began to cry, as my body swayed against his. "I love you too, Blair. Why won't you tell me what's wrong?" I asked as my lips brushed against his.

"Because time is running out, I have to get you out of the house, now."

"Blair, you're scaring me. Baby, what's happening?" I asked as I held him close.

"Everything is going to be okay, I'll explain everything to you later." Then Blair did something I had never seen him do before, he removed the necklace with the heavy gold locket from around his neck and quickly placed it around my neck. The locket now hung next to the diamond heart Blair had given me that day in Yuma. "Baby, you have to go now, it isn't safe here any more. You have to go quickly. Once you've reach the ravine, call 9-1-1. Do not turn on the flashlight until after I've closed the hatch, and watch your step," Blair smiled and kissed me again.

"Blair, I'm not leaving you," I said as I clung to him.

He stuck a cell phone into the pocket of my sweater before reaching up and removing my arms from around his neck. Once again he turned me toward the opening in the fireplace and gave me a gentle push in the small of my back.

"Remember, let Eurydice led you, watch your head, and be safe. I promise I'll follow you as soon as I can. Eurydice, *safe walk*," Blair instructed.

I stumbled a bit as Blair's little push propelled me forward. The opening creaked and groaned shut behind me, separating me from Blair. I gave Eurydice's leash a tug and instructed her to lie down. I fumbled with the flashlight, my fingers searching for the switch in the darkness, while at the same time questioning if I really wanted to see this place or not, as my mind played out the different kinds of creepy crawlers the darkness might harbor. I clicked on the flashlight, and shone the light back at the now closed opening. I pushed at the hard rock, but nothing happened, and then I turned and shone the flashlight in the opposite direction. The whole area was made of rough stone, right down to the uneven rough-cut stone steps leading down into the darkness. Eurydice was ready to start on our trek the instant I turned on the flashlight she stood, but I held her back as I took a good look around. "Let's go", I said as Eurydice started down the stairs with me following along behind her. The tunnel wasn't as bad as I'd thought, it had a strong musty smell to it but for the moment the area seemed to be free from any creepy crawlers, but that was the least of my problems, for my thoughts were still on Blair.

So engrossed in my surroundings, I'd misjudged the width of one of the steps and took a larger step than necessary. I found myself tumbling head over heels down the stairs. I let out a scream as I tumbled down seven or eight steps, before coming to a stop, bumping my head up against the hard roughen stonewall. I don't know how long I'd lain there, dazed, and disoriented, but as my senses finally hit full force again, I panicked as I looked around searching for Eurydice, after noticing that I was no longer holding onto her leash. The flashlight had landed just a few steps below me and I breathed a sigh of relief as Eurydice ran up to me and began to lick my face. I longed to go back up the steps and back to Blair, knowing he was back there facing only God knew what all by himself, but the space was beginning to fill with smoke. Taking several deep calming breaths, I checked for broken bones before slowly rising to my feet. My head felt like hell but I shoved forward, in a hurry to get out of this confined place. Blair had told me not to look back, so with one hand on the wall and the other one holding the leash and flashlight I carefully advanced down the steps. I wasn't good at judging distances so I'm not sure how far we'd traveled before the tunnel ended. All that lay ahead was a thick growth of bushes. Damn- now what? I thought as tears stung at my eyes, it looked like a dead end to me. I was pondering my next move and wishing Blair was here with me, when Eurydice got down on her stomach and started to scoot forward toward a small opening I hadn't notice before. I gave her leash a tug, instructing her to stay and got down on my hands and knees shining the flashlight at the opening.

The bushes were so dense I couldn't see through the other side. Suddenly, I jumped back; stifling a scream as the bushes trembled, letting me know that something was indeed alive inside of them. Eurydice gave a sharp bark and placed herself in front of me. I sat still, hardly breathing at all as I waited to see what was going to jump from the dense foliage. I sat as still as a log, as though in a trance, staring at the foliage for what seemed like forever. All was quiet for a long time with no more movement coming from the clump of bushes. I moved forward again thinking my choices were limited. One was to say put and suffocate to death from the smoke that was now pouring through the tunnel, or get down on my hands and knees and crawl into the bushes.

My imagination began to run wild as I envisioned poisonous spiders or worse, poisonous snakes slithering around in the bushes just waiting for me. My head was throbbing like mad, and I wasn't sure if it was because of my escalating fear or, the result of my fall. I started coughing from the smoke, but still I just sat there afraid to go forward and knowing that there was no going back. The smoke was growing thicker now, and soon I wouldn't be able to see the opening at all if I didn't get a move on. I wasn't sure if I should send Eurydice through first and follow her or if I should go first. The smoke was getting thicker, and I still didn't move. It was a fit of coughing that finally made my mind up for me. I sent Eurydice though the opening and then practically threw my body in behind hers. The bushes were thicker than I'd anticipated as I followed along behind Eurydice flat on my stomach. The branches of the bushes seem to reach out and grab me, snagging at my clothing and my hair. Eurydice was a smart dog, and having sensed my fear of the unknown, she'd look back over her shoulders at me from time to time, I'm guessing to make sure I was still behind her as I used my elbows and my feet to inch my body slowly and cautiously through the growth. It was a slow process, for my sweater and hair kept getting caught up on the many branches that reached out and grabbed me, making our progress much more difficult. I had to keep stopping to free myself from the tangled mess and to top it all off, I couldn't seem to stop coughing. For someone with a fear of insects, maneuvering through this shrubbery was pure hell for me, but eventually Eurydice and I finally crawled out into the opened night.

I sobbed with relief as we emerged into the cold damp dark night. I turned around and looked back at the way we'd come, and all I saw were the thick bushes. There was nothing to show that there had been an opening on the other side of the thick shrubbery. I looked up and saw the reddish glow in the sky from the fire. I quickly turned and headed in the direction I thought the ravine was. Luckily, I had picked up Eurydice's leash again, for she turn and headed in the opposite direction. Eurydice led the way through the darkness, guiding me to the ravine, which if I remembered correctly was less than a half a mile or so from the front gate. I reached into my pocket and pulled out the cell phone and dialed 9-I-I, just as Eurydice begin to bark, and a shadowy figure emerged from the night. I screamed before I heard my name being called and then I rushed into Sonny's opened arms.

"Mia. Oh thank God you're okay. What happened?" he asked, as he squeezed me against him.

"I don't know, Blair woke me and said burglars had invaded the house, and that the house was on fire," I said just before an outbreak of coughing hit me. Sonny looked down at me with concern, as the coughing racked through my body. I looked up at him with watery eyes, and a running nose, and it struck me again what a relief it was to see Sonny's familiar face standing here before me. "I'm so happy to see you, what are you doing here?" I was finally able to ask.

"Blair called me-"

I grabbed him by his jacket as he said this, with tears of joy in my eyes. "Is he okay?"

"I don't know; he called me over an hour ago. How long have you been out here?"

"I'm not sure," I replied as we heard sirens in the distance. One of the neighbors must have called 9-I-I because in all the excitement upon seeing Sonny, I'd forgotten about my cell phone.

"My car is over there," he said leading me away. "Mia, why don't you wait in the car for me and I'll go back to the house and find Blair."

"I'm coming with you. Let's put Eurydice in the car," I said as we made our way to Sonny's car. For a brief second I felt dizzy and started to cough again. I looked up and observed sparks and ashes from the fire flying everywhere, the ashes covering everything in their path.

Sonny reached out to steady me, peering into my face with concern. "I really think you should wait in the car."

"No, I'm coming with you," I said catching my breath. I handed Sonny Eurydice's leash and he placed her in the car. We could now see the lights from the fire trucks.

"Get in the car."

"Sonny, I'm not going to sit in the car." I looked at him in the light, noticing his face was smudge with soot and he was covered in ashes as well.

"I know you're not, I'm going to drive and park the car closer to house, that's all."

Sonny decided to remain on the far side of the ravine, to stay out of the way of the fire trucks. The smoke was billowing as black as the night. An ambulance pulled up next to us and Sonny ushered me over to the truck. I explained to them how I had fallen escaping the fire and that my husband may still be up at the house, as they checked me out. I was sucking on 100% oxygen when, suddenly, several loud explosions shook the night. The sound of the first one made us all jump to our feet, and sent Sonny running toward the house. I turned to go in pursuit of Sonny, but one of the paramedics held me back preventing me from following him.

"Probably the gas tanks of your vehicles," the paramedic explained.

I looked across the smoke filled ravine as a figure emerged. With my face streaked with soot, dirt and tears streaming down my face I held my breath until the figure became recognizable. It was one of the firefighters and he was carrying something in his arms. Oh God, I thought, thinking the worse, before noticing the object that the fireman carried was too small to be that of a man, so what or who...

"Orpheus," I screamed and stumbled forward. Someone grabbed me my arms and prevented me from going any further.

"Wait there, it's safer," Sonny shouted as he started over to the other side of the ravine, meeting up with the fireman who was carrying Orpheus. They stopped and knelt down, placing Orpheus on the ground between them.

I was moving forward as Sonny said this, pulling along whomever it was that was trying to hold me back. "Orpheus!" Orpheus ears twitched and he began to squirm around on the ground upon hearing my voice. The paramedic, who was trying to hold me back, finally let go of me, and I followed Sonny across the ravine.

As I got closer, the firefighter who had carried the big dog was speaking softly to Orpheus as he examined him. I stopped and turned away for as I'd gotten nearer to the vehicles and the lights, which now shone brightly upon Orpheus, I noticed how badly he'd been burned, and I couldn't stand to see him suffer. Orpheus looked over at me with his big brown doggy eyes, as Sonny dropped down beside him. "He isn't going to make it," Sonny said as he reached out and patted Orpheus on the nose.

I moved forward and knelt down next to Sonny, but I couldn't bring myself to touch Orpheus, as he whined with pain. A paramedic open what look like a bag of saline and poured it over the dog's body. "I think you're right," he said as his hands examined the dog. He looked over at me with a shake of his head as if to confirm his statement, and just as quickly, Orpheus went into a seizure. I stood up and quickly backed away, covering my face as my loud sobbing filled the night air. Sonny rose and came to me, holding me in his arms, rubbing my back as I cried on his shoulder. Again, Sonny attempted to steer me to his car, but I stood firm.

"Did you see Orpheus back? It looked like gunshots." Sonny said.

I shook my head and looked back over my shoulder just as a shout came from across the ravine. Sonny and I ran forward, but when Sonny realized I was with him, he stopped to halt my pursuit. Paramedics rushed out from behind us and ran toward the others. "Please, please let him be okay," I prayed out loud over and over again. All I could see was the shaking of heads the firemen before I turned and buried my scream in Sonny's chest. I repeatedly stumped my foot upon the ground, shouting no, no, no.

I could hear Sonny talking, but I couldn't quite make out what he was saying because of loud roar of the fire. Sonny moved away and another pair of hands replaced his, holding onto me. I turned and watched Sonny walk away toward the group of firefighters. It seemed like hours passed as the firemen continued to fight the blaze and from what I was told later, they would not be able to search the smoldering ruins. That would have to wait until after the ashes had cooled down. Finally one returned and beckoned to us.

CHAPTER TWENTY

Blair was dead. I lay in the hospital bed, my eyes red and puffy from the constant crying I'd been doing. The curtains of the hospital room had been pulled back, and the view outside the window was of the California coastline. It was the month of December and the weather had changed drastically overnight. Where there had been blue skies and billowing cumulus clouds just the day before, now lay way to dark heavy clouds verging on rain. The wind was blowing so hard outside my window that the trees near my room were beating a furious rhythm against the windowpane. What was going on outside didn't faze me at all, for the storm inside my head was far greater than any show that Mother Nature could put on. Even without a mirror I was certain the look on my face was one of pure pain and misery. Although my injuries had not been life threatening, anyone viewing my hospital chart would simply see what was written down, that I was recovering from a light case of smoke inhalation, a mild concussion, and multiple scratches and bruises to my lower extremities. What wasn't written was the mention of my husband Blair, of whom I'd been married to for two fantastic years. Blair, who had died that horrible night in what the papers had describe as one of the deadliest fires ever in the area. It had never been confirmed, but the authorities thought they had discovered the remains of two or three bodies and the scene was still under investigation as I lay here. They weren't sure because of the devastation and the intensity of the fire which had consumed everything in its path. The police had filed the incident as a home invasion.

The memory of that night assaulted my thoughts, hard and furious, but I no longer wanted to think anymore, as I tossed my head from side to side. Even with the curtains opened to the outside world, I was feeling claustrophobic as the walls of the hospital room closed in on me. I knew it was all in my mind, but my throat seemed to tighten up on me as well. The oxygen tubes in my nose only made matters worse, for they were uncomfortable, and burdensome. Stealing against the nausea that usually followed whenever the tubing was removed, I reached up and with two fingers, grasped the tubing between my fingers, and slowly pulled it from my nose. This would be the second time I had removed the tubing. The last time I had removed the tubes, one of the floor nurses had replaced them, chastising me, taking her job very serious, insisting that the tubing remain because the pure oxygen would be good for my lungs, but to me it was merely a nuisance. I took several deep-calming breaths through my mouth, trying to quell the bout of nausea, as I turned to face the window again. I lay still, mentally willing the nausea away, as my mouth filled with saliva, and the bitter tasting bile began to creep up my throat. I kept inhaling, taking large deep cleansing breathes until the urge had passed.

Letting out a loud sigh, I searched the panes of glass for my reflection, as a single tear made its' way down my cheek. "Blair." His name came out in a croaking sound, my vocal chords raw and bruised from all the yelling and screaming I'd done that horrible night. Blair's name was the first word I'd spoken in hours. I had been admitted to the hospital not because of my physical injuries, but because I had fainted at the scene and had been in shock when I had finally became conscious again. My chest tightened, as I tried to control my urge to weep, for the tears I wept were for Blair, because the pain that was in my heart, far out shadowed the pain of my insignificant injuries. The amount of weeping I'd been doing surely could not be healthy for me; however, as hard as I try, I could not halt the flow of tears. I felt as though I had cried enough to fill a river, and still the tears continued to fall. I quickly closed my eyes in a vain attempt to hold back the flood of tears that threaten to spill from my eyes. And as though to disrupt my feeble attempt, a bolt of lightning lit the darken and bruised sky. A series of bright colors flashed across the skyline, brilliant in the night, followed by a loud downpour of rain. It was a magnificent show of force from Mother Nature; her way of letting me know that she would not be ignored.

Blair, he had been my love, my heart, and my soul. How could this have happened- I asked myself for what had to have been the hundredth time? A high whining sound filled the room, and it took a second for me to realize the sound was coming from me, as a mental vision of that horrific night filled my thoughts, the same images that prevented me from sleeping at night. I was alone again, and as always, heartache, and tears followed those painful memories. I thought back on that frightful night, and it all appeared so unreal to me, like a bad dream that wouldn't end. I was at my wits end, persistently searching for details of that night, trying to come up with an explanation of why Blair had chosen to remain behind instead of escaping with me. How could it have happened? Who were the men who had invaded our home, and why where they there? What did they want? What happened to the smoke alarms, what about the house alarm? I remembered Blair had armed the house after he had returned from letting the dogs out. Why hadn't any of the alarms gone off? These questions and more circulated through my mind, but the most important question of all was, what had prevented Blair from leaving the house that night? The last time I'd seen Blair, he was alive and whole with a big ole silly grin upon his face, as he pushed me toward the hidden exit in the bedroom fireplace, which I'd never knew had existed until that night.

It was Christmas day, and for the moment I lay in the cold sterile hospital room alone, my mind in a jumble and I felt as though I would go stark raving mad. The one time I'd actually slept since my admission into the hospital had been drug induced. If I didn't receive medication to help me sleep, the sleep would not come to me. Last night I hadn't slept at all. I knew I couldn't rely on medication forever, so I had turned down all medications last night. Anthony and Maurice had arrived at the hospital bright and early this morning, spending most of the day with me, until I'd written them a note, sending them out for some fresh air, away from this stuffy and sterile hospital room, and to find themselves some dinner. I knew I wouldn't be alone for too long; they would return, as well as Sonny, Sonny, my dearest friend. He was probably on his way to see me now, because Sonny was like that, a true friend to the end. I would always be grateful to him for introducing me to Blair.

My tears fell in earnest now as I cried loud wrenching sobs. It hurt so much to loose Blair, and to recall that night, as well as the pain in my heart was becoming far too great for me to bear. I remembered how thick the smoke was in the air, and how it had become increasingly difficult for me to breathe. The heat from the fire had been so intense; I could feel its warmth upon my skin from where I stood across the ravine, which was about a half a mile from the house. Why him, why Blair? I was on a roll now, a river of tears flowing down my face.

I clutched at the pillow, my body rocking from side to side, as the recollections of that night flooded my thoughts. I could practically smell the smoke from the fire and I would never be able to rid my mind of the loud roaring noise that the fire had made as it took my husband from me and devoured our home. Afterward, Sonny and I had been told the fire had been too intense for the firemen to enter the house. I remembered I'd screamed, and clawed at the paramedic holding me at bay. I wanted to get away from him, back across the ravine and into the house, to my husband. I remembered hitting the individual who been restraining me that night, as I struggled to free myself. When that hadn't work, I'd done the next best thing; I'd pleaded, and begged him to release me so that I could go in search for Blair. I recalled being in Sonny's arms and disorientation followed as the darkness engulfed me.

I'd awakened in this hospital, with my dear friend Sonny hovering over me, as I called out Blair's name over and over again. The fresh assault of pain from that night was hard to resist as it racked my body, like a fierce storm as I lashed out at the empty room. Suddenly, I felt arms about me, and the pillow was removed from my grip, replaced by a warm body.

"Can't you give her something?" It was Macey, speaking to the nurse who had rushed into the room at the sound of my screams. Macey smoothed my hair back, and away from my face and then I felt a much tighter grip on my hand, it was Sonny, forcing his strength into me. I was so grateful for them, because I would need all their strength and more to get through this night.

"Mrs. Freeman has declined all prescribed medications, and Dr. Simon supports her decision. She won't take anything stronger than an aspirin."

"When will she be discharged?" Sonny asked sternly, as he peered into my face.

"I'm not sure, but Dr. Simon feels Mrs. Freeman isn't ready to be released yet, but you will have to speak with him. He is a bit concerned because she hasn't eaten anything since she was admitted."

"She isn't going to eat anything while she's here. Have her sons been in to see her today?" Sonny asked as he squeezed my hand, his eyes never breaking contact with mine.

"Yes, they were here earlier but they left about an hour ago."

"Maybe her physician will release her today for Mia has business to attend to. She needs to bury her husband to have closure, and to get on with her life."

I screamed at his harsh words, my head thrashing back and forth on the pillow as I tried to pulled away from Sonny, but his grip was hard and tight, just like his words had been. Why was Sonny saying those things to me? Oh God, how could you take my love away from me?

"Sonny! What are you saying?" Macey shouted, as she put her hand to her mouth, turning away from the bed as she was overcome with her own tears.

"Macey, Mia is stronger than this. She needs to get out of this place. She has business to take care of, that's the only way she's going to go forward. Mia," Sonny said as he lowered his head level with mine, his eyes searching my face. As he began to speak, his voice took on a softer tone, almost a whisper as he bent closer. "Mia, my light, I love you, and I don't want to see you do this to yourself. Blair would not want you to do this to yourself. You have two sons that love you as well, and they want to see their *mother* whole and healthy again. There is nothing more that anyone can do for you. This is something you *must* do for yourself. Baby, I can hold you; offer you my shoulder to cry on. I can love you, and I can even get you drunk," Sonny said, flashing a strained smile at me. "But, what you want the most in life,

I cannot give you. My love, Blair is dead, and as much as I *want* to, I cannot bring him back to you. I can be with you, and help you heal, but I can't bring him back! Mia, you're going home! Do you hear me?" Sonny asked, wrapping his arms around me, as we cried together.

For a long time, the only sound in the room was the sniffing sounds of our weeping. I looked passed Sonny, over at Macey as her tears flowed down her cheeks. I raised my hand and touch Sonny's face. A long time ago I had loved him more than he ever knew. But that was a long time ago and things were different now. But Sonny was right; the reality of his words suddenly struck a cord in me, and I knew exactly what he'd meant. I had business to attend to. How could I ask someone else to take on the responsibility of burying *my* husband? This was something that I must do, for I would need the closure. As devastating as that night had been, I knew I had to call upon forces deep within me to help me gather the strength which dwelled inside and put my life back together.

I looked around at the squeaking sound of rubber soles on the linoleum floor, into the anxious faces of my sons as they entered the room, each carrying bags of fast food. The smiles on their faces disappeared as they took in the crying huddle around my bed. I took a long shuddering breath, and briefly closed my eyes before speaking. "I'm ready to go home now,' I said, profoundly composed as my raspy voice filled the room. "Can somebody bring me my clothes, please?"

Per Blair's instructions, he wanted his remains cremated, but since the fire had been so intense, there had been nothing left of him to cremate. It had been a small private gathering, just family, along with Macey, Sonny, Blair's employees, Sonya, and Claudia. I would have to find a way to reach out to Blair's sister to let her know of his death. All the information I had collected on her was now just a pile of ashes along with the rest of my things. I was sad at the thought of contacting Lawanda and giving her this devastating news about her brother. I could only imagine how awful this news would be to Lawanda and her family.

With my home nothing more than piles of ashes, I had moved back into the condo with my sons. It had been seven long heart wrenching days since Blair's death and my discharge from the hospital and I didn't know what to do with myself. The police had questioned me extensively regarding the break-in that night. Over a course of the next few days, it had grown tiresome, as I'd repeated to them what Blair had conveyed to me that night. I believe I passed on the same information to a minimum of five different investigators, over and over again, then, finally after many days of intermittent questioning, they had come to the conclusion that it had been a botched home invasion.

Maurice was returning back to school, he'd wanted to take some more time off to stay with me, but I of all people knew that life goes on, so I had insisted that he return to school.

"Maurice, if you need to take more time off for yourself then stay, but don't stay on my account. I'll be fine, it'll take awhile, but I'll be okay." I knew how close he and Blair had become and how Blair's death had devastated him as well. I knew Maurice was missing Blair and that he was being strong for me.

"I want to stay for you, Mom. Don't worry about me, I'm okay. It's you I'm worried about, you...I know how much you loved Blair," Maurice said as he rubbed my back. "Call me anytime if you need to talk, okay?"

"That's so sweet of you, Maurice." We hugged and said our good-byes as he and Anthony headed out for the short drive to the airport. Anthony had vacated the master bedroom and had moved his things into the loft so I could have my old room back.

Later that day, Sonya had stopped by insisting I go shopping with her. She and Macey had shopped for me while I lay in the hospital, purchasing a few essential items for me. Sonya had to practically drag me out to the mall to buy some much-needed clothing. No matter how much I protested, Sonya would not take no for an answer. After finally consenting to go with her, I barely had the strength to visit one store before my energy gave out. I didn't care to spend a whole lot of time at the mall, because mentally I just wasn't up to being outside, for I was feeling way too vulnerable and exposed. Now as I gave a fleeting look around my bedroom at the clutter of shopping bags and shoeboxes littering the room, I let out a loud sigh and prepared to organize the mess just as the buzzer sounded.

Talk about bad timing. I certainly wasn't in the mood for company at this time. All I wanted was to be alone. I closed the bedroom door ignoring the noise of the buzzing intercom. I picked up a shopping bag, dumping the contents onto the bed. Retrieving hangers from the closet I was in the process of hanging up a skirt, just as my bedroom door swung opened, making me jump from fright.

"Why didn't you buzz me up?" Sonny asked as he rushed into the room carrying a large package under his arm.

"Sonny, you scared the shit out of me. Man, don't you know how to knock?" I asked as I threw a hanger at him. "How did you get in here anyway?"

"I used my key," he replied dodging the hanger and presenting a key, as he walked over and gave me a long hug and his customary kiss upon my lips. "Sorry I frighten you, but remember when you first bought this place you gave me a key for emergencies? I thought it would be okay if I used it today, you know, when you didn't reply I thought you…oh I don't know- where's Eurydice?" Sonny asked, scanning the room.

"You thought I was maybe sleeping or something? She's upstairs, out on the balcony. Want something to drink?" I asked, as I headed for the kitchen. "I think there's some wine in here."

"Mia, I didn't mean anything," Sonny said as he reached out and rubbed my arm.

I patted his hand, knowing exactly what he was thinking. "I know."

"Got anything stronger than wine?" Sonny asked as he followed me into the kitchen. "I think we're going to need it."

"Why? What is that?" I asked pointing to the package he was carrying. I pulled out a bottle of whiskey. "Sonya dropped by today baring gifts." I said as I placed the bottle on the counter. "Will this do?"

"That'll work, and to answer your question, this was delivered to me this morning," he said as he dropped the package on the counter.

"What is it?"

"Don't know yet. I receive a call from Blair's attorney to meet me at Blair's office. When I got there, Jeremy was waiting as well.

Blair's attorney had instructions to open the safe that Blair had in his office with the two of us present and I was to have access to the package inside if anything should ever happen to him. The attorney also dropped off the insurance policy for the office," Sonny said as he dropped a thick manila envelope on the counter. "Here, this was attached to the package." Sonny pulled a letter from the back pocket of his jeans and held it out to me. "The letter's dated the day after the two of you got married. Blair wanted the two of us to be together when we opened this," he said giving the brown wrapping that covered the box a thump.

I quickly rounded the bar and with trembling hands, and took the letter from Sonny. And true to his word, the letter was written by Blair, with his own hand. With tears in my eyes I looked over at Sonny, who had moved to the other side of bar. He was in the process of retrieving glasses from the cupboard and then busied himself with getting ice from the freezer for his drink. I quickly scanned the letter. In it, Blair had written that I should view the contents of the package with Sonny and for me to be strong. He also confessed his love for me and apologized for leaving me. I held it to my chest for a few precious seconds, as though the piece of paper with Blair's handwriting on it would bring him back to me. I couldn't guess what was in the package; I thought that everything had been settled. I'd met with Blair's attorneys yesterday, and aside from the fact that Blair was no longer here, everything was as it should be. Financially, Blair had left me very well off; there was his insurance policy, which was for a million dollars, because of the accidental death clause, the insurance on the house, the cars and all his other assets. Blair had been an excellent businessman, and he'd made a few investments that had made him a lot of money. In addition, I was now the sole proprietor of a pool and lawn service, as well as the staffing agency. Blair's will had also stipulated that in the event if anything should happen to me, all of his assets would then go to Anthony and Maurice equally. Per Blair's instructions, Jeremy would continue to operate the pool and lawn business, which was fine with me.

With shaking hands I tore away the covering from the package. Besides the four notebooks, there were also several videotapes. One of the notebooks had my name on it and the other three were numbered one through three.

"You might want to read that one when you're alone, it might be private," Sonny said gesturing with his glass at the notebook with my name upon it. "Let's sit in here," he said as he scooped up the other three notebooks and headed for the living room.

I slowly followed along behind Sonny, with shaking hands, and lead feet, and to top it all off, I felt sick to my stomach. I took a deep breath and slowly sat down on the sofa. The palms of my hands had broken out into a sweat, and I rubbed them along the leg of my slacks to dry them off. I could not imagine what was inside the notebooks or on the videotapes, and I felt dread as I fought about whether or not I should read what was in them. Blair was dead, dead and gone, what did I care about words written on a piece of paper. Would words bring my husband back to me? I looked up to find Sonny staring at me over the top of his glass.

"It's going to be all right, Mia. Whatever is in these notebooks and on those tapes, I'm here for you," Sonny said as he walked over to me and sat down beside me. Sonny sat his glass on the table and placed his arms around me, hugging me close.

"What do you think it all means?" I asked with a catch in my voice.

"I don't know, and we'll never find out if we don't open them. Mia, we don't have to do it now if you don't want to. Would you rather wait until another time?"

With tears blurring my vision, I flipped opened the notebook with my name on it, and almost died right there. Blair's handwriting flowed over the page, and as I began to read, it felt as though Blair was right here in the room with me.

CHAPTER TWENTY-ONE

Blair's Journal

My darling, Mia, if you're reading this journal, then something has happened to me. Let me restate that. Something *bad* has happened to me, and it could only mean I am no longer with you in this life. Baby, having you in my life was one of the best things that ever happened to me, and I want to stress, in my whole life. I want to take this time to thank you for sharing yourself, and your two young men with me. I hope, no, I pray that you, Anthony and Maurice came to no harm. What I want for you, my darling Mia is for you to live a full healthy life. Remember, my love, that even though we have been separated by death, my love for you will always be strong.

I remember the first day we met and Sonny turned to me and asked me the fifty million dollar question, and that was "So what do you think?" What did I think? You, lovely lady, floored me. You were everything I could ever hope for. I think my reply to Sonny was, "Pretty lady, pretty smile. She seems to have a nice personality, and uh, pleasant too, I like that. How old did you say her two sons were?" I was dumbfounded, didn't know what I was saying because you took my breath away.

Then Sonny proceeded to tell me how great your sons were, no attitude, just like their mom. They are super kids, he said, and then he told me to trust him. Well, Maurice fit the description, but I don't know about Anthony. I don't think Anthony ever trusted me, and I can't say that I blame him, because if Anthony knew the truth about me then, I believe he would have done his best to prevent us from being together. They are great kids, Mia. You did one hell of a job raising them. They love you, and they have a lot of respect for you as well.

I was glad to be around to see Maurice graduate from high school, and I hope he excels in whatever his career of choice may be, whether it is basketball or physician. And let's not forget our boy with the attitude, Anthony. Sonny was partially right about Anthony too. He is an artist and he should pursue that career, tell him I said to stay with it (yeah right, like Anthony would ever do anything I told him to do). Tell Sonny I wouldn't go as far and say that Anthony's going to be the black *Picasso* (those were Sonny's words not mine) but I do agree that Anthony is a good artist and one hell of a karate instructor. I think Sonny was trying to sell me on you and your ready-made family, but tell him he was wasting his time. Because after hearing all the good things about you, I was ready to buy, sight unseen. Now, Mia, don't go getting yourself all in a huff about that sentence, it was just a metaphor. I was interested in meeting you ever since the first time I saw you at The Egg Roll, and all those many photos of you in Sonny's old bachelor pad, I couldn't wait to meet the real thing.

Sonny couldn't stand the professor. Every time I'd ask him to introduce you to me, he'd tell me you were still dating that old fart, the college professor. Sonny never tired of reminding me that if I had showed up at his wedding I would have had the opportunity to meet you then.

To be honest with you, the real reason I offered to give Sonny and Macey a party at my place was for the opportunity to meet you. I didn't know any of those people that night, except for Sonny's father. A funny thing happened that night while Sonny and I where in the kitchen discussing you. Sonny got kind of emotional and gave me a hug, and one of the caterers (whom I believed was gay) started batting his eyes at us, gazing at us all funny, and smiling and shit. I had to tell Sonny to watch out with the damn hugging mess. Sonny asked me in a joking way, what was the matter? Was I afraid you might think I was gay? And when the caterers stated to laugh, Sonny played it up by saying, come on, big guy, give us a kiss, and then he made a grab for me.

What was funny was, later on that night you ask me if I was gay. Anyway, Sonny and I started playing around and we got into some fake sparing, and I told Sonny to watch out because I was better at jujutsu than he was and I don't know if you remember or not, but that's how that whole mess started about how to spell jujutsu. This was also when Sonny told me not to mess up or he was going to kick my ass. Sonny explained to me how much he cared for you and your sons and how much you were all like family to him, and how he felt you deserved the best because you were the best and I couldn't have agreed with him more.

Then there was the time you and I had our first big argument and Sonny and I had that fight. I called Sonny over that day. I don't know what made me do it, but I just had to hit something, someone, and that day I decided it should be Sonny. I thought you would never speak to me again for what I did that day. It really pissed me off to see you defending Sonny like that, but later, I saw your side of the whole thing and you were right, it was a childish thing for me to do. But you have to realize how I was feeling that day. It was like you were not appreciating my love for you. My feelings for you have always been genuine. Mia, you have to understand, you had me wrapped around your little finger from the very first time we met. I've told you many, many times before how much you meant to me. Only one other woman has held a piece of my heart and that was my grandmother. Until I met you, there has never been anyone that I have been this close to. But that day, it was like the closer I became to you, the more distant you became towards me. I did not want to lose you and it felt like we were drifting apart. It was like even when he wasn't there I always felt that Sonny was between us. Call it what you want, but I was never sure if I had your love one hundred percent of the time. I could write about this for hours, but what good would it do me now, right?

You don't know how many times I wanted to share with you my life before you, Mia. I don't know how to begin, so I'll just start at the beginning of the first day of my new life as Blair Janús Freeman, I'll never forget that day because that was the day I turned my back on all that I'd grown to know. So here is my story, beginning with day one of my new life.

I checked out my eighth floor two-bedroom apartment for the last time, making sure everything looked as it should be, with everything in its rightful place. The one thing I was taking with me was my usual garment bag, which held my customary two suits, a pair of dress shoes, and two days worth of clean underwear. All personal items, such as my toothbrush, deodorant and the rest of my toiletries, I had stuffed in the side pocket of my bag. Everything looked ordinary, to the casual observer as well as those with a more discerning eye.

Although I'd never invited anyone up to my apartment before, I knew the Goodbyte brothers had visited, as well as a couple of their minions whenever I was away doing a drop or a pick up out on the West Coast, and let's not forget the Federal Agents, I'm sure they've given me the good housekeeping seal of approval. For you see, I'd had installed four miniature video recorders in my apartment and could at any day and time pinpoint who had visited me while I was away from my apartment. I had removed the electronic surveillance equipment the day before my departure, and it was already on its way to a post office box in Sterling, Texas, and from Texas to Vancouver, B.C. I really didn't care who visited this place after today, because I would never be returning to this apartment or to the state of New York for that matter. I'd had my fill of this place and my lifestyle here. After fifteen years of working for the Goodbyte brothers I was ready to leave this business for good. I'd been planning my disappearance for years and now it was all coming into play; Dwight, AKA Smithy, Smith was disappearing from the face of the earth.

I was going to miss my apartment, in the years since I'd lived here, I'd made it my haven away from the hard street-life and the business I'd been forced into. I'd always been adamant about not doing business where I laid my head at night, and since moving up in ranks and having people under me, rarely was I seen on the streets anymore. I had a tendency of setting up different meeting places for all of my transactions, and no one but me knew of the actual locations until the day of the meeting. Rarely did I attend any of these meetings. Usually one or two of my Lieutenants would attend in my place. My clients never found out about the location of the meeting place until fifteen minutes before hand, and if they were late, or missed their appointed time then they would have to deal with my underlings. In all the time I'd been in this business, I'd never once had to do any of the dirty work. The Goodbyte brothers issued the orders, and I was the one who made it happen via one of my Lieutenants. I made it a habit to never look back once I'd assigned a hit. Of course I was capable of doing my own jobs, but a long time ago I'd chosen not to. I was an excellent shot, and even carried my own specially welded weapon, which a highly skilled gunsmith had made for my hands only. I have a seventh degree black belt in karate, and although I had kept it a secret from the Goodbyte brothers, I was also highly skilled in kickboxing and jujutsu. I wasn't sure if anyone was aware of my fighting skills, and when sparring at one of the local gyms, I would usually keep a low profile, while at the same time try to get a good workout. I made sure I kept my body in top condition.

Today was different though, at least for me it was. But as far as anyone else was concerned it was just like any other day in middle of the month, nothing out of the ordinary to show I wasn't coming back. I was off to Los Angeles for a major cash pickup, something I'd been doing for almost six years now. I glanced around the room one more time, making sure that nothing was out of the place. As a habit, I generally kept a clean apartment, with everything in its place; I even did my own cooking, and rarely ate out. When I did venture out to eat it was usually Italian food, and the places I frequented the most where located in my neighborhood, not far from my apartment. One good thing I had to say about New York City was you could always find a good Italian restaurant on just about every corner.

I started playing the sax in grade school, and I knew I was going to have to leave it behind. I looked longingly over at my saxophone, which was sitting in the corner of the living room on its stand. I loved my sax, and for the past ten years it had been my only salvation from my occupation, but my saxophone would be staying behind too. After all, it would be completely out of the ordinary for me to take it with me on my trip today. Everyone would surely suspect something then. I'd also made up my mind that there would be no room for my saxophone in my new life. Maybe I'd purchase a new one once I'd settled down, but then maybe not. After all that would be too much like Smithy, and after today I would no longer be that person.

As I stood in the foyer, I checked out Dwight for the last time. I ran my fingers through my shoulder length dreadlocks. These were going to have to disappear too; for my hair would become a part of my past as well. I'd grown fond of my dreadlocks and I wasn't too eager about the idea of cutting my hair. But, I knew that my hair, among other things would be a small price to pay in order for me to leave this lifestyle behind.

It was going to be nice not having to look over my shoulders all the time, and it would probably be a hard habit for me to break. In the beginning, when I'd been chosen to undertake these little jaunts, I'd been followed and watched. No one had to tell me I was being followed, or that there was someone watching me, because I could feel it. It was like the sun suddenly going behind a cloud, and the little hairs on the back of my neck would stand at attention. I would get a sudden chill and when I looked around, nine times out of ten there would be someone watching me. As far as being tailed, well it never bothered me because I could always spot them in a crowd. They all looked alike and just like any other lackey; they could always be ditched. I played their little game, and I played it well. I was one hell of a player too; after all I had been playing this same game since I was fourteen. The one difference was, I played by my own set of rules, even inventing new ways to do so. My first boss, Eddie, used to always advise me to keep my guard up, my ears opened, and to never volunteer for anything, that way I wouldn't look to eager, and never let the other guy know what I was thinking. But, the most important rule of all, which Eddie had instilled on me, was not to trust anyone but the man looking back at you in the mirror.

I knew the ones who followed me, for I could always pick them out in the crowd, no matter how hard they tried to blend in with the crowd. I knew how they moved, because I was moving the same way. Sometimes I thought I could even smell them. Right about now you're probably asking how I knew all of this? Well, that's because I used to have their jobs. I'd watched a few couriers on different occasions, so I knew whether or not I was being tailed and not just by my own people; but the Feds too. But over the years, and after my stepsister Lawanda had married into the Goodbyte family, I was watched less and less by the Family, and eventually, they had removed all tails from me a few years back. The Goodbyte brothers had started in the business at the early ages of 16 and 17, after their uncle had been injured in a failed takeover by a rival gang. Their family practically dominated the East coast drug business. I guess the Goodbyte brothers probably figured since I was a part of the family; they could now trust me with their goods and money. I smiled at my reflection, thinking if they only knew what I was about to do.

The Feds, well that's a different story, because they didn't exactly want me; they were after my employers, the Goodbyte brothers. I could have given up both brothers to the Feds a long time ago, all wrapped up like Christmas presents, but that wasn't the way I played the game. That would be my trump card against them if the Feds or the Goodbyte brothers ever ran across my path in my other life, which I doubted very much, because like I said earlier, I'd been planning my disappearance from this lifestyle since I was seventeen years old.

It was time to leave, so I quickly picked up my garment bag and headed out the door of my apartment for the last time. It was time to get this part of the day over and done with. I took the elevator down to the underground parking garage and made my way over to my Nissan. I could have had any car I wanted, but I only drove practical cars, nothing too showy, I left the glimmer and glamour up to the Goodbyte brothers. I always drove my own car to the airport when making a run, and I always parked my car in the long-term parking lot. I would then take a shuttle over to LaGuardia, and today was no different, except for my gun, which I normally left hidden in my apartment.

When I wasn't carrying it, I usually kept it in a small floor safe I'd built into the floor of my apartment. Once, when the unit beneath me had been vacant, and since the apartment building had hardwood floors, I'd simply removed a couple sections of the floor and had dropped in a small lead safe into the open hole. It was hard to see unless you knew exactly where to look, and to make it even harder to find, I'd put my old antique cherry wood desk, which sat flushed on the floor over that section of the floor. I was still able to access the safe by pulling out the bottom left-hand drawer. The rollers for the bottom drawers had been nailed and glued onto the wooden bottom. It was easy for me to remove the bottom section, allowing me access to the safe whenever there was a need, and at the same time keeping the safe out of sight from prying eyes. I also had the conventional safe, the one that I wanted everyone to notice, located in the wall behind the mirror, in the foyer.

Earlier that week I'd broken my gun down, and packed it and shipped it to Texas with my surveillance equipment. My weapon was one of a kind, melded from my specifications for my hand only. Even the bullets had to be specially ordered, just for this individual gun, and the only times I'd used it was at the shooting range.

I stepped off the parking shuttle bus and made my way to the curbside ticket booth, showed my I.D. to the attendant, confirming my e-ticket and checked in my luggage. Over the years since I'd been doing the pickups I'd become a creature of habit, not drifting off of my routine, oh no, nothing suspicious about good old trustworthy Smithy, just the usual routine for me. Out of the corner of my eye I spotted my first tail, he appeared quite bored with it all, and probably pissed off about being assigned to watch me. They were always very obvious to me, because they were the ones trying the hardest to blend in, but I had been expecting this. There would probably be two more at this airport and a couple of new ones once I reached LAX. It didn't matter though; I would lose them all when the time came.

After clearing security, I handed my first class ticket to the flight attendant and boarded the plane. Once on the plane I buckled my seat belt and settled back into my seat for the long flight ahead of me. I usually carried my own bottled water, and never ate or drank anything on the plane. I informed the flight attendant not to wake me, inserted a CD into my portable CD player, closed my eyes and drifted off to sleep with memories of long ago on my mind.

After my grandmother had passed away, and since the whereabouts of my Father was unknown, I was packed up and shipped off to my nearest living relative, who in this case happened to be Brenda, the Mother whom I never knew, and the Mother who would always be just plain Brenda to me.

My grandmother had raised me, the one real parent I'd ever known, in Atlanta, Georgia. She'd had custody of me since I was an infant. The story that my grandmother use to tell me, her son, Leon, who was my Father, had taken me from Brenda when I was barely three months old, putting me in the care of his mother until he could find employment. Ten years later he still had not returned for me and from what I was told he never went back to Brenda and her daughter Lawanda either. No one ever knew what really happened to Leon Smith after he had left my grandmothers' house. He just disappeared into the night. Years later, my grandmother had informed me that at the time there had been plenty of speculations concerning my Father's disappearance, but nothing was ever confirmed. That's how I had gotten the idea of disappearing. I figured if my father could do it, then so could I.

At the time of his disappearance, several people in the neighborhood had informed my grandmother about her son's drug problem, and how he would regularly get into trouble, searching for the perfect high. Some even said my father had probably met his demise caught up in a drug deal that had gone bad. Me, well I never had a thought about him, one way or the other. Although I'd seen pictures of him around my grandmother's house, I never knew him and my grandmother had given up on him going clean a long time ago.

While my grandmother had lain in the hospital dying of cancer, several attempts had been made by several different agencies, to contact her son. Even before she had become too ill to leave the house, my grandmother had put out a missing person report in an attempt to locate my father. It was if Leon had just dropped off the face of the earth, and after my grandmother had passed away, I was placed in the custody of Brenda.

Brenda was located by an old address that my grandmother had kept. I understand that right after I'd been dropped off by my dad, Brenda would call collect hoping to contact Leon for the first month or two after he'd disappeared from Atlanta, and my grandmother would always ask Brenda if she wanted her baby back. My grandmother had said that Brenda would never ask about me, and the few times when she had called were only to inquire whether or not if my grandma knew the whereabouts of Leon, and after a while, the calls finally stopped. Brenda did call back a year or so later, to tell my grandmother to stop sending pictures of me to her.

So with my suitcase full of clothing and ten, ten-dollar bills stuck in each sock, I arrived at Grand Central Station feeling lost and alone. The Department of Social Services had arranged my trip and a social worker had picked me up from the station. Brenda was supposed to meet me at Social Services to fill out the necessary paperwork and to arrange for her to collect a welfare check and medical benefits for me. Although Brenda had been contacted well in advance with the notice of my arrival, the office doors of Social Services were just about ready to close by the time she arrived to collect me.

At age ten, I was considered a very bright and intelligent child, and wise for my age. While other ten year olds were still in the fourth grade, I had been placed two grades ahead with the sixth graders, and had been on the honor roll at my school in Atlanta. I guess that came from living with my grandmother who had been a schoolteacher for over forty years, and although I was a bright child, her death had taken me quite by surprise.

My grandmother had hidden her illness well, right to the end, and it had saddened me when she had died from breast cancer. I didn't utter a word for the rest of the week after her death. Even my ten-year-old brain knew that with my grandmothers' death, went all my dreams and hopes of a bright future. Social services had searched high and low for Leon, but he was never to be found. With Leon being an only child, and my grandfather who had died in a car accident ten years before my birth, left me with one living relative; my birth mother Brenda and she didn't want anything to do with me. The child services department finally tracked Brenda down, but she flat out refused to accept me, and only after much prompting, did she finally offer to take me in.

The one good thing that happened out of all of this was the fact that I was my grandmothers' sole beneficiary to her estate. Although I didn't see the benefits of being my grandmothers' sole heir at that time, as I matured, I realized how much her gift to me mattered. In her will, my grandmother had left me everything she owned, which consisted of the sale of her modest three bedroom ranch-style house, and her life insurance policy. All were being held in a trust fund for me until I reached the ripe old age of twenty-one.

I can still remember my first day in New York, like it was yesterday. Even to my young eyes it was quite evident that everyone in the office was feeling sorry for me, and there were some whispers about me becoming a ward of the State if my absentee mother didn't come to claim me. Well Brenda finally showed up, and when she walked into the office, it was quite obvious what kind of a parent she would be. From the looks of her, I knew right then and there I had gotten my genes from my Father's side of the family. After filling out all the required paperwork and signing the necessary forms, Brenda practically drugged me out the door. I remembered how she had fussed the entire time, about how she had to come all the way downtown to pick up my black ass. I hadn't known it at that time, but that was her first indirect sentence to me. She would never speak directly to me, only at me. As we rode the subway to my new home, she sat across from me with an unreadable expression upon her face.

Once we had reached the apartment, Brenda took my suitcase from me and dumped everything out onto the filthy apartment floor. On her hands and knees she had gone through my things like a mad woman, shaking out my shirts and pants as though she was searching for something. After she'd gone through every single item in my suitcase, Brenda had looked up at me and mumbled something. I'd just stood there staring at her because I couldn't understand a word she had said.

"They told me that old woman was rich and that he was going to have some money, how come he ain't got no money?"

I shrugged my shoulders, reached into the breast pocket of my jacket and held out the letter my grandmother's attorney had given to me. The letter that I'd given Brenda was just a copy of the one the attorney had mailed to her. I knew this because my grandmother's attorney had been a good friend of my grandmothers'. He would come by on Sundays for dinner, and sometimes we would visit with him at his large farmhouse. He'd been the friend of my grandmother's who raised orchids. After my grandmothers' death, he had sat down with me and explained every little detail of my grandmothers will to me, in terms that I could relate to.

Brenda didn't take the letter from my hand, but just gave me a look of disgust before she told me, in her roundabout way, that she didn't know how to read. I unfolded the letter and read it to her and it stated what I already knew. The contents of my grandmother's estate were being held in trust for me until I reached the legal age of twenty-one. Brenda snatched the letter from my hand and demanded to know if there was a phone number where she could call and speak with the lawyer. I nodded my head and informed her that there was a number listed. After a few minutes of chewing on her bottom lip, and staring into space, Brenda returned the letter to me.

"Somebody will have to hold it til tomorrow," Brenda said in her uneducated voice, before turning and leaving the apartment, and I didn't see her again until almost dawn of the next morning. It was a good thing I had money of my own for there was nothing in the apartment to eat. I'd gone down to the corner market to buy a can of chili and a box of crackers. I slept curled up on the old worn sofa because there was so much soiled clothing upon the bed that you could hardly see the bed, and anyway I wasn't sure if I was supposed to sleep there or not. This routine went on for the first week I was there. I'd always clean up after my meal so Brenda never knew if I'd eaten or not, and she never asked. It was a good thing my grandmother had taught me the value of a dollar, and since math was my favorite subject in school, I'd calculated a budget in my head on how much money I could spend a day on meals to last me for a while.

In my suitcase, I had a bar of soap, deodorant and a tube of toothpaste, which would last me for a few weeks, since it was obvious I was the only one in the apartment with a hygiene routine. My first three months there I never once saw Brenda take a bath or shower.

As for my sister Lawanda, well I would not meet her for almost a year after being placed in Brenda's custody. I didn't know it at the time but Lawanda was in jail on charges of solicitation. After two weeks in Brenda's custody, she still hadn't enrolled me into school, until one day a social worker came out to the apartment and informed Brenda that if I wasn't place in school by the end of the week she would no longer receive benefits for me. The next day I was promptly enrolled in school and I loved it, because it was my haven away from the roach infested apartment where I had to live. I never considered the apartment my home, just a place to rest my head, for even at my young age I was determined to get out of this place just as quickly as I could.

Since I was living there, and thanks to my grandmothers' strict upbringing, I keep the apartment clean, even went in and straightened up the bedroom one day, but when Brenda came home she had yelled at me to stay the hell out of her room. So now I just kept the bathroom, living area, and kitchen clean which was easy since I did all of the cooking. I did my own laundry too, right in the bathroom in the old rusty tub. I usually hung my laundry out to dry on the tiny balcony off the living room in the summer, and during the winter I would string a rope over the tub to dry my clothes.

Once, after receiving her monthly supply of food stamps, Brenda had given me ten dollars worth and sent me out to buy food. I returned home from the store with two bags of groceries, and I could tell that she had been impressed with my purchases, and following the first time Brenda started giving me twenty dollars in food stamps and I'd go out and buy groceries for the apartment. I never knew what she did with the rest of the food stamps and she never told me.

When the check came in the mail, Brenda would take me along with her when she went to cash it. She would ask me how much of it would be left over after the rent and utilities had been paid. She found out that I was great with figures and I could do calculations in my head and quickly too. She may not have been good at parenting, but Brenda did understand the basic needs, and she would always make sure the rent and utilities got paid. She would hand me the money orders right then and there and I would address the envelopes and drop them into the mail.

Brenda started staying away longer and longer. I was never sure if she came home during the day while I was away at school or not, and I really couldn't tell because the bedroom always looked the same, messy. Sometimes I didn't see her until the end of the week, especially after she'd gotten her welfare check, and I was spending more and more of my time at the library after school. I even joined the school band, forging Brenda's name and using ten dollars of my sock money to pay the band fee for my instrument, which I never brought home with me. I would stay after school for an hour practicing on the saxophone, and then spend an hour at the library. I always made sure to be back at the apartment before dark, that lesson I'd learned the hard way.

One day I had lingered too long at the library and it had grown dark outside. On my way home, two teenage boys had accosted me and they started to beat the crap out of me. I do believe they would have killed me if this man in a big car hadn't stop and ran them off. I never knew it then, but the man who had saved me that night would turn out to be my mentor and friend. So, I made a promise to myself that it would never happen again, and everyday I would run home from the library as fast as I could run. I avoided anyone walking down the street, and you couldn't catch me standing still waiting for a red light to change either. I'd dash across the street at the first green light, and kept right on running until I reached the eight-unit brownstone on the corner of Fourth and Hood.

An elderly couple lived in the apartment on the first floor of the brownstone and they would look out for me when I was home alone, which was most of the time. On weekends I usually ran errands for them or went with them on their shopping days to help carry home their bags. They owned the one television set in the entire building, and on Friday and Saturday nights they would allow me to watch television, until it was time for me to head upstairs to bed.

I'll never forget the day I met my mentor, Eddie, for the second time. Mentor was what I called him, even though he was a drug dealer. Eddie took me under his wings and taught me about the mean life on the streets of New York. Eddie had also been the one who introduced me to martial arts, as well as being the one true friend that I could talk to about how much I missed my grandmother and my life back in Atlanta. Eddie was also Brenda's supplier.

"Brenda, I just can't be giving my shit away. It costs me money and I'm not going to be giving it away for free. I gots to go, I gotta couple of drop offs to make and old Goodbyte will have my ass if I ain't done with my run. He doesn't like it when I'm late dropping off his money." The tall man said. He looked down at me, and then at Brenda as we stood in the door of our shabby one bedroom apartment.

I suddenly felt ashamed, as the man's eyes took on Brenda's appearance. She hadn't bathed in days, and her breath, along with the crap on her teeth confirmed the fact that her teeth hadn't seen a toothbrush for a while either. Her eyes were all crusty and I doubt if she could get a comb through her hair, which was a tangled mess.

"Brenda, don't you be calling me if you can't pay. Woman, I ain't got time for none of your games."

"I told you last week that when I gets my check on Wednesday I'll pay up then," Brenda said wringing her hands around the hem of her shabby dress.

"Then I guess I'll catch you Wednesday then."

"Maybe we can work something out...?" she had a smile on her face as she asked this question.

"Woman, I said I'd catch you Wednesday, and feed that boy, he so skinny I can see right through him."

I looked up at her, but as usual Brenda never acknowledged the fact that I was even present. I'd been living with Brenda for five months now, and she hadn't said more than two whole sentences to me since the time I'd been here. Although there had been plenty of times when I'd caught her staring at me, her eyes always lifeless.

Brenda waved me aside with her hand; then it suddenly dawned on her that I was there. She paused as a look of what I could only describe as pure happiness crossed her face. "Take him!" Brenda said giving me a push forward. "Dwight might look skinny, but he can run, he can run real fast. He real good with numbers too. He'll do anything I tell him to. Dwight, go with this man and help him with his bizness," Brenda, said as she gave me another nudge out the door. "Dwight can make your drop offs for you, Eddie," Brenda said with an excitement in her lifeless voice that I'd never heard before.

The man looked down at me with a thoughtful look on his face. "I do have a lot on my plate today, and I have to be in two places at once. Boy, how old is you?"

"I'm ten, sir," I replied as I looked down at his shiny black and white shoes.

The man had laughed. "Sir? Boy, who you calling sir, my names Eddie," he said peering down at me, pushing his black hat back and away from his eyes. A squinting Eddie grinned down at me, like he didn't believe what he was seeing. Eddie had three gold teeth, and an infectious grin. "Boy," he begins, as he starched his head. "Don't I know you from some wheres? Ah, now I remember, you that skinny little boy that was gettin beat up a few weeks back. Them boys ever give you any more hard times?"

"No, sir."

Eddie laughed, as he placed his hat back on his head.

"Eddie, don't pay him no never mind, his grandmama got him like that." Brenda hated it when I spoke, she said I sounded funny, like a rich white person from down South, but I thought she sounded even funnier. So around her I spoke only when spoken to, which wasn't a lot. "His names Eddie, Dwight."

"Yes, Ma'am," I replied as I looked down at my feet.

So five months after arriving in the Bronx, I was working for a drug dealer. Brenda started staying home a lot more often after I started helping Eddie out. But that meant more for me to clean up once I got home from school. I continued with my band practice and still visited the library every day for an hour after school to do my homework and to reread my favorite books like, *The Three Musketeers* and *The Swiss Family Robinson*. One day Eddie questioned me about why

I was always late getting home from school. I'd lied and told him that I had to stay after school every day and spend time with my tutor, but somehow I knew Eddie didn't believe me, but he never commented on it. But I could always count on Eddie to be waiting for me in his big car everyday at the corner down the street from the library.

I would sit in the back seat of his big car and count out money into bundles of one hundred dollars each. I kept a log for him too, recording how much of each drug had been sold or picked up for the day. I guess you could say that thanks to Eddie, I learned at an early age all there was to know about cocaine, marijuana, crack, and heroin, which I discovered was Brenda's drug of choice. Eddie told me he'd been supplying her for over five years. Brenda had started off with marijuana, then crack, and finally she had worked her way up to the big horse, heroin. To keep the social workers off of her trail, Eddie said that Brenda would shoot up between her toes.

I guess you could also say that thanks to Eddie I knew this was not the life for me. My grandmother had wanted me to become a doctor and that was my goal, which I had shared with Eddie one day.

"Smithy," that's what Eddie had started calling me the second day I started working for him, and soon everyone else was calling me Smithy too. "With a head for numbers like yours, boy you can be just about anything you wanna be. Just don't get caught up in this game," he said waving his hand. "Get out fore you get sucked in too deep. I know you ain't had much of a say about any of this, being pushed into this shit by your own mama and all, but, Smithy, I must admit you gots smarts for someone as young as you are. Young man with a gift like yours, I know you'll do right and get out of the business while you're still young."

"Mr. Eddie, how long have you been in this business," I'd asked him one day.

"Since I was seventeen." He looked down at his big hands as they begin to shake. "I dropped outta school when I was twelve and got mix up with the wrong crowd, got into some shit, and spent some time in jail and prison too. Do you know how old I am, Smithy?"

"No sir."

"Not quite forty, but I look bout fifty. I'm the one who showed your mama how to shoot up tween her toes."

I found out later that Eddie was only thirty-five years old. He was never aware of it, but Eddie was the fortifying force in my life during those years. Even with no more than a sixth grade education, and having practically grown up on the streets of New York, Eddie was still able to show and tell me more about life than anyone else. Even at my impressionable young age, I was almost certain that I would have never grown into adulthood if it hadn't been for Eddie. He was even responsible for me attending a private school during my second year in New York. No more running home for me, and I no longer had to hide my interest in playing the saxophone, and I owed it all to Eddie.

Eddie had been my savior. Eddie had been the one who had talked Brenda into placing me into a private school, which he agreed to pay for. But being in a better school system and having Eddie to talk to still didn't stop me from longing for my old life back in Atlanta, especially when I had to return to the apartment every night. But at my new school, there were others that I could relate to, because there were a few other wiz kids attending that school beside me. Then there were those days during certain times of the year, like holidays and my birthdays. Those were the times that had been the worse for me, and it was during holidays when I missed my old lifestyle and my grandmother, who always made holidays and my birthdays special. Those were some lonely times for me, and it didn't change much as I grew up. The one big difference was I was able to change the way I was living, but by then I was a loner.

Exactly one year later, I came home from work one Friday evening and found Lawanda sitting in the living room on the old battered sofa that I used as a bed. She was smoking a cigarette and laughing and talking with Brenda who stood in the small kitchen preparing something on the stove. Neither was aware that I had entered apartment, which was another one of my traits, I was good at being invisible, blending in and observing my surroundings even at an early age. Although I had never laid eyes on Lawanda before that day, the moment I saw her, there was no doubt whatsoever who she was because she looked just like Brenda. The one difference was Lawanda was a younger, healthier version of her mother.

I was in for a couple of first occurrences that day as well, for Brenda was in the kitchen cooking something that smelled good, and that was rare in itself, because Brenda had never cooked a meal in the whole year I'd lived with her.

Before I entered the apartment, I could hear loud talking and laughing coming from the other side of the door, which made me stop in my tracks. I hesitated before entering the apartment, as I stood there listening to the festive sounds for a few seconds more. Although I recognized Brenda's hoarse voice, I had never heard her laugh before, which sounded like her speaking voice hoarse and raspy like.

I'd been shocked to hear Brenda's voice coming from the other side of the door, as it was full of hilarity and I was even more shocked when I heard another voice joining hers. Company was something we rarely got, except for the social worker and Eddie, but lately even Eddies' visits were rare because I delivered Brenda's daily fix home at the end of my day.

For the first month Eddie didn't pay me for my services because there had been a negative mark beside Brenda's name, but after Brenda's tab had been paid, I would sometimes get up to one hundred dollars a day which Eddie made sure that most of it went straight into my savings account and leaving me with an extra twenty in my pocket. I was certain that I was the only eleven year old at my old school with a savings account. Upon discovering that Brenda would take most of what I brought home, Eddie would make sure that I always had an extra twenty to give to Brenda because that was the amount she thought I was making. At first I didn't mind working for Eddie, it got me out of the apartment, and Eddie took me places and showed me things that I would have never had an opportunity to see and do if it hadn't been for him. Even though I had enough sense to stay out of trouble, I do believe if left up to my own devices I would have ended up as one of the many statistics like so many other black men at the time; ending up in prison, or I probably would have died on the streets of New York.

I stepped into the apartment and stood in one spot, waiting for Brenda and her daughter to acknowledge me. The room was smoke filled from their cigarettes and the air filled with the scent of grease from chicken Brenda was frying. "Smithy, say hi to your sister," Brenda finally said in a fit of laughter after she had noticed me standing by the door. Lawanda turned toward the door, with her horse-like features, a wide grin on her face. As I grew older and wiser, it didn't take me a long time to realize that most prostitutes were not being paid for their looks. Brenda sat a platter of fried chicken on the table, wiping her hands on her clothes, with a big grin upon her face.

"Ma'am?" They laughed as I looked from one to the other.

"This yo big sister Lawanda and she come home to stay." Brenda had a proud look on her face as she said this and to this day I could never figure out why she had been so proud of her daughter that day. Was it just the idea of Lawanda finally being home that had put that look upon Brenda's face? When Brenda had discovered I'd been placed two grades ahead of other kids my age, what I'd seen on her face at that time was disinterest.

I stood there staring at them.

"Well, hey there, little bro," Lawanda said as she rose and walked toward me. "He kind of cute mama, but, he too skinny," Lawanda commented as she reached out twisted my right ear. I yelped and jumped back, one hand up to my ear.

"Smithy, you got something for me?" Brenda asked.

"Yes, Ma'am."

"Boy don't just stand there like you ah ole lump on ah log."

I handed her two small Baggies, and then I headed for the bathroom to wash up for dinner. Upon entering the bathroom, I discovered that Lawanda had her personal things lying around the small bathroom, adding clutter to the normally bare room. I kept my personal things in a box, hidden away behind the living room sofa, along with my suitcase which contained all of my clothing. I left the bathroom returning to the living room to find only Lawanda left in the room.

"So, lil bro, how you like living in the big city? I know there's lot more things to do here than living in that ole hick town with your old grandma."

I was in the kitchen preparing a plate of food that Brenda had prepared. Besides the fried chicken, she had also prepared a box of Kraft macaroni and cheese, some canned string beans and a pan of cornbread. The food brought back memories of the way my grandmother used to cook. We always had a big meal on Sundays after church. I picked up a chicken leg and stared at the grease dripping from it. I dropped it back down onto the plate, and went in search of a dishtowel. I returned back to the table, picked up my chicken leg and plopped in down on the towel, rolling it around soaking up the grease. Of course my grandmother had been a much better cook than Brenda, I thought, as I took a bite of chicken before answering Lawanda's question. I was hungry and lately it seemed like I was hungry all the time. Eddie said that was because I was a growing boy, and that I needed to eat three healthy meals a day. So, Eddie had started going grocery shopping with me, making sure that I bought lots of fruits and vegetables. He knew all of the best soul food restaurants, which was his favorite and lots of times we would have dinner at one of the restaurants before he dropped me off at the apartment.

I wiped my mouth on the back of my hand and looked over at Lawanda. "I prefer living in Atlanta than New York any day. It's too crowded and dirty here, and all the Black people are on drugs."

Lawanda threw her head back and laughed. She laughed so hard that she almost choked on her own spit. "What you know bout drugs 'cept what Eddie tells you? Besides, not all of us are on drugs. I'm not doing them," she said taking a drag of her cigarette.

I watched as she leaned her head back and blew the smoke into the air. I hated the smell of cigarette smoke. Usually when Brenda smoked she would go into her room and close the door. I wanted to ask Lawanda to step out on the balcony, but decided to ignore it for the moment. "You may be right, Lawanda, but then you're a *whore*."

"What! Why you 'lil shit!" Lawanda shouted as she came running toward me, with her hands balled into fists, and anger in her eyes.

"Lawanda, leave that boy 'lone," Brenda said as she stepped back into the room with the dreamy look on her face she normally wore after she'd had her fix.

"Mama, did you hear what this 'lil punk called me?" Lawanda was still advancing on me, but I didn't move from my spot. My hand hung in mid-air over the pan of cornbread I was about to get into, and I had no idea what Lawanda would have done to me if Brenda hadn't spoken up.

"Hell, it's true ain't it? I said leave him lone," she repeated before picking up her pack of cigarettes and heading back toward her bedroom.

"One of these days mama won't be around and when that day comes, you'd better watch out," Lawanda said as she sat down and started putting on her shoes.

"You don't even know me, why do you dislike me?" I asked her.

"Because you're a little punk, that's why."

"Is it because I called you a *whore?*"

"Look you little shit, you call me a *whore* again and I'm kicking your ass, and I don't give a damn what mama says!" Lawanda jumped up and snatched her purse up from the table and headed for the door.

"Lawanda?"

"What!"

"If you don't like being called a *whore*, then why
do you do it?"

"*Fuck you*, you little punk!"

I heard a snicker of laughter and turned to find Brenda standing in the bedroom door with her cigarette dangling from her lips, and in her hand she held a pint of whiskey. "Your sister's a *whore* cause she likes to fuck," Brenda said removing her cigarette and taking a long drink from the bottle. She turned around and retreated back into her room, still chuckling to herself as she closed the door behind her.

I sat at the table and ate my dinner alone. I hadn't meant to make Lawanda angry with me, but everyone who knew her always called her a whore. I ran into people everyday who would ask me when that *whore* of a sister of mine was coming home. I didn't know she hated being called a whore, but Brenda had answered my question. I'd thought that maybe Lawanda was turning tricks for the money and I was willing to help her out by giving her some of the money from my daily pay. But since Lawanda was doing it for other reasons besides money, I couldn't help her.

I knew all about sex. My grandmother's attorney lived on a farm and I saw the animals doing it all the time. And since I had been living with Brenda, I had even walked in on her and one of her Johns once. But now, since I was bringing her daily fix home she no longer had to turn tricks, as Eddie had explained to me. But Brenda still disappeared from time to time and during those times I never knew where she was. Eddie said that she was probably hanging out at one of the numerous crack houses that practically dominated the neighborhood.

I hated living here and I thought about how to leave this place every single day of my young existence. The whole neighborhood had an odor to it as well as the people. By the age of fourteen I was finally able to move out of that roach and rat infested building and into a different area. Due to my income from Eddie, which had grown considerably, we were now able to afford something a lot better, so I moved Brenda and Lawanda into Eddies' neighborhood and I found a large studio apartment for myself not too far away. Since I was under-age, Eddie leased the studio for me in his name. At first Brenda had complained, and in the end she had downright refused to leave, but after I'd explained to her that I was leaving regardless if she wanted to or not and without me she would no longer receive her monthly welfare checks and food stamps. I also reminded her that she would not have the funds to pay the rent to continue to live in our old apartment. After I'd explained this to her, Brenda finally decided to move in with Lawanda.

Brenda died from an overdose of heroin two months before my seventeenth birthday. The night she died, Brenda had been visiting the old neighborhood at one of her regular hangouts. Her body was found the next day in an alley, with a piece of elastic still tied around her arm, she'd starting shooting up in her arm about six months before her death.

Lawanda got the call; she was also the one who went down to the morgue to identify the body. When the time came, I paid for the funeral arrangements, but I did not attend the funeral. There had never been any love between us, so I doubted if I was missed at the funeral. I had tried to do everything in my power to make Brenda comfortable by providing a decent roof over her head and food on the table, but Brenda would always be just another junkie to me, nothing more.

After graduating early from high school, I received several scholarships toward college, and decided to accept one from NYU. I no longer wanted to be a physician, and took business management and finance classes instead. I still didn't enjoy the lifestyle I was living, but I guess you could say that the money was good and it would also be my ticket out of this life. Although I was staying on campus, I still worked with Eddie after classes and on weekends. While working for Eddie, I was raking in more than four grand a month. Eddies' addiction was slowly killing him as well. He had been diagnosed with HIV three years ago and full blown AIDS by the time I had completed my first year of college. Contrary to his doctors' orders, Eddie didn't stop his old habits, the same habit that was killing him. He refused any type of medication as well, which would have prolonged his life. I believe this was Eddie's way of getting out of the business. Eddie told me he was tired, and he was ready to lie down and rest his head. After his recommendation to the Goodbyte brothers, I was assigned his full route, and another area as well, which made my earnings triple.

Three years later, I graduated at the top of my class, and moved into a two-bedroom apartment in downtown Manhattan, miles away from everyone and everything that I had grown to know. Eddie wasn't around at my graduation, for he had died during my second year in college. A few weeks before his death, Eddie had given me documents stating I was the beneficiary to all of his assets, which included a safe deposit box containing over half a million dollars as well as instructions for his burial. A couple of days before he died, Eddie had informed me he had no family or relatives and that I was the son he never had. He then advised me to get out of the business, and to live my dreams. Twenty-hours later, Eddie went into a coma and never woke up. Eddie hadn't known it at the time, but I already had one foot out the door.

Eddies' remains were cremated as per his request, and I scattered his ashes in Niagara Falls. Eddie had always wanted to visit Niagara Falls, but during his whole tenure as a drug dealer he'd never traveled outside of his territory. His apartment contained travel magazines, and other books on Niagara Falls, which was only a few hours drive north of the New York City. I never understood why he never visited, and now he was there to stay.

I was still paying the rent for Lawanda, but the word around town that she was seeing Webster Goodbyte, the younger of the two Goodbyte brothers, and I was looking forward to not supporting her any more. Lawanda and I were never really close. The one thing we had in common was Brenda, and in my book that wasn't much to warrant any affection between the two of us. Occasionally when she was broke or needed something, Lawanda would try the sister act and I'd just give her whatever it was she wanted just to be rid of her. I was quite happy when she and Webster Goodbyte finally got married two weeks after my twenty-first birthday.

Per my instructions, my grandmother's inheritance was placed into a Swiss account the day I turned twenty-one. The amount deposited was a considerably large amount of money. There was her life insurance policy, and the cash from the sale of her estate had been another seventy-five thousand dollars, plus whatever interest had accrued over the last eleven years. Then there was the college fund my grandmother had started for me, which I hadn't used because of my scholarships and Eddie's generosity. My college fund account had over seventy-five thousand in it, some of it I had used to buy myself a car. So that amount of cash, plus eleven years of interest was sitting in my Swiss account along with other funds I had accumulated over the years.

I was never hurting for money, and my Swiss account would be my ticket out of this business. I'd also planned on taking my last pickup with me, because I felt I'd earned it along with the usual ten percent I'd been skimming from the top over the span of the past five years.

So, Mia, that's pretty much my life story, the condensed version or the *PG* rating if you will. Mia, please don't hate me for not sharing my story with you before now, but I just could never find the right time to share this ugliness with you. I assumed the least you knew about my past the better.

Do me a favor will you, tell the guys they will always be my *boys.* One more thing, and then I'll bid you *adieu.* The day I met you at the hospital when Maurice became ill, I can't tell you how I almost died that night. It tore me apart when Sonny came into the room and you and Anthony just fell into his arms. I consider myself to be a tough guy, street smart and dangerous to some. But that day, when I saw the three of you together, I asked myself if I'd ever seen a normal happy family before, because there was one standing right in front of me. Even though it was a sad day for everyone, and the three of you were bawling your eyes out- you had each other, and it came to me how truly alone I was. I have been on the run for a long time, hiding and lying for such a long time, I didn't even know what normal was anymore. I had to leave the room to compose myself, because what I saw that night was a normal family unit, supporting each other and I wanted to be a part of that family. You'll never understand how much I hungered for what you and Sonny had. I wanted to be normal again and I saw myself in Sonny's place, and it was then that I knew I would ask for your hand in marriage. There's so much more I want to write, so many things I want to say to you, and do to you one last time. I want to hold you close and kiss your wonderful lips. Make love to you, breathe your scent, and hold your hand and so much more. But, baby, if you're reading this, my time has run out.

Dearest, Mia, I want you to know that you will always be my heart, my love, and my joy. I loved you the best I knew how and my only regret is I'm not with you now. I'll love you forever and always. Take care, my love, and live your life to the fullest, and remember, beauty is in the eye of the beholder, and I'm beholding you.

All my love, Blair Janus Freeman aka Dwight Smith

CHAPTER TWENTY-TWO

Going through Blair's notebooks made that night the second longest night in my life, and by nightfall, Sonny and I had gone through all the notebooks and I had succeeded in watching only about the first five minutes of the first videotape, because of the violence it contained. There were people being executed, drugs being used, sold, and produced, money laundering, and the raping of young girls and women. Sonny watched all the tapes, wearing headphones, because I didn't want to hear what was happening on them. While he had watched the tapes in the living room, I had retired to my bedroom and reread the notebook Blair had left for me.

Between the two of us, we'd damn near finished off the entire bottle of whiskey, and a large pepperoni and sausage pizza. Sonny and I had taken turns reading the contents of the other three notebooks, which were like journals, with names, dates, time, and places where executions had taken place, money laundering drop houses, crack houses, prostitution rings, law enforcement officers and government officials on the payroll, rival gang territories, names, ages, and addresses of family members of everyone listed, and the list went on and on.

I looked up from my place on the bed when Sonny entered the room.

"Done," Sonny said as he turned and headed back into the living room. By the time I'd entered the living room Sonny was standing at the window, silently staring out at the night. Stopping next to him, I reached out for his hand as I too stared out into the night. Life below us continued on as pedestrians, cars, trolleys and buses navigated through the busy streets. The people below living their normal lives, as my mind took in all that had happened in these last few weeks, and the years of turmoil Blair must have endured trying to live a life of normalcy. And I wondered how many of those strangers on the streets below were living a secret life. Sonny and I stood quietly for about ten minutes. I think we were pretty much in shock from what we had discovered about Blair.

Sonny spoke first, giving my hand a reassuring squeeze before releasing it. "Shit, I can't believe this stuff. This kind of shit only happens in the movies," Sonny said, as he stretched, yawning loudly as he raised his arms high in the air over his head, before he begin to pace back and forth. "I had no idea shit like this could happen in real life. Who would have thought, Blair Freeman, AKA Dwight 'Smithy' Smith was into some shit like this. Those tapes were brutal, just brutal! Mind boggling, brutal shit! Fucking blew me away! This is some way out mother fucking shit," Sonny said slamming his fist into the wall. "Damn! Shit so deep, I want to change my name and go into hiding. After reading and watching those tapes, I feel like I was a part of that filthy mess."

I sat down on the sofa, my hands covering my face listening to Sonny, who had been just as verbal during the time we were reading the notebooks and while he had watched the video tapes. Then it all hit me, and I burst into tears.

"Mia, I'm sorry," Sonny said as he sat down next to me, hugging me close. "I can't believe I introduced you to Blair."

"How could you have known about his past? Blair had us all fooled, Sonny," I replied before going into details about Blair's life.

After I'd finished giving Sonny a brief look into Blair's life, he said something I thought I'd never hear him say and he was actually taking Blair's side. "Mia, I don't think that Blair was trying to fool us, like he said, he was weary of his old lifestyle and he wanted out. Falling in love with you was the real thing. I guess Blair assumed the least we knew of his past, the better off we'd all be. I don't believe Blair was involved in any of that mess, other than being the moneyman. Those tapes, the focus was off a bit on them all. I think Blair may have been doing some undercover filming, putting his own life at risk just to get this information on tape. And those logs...it's all so mind boggling. Did you notice the dates; he's been keeping records for years. This *shit* is deep!"

I agreed. "It's horrible, his own mother. If Blair had told me about all of this in the beginning he would still be alive today. I would have never called his sister if I'd known about his past. Blair should have trusted me. Why didn't he trust me, Sonny?" Then it all hit me, I'd killed my own husband by calling his sister and informing her of Blair's whereabouts. "God, why didn't I listen to him and leave well enough alone? I can't believe I was worried about not being able to contact Lawanda to tell her that her brother was dead. She was the one behind all of this in the first place."

"Don't do this to yourself, Mia. Blair trusted you, and he loved you very much. I don't know, I guess Blair figured you wouldn't love him anymore if you found out about his past."

"I *killed* him, Sonny, I killed Blair and I'll never forgive myself, never." The tears started flowing again as the realization from the impact of my words shook me up even more. "I should've stayed out of his affairs. What the hell was I thinking? I didn't know the magnitude of all this, if I'd known, I- I- I don't know if I would have stayed with him or not. Maybe, yes, I can't say. By trying to repair Blair's relationship with his sister, my actions had only lead to his death, and I'm sure Blair had known how his sister's husband had found him in the end. And poor sweet Blair, loving me as he did, he never questioned me about it; his one concern that night had been to see me to safety. Dear God, I'm responsible for my husband's death." I looked up at Sonny through teary eyes at his blurred image.

"Listen to you, stop it. Stop talking like that. You didn't know. Mia, Blair loved you with all his heart he would never blame you for what happened. If anyone was at fault then it was Blair."

"Blair knew I would never stop loving him. All that was in the past, long before any of us met. I don't know, maybe it would have made a difference, but he should have told me regardless, and maybe, just maybe he- he would still be alive today," I sobbed crocodile tears, missing Blair more than ever. The realization of what Blair must have gone through tearing away at my heart.

"Please don't do this to yourself, Mia. Blair knew eventually they would find him, look at this stuff," Sonny said with a wave of his hand. "There's enough evidence here to put the Goodbyte brothers and their minions in prison for the rest of their natural born lives! And remember the list of names of all the government officials and policemen on the take. This shit is big, way bigger than anything we could ever imagine!"

I stepped back from him as his words started me to thinking. I wipe away the tears from my face. "*Oh my God!* Sonny, do you know what this means? The information from these notebooks will prove that the fire and Blair's death was not an accident. If we give the notebooks and tapes to the police there'll be an investigation, everything will come out in the open."

"Mia, we should give this some more thought. If there is an investigation, your name and your face will be in all the papers and on TV, and then who knows, the Goodbyte brothers might come searching for you next. Remember, Blair took large sums of money from them and I'm sure they're looking to get their money back."

"Sonny, I just can't let them get away with *murdering* Blair."

"I don't know what to tell you, baby. Even if we mailed all this stuff anonymously to the FBI, there would still probably be an investigation."

"But how will they know that Blair was a part of this? Blair's name isn't mentioned in any of these journals. He's only known as *Smithy*. We can drop them off in the mail and let the FBI handle the rest." My tears had ceased, as this idea came to light.

Sonny had resumed his pacing back and forth about the room, his right hand tapping the right side of his leg. "I don't know. Maybe we should just call his sister and tell her exactly what we have here, and then let her husband know that if anything should ever happen to you, then this information falls in the hands of the FBI."

I started pacing back and forth along with Sonny, as Sonny's words hit home. "You think they're watching me?" I asked suddenly aware of the possibility.

"Maybe not. Why should they, Blair's dead..."

"Oh shit! Sonny, what's going on here? I didn't want to know about his past. I didn't want to know about the Goodbyte brothers, and I damn sure didn't want a set of crime videotapes," I said raking the whole lot of it off the table and down onto the floor. Sonny was by my side in an instant, holding onto me. "It's bad enough that I have to deal with Blair's death, now I have to deal with this *shit* as well. Sonny, what am I going to do?"

"First we're going to find a safe place to put all of this in-"

"Safe place?" I let out a loud puff of air. "Who cares about this shit, what about me, Sonny? What happens to me now? Will I ever be safe?" Sonny's words came back to haunt me over and over again later that night. Now that I had it, what was I going to do with the information Blair had left me? Should I give it to the local authorities? Or should I just destroy the whole lot and go on as if it all never happened? Or, was there someone out there watching me?

CHAPTER TWENTY THREE

Days later Sonny and I went with his idea of anonymously send-ing all the notebooks, except the one Blair had written exclusively for me, as well as the videotapes to the FBI, then we had held our breath as we waited and watched CNN and read the NY Times for any reference to the Goodbyte brothers. Sonny wanted to make copies of everything before sending it away. I didn't care what he did with it all, just as long as he took it out of my sight.

It was a long wait, but seven weeks after mailing off the package, the two Goodbyte brothers were arrested for drug trafficking and numerous murder charges spread out over a period of several years. The FBI took all the credit, claiming that after years of being under investigation, they had now accumulated enough evidence to convict the Goodbyte brothers, and to break up their ring of drug trafficking. The bust shook up New York City, because the investigation incrimi-nated high ranking State, City, and Federal officials as well.

Six months later, Anthony's job transfer finally came through and he moved to Atlanta. Although with me now living at the condo, Anthony was no longer in a hurry to leave, not wanting to leave me on my own. He kept changing his mind, claiming he wanted to stay in San Diego instead. But after many discussions, I finally convinced Anthony that it would best if we all got on with our lives.

I knew I would be okay on my own, and after Sonny and Macey had promised Anthony that one of them would stop by to check on me, Anthony had left for Atlanta. Maurice was taking some sum-mer classes to make up for the time off he'd taken in December, so I wouldn't be seeing him this summer unless I took a trip to Atlanta. I never confided with either of my sons about Blair's past life, or about the contents of the package, and Sonny had opted to keep it from Macey as well.

I'd returned back to work at the agency and things were slowly getting back to normal. I was still experiencing sleepless nights from time to time, and when morning came I would call Sonya and inform her I wouldn't be able to make it into work or, arriving to work midday or sometimes not at all. But these occurrences happened less and less as I got on with my life. I had no idea what I was going to do now, and I tried not to think too far into the future taking it one day at a time.

True to their word, Sonny and Macey routinely stopped by for a visit. Sonny's visits were more frequent than Maceys', since The Egg Roll was not far from the downtown area. Sonny and Maceys' relationship seemed to be doing much better these days now that Macey was pregnant. There would be a little Steward running around this time next year.

Claudia had slowly inched her way back into my life. She'd started off by calling me every evening right after Blair's death to see how I was getting on, and one night during one of our many conversations; Claudia had even apologized for her behavior the night of my wedding reception. After realizing that I had harbored no bad feelings toward her, Claudia finally got around to inviting me to lunch and we even caught a movie once. Claudia was with me when I finally went shopping for new furniture and Sonya tagged along as well.

Now, here it was the middle of summer and today I was having a girl's day out. I had invited Claudia, Macey, and Sonya over for brunch. It was my way of thanking them for being there for me in my time of sorrow and to invite them to my house warming, even if it was my old place. This was the beginning of my new life and my newly decorated condo would be a reflection of my new beginning.

"Hey, Mia, what's new?" Claudia asked as I held the door open for her.

"Claudia, you're a little early aren't you? How are you?" Actually she was about thirty minutes early.

"Can't complain," she said as we exchanged hugs and a quick peck to the other's cheek. "This is for you." She handed me a package all wrapped up in bright colorful paper with a big fat red bow.

"Thank you. This paper is very festive, what's the occasion?" I asked her as I lead the way down the hall and into the dining area. Claudia had begun to dress very modest of late, almost like one of those old fashioned eighteen-century school teachers. Her skirts and dresses were down to her knees, and I'm not talking about the stylish kind either. Claudia's new look was spinster in appearance. Every since Claudia had started dating her new man, she had changed overnight. Even though her style had change, at least this guy really seem to really care about her, and that was the biggest change in Claudia's life, she had finally found someone who really cared for her. I'm not sure whose idea her new wardrobe was.

"House warming present. Nice table, nice spread," Claudia said as she picked up a raisin muffin and bit into it.

"You didn't have to bring me anything; all that was required was your company." I'd gone all out in setting the table for our brunch. On my last shopping expedition, I'd bought all new china, tablecloths, placemats, and candlesticks. I'd even replaced the old silverware, and gotten rid of all the old kitchen clutter and replaced everything, right down to the dishtowels. Right now my new beveled glass dining room table was sporting my new set of placemats, along with a pretty floral centerpiece gracing the center of the table. I'd placed candles and flowers throughout the room, which gave the whole area a soft feminine appearance, which was just the right ambiance for an all female brunch. "Thank you," I replied as I opened her gift. It was a lovely vase of oriental design, to match my décor.

"You're welcome," Claudia replied as she glanced nervously about the room. "Mia, I wanted to get here before the others because I wanted to tell you- to let you know I'm here for you. If you ever need anything or should you want to talk I'll always be here for you. I know I wasn't much of a friend to you during my *downtime*," Claudia said with a smile. That's what Claudia called her addiction days, "*downtime*." She reached out for my hand as she continued. "I know how much you loved Blair and I know you're missing him right now, but it will get better with time. After my grandfather passed away you were a *true* friend to me, even after all the horrible stuff I did and said to you and Blair. You were there for me after you found out about my addiction, and it is because of you that I'm clean today, if you hadn't been there for me, there's no telling what or where I'd be-" Claudia couldn't finish her sentence, as tears clouded her eyes.

"You'd be right here where you are now. Eventually you would have figured it out on your own, Claudia, and found the help you needed," I said as I gave her hand a gentle squeeze. Claudia had finally found her niche in life. She was a counselor for a substance abuse rehabilitation center, counseling those who had fallen through the cracks. For the first time since I'd known her, Claudia seemed to be happy; even her language had cleaned up considerably, and she was dating a decent man, who was the director at the facility where she worked. Life works in mysterious ways, I'd lost my love and Claudia had found hers.

"I used to be so jealous of what you had with Blair. I thought I could never be happy, that is until I met Gary, and then everything *came* together for me."

"You don't have to say another word-"

"But I do," Claudia replied as she looked down at her feet. "I hated you, Mia. After you and Blair starting dating, I couldn't *stand* you. You were always smiling and so happy go lucky, and it just irked the hell out of me seeing you so happy all the time. You had what I wanted, Mia. You had a good man and here I was laying around with the scum of the earth, and I thought- I thought I had so much more than you, and I did, too. I had money, I had the looks, every-thing...but you got what I've always wanted, you got the *man!* Blair should've been my *man*, not yours and I hated him as well, coming into your life and giving you what I've always wanted. I know now that you two were in love, and you didn't marry him because of your business." Claudia sat down heavily in a chair at the table, head in her hands, shaking her head from side to side.

I was speechless, and angry as hell because she was bringing this shit up all over again. After a few minutes of silence, Claudia finally looked up at me, and I saw the tears streaming down her face. But her tears didn't move me, not as much as her words had. "It's all water under the bridge, Claudia," I said with a shake of my head. "All those times Blair would tell me how you would try and throw yourself on him. Blair would always tell me what transpired after each incident he had with you, and I thought it was just a little friendly flirting. Oh, don't get me wrong," I said to Claudia, as her tears were replaced with a surprised look on her face. "I've always believed him, but at times I thought he was exaggerating, but after that night at our wedding reception-" I said with a shake of my head. "At first I thought it was some kind of male testosterone thing going on, you know? I never dreamed it was as bad as Blair made it out to be. Why? Because I thought you were my *friend*, Claudia, and *friends* would never do anything as low down and dirty as what you tried to do to me. Why would you do something like that anyway, Claudia! Huh? Why would you do something like that?" I asked again, as I snorted loudly through my nose, before twirling around and heading back into the kitchen. I began to bang pots and pans and dishes around the countertop like they were plastic.

"I'm sorry, Mia, I know I should've told you all of this a long time ago," Claudia said from behind me. "I knew you'd be angry with me and I didn't- I couldn't risk losing your friendship. Mia, you're the one true friend I have."

I spun around to face Claudia, so quickly, that I became dizzy, and made Claudia jump about a foot away from me. "Well, I guess you can say that we're even now, huh, Claudia? I fired you and you tried to sleep with my husband. Does that sound about even to you, Claudia? Even though I fired you only once, I understand that you came on to Blair numerous times."

"Mia, I never meant to hurt you-"

"So, what was it, Claudia? You thought I was too old and too fat to keep a man like Blair? Was that what you thought, Claudia? Old fat Mia doesn't need a man like Blair. You would have been a much better catch, right? Biracial, rich, thin, just what every Black man dreams of, right! Except for one, and that was Blair."

"Mia, I said I was sorry-"

"Well, Claudia, here's a news flash for you as well, I could only tolerate you up to a point. Shocking huh? Most of the time I felt sorry for you because I knew you were only seeking attention, something I don't believe you got a lot of as a child. When I invited you over, or hung out with you, I was trying to show you the other side of life. Trying to prove to you that those without and those not as well off as you could live a pretty decent life. I included you in of my life only because I thought eventually you would realized that everyone who hung out with you didn't always want something from you, Claudia. I thought maybe Sonya and I would rub off on you, and to prove that you could be happy with a little as well as with a lot, something I learned the hard way. In my book, you had everything, and you still wanted what I had," I said with a wave of my hand, making Claudia take another step back. "But Blair's dead and there is nothing you or I can do to bring him back." I smiled as tears stung my eyes. "You should've kept this shit to yourself. It's old news and nobody wants to hear it anyway, Claudia." Neither of us said a word for the longest time, me staring at Claudia, and Claudia with her head bowed, staring down at the kitchen floor. The front door buzzer sounded, bringing us out of our zombie-like stances.

I took a deep breath, stepped over to Claudia and wrapped her in a long embrace. After a brief second, Claudia returned my hug and we didn't break our embrace until the buzzer sounded again, announcing the arrival of Macey and Sonya, who had carpooled to the downtown area. I didn't care about what went on then, this was another life for me and I doubt I would ever see Claudia again after today anyway. I'm glad she had found happiness with her new man, but I wasn't in the mood to tolerate her anymore.

After a round of hugs and kisses, the four of us sat down to a pitcher of Mimosas. After catching up on current events, we started in on brunch. Earlier that morning I had purchased several different types of pastries from the neighborhood bakery, and we munched on those, as well as the homemade waffles I'd prepared earlier in my brand new state of the art waffle maker, along with several different toppings ranging from strawberries to peaches, and to top that, there was plenty of fresh whipped cream. For the traditionalists amongst us, I also had warm maple syrup. I'd fried some bacon, sausage, and ham, along with some home-style potatoes and scrambled eggs. The food was plenty and the level of noise in the room made us sound like a group of twelve instead of four.

The room was abuzz with the sounds of our loud talking and laugher, and in the background my CD player was bumping out a Sade tune. I suddenly realized my place hadn't seen this much action in months. My earlier conservation with Claudia was now pushed to the back of my mind, as I glanced around the room at my friends, smiling at the fun-loving atmosphere of the room. I couldn't remember the last time I'd truly smiled, or enjoyed the company of others for that matter. Blair was dead, and as I had reminded Claudia, there was nothing in the world that would bring him back to me. Blair had been my greatest love, and I would always hold the memory of him in my heart, but it was time to join the living again. I knew it was going to take some time for me to fully recover from his death, and I wouldn't be able to enjoy events like this everyday, but when good times like this came along I was going to roll with the flow.

I rose from my chair, tapping on the crystal glass of Mimosas; the gentle tinkling sound of the spoon hitting the lead crystal got the attention of the others. Standing at the head of the table, I glanced around the table my smile growing larger by the second, as I looked at my circle of friends.

"I shall keep this short and sweet," I begin as Sonya laughed from behind her napkin.

"That's how she always starts our meetings at work and they usually run an hour or two," Sonya snickered, as Claudia and Macey joined her.

"Okay, I can take a hint. This is going to be short and sweet," I said with a smile. "I want you all to know that the three of you have been terrific friends to me during my time of need, and this little gathering is just my way of saying thank you, thank you all for being there for me. Thank you for letting me cry on your shoulders, and for listening to me rant and rave at all hours of the night, but most of all,

I would like to thank you all for being my friend. For without you three beautiful women by my side, I don't believe I could have made it this far." I raised my champagne glass high in the air, and I waited until the three of them had raised their glasses. "To friendship."

"Friendship," Claudia spoke as she raised her glass.

"Friendship," Macey said as she took a sip from her glass.

"To Mia, stay strong my, *sistah*," Sonya toasted.

After brunch I gave them a tour of my newly decorated condo, I'd even redecorated the loft, and they all commented on how it looked like a different place.

"Mia, I really like what you've done to the place," Sonya remarked later as she helped me load the dishwasher. "Tell me if it's none of my business, but has Claudia spoken to you?"

"About?"

"You and Blair, and how she was always throwing herself on Blair."

I was about to place a glass into the dish rack, and I stopped to look at her. "You knew about that?"

"Claudia stopped by the office one day and told me. She was feeling all guilty and she asked me what she should do."

"And I suppose you told Claudia to speak with me?"

"Yes, I did. I told her to talk to you, get the shit out in the open. Mia, you and Claudia have been friends for a long time, and Blair is dead. I mean, what's the worse that could happen?"

I turned around and resumed my task of loading the dishwasher thinking the worse had already happened.

"Are you planning on selling your condo and moving to Atlanta?" Sonya asked after a long silence.

"I really haven't planned that far out ahead yet, Sonya. I was thinking of maybe buying a home in Atlanta, that way Anthony and Maurice would have a place to stay," I said as I stopped and slowly glanced about the room. "To be honest with you, Sonya, I don't know what I'm going to do."

Sonya nodded. "Mia, don't worry about it, everything's going to be all right. You just have to take it slow, Mia, one day at a time," Sonya said as she pulled me into her arms.

Later, we all piled into my new SUV and headed out to the mall in Mission Valley. We did a little shopping and after that we took in a movie before heading back downtown as our delightful day came to an end. Unbeknownst to my three friends, as a thank you gift to them all, I had made arrangements with a local florist to have a bouquet of flowers delivered to them once a month, for the remainder of the year.

It wasn't too long after that day that I started receiving fresh orchids on a monthly basis. At first I thought one of my sons was sending them to me, but after much questioning from me, and denials from them, I moved in on to Sonny next and he also denied sending me flowers. I finally came to the conclusion that maybe it was Claudia, Macey, or Sonya, reciprocating my gift of flowers to them. So I decided to stop playing private detective and just let them keep their little secret since it was such a sweet gesture, even if the orchids reminded me of Blair.

"You'd better start eating and put some meat back on those bones."

"I don't have much of an appetite these days."

Sonya shook her head, as she placed a file on my desk. "You know Blair wouldn't want you wasting away like that."

"Thanks for the advice," I said as I sat down.

"When was the last time you spoke to your sons?"

"I call my sons every night, thank you very much. Don't you have some work to do?"

"Uh hum, don't try and change the subject. They know you're not eating?"

"Sonya, I'm okay, stop worrying about me," I replied as I gave her a pat on the shoulder, just as the buzzer on the office door sounded. I peeked out into the hall as Sonny walked up.

"Hey, Sonny, how you doing? How's Macey?" Sonya asked

"Sonya, how are you? I'm doing okay, and Macey is doing well, too," Sonny replied, as he gave her a hug. "I just stopped by to see how my girl is doing."

"You don't have to check up on me, Sonny."

"Feel like lunch?"

"Yeah, take her butt out to lunch, Sonny, and make her eat something. *Look* how skinny she's getting," Sonya added, as she gave my arm a squeeze.

"Sonya, don't you have an appointment or something?"

"I can take a hint," Sonya said as she left the room.

"She's right, you know, you're losing too much weight."

"Sonny, I'm fine. Don't you have something to do?"

"Okay, I can take a hint too. Walk me out to my car."

After seeing Sonny to his car, I ran into Sonya, as she was on her way out. "I'm leaving early today, I'll see you tomorrow," I said as I headed for my office.

"You know what?" Sonya said as she followed me back inside.

"What?"

"That man's in love with you."

"Sonya, Sonny and I have been friends for a long time," I said wearily as I sat down.

"I'm not talking about that kind of love; I'm talking about real love."

A few weeks after I started receiving the orchids, I had of one the worse nights ever since Blair's death. When morning came around, I called Sonya, informing her I would not be coming in at all that day. It had been such a bad night I couldn't get my gears in working order that morning. I was feeling so wretched, that I spent most of the morning in bed alternating between crying and eating or just feeling plan miserable. I was missing my sons, but most of all I was missing Blair, and I wondered if the pain would ever go away?

The CD player in my bedroom was on, and it was belting out the best of Peabo Bryson, and the old love songs were playing over and over again. I knew the melancholy songs were just adding to my misery, but I was too depressed to get up and change it. It was almost eleven in the morning, and I'd just polished off a pint of pistachio ice cream and some microwave popcorn when the phone rang. Anthony or Maurice had a habit of calling me, sometimes three four times a day, and without giving it a second thought, I reached out and picked up the phone.

"Mia, why aren't you at work?"

It had to be the last person in the world I wanted to speak with. "Because I didn't feel like going in."

"Did you have a bad night?"

"*Yes.*"

"Are you still seeing your therapist?"

"*Yes.*"

"Did you tell her you were having trouble sleeping at night?"

"*Yes.*"

"Come on, Mia, talk to me. So, what else did she say?" Sonny asked patiently.

"She told me what I already knew; I'm depressed and I should be taking *Prozac* or some other anti-depressant medication. She doesn't want to prescribe sleeping pills because of my previous history with them."

"No, you don't need any of that shit. I'm coming over."

"Sonny, I'm really not in the mood for company right now."

"Okay, see you in about twenty minutes and remember I have a key."

"Then you can let yourself in," I said as I hung up the phone. Exactly twenty minutes later, Sonny knocked on the front door before inserting his key and unlocking the door. Eurydice met him in the foyer; I could hear her big paws flapping on the tiled floor and from the sound of Eurydice's jingling dog tags, she was obviously happy to see Sonny, and as they came into my view, her little stub of a tail was wagging faster than she normally did when she greeted me at the end of my day.

"Hey, E, how are you today?" Sonny asked as he tickled Eurydice behind one ear. "Has she been out this morning?" he asked as he approached my bedroom door.

"No," I replied as I rolled over in bed, feeling a little guilty about not taking Eurydice out for her morning walk. I picked up the television remote, turning it on and making sure the sound was on mute, so it wouldn't drown out the music from the CD player. Sonny made a quick about face and I could hear him as he fussed around with Eurydice's leash, as he prepared her for her morning walk.

"I'll be right back," Sonny said, as he poked his head back into my room. "Don't go anywhere," he said pointing his finger at me.

I must have dozed, because Sonny was back and he was in the process of raising the blinds in my room. "Have you eaten anything?" he asked.

"Yes," I replied closing my eyes and rolling away from the sudden light. "Please, close the blinds."

"What did you eat?" he asked as he closed the blinds.

"My usual," I replied as Sonny stepped into my bathroom and proceeded to wash his hands.

Sonny stood in the bathroom door drying his hands on a towel with a look of concern on his face. "Popcorn and ice cream again, huh?" He sat down on the edge of the bed next to me, reaching out and gave my leg a rub through the sheet. "You want me to prepare you something to eat?" he asked, as I replied with a shake of my head. "I don't like seeing you this way."

"Then go away."

"Mia, please talk to me, tell me what's going on inside of you."

"So who are you now, Sonny, my therapist? You want me to talk to you? You want to know what's going on inside of me? Is that what you want, Sonny? Okay, I'll talk to you," I said as I sat up in bed. "First of all, I want you to go away and leave me the hell alone. Right now I'm feeling a little sad, no, not a little, I'm feeling a lot of sadness right now, but it's okay for me to feel this way. You don't have to worry; I'm not going to do anything stupid, Sonny."

"I'm not worried about that, I just don't like to see you this way, babe."

"Then go away, Sonny! This is me, healing. This is how I heal; so let me do this, okay! If this is how I want to do it, then let it be my way. I'll come out of it tomorrow and I'll call you first thing in the morning," I said as a fresh wave of tears streamed down my face. "Oh, Sonny, I don't know what to do anymore. I read Blair's journal almost every night, and I can't stop thinking about the fact that it's my fault he's dead. Blair thought I didn't love him, but I did Sonny." I spoke in a whisper.

"I know, babe. I don't want to leave you alone today."

"Sonny, don't you understand? I want to be alone right now."

"No you don't. Mia-"

"I do, Sonny, please go. Go!"

"But you don't have to be alone, Mia. I'm here and I will always be here for you."

I'll never know who made the first move, but before I knew it Sonny and I were lock in a heated embrace. Although we had comforted each other many, many times before, this was more than just friends comforting one another, as his mouth sought out mine. Sonny's mouth was searing hot, as his lips crushed against mine. It was a hungry kiss, as though we were trying to kiss the skin from the other's lips, before he slid his tongue into my opened mouth. Sonny's hands where all over me, in my hair, on my breasts, and then his hands were tugging at my underwear, as his head dipped down and he brought his lips to my neck. His mouth seared a hot path down to the valley between my breasts, before finding his its way to one of my nipples. I moaned loudly, and I was shocked, then surprised as I discovered that I was wet and ready for whatever was to come.

Lately I'd taken to sleeping in large tee shirts and I heard a loud ripping noise, as Sonny ripped it down the middle and flung the ruined shirt away from my body. His mouth was everywhere, as he kissed, touched, caressed, and nibbled every inch of my skin. It felt so good, so right.

I can't do this! I was about to ask him to stop this before Sonny slipped one of his fingers into my mouth. That simple act sent shockwaves though my body. It made the hair on my arms, legs, and head stand straight up. Even my skin became more sensitive. It was the most erotic feeling, as he began to rub his fingertip along the tip of my tongue, then over my teeth and gums. I never knew a man's finger in my mouth was such a turn on, bringing out so much passion in me. *Dear God, make him stop!* I couldn't do it. How was I going to make Sonny stop if I couldn't stop? I thought as I moaned loudly. Sonny's lips made their way back up to mine, his mouth replacing his finger. Sonny's shirt came off followed by his pants and lastly his underwear.

We where on our knees in bed, naked, facing one another. Our fingers entwined, nose to nose. I could feel his hardness against my thigh, as our bodies leaned against the other, and I was wet with anticipation. On the outside, our kissing and movements were calmer now, but inside I could feel his heart beating wildly against my chest, and my own heart was furiously beating in my chest. I was trembling, from what, I did not know, as we slowly parted, but not too far, as Sonny wrapped his arms around my waist. I looked deep into his eyes, and shivered with desire as I recognized the lust in them.

"Tell me now if you want me to stop," he said. His voice was low and gravelly.

I was weak from wanting him. It had been far too long. I loved the feel of him, his scent, his touch, and his warm breath on my face. I was back in his arms again. I'm so weak, dear God, help me. I am so weak. Seconds felt like an eternity, as we held onto one another for what seemed like dear life, each of us silent. I've never been good at praying, but right now I was praying for God to give me the strength I needed to tell Sonny to stop. I knew I did not have the strength to do so, because to be loved by Sonny, even if it was wrong, it was what I needed- really needed at this time. I wasn't sure how Sonny was feeling, but for me, deep within my heart I knew this was all wrong. I knew it, but for the moment it felt so right for me to be in his arms again, and right now to be held by Sonny was what I wanted, for I would be safe in his arms. But, in my heart, I knew when the morning sun came; I- we would have to pay the consequences…but for right now, nothing else really mattered.

I couldn't quite get my mouth to say the words that would let Sonny know I didn't want him to stop. I was afraid that if I spoke out loud, the ethical side of me would say the right thing, so, I just let my hands do the talking and our joining was powerful, wonderful, and magical, like two stars colliding high above in the night sky. Sonny's slow sensuous caresses started from the nape of my neck to the bottom of my feet. His touch ignited the depths of my soul making me ache with pleasure and removing all doubt from my mind. We were both wide eyed, me, because I didn't want to miss out on watching his handsome face as he gave himself to me. I felt revived, marvelous, as Sonny looked down at me, his eyes full of desire. I wrapped my legs around his back rising to meet his thrust, and my movements seemed to send him into frenzy as we rolled into a new position. I was now sitting in his lap. I raised my hands to his face, kissing him until we were both breathless. I'm holding him and I'm loving him and I'm giving him my all as I should have done so many years ago. His hands drifted down to the small of my back bringing me to my peak. He now belonged to me, mind, body and soul and I was his. And when it was over, our limp bodies seemed to float above the bed as we drifted among the stars.

In the wee hours of the morning, I awoke in a panic, not knowing the reason why as I quickly sat up in bed. Then it all came back to me, and it suddenly dawned on me what it was that had awakened me as I slowly looked down at the prone figure lying beside me. My sudden movement must have awakened Sonny, for he brought his hand up and pulled me back down to lie beside him, wrapping his arms tightly around me. The scent of sex was heavy in the room, as well as on me and Sonny. I lay there stiff as a board, afraid even to breathe as the realization of what we had done slapped me full in the face like a ton of bricks. *Oh-my-God!* What had I done? What had we done? Sonny ran his hand up and down my thigh, before bringing his hand up to cup one of my breasts. I pushed his hand away, and jumped out of bed as though I'd been burned, and raced into the bathroom, banging the door shut behind me. I locked it just in time, for Sonny was up in a flash trying the doorknob.

"Mia, you all right in there? Mia!"

I didn't answer right away, because I didn't know what to say. I just stood there frozen to one spot as I stared at the mirror. Am I all right? "What?" I finally called out to him.

"Mia, unlock the door," Sonny called out from the other side, as he gave the door a vicious shake.

I was breathing hard, my heart pounding in my chest. I guess this is what guilt feels like. I turned away from the mirror, ashamed, and consumed by guilt, and with shaking hands I turned on the shower. I stepped into the tub before the water even had a chance to get warm. Picking up my loofah, I frantically began scrubbing my body in a vain attempt to scrub away the smell from the hours of hot, raw, sex. The rough texture of the dried sponge, left marks on my body as I tried to scrub away his lingering touch and erase the sounds of our moaning and groaning as we pleasured one another. To scrub away the fact that I'd enjoyed every glorious minute of our lovemaking as we thrashed around on the bed together. I tried, and I tried to scrub everything that had happened for the past eleven hours or so. It was a foolish effort, because I knew I could stand here and scrub all day long, scrub my body from head to toe until I was red and raw and still it would never erase the *senselessness* of our act. Then I cried, long racking sobs, I cried for Macey and Sonny, but most of all I cried for me! Allowing this to happen had been a foolish, foolish thing to do, all because I was feeling sorry myself, now I had ruined two lives just for one night of passion. The guilt of what we had done was running through me like a locomotive and I kept right on scrubbing and scrubbing as the shame knocked me to my knees.

"What did we do? God, what did I do?" I cried out into the room, as I rubbed and rubbed the loofah over my body over and over again.

It didn't take long for Sonny to realize the key to the bathroom door was stuck in the doorframe, just above the door. Sonny entered the bathroom like a hurricane, slipping and sliding on the wet floor, for I had not closed the shower door and water from the shower was all over the bathroom floor. Sonny turned off the water and grabbed the loofah from my hands tossing it into the room. He shook me before pulling me into his arms, holding me close.

"Mia, listen to me, we did nothing wrong! Do you hear me? What we did wasn't wrong," he said in a harsh voice breaking through the haze in my head as he tried to get through to me.

"But Macey-"

"Mia, I do not love Macey, I love you!"

I leaned away from him, shaking my head from side to side. "What we did was wrong, Sonny. Wrong and selfish, I was thinking about my own needs. I should've stopped you." Now that I'd said it out loud, I felt worse then ever. It was true; I should've stopped him before the first kiss. I pulled away from Sonny, reached over and grabbed a towel from the towel rack. I wrapped it around me, as I slowly made my way back into the bedroom. I needed a drink, a big one. I could hear Sonny as he followed along behind me.

"Mia, we were destined to be together. Don't you see? It was bound to happen." Sonny stepped in my path, blocking me from leaving the room. He reached out and placed his hands upon my shoulders. "Where are you going?" He asked, his eyes frantically searching my face.

"I don't know, in the other room," I replied with a shake of my head as I waved him away. "I need a drink."

"Talk to me."

"Sonny you should leave, Maceys' probably worried sick about your whereabouts." Just looking at Sonny made me feel even more guiltier. *God, I loved this man.* He stood naked before me in all his magnificent glory. His toned muscular body evoked maleness, luring me to him. In a way, I felt horrible about what had transpired between us, but then the other half of me, the less respectable half, wanted him over, and over again. I looked down at my feet, and watched as droplets of water dripped from my wet hair, splashing down onto the floor.

Sonny placed two fingers under my chin, at first I resisted, but then I raised my head until my eyes met his. "Mia, did you hear what I said back there? I love you, always have and I always will. Every since that night so long ago, when I pulled you from that gas filled apartment, I knew then and there that you and I would be together one day, and this is that day. You don't have to worry about anything-"

"No! Sonny, we can't do this." I turned away from him and sat down heavily upon the bed. My head hurt, for with each hammering of my heart, it was like a loud bong going off inside of my head. Bong. Bong. Bong. Guilty. Guilty. Home wrecker.

Sonny sat down on the bed beside me, then he pulled me into his lap, and my traitorous head rested upon his bare shoulder. "You're not going to do this to me, Mia."

"What?" I asked, drained and worn-out from this verbal battle.

"Make me feel guilty about what happen between us. I refuse to feel any kind of regret."

"Macey-"

"Macey isn't home. Her aunt was hospitalized yesterday morning and the doctors don't think she's going to make it. Macey and her mother flew to San Francisco early this morning."

I sat up and looked at him. "What? You planned this whole thing, didn't you? Coming over here knowing that your wife would be out of town?"

"No!" Sonny cried out with a hurt look upon his face. "Mia, you know me better than that. If Macey had been at home I would still be here. Right here!" Sonny said as he punched the mattress with his fist.

I covered my ears, not wanting to hear. "How could you say that?" I asked after a while. "How could we do this to Macey, she's my friend- your wife?" I shouted.

"You know how I feel about you, Mia, and I know you feel the same for me. We've denied it for far too long. It's time for us to be together."

"No, I'm not going to do this to Macey." We could argue all night about this and no matter how rational Sonny sounded I would continue to feel the guilt of our passion. Why Macey or anyone else had to suffer for our benefit was the question I knew would not let me sleep tonight. I was annoyed at myself for allowing my passionate heart to sabotage not only my own life but those of two others. Why didn't I stop Sonny? Why didn't I stop? I had no answer to my questions and I couldn't think with Sonny in such close proximity. It was useless to tell Sonny *no* or *stop* when I wanted him over and over again. The feel of his hard body in my arms and his scent was entrancing me, tantalizing me all the more.

"Sex feels so much better when you love the person you're with," Sonny replied as he ran a fingertip over my bare shoulder.

What was wrong with me? Why was I so weak when it came to Sonny? I scooted out of his lap, taking a deep breath as I backed away from him. Somehow I had to convince Sonny to leave because I could no longer control myself. "I'm not listening to you anymore, Sonny. This will never happen again. I will not be the one to come between you and Macey."

"Well it's way too late for that, sweetheart. You're always there, Mia. Every time I kiss my wife, I'm kissing you. Every time I take Macey to bed, you're lying there next to me."

"Sonny, we cannot do this to Macey!" I covered my face with my hands. I knew everything that he said was true. Although I had loved Blair, now that he was gone from my life, my love for Sonny was in full bloom again, but I couldn't tell him, it wasn't right. "Sonny, what we did was wrong and it shouldn't have happened. I'm sorry but I think you should leave," I said as I lowered my hands from my face.

"I don't want to leave you alone."

"It's okay, it really is okay. Go home, Sonny, go home to your wife." I walked away, toward the bedroom window. I stopped and stood before the window, my arms wrapped around me.

Sonny approached me from behind, placing his hands on my arms. He rubbed my bare arms and then his hand drifted down to my waist.

"Sonny, don't, please don't do that," I said as I hesitantly stepped away from him, when all I really wanted to do was wrap my arms around him and never let him go.

"You can't tell me that after all these years you've never thought what it would be like? Ever since that first night we were together I would question whether we had done the right thing by denying ourselves? The question has never left my mind, it's always there, Mia, floating around and around," he said as he thumped his forehead. "Don't tell me you've never questioned yourself about that night! Do you ever think about what if we had gone all the way the first time; would we be married to each other today? You can't tell me you don't think what we have is- will always be special." He spun me around, pulling me into his arms again. "I'll divorce Macey and move to Atlanta with you and the boys. I could open up another restaurant there and start all over again."

"No! Baby, please don't say that. Stop talking like that. I can't let you do that," I said pulling away from him. "Sonny, I'm sorry, but I don't know what I want right now, and anyway Macey is carrying your child. I couldn't do that to her, Sonny."

"I'll support my child."

"I'm not talking about supporting your child. What about being there to watch your son or daughter grow up? Think of the lives we will ruin if we continue this way. But, most importantly, what about Maceys' feelings? She trusted you, she trusted us! After all the doubts she's ever had about us over the years she's finally able to trust us and look what we did to her."

"Do you love me?" Sonny asked as he raised a finger to my face and gently wiped away a lone tear as it crept down my face.

"Yes, with every beat of my heart," I shook my head, raising my eyes to the ceiling, as I used the edge of the towel to wipe my face. "But it doesn't matter; it's much too late for us," I said in a whisper as I took his hand and kissed the palm of his hand. I held his hand close to my cheek as I spoke. "We cannot hurt others to satisfy our own needs."

"What about our *fucking* needs, Mia! What about our feelings for each other? Are we supposed to just forget about us? After all these years we're finally able to admit that our love for one another is real and you just want to chuck it all? Shit! Mia, people get divorced every single day."

I cringed at his words for what he said was true. "But, Sonny, can't you see this is different!"

"No! It isn't any different than any other divorce. Stop trying to make my decisions for me." Sonny quickly turned from me and began picking up his discarded clothing from the floor, and began to get dressed.

"That's not what I'm doing, Sonny. I'm not trying to make your decisions for you. I just don't think this is right."

"If I decide to divorce Macey, that's my business."

"We slept together, which influenced your decision, which makes it my business *too*."

"Mia, are you telling me that you do not love me?"

"Sonny, that's not what I'm saying. I love you so much it hurts, but I can't stand the thought of destroying your marriage-"

"So, what are you suggesting, Mia, that I stay in my marriage and we sleep around on the side?"

"No, that's not what I meant."

Sonny had finished dressing by now, and he was pulling on his shoes. "I didn't think so." Sonny stood and stuck his shirt inside his pants, leaned over gave me a long kiss. "I'll call you tomorrow," he said as he hastily left the room. The front door closed with a bang, and I could hear the sound of his key in the lock as he locked the dead bolt.

I was at work bright and early the next day, mainly because I didn't want Sonny to catch me at home alone. I knew I would not be able to resist him ever again, not after a night like last night. Our lovemaking had been exactly as I've always known it would be, and it had been our special time. Part of me was intent on making it just a one time event, but my heart knew differently.

I wasn't in the mood to see clients outside the office, so I decided to let Sonya handle my off site appointments. I directed my energy into running the office, and dealing with the potential applicants as they drifted in that day.

Sonny called twice that morning, and I had put him off each time, by telling him I was busy, and promising to call him back at a later time. I was sitting out front at Sonya's cubicle when exactly at noon the door buzzer sounded, announcing that we had a visitor. I looked up just as Sonny entered. Sonny nodded at the receptionist before making his way back to me, wearing what came across as a cocky smile upon his face. He was so handsome in a floral Hawaiian shirt, the kind I loved to see him wear. It was loose fitting, but one could still make out his large chest beneath his shirt. He was sporting a pair of khaki shorts, along with a pair of leather sandals, and in spite of it all, I returned his smile.

"Still busy?" he asked

"Things are kind of winding down right now," I replied as I rose from my chair, and hugged him. Despite the mess that we had created, he would always be my Sonny.

"Feel like a little lunch and a lot of conversation?"

"Okay. Carla, I'm leaving for lunch, Sonya should be back any minute now. Tell her I'll give her a call if I'm going to be late."

"Okay, Mrs. Freeman. Enjoy your lunch."

As I climbed into the car, I saw a picnic basket sitting in the back seat. "Picnic?" I asked as Sonny climbed into the front seat.

"I thought it would be a nice change to eat out in the sunshine." We were silent as we drove the short distance from my office to Balboa Park. After retrieving a blanket from the trunk of his car, we hiked to a spot beneath a large tree and spread our blanket out on the grass.

I laughed, when upon opening the containers I found corn dogs and tater tots. There was also a salad and oatmeal raisin cookies, still warm from the oven, for dessert.

"Corn dogs, just the way you like them, crispy on the outside, cheese on the inside and plenty of mustard," Sonny said as he handed me a corndog. He picked up one up for himself, and leaned back on one elbow. "Remember when we used to take Anthony and Maurice to the park?"

"Sonny-," I started.

"Mia, about last night," he began at the same time. "I just- I want you to know that I'm not sorry about what happened, and I meant every word I said to you. It's unfortunate that Macey will be hurt by all of this, but I can't stay in my marriage. It would be a lie if I stayed and I think that would hurt Macey even more than if I just left."

I said nothing as I chewed on my corndog, dipping the tip of it into the mustard. What do you say to something like that anyway? I knew Sonny was expecting me to give in to his views, but I couldn't do that to Macey. "Maybe we shouldn't see each other for a while. I think we need to give each other some...some breathing space, and see what happens."

"Here you go again," Sonny said as he tossed his corndog into the bushes.

"No, Sonny, wait. Give me a minute and just listen to what I have to say. I was thinking about visiting the boys in Atlanta in a few days. I've never been there before and this would be an excellent time for me to visit. I was planning on staying for a couple of weeks; that way we can think about what we really want to do. I won't be here to influence you, and not seeing you will help me think more clearly as well."

Sonny laughed, with a sneer on his face. "You think that's really going to work? Mia, it's been years since that first night we almost slept together and my yearning for you never went away. I went out there and I found someone the exact opposite of you, and although eventually I grew to love Macey, it's you that I'm in love with. Mia, you do what you have to do, but two weeks is not going to change my feelings for you one way or the other."

"Well, Sonny, I don't know what else to do. I don't want to see you do something you will regret later on. I don't want to be the person responsible for destroying your marriage."

"Mia, you're not listening to me. There is no marriage anymore!"

"What are you talking about, Sonny?"

"I called Macey this morning and I told her I wanted a divorce."

I jumped up and began to stomp around on the grass, as his words sunk in. "Shit, why did you do that? You called Macey up on the phone? You asked your wife for a divorce over the damn telephone?" I couldn't believe this. Sonny rose and walked toward me, reaching out for me. "Just stay away from me, how could...how could you do that to her? At least you could have given Macey the dignity and respect that she deserved by meeting with her face-to-face."

"Mia, it really doesn't matter how it's said, in the end it all has the same results. Regardless if I asked Macey for a divorce to her face, or over the phone it's all the same thing. I don't understand what difference it would've have made."

"You don't understand? That's what's wrong with you men, you all think with your fucking penises!"

"You weren't complaining about it last night."

"Fuck you, Sonny."

"Okay, okay let's stop," he said holding his hands in the air. "Listen, if it will make you feel any better, I will fly to San Francisco tonight and speak with Macey."

"Did you tell her why? Did you tell her it was because of me?"

"No, I did not. She'll find out for herself sooner or later, that is if she hasn't already figured it out."

"Shit." I cried out for I knew all to well the pain and hurt Macey must be feeling, because of what Sonny and I had did. This time when Sonny came to me I didn't send him away. "This is so wrong, we cannot do this. I'm sorry you had to ask Macey for a divorce, but we can't ever be together like last night ever again. It was so wrong. I'm leaving for Atlanta on Friday, and Sonny, please don't call me."

CHAPTER TWENTY FIVE

"Mom, telephone, it's Macey," Maurice called from the living room.

I'd been in Atlanta for few days now, and was in the kitchen of the three-bedroom rental preparing meatloaf for our Sunday dinner. I wiped my hands on a towel and pick up the phone. "Hello?" I spoke into the phone as I absently brushed away a few stray hairs from my face.

"Mia, Sonny wants a divorce."

I was silent for a long time. I had no idea what I was expecting Macey to say. I guess I thought Macey would start off with some small talk first, giving me time to prepare for what was to come next, not just blurting it out and catching me off guard. It wasn't hard to act surprise, because her straightforwardness had definitely put me at a disadvantage. "What?" I finally managed to say.

"You didn't know?" Macey asked, her voice barely above a whisper, as she took my silence for ignorance. "I guess you didn't know, being there in Atlanta with the boys. I hope you don't mind; Sonya gave me this number. I don't know what happened. Wednesday morning, just, out of the blue, Sonny calls and asked me for a divorce. Then Thursday morning, he flew out to San Francisco. We talked, and I even suggested that we get some counseling, but all Sonny kept saying to me, was our marriage was over. He- he left that same day, and told me...that- that when he got back to San Diego, he was moving out of the house," Macey cried. "Mia? Mia, are you there?" Macey asked, as I'd grown quiet.

"Macey, I'm so sorry," I said trying to hold my tears at bay. How could I tell her it was my fault that her marriage to Sonny had ended? My head ached from the thought that I was the reason for her marriage being over. How could I tell Macey I was the cause of her pain?

I was afraid of what she would think of me, when all she ever wanted from me was my friendship.

"He told me, it had been a mistake for us to get married in the first place, and it was best to end it now before we wasted any more of our lives." Macey started to cry again.

"Macey, I'm so sorry," I was finally able to speak after hearing her cry on the other end of the phone. And I was generally sorry for what I had done to her, I had to tell her about what Sonny and I had done. "Macey, I-

"Mia, would you talk to Sonny for me, please, find out what I did wrong. You are his *friend*, he will tell you. Please tell Sonny…tell him I love him, please call for me, Mia, please?"

"Macey, I'm so sorry-"

"Mia, please? I don't know what else to do," she sobbed.

"Macey, I have something to-"

"Mia, please don't say no, he'll talk to you. He tells you *everything!*"

I was at a dead end. I knew I wouldn't be able talk Sonny out of leaving her. Not after the things he told me about how he felt for me. "Okay. Okay, I'll talk to him. Sonny offered to take care of Eurydice during my stay here in Atlanta. Maybe I can catch him at the condo. I'll call and speak to him, Macey." My nerves were a wreck by the time I'd ended the conversation. I left the kitchen and took a stroll around the large back yard of the rental. The brightness from the sun dried my tears, and the greenness of the well-maintained grounds strengthened my heart. The garden was a typical southern garden, filled with lots of flowers and green shrubbery. The air was scented with floral smells and freshly cut lawns. It was early evening, the sun low in the sky. I was sure most of the neighbors were busy preparing for the dinner hour or sitting down to their Sunday dinner. There was not a lot of traffic on the quiet residential street, so through the opened windows you could hear the sound of the evening news on TV, a baby crying, a dog barking in the distance and a mother calling her family to the dinner table. I lingered around in the backyard until calmness had settled over me. I looked up at the house; it was a nice old two-story home, with plenty of backyard and room for several dogs. Maurice had hinted about letting Eurydice come out to live with them, and after checking out the place, I was certain that she would love it here. It was sometime later that I went back inside the house and up to my room to call Sonny. He answered on the first ring.

"Macey called me."

"I figured she would. I didn't tell her anything about us."

"She wanted me to call you, find out what she had done wrong. I wanted to tell Macey it wasn't her, but me. I was the one who had done wrong."

"Macey knows it was nothing she did. I already told her that. Macey feels I am divorcing her because she is pregnant, and she knows I didn't want any children. And, Mia, it was nothing you did either. It was me; I never should have married Macey in the first place."

"I had such a difficult time speaking with her because of all my guilt. Sonny, I felt her pain."

"Mia, I'm so sorry you have to go through this. I'll give Macey a call and ask her not to bother you anymore."

"No, don't do that. She told me you moved out of the house."

"I moved into your condo last night."

"Sonny, you can't stay there."

"I know it's just temporary. I'll be out by the time you get back. How are the boys?" he asked, changing the subject.

His tactic worked, as I filled him in on their new lives here in Atlanta. "Great, both are doing just great." I then proceeded to tell him all about the house they had rented.

"Good, I'm glad everything is going well for them. What's for dinner?"

"Meatloaf."

"I love your meatloaf. Mia, have you thought about us?"

"Every single day, Sonny, every single day," I replied. And it was the truth. I thought more about him now than anything else. Our separation brought Sonny more to mind than if I had never left San Diego. I was surprised at how my thoughts of Blair were becoming less and less every day. "I love you."

"Love you."

I was well into my second week in Atlanta, searching for a home to buy so the boys wouldn't have to worry about whether or not their landlord would allow them to have a pet in the house, and seriously thinking of extending my stay for another week. I was breathing a little easier these days, and thought all was going well with Sonny and Macey. Sonny and I spoken quite often after my initial phone call from Macey, even though I had told him not to call me. But, deep inside, I was beginning to enjoy our conversations, for they reminded me of our times together, before Blair and Macey when Sonny and I used to spend long nights sitting around and talking about our future. During our last exchange, Sonny had even mentioned how he might drive out to Atlanta with Eurydice and he wanted to know if he did decide to drive out would I be willing to drive back to San Diego with him. So it had been a complete shock to me when one morning after I'd just finished making my bed, and was on my way downstairs to make a pot of coffee, I ran into Anthony who was on his way to work.

"Mom, Macey called you last night or should I say, around two this morning, demanding to speak with you. I told her you were asleep and for her to call you back at a more decent hour, and she practically cussed me out. Mom, Macey sounded like she was drunk, crying or something, I don't know which; but I do know I had to hang up on her twice. I know she and Uncle Sonny are getting a divorce but why drag you into it?"

I had stopped walking, frozen at the bottom landing; my grip on the railing was so tight my hand began to shake. Anthony, who was headed out the door didn't seem to notice the look on my face as he bid me good-bye and headed off for work. I called The Egg Roll and was told that Sonny wouldn't be in until the afternoon. Next, I called the condo; the phone must have ringed about twelve or more times. I was ready to hang up and try to reach Sonny on his cell phone when Sonny finally picked up the telephone. "Hi, what's going on? Anthony said Macey called a couple of times, ranting and raving about something. Has she called you?"

"She's right here in front of me," Sonny said, and that was when I heard Macey in the background calling Sonny every four letter word in the book and then some. "Mia, let me call you back after it's quieted down here."

Why did he have to say my name? At the sound of my name I heard Macey *scream*, and then I heard a crashing sound. "What the hell?"

"I'll call you back, bye," Sonny said hastily.

An hour later the phone rang, it was Sonny returning my call. Sonny explained to me how Macey had finally asked him the right question, and he had told her the truth, and thus the tantrum. They'd discussed it the night before over the telephone, and after Macey had processed it all, she had made a call to me here in Atlanta. Not being able to reach me, Macey had driven over to the condo and had let Sonny have it with both barrels. By the time I'd called the condo, he and Macey had been in a shouting match for hours. Luckily, old Mrs. Jamison from downstairs finally called the police, before things had gotten out of hand.

True to his word, by the end of the week Sonny had driven to Atlanta with Eurydice in tow. Since this was his first trip to the Atlanta area, we spent most of our time sightseeing. Anthony and Maurice enjoyed spending time with Sonny and both did their best to squeeze in as much time with him as their schedules would allow. Sonny and I visited all the places that I'd visited during my stay, as well as some of the nightclubs and restaurants that were on Sonny's list of things to do. We discovered a charming supper club in the Peachtree district, which featured some great local jazz musicians. Sonny could only stay a week, for we had a long drive ahead of us back to the San Diego.

On the drive back, Sonny had insisted on doing all the driving. We drove during the day, and stopped in the evenings, spending the night at hotels along Interstate 10. On the last leg of our journey, we pulled out of Texas, bright and early in the morning. Sonny was determined to drive non-stop through New Mexico, with no more than a quick restroom break during our stops for gas.

I'd offered to help him drive, but Sonny insisted on doing it alone. I'd slept all the way through New Mexico, and by the time we'd reached Phoenix I was well rested and again I offered to do my part and drive the rest of the way, but Sonny wanted to stretch out in a bed, get some sleep, so we found a decent hotel off of Interstate 10. After checking in, we retreated to our rooms to clean up before meeting down in the hotel lobby for dinner. It was a fairly large hotel, and we were lucky to discover that the hotel restaurant was still serving dinner. Sonny was in the lobby waiting for me as I stepped off the elevator.

After placing our orders, we remained silent, as we each sipped on glasses of wine. I'd ordered soup and a Caesars salad with grilled chicken. Sonny had ordered a large steak, a baked potato with the works, and a side salad. He was smiling, giving me a side-glance, every now and again.

"What are you up to?" I finally asked.

"I knew we were meant for each other the night you threw up in my mouth as I did CPR on you," Sonny said with a smile.

"Sonny, that is so disgusting," I replied and feeling uncomfortable about the subject.

"That's closer than I've ever been with anyone else."

"Okay, enough!"

"Why?" Sonny asked as he raised his glass and drained it.

"Cause you're being silly," I replied.

"You really gave me a scare that night."

"Sonny, why are you bringing this up?" I asked as I looked down and dusted an imaginary piece of lint from my lap.

"Because we've only spoken about that night once, and then you locked it away as if it never happened."

"I wish it hadn't," I replied as I looked around the room, anything to avoid looking at Sonny.

"But it did and you never told me why you-,"

"Sonny if you don't mind I would rather not discuss it at this time. I received several years of *professional* counseling and enough medication to plug up a toilet, it's over, okay."

"You knew I was there for you, right?"

This time I met his stare with a challenge of my own. "Why, Sonny? Why bring it up now after all those years?"

"You never told me why. You told Blair the reason you tried to take your life that night, right?" he asked, as his stare drilled into me.

"I'm not doing this, not tonight," I said with a shake of my head as I started to scoot out of the booth. I had reach the edge of the red leather seat, was about to stand before Sonny reached out to stop me.

"Mia, don't go. Please stay and I swear I won't bring it up again if you promise me one thing, okay? Come on, come on stay. Our food will be here soon," he pleaded as I hesitated before taking my seat as the waiter returned to refill our wine glasses. "Mia, promise me one day you will share with me the reason why you tried to take your life, okay? Until then, I won't talk about ever again, not until you are ready."

I nodded my head as I picked up my glass of wine. "Okay, one day I will share that with you," I replied as I raise my glass in the air, "I promise."

Sonny reached out and brushed the back of his hand against my chin. "You look nice tonight. Not that you don't look nice all the time. But there's something about the way your face looks in candlelight, you look all soft and pretty."

"Thank you," He smiled, his slightly almond shaped eyes crinkling at the corners, and his violet eyes now more dark blue in the candlelight. "You look pretty good by candlelight yourself." He hadn't shaved today, and he was sporting a five o'clock shadow.

Sonny raised his eyebrows. "What will it take?"

"Excuse me?"

"What will it take to make you love me?" he asked.

"Sonny, I have always loved you, but not at the expense of Maceys' happiness."

"It was over between Macey and me a long time ago."

"You don't know how much I want to believe you."

"I don't know why I even married her. Trying to be a good son for my mother I suppose. If only I'd waited a while longer."

"Why?"

"Well, look what happened. I get come back from my honeymoon and you and the professor are history. I should have waited," he repeated.

I said nothing as the waiter placed our food on the table. Sonny's eyes were boring into mine.

"You fall in love too quickly," Sonny blurted out. "I had no idea that you would fall for Blair that quickly. I mean, he was a nice guy and all, but you just went head over heels."

"Isn't that the whole idea of falling in love?"

"Not for me. You don't know love until you've tasted the vomit of your loved one." Sonny laughed as he cut into his steak.

"You're drunk."

"Not yet, but I'm working on it," Sonny said as he finished off another glass of wine.

"You had me, you know? I was there for you."

I cringed, because I thought he had forgotten his promise to me earlier and I wasn't ready to tell him why. "I know."

"So now you know how I feel?"

"Not the same," I replied.

"The hell it is."

"Sonny-"

"Mia-"

"What would you do if it didn't work out? Would you go back to Macey."

"Too late. You know what they say, once you've had *Black* you ca-"

"Oh stop it." I said as I threw my napkin at him. Sonny ducked his head and laughed out loud. I shook my head, chuckling along with him.

"Remember the good old days, and our good times we had together?"

"Yes." It did feel like old times. I thought we'd lost this feeling the night we'd crossed the line and slept together.

"Feels good, huh?"

"Yes, just like before."

Sonny laid his fork to the side. "I've missed you, Mia. I want you back in my life."

"We were too close," I said. "Marriage to other people was good for us. That's what we needed, relationships to work on." I was beginning to sound like a counselor.

"It didn't work."

"It would have if Blair were alive."

"Mia, Blair's dead and you're alive. It's our time for love."

"Sonny, I don't know if I'm ready to jump back into a relationship."

"I'm not going to wait around forever you know?"

"So, you're going back to Macey?"

With a shake of his head Sonny picked up his fork. "No."

"Where are you going?"

"I'll know when the time comes," he replied as he sat his fork back down and reached out for my hand. "I do know my marriage is over. It wasn't right to begin with. You were always in my thoughts." He brushed his thumb over the back of my hand. "Life goes on; the clock on the wall is still ticking. Macey will carry on, have the baby, and the wheel of life will keep right on spinning. This is our time, right now."

"Sonny, I'm not the *only* woman in this world."

"You're the *only* woman for me."

We ate the rest of our meal in silence, and we turned down dessert. As we made our way across the lobby and to the elevator, Sonny reached for my hand.

We stopped before my room, my door card in Sonny's hand. Sonny lowered his head and kissed me on the lips, and I returned his kiss. Unexpectedly, Sonny's arms went around me, and I whimpered as he pulled me closer. His body hard against mine, making me weak in the knees. The smell and the touch of him was enough to make any women weak. Sonny pulled away and inserted the door card into the key slot and opened the door. I was in his arms before the door had a chance to close properly. Sonny's hands seemed to be everywhere, and my hands were doing a little exploring of their own. We did a slow waltz to the bed accompanied by the sound of our moans and groans. By the time the back of my legs brushed up against the bed, my top was off, and Sonny's jeans were practically down to his knees. Off came his shirt, buttons flying into the air. My hand went in search of his hardness, as his lips ravaged mine. With my hand deep inside his underwear, I met up with soft springy hair. Sonny's kisses were hot, long, and sensual. One of his hands went to the back of my bra, it popped off, my breasts heavy, and my nipples hard, as Sonny planted kisses upon each one before taking a nipple between his teeth. Sonny bent slightly, as he administered long kisses to my breast, nibbling and gently pulling on my nipples with his teeth.

"Delicious," Sonny mumbled, as he moved to the next nipple.

More like torture. I wanted to scream, as I placed my hands on his head, holding him to me.

Sonny went lower, planting kisses on my stomach, as he pushed my slacks down to my ankles. His lips went lower still. My knees buckled, and I sat down on the bed. Sonny pulled my slacks off in an exaggerated movement, sending them flying across the room. Stripping me of my underwear, he pushed me backwards, flat onto the bed. I gasped as his mouth came down on me. My hands were on the back of his head, my feet rising to the bed, as Sonny pushed my knees back and up onto the bed. I was still throbbing from his first assault when he entered me. One leg went around his broad back, Sonny held my other leg in his hand just at the bend of my knee. Sonny lowered his head planting kisses to the inside of my thigh. I cried out his name as I lost myself again. Somehow I ended up on top, and it was now my time to ride him, and I rode him long and hard.

"Damn, baby, what was that?" Sonny asked afterward, with a wide-eyed expression.

"What?"

"I believe I've just been *pussy whipped!* Where do you want me to go, what do you want me to do. Baby, I'll follow you anywhere!" Sonny said playfully as we rolled around the bed laughing at his theatrics. We then raided the mini bar, ravenous, from our recent escapade and afterward I lay wrapped in his cocoon like embrace in the midst of his arms and legs. I nibbled on his ear while Sonny gentled caressed my back. My thoughts drifted to another time and place similar to this night as we lay snuggled in each other's warmth, but it was also different in so many ways. I thought about Sonny's conversation at dinner and I questioned if we were meant to be together as man and woman? Was this our destiny? Or was it just my hormones talking- loudly?

"Can I tell you something?" Sonny asked as we snuggled.

"What?"

"About Blair."

"What?" I asked as I sat up."

"About the *girls*," he replied with a smile.

"Sonny, what are you talking about?" Sonny and I started referring to my breasts as *girls* soon after my plastic surgery.

"How much he liked them."

I shook my head. "Don't tell me you two talked about that?"

"Yes. He mentioned it, once or twice. Actually, he was bragging, telling me how nice they were. Even asked me if I knew you'd had them done?"

"I can't believe you two actually discussed the *girls*."

"Of course we talk about *breasts* we're guys, remember? Anyway I lied and told him I knew nothing about it, only because I knew he'd be jealous if he knew I was the one who paid for your surgery. After you told me about all the grief Blair had given you about Anthony's truck, just think what Blair would have done if he'd known that I knew about your surgery?"

I was silent for a minute as I thought about what Sonny had said. He was right; Blair would have thrown a fit if he'd known I'd borrowed the money from Sonny to have my breast lift surgery. "I paid you back."

"I know, but do you think that would have stopped Blair from having a fit? Could you picture Blair and I having a discussion about you, and me telling him I paid for your plastic surgery and took care of you while you recuperated? I can just see his face now, 'hey Blair, I took off the bandages and saw the job first hand. Even took Mia to the store to be fitted for her new bras!'"

"Sonny, please give it a rest."

"Why? Tell me why should I stop? There's so much that *we* know about one another, more than Blair or Macey could ever learn in an entire lifetime. Blair had no knowledge of who you were ten years ago, and neither does Macey. She didn't care what my life was like before, she was only interested in now, today."

"We got to know each other well because we talked."

"Exactly my point! We talked. So tell me, how come Blair never spoke to you about his family before? He was so strong on being honest and putting everything out in the open and he had ghosts in his own damn closet."

I was feeling uncomfortable discussing Blair while I lay in another man's arms. Even though Blair was dead, I didn't like the taste this discussion was leaving in my mouth. "Why are we talking about this? Let it rest, Sonny. Let bygones be gone."

"Because, I want to know why, okay? I don't think that's such a difficult question, is it? After knowing everything about Blair that I know now, I really admire him. He went through hell and back. He defied the odds and came out of it alive. I've heard stories before, and believe me not too many guys who did what Blair did get a chance to live another life and tell about it, even if that life was in secret. I admire him," Sonny said with nod of his head.

I was scooting across the bed as Sonny spoke, the top sheet from the bed wrapped about me. "You're right. But the person you should be asking that question to is not here at the moment. And, he didn't live to tell about it. Just in case you hadn't noticed, Blair is dead. We read about his life in his journals not from him. He's dead!" I shouted as I stormed into the bathroom.

Sonny found an apartment not too far from my condo, and in

the weeks to come, we would meet for dinner a couple of times a week and if he had the weekend off, we'd take in a movie. Sonny had cut back on working at the restaurant, taking more time off in the evenings, giving his sous chef more freedom with the place.

It was the end of September and the days and nights had been unusually warm. During one of these balmy nights Sonny and I walked the few blocks over to the Gaslamp Quarter for dinner and to listen to the local talent. It was a beautiful night, and there was a light breeze as it gently brought with it the smell of the ocean at a vain attempt to cool down the warm night. The stroll back was uneventful and we talked about our Atlanta trip, walking hand in hand. The streets were bustling with weekend pedestrian traffic as well as the many courageous drivers who had thrown caution to the wind at the usual downtown congestion and had driven in to enjoy the nightlife in the many restaurants and nightclubs in the area. The unseasonably warm evening had brought people outside in hordes making it a bad night for finding a parking spot. The few parking lots in the area had begun to post their *Lot Full* signs, causing some cars to do the once around the block in search of the next available spot on the side streets. The night was filled with the sounds of car horns, and squealing tires on the asphalt from breaking cars, shouting, and music from a live band as we neared a local jazz club. A couple, laughing as they ran to catch the trolley as it pulled to a stop before us. It had been a truly wonderful evening and a perfect night for a walk. Sonny and I had only just stepped back into my condo when the phone rang, and as I reached to pick it up I suddenly pulled back. Sonny gave me a curious look before he reached out and answered the phone. After a couple of hellos from him, he hung up.

"For the past few weeks someone has been calling here and not saying anything. At first I thought it was Macey."

"No, she wouldn't do that to you, to me maybe, but not to you," Sonny said with a chuckle.

"Has Macey been calling you and hanging up without saying anything?"

"No she hasn't. Did you try star sixty-nine?"

"Yes I have. That's why I know it isn't Macey. The few times

I've used that option the line on the other end just rings and rings, once someone answered and they told me I had ranged a pay phone, and you know what, each time I've called back, it's always a different number and it's not always here in San Diego."

"What?"

"Sometimes it's a different area code. When I do answer the phone, the person on the other end of the line never says a word. They just stay on the line until I hang up. And it's the same even when my answering machine picks up."

Sonny reached out and picked up the phone, and entered star sixty-nine. "No answer," he said hanging up the phone. "It was a '905' area code."

I folded my arms across my chest and stood before the window staring out into the night. I had lost my good mood and what had started off as a great evening with Sonny had suddenly gone downhill because of one lousy phone call. "Do you think it has anything to do with the Goodbyte brothers?" I asked. The question had been floating around inside my mind ever since the phone calls started. I got chills just from thinking about the Goodbyte clan, because the thought of someone out there trying to kill me was scary as hell.

"Why would they do something like that? Remember those people don't know who turned them in to the FBI. They probably think Blair had it set up that way. You know if anything should ever happen to him then a certain package would conveniently arrive at FBI headquarters and in this case that's exactly what happened." Sonny walked up behind me and began to rub my shoulders. "No, I don't think you'll have to worry about them ever again. Right now all you have to worry about is me," he said as he quickly spun me around and kissed me.

"Sonny," I said pulling away from him. I was not in the frame of mind for a tumble between the sheets. "If you want the stay the night you're welcome to stay. Those hang ups really creep me out. Actually, I would welcome the company tonight, but remember what I said the last time, no more sex," I continued as I rubbed my arm.

"Yeah right. And which time was that, the first time, second time, third, or the fourth time? Mia, why? I know you want me. Why won't you just give in to your feelings?"

"Sonny, this isn't going to work, I will always be consumed by all the guilt of knowing that I broke up your marriage."

"Mia, you didn't break up my marriage. It wasn't working out in the first place."

"But the two of you always seem so happy together, that is, be-fore-"

"Macey was the one that was happy and she got what she want-ed; she's having her baby!"

"So if you and I hadn't made love, you would still be together, right?"

"No, I was thinking about ending my marriage long before Blair's death. But during the time all of that was going on, I just put it into the back of my mind. But I knew it wasn't working out. As a matter of fact, I was planning on asking Macey for a divorce after she had returned home from San Francisco." Gripping my shoulders Sonny leaned in close to me, our noses almost touching, "Mia, you have nothing to feel guilty about. It was over long before you and I made love." Sonny moved away and stood with his back to me as he stared out of the window.

"Mia, I cannot force you into a relationship you do not want. I know you and Macey were friends, but you have nothing to feel guilty about. If anything, I'm the one who has been living a lie all this time. I am the one who should apologize to Macey for hurting her, because I should have never married Macey in the first place."

I moved toward him. "Maybe if we waited awhile-"

Sonny spun around so quickly that I had to take a step back or else we would have collided into one another. "Why must we always be the ones to wait? We waited before and look what happened, you started dating *what's* his name, and then that other guy with the afro, and then there was the professor. Then after the professor it was Blair. And what about me, first it was off again and on again with Tina, and then Macey. When will the time be right for us, Mia? When will you be able to say fuck everything and everybody and let your heart guide you? Why won't you just let it happen?" Sonny asked as he reached down for my hand, practically thrusting it under my nose. "You still wear his ring. Why do you still wear his ring and those necklaces?" he asked as he released my hand.

These three pieces of jewelry were the only pieces I owned. The sterling silver and diamond necklace Blair had given me in Yuma, my wedding ring, and the gold necklace with the locket, which Blair had placed around my neck before I had entered the secret opening in the fireplace the night of his death. For a time I never had the heart to open the locket. When I did find the courage to open the locket, I discovered one side contained a photograph of Blair's grandmother and on the other side was a photo of me. "I don't know, Sonny, I just don't know."

I had difficulty sleeping that night. Sonny had left for home, shortly after our conversation and still I couldn't come up with an answer to his question. Why didn't I just let it happen? Was it our destiny to be together? Was my indecisiveness because of the guilt I was carrying around, blaming myself for destroying Maceys' marriage? Had Sonny told me the truth about his love for Macey ending long before Blair's death? After much tossing and turning, I finally gave up trying to sleep. I threw off the top sheet and rose from bed. Who was I fooling; I wasn't going to get any sleep tonight. I loved Sonny, but I was I in love with him? Was it lust or love? Usually I only had thoughts of Blair and all of the unanswered questions that he would never be able to answer. Now my thoughts were in chaos for an entirely different reason. I made my way into the kitchen for a drink of water. Here I was thinking of another man when my husband had been dead for less than a year. Hell, six months had barely gone by before Sonny and I had slept together; so much for being the faithful widow. I was giving myself a mental beating when the phone rang. I glanced at the clock; it was one thirty. Immediately my thoughts went to Anthony and Maurice in Atlanta, as I reached out for the phone. "Hello? Hello...who is this!" I shouted into the receiver. In utter frustration, I slammed the receiver down knocking the phone onto the floor. I wanted to leave it there on the floor; at least I wouldn't be able to receive any more phone calls tonight. I stood there looking at the phone lying on its side on the floor. The beeping sounding from the phone being off the receiver would drive me insane and anyway what if my sons should call. They had my cell phone if they needed to reach me, but I usually turned it off at night while it charged. With one final sigh, I retrieved the phone from the floor and placed the receiver in its place. I went back to bed for what would be a long night of tossing and turning.

The next morning didn't fare too well for me either, after getting a total of two hours sleep I stormed into the office like Attila the Hun. I should have stayed by butt at home, because nothing went right that day. Even my usual cup of extra strong coffee did nothing to soothe my troubled soul. Just a little before noon, I finally decided to call it quits for the day and headed for home.

There was a FedEx package waiting for me by my front door, and once I was inside, I kicked off my shoes, followed by every stitch of clothing that I had on. I ran a tub full of hot water, added bath salts, oils and my favorite scented bubble bath. I let out a loud "Ahhh," as I slid into the foaming concoction. I reached down for the glass of wine I'd poured earlier and leaned my head back, taking a long sip from the glass. "Damn, I should have brought the bottle with me," I said out loud, after discovering if I didn't go easy my glass would be empty before my bath water had a chance to grow cold. I took another sip of wine, returned the glass to the floor, prepared a wet cloth for my eyes, and closed my eyes to clear my thoughts so I could relax. It was total relaxation. This was nice, I thought as I soaked amongst the scented water and bubbles. I soaked until the hot water grew tepid and the glass of wine, which had made my body go limp, was empty. Much later, it was the shrilling of the phone that jarred me from my relaxing bath. Glancing over at my nightstand, where the telephone, along with the answering machine sat, I waited. After four rings the answering machine finally picked up, but there was only silence on the other end of the line until the answering machine beeped and clicked off. "Who is that?" I asked out loud. It must have something to do with Blair's sister, but wait; I thought as I stood up and reached for my towel. This was something that neither Sonny nor I had thought about, this phone number was in Anthony's name not mine, so how could anyone have known about this telephone number or the condo? The last time I'd called Lawanda I'd been out at the house and it was that number that I'd given her along with the address in Alpine. Anthony had taken care of making sure everything related to the house had been disconnected. So, whoever was calling couldn't have any kind of connection to the Goodbyte clan and even if they had somehow connected this number with me, was that their forte, to call and do a lot of heavy breathing on the telephone? It was frightening and irritating as hell.

I finished drying off, pulled on my robe and stepped into the kitchen for another glass of wine. The FedEx package lying on the kitchen counter caught my attention. It was from a travel agency in the city. Curious, I opened the package and pulled out the contents. "What? Was this a prank?" It seemed I'd had won a free round trip ticket with accommodations to the Caribbean island of St. Lucia for seven nights. I quickly scanned the rest of the letter, as well as the contents of the package, which included lots of information about the island. Apparently I had entered a contest a year ago, last November, and I'd won the grand prize which was a trip to the island of St Lucia. I raked my brain trying to remember a contest such as this. Normally I was not one to enter contests of any kind and thought maybe Blair or one of my sons may have entered my name into a drawing.

I called the number on the letterhead and spoke to one of the travel agents. It seemed that all was legit, and I had until November to use the ticket. I thanked the travel agent and returned to my wine as I digested this bit of news. I had less than a month to use this ticket, hmmm, I thought, as I roamed about the room, maybe this was just what the doctor order. Could this trip be a blessing in disguise? This trip would allow me to spend some time alone to think about my future and my next move. I still wasn't one hundred percent sure if I wanted to stay in San Diego, but I wasn't sure if Atlanta was the place I wanted to be either. And what about Sonny, was I ready to spend the remainder of my life with him? Not that it was a bad idea, after all he had my love, but I needed to spend some time away from him, at least until after his divorce was final. I picked up the phone and called the travel agency again, scheduling the trip for the end of October, four weeks from today. This was definitely not something I would normally do; this was more in line of something that Blair would do. Blair loved to do spur of the moment trips. Now, I guess it was my time. Hell, I thought as I twirled the wine glass around in my hand, it was past my time, St. Lucia here I come! I closed my eyes and thought of Blair, but all I could see was Sonny's smiling face, and I quickly opened my eyes again. Blair was fading from my memory and he was no longer with me wherever I went. This would be the perfect trip to say my final goodbye to him as well.

CHAPTER TWENTY SEVEN

"In natural beauty St. Lucia is like an island plucked from the South Pacific and set down in the Carib-"

"I know all about the *island* of St Lucia. I researched it on the Internet, remember? Mia, you're evading the question again. You still haven't answered my question about the reason you're taking this trip?" Sonny asked as we drove to the airport. Sonny had insisted on dropping me off at the airport and he kept repeating the same question over and over again, during our drive. "Why are you running away from me?" Sonny asked again.

Pretending to be preoccupied with the information in the brochure I'd kept right on reading about the island of St. Lucia, with Sonny interrupting me, demanding an answer to his question.

"Because," I begin, as I reached out and rubbed his thigh. "I need to get away for a while, and Sonny, if it's any consolation, I am not running away from you," I finally replied.

"So what happens to us?"

"Think about it, Sonny, was there ever an '*us*' to begin with?"

"Okay. So tell me *what* do I *have* to do for us to be together?"

I looked out over at the line of cars as we slowly made our way toward the terminal, letting out a loud sigh. "Sonny, this is the reason why I'm taking this trip. I want to be sure I'm making the right decision about us.'

"Mia, Blair's dead. It's time for you to get on with your life." Sonny swung into an empty spot at the curb, and quickly exited the car. I stepped out onto the curb as he pulled my luggage from the trunk of the car and set the suitcases down at my feet. "Mia, are you sure you don't want me to come in and wait with you for a while?"

"I'm sure," I said as I reached up and placed my hand on his face. "Sonny, I'm going away because I need this time to think. If you can give me this time alone, when I get back you'll know my decision. Can you give me this time for myself?" It must have been something in my eyes, because suddenly Sonny seemed to back down, and his whole mood was lighter.

"Take as long as you want, I'll be here when you get back."

"Really? Correct me if I'm wrong, but is this coming from the same guy who said he was not going to be around forever?"

"I lied, call me when you get there," Sonny said, as he leaned over and kissed me.

We kissed and I held onto him, suddenly afraid to let go. "I love you," I whispered into his ear as I held him tighter. He smelled of the wind, the ocean, and of our early morning lovemaking session.

"Always." Sonny replied, giving me one last squeeze before turning and heading back to his car. I wanted to call out to him as he walked away, for in that instance, I had made up my mind. But instead, I turned and slowly entered the terminal.

My flight landed hours later. I was staying at Paradise Villa on Marigot Bay. It was a privately owned villa with three bedrooms, three full baths, a full kitchen, living room, dining room, and it even included a maid and my own personal chef, how great was that? A driver met me at the airport, and we headed out for the long drive to Marigot Bay. I was too exhausted from the flight to even notice the beautiful surroundings on the drive to the villa, and upon reaching the villa I went straight to bed. I awoke bright and early the next day to a spectacular sunrise and a mesmerizing view of the bay.

The maid and chef, Enid and Tomas, whom I believed to be mother and son, where waiting in the kitchen for me the next morning. They informed me they would be onsite during the day, and usually left right after the dinner dishes had been cleaned and put away, but they would return early the next morning. If I should require their services for a longer time, say for instance a social gathering, they would be more than willing to stay for as long as I needed them to stay. I assured them that I would not be holding any social events for I was alone here at the villa, and I would not need their services after dinner. And of course, I thanked them for their offer.

My first day at the villa was uneventful; I hung out around the large hibiscus shaped pool and caught up on my sleep. I'd brought several books and a few magazines with me to read; and I had piled them up on the nightstand next to my bed. Right now reading was the last thing on my mind because after catching up on my sleep I was too busy exploring the nearby area to sit still long enough to read a book.

I was beginning to enjoy my solitude here at the villa. No phones, faxes, or television, just me and my thoughts. I was spending a lot of time thinking about Sonny and I could no longer deny the fact that I loved him more now than before. There would always be a place in my heart for Blair, but as Sonny had pointed out so many times before, it was our time for love. I was even considering leaving the island earlier than planned and surprising Sonny. This day was also special, because this was the day that I finally decided to remove my wedding ring and the two necklaces.

My second day on the island started out pretty much like the first one. Tomas prepared a very satisfying breakfast of eggs Benedict, home style potatoes with sweet onions, red and green bell peppers, and a side of fruit salad, made with fresh fruit from the island. I enjoyed several cups of the superbly strong coffee and even convinced Enid to sit and visit with me for a bit. Afterward, I complimented Tomas on the delightful breakfast and when he asked me about lunch, I requested something light, a salad maybe, and Tomas had smiled and nodded. I changed into my bathing suit and took a few laps around the pool. After my swim, I showered and changed, then took a short stroll down the curved dirt road to see some of the other villas Enid had spoken to me about. Apparently most of the villas were privately owned, and leased out during certain times of the year. I was only able to glimpse parts of the villas because most were similar to the one I was staying in with long driveways leading to stark white houses hidden behind banana trees and other green tropical foliage. The area was very secluded and private with no traffic of any kind.

Returning to the villa, Tomas greeted me at the door with a tall tropical blended drink laced with spiced rum. The tall frosty glass was shaped like a hurricane lamp, and a thick slice of pineapple and a small orange flower with a straw up the center almost made it too pretty to drink. But I was thirsty from my hike on the winding road and took delight in taking a long satisfying first sip. It was delightfully cold and I closed my eyes as the icy concoction made its way down my throat. Tomas informed me that lunch was being served out on the terrace, so I kicked off my sandals and made my way out back. The tiled floor was cool to the touch, and the French doors leading out to the terrace stood wide opened, letting in the ocean breeze scented with floral scents from the different blossoms crowding the terrace and from the hill out back, sending the sheer white curtains hanging at the doors floating through the air. The glass topped table was elegantly set for one, with more tropical flowers, gleaming silverware, tall crystal glasses, and delicate china. Taking another sip from my frothy glass, I sat down in the chair Tomas was holding out for me. A small salad sat in front of me, the greens so bright in color that they didn't quite look real. Thinly sliced bright red tomatoes with cucumbers sat on top of the bed of lettuce. It was a homemade vinaigrette dressing, Tomas informed me as he left me on my own to enjoy my salad. His timing was perfect, as he returned later with the second course. He removed my empty salad plate, and in its place sat down a large conch shell with a milky smooth creamy looking soup inside.

"Conch soup with shredded coconut," Tomas remarked with a nod of his head. He returned a short while later with a plate of bread and butter, the bread still warm from the oven and a bottle of Tabasco sauce. "This," Tomas begin in his strong West Indies accent, "will give it an excellent kick."

Well, Tomas had followed my instructions in preparing a light lunch, but I had been a bit piggish and finished off all the soup, dipping my bread in the bottom of the shell to make sure that I got every bit of the delicious tasting soup. I was stuffed, but it didn't stop me from asking what was for dinner.

My third day on the island started out pretty much like the first two. A nice big breakfast, fit for a queen and an excellent lunch, prepared by Tomas. I must admit everything tasted a lot better when you didn't have to cook for yourself. After my splendid lunch yesterday,

I'd decided to let Tomas have free control in the kitchen. Whatever he prepared I would eat, no questions asked for he was an excellent cook. There was a small blackboard in the kitchen which Tomas wrote down the menu for the day. "If you do not like what you see, please go right ahead and change it to something that you desire." He had informed me on the second night.

After lunch, I decided to visit the beach. This would be my first trip down to the private beach which was shared by the other villas. Wearing a pair of loose beige shorts and a long flowing top and a big floppy hat, which Enid insisted I should wear, I made my way around the pool to the edge of the terrace to the many small steps leading down to the Bay. It was slow going as I carefully maneuvered the small stairs one by one, watching my footing or chance slipping on the sand covered wooden stairs and tumbling to the bottom, and lucky for me the large hat came with a chin strap least it end up high in the air with the birds. There was no way I would have been able to maneuver while clutching my hat. As I zigzagged down the hill I would stop from time to time and take in the sites. The beautiful sapphire colored ocean ending at the white sandy beaches. The sandy hill was covered with plant life indigenous to the island. Flora bloomed in their splendor and the air was filled from a mixture of fragrances from the many different flowers growing wildly on the hillside. Most of the plants laid low on the hillside, probably due to the warm wind which constantly blew in from the beach. The plants came in a variety of shapes, sizes, and colors, blanketing the entire hillside, except for the area occupied by the small uneven wooden stairs, which were half the size of a human foot, zigzagging their way down the hill. The only plants I could identify were the small palm tress, clinging precariously to the sides of the hill and a few of the blooms gracing the area. The sky was also filled with the sounds of sea gulls and other waterfowl which I could not identify, and the sky above was filled with their noise as they swooped and dived high above in the clear blue skies. It was all quite breathtaking, the clean air, the ocean breeze, the plant life, and the birds making me wonder why I hadn't vacationed here before or any of the other tropical isles before. I marveled at the many sights, taking in the fresh air and loving every minute of this beautiful island and the noise and hustle of bustle of the busy downtown streets of San Diego was just a distant memory compared to this peaceful little inlet. Maybe investing in a vacation home on St. Lucia might be a good idea.

Once I'd reached the bottom I walked the length of the private beach, and then back again, taking in the picturesque view. A handful of sunbathers, some clothed, some nude, dotted the beach, while others splashed around in the water, and all very friendly. I stopped to chat with a couple who leased the villa to the right of the one I was staying in, and they invited me to stop by for drinks before I left the island. Several boats and yachts of various sizes dotted the bay, and occasionally I would get a loud, *"Hello on the beach,"* from one of them. Earlier, Tomas had taken the trek down the hill and left some snorkeling gear for me to use. He had also set up an umbrella to provide some shade from the fierceness of the sun beating down upon the white sandy beach, a small folding table and chair for me and over the back of the chair was a brightly colored towel, and sitting in the shade of the umbrella was a medium sized ice chest filled with ice, a bottle of orange juice, and bottled water. Tucked along inside the chest was a large baggie filled with grapes, and bite sized pieces of cantaloupe and honeydew melon. After relaxing in the shade from the umbrella and sipping the cold bottled water, I decided it was time I took a dip in the warm ocean. I removed my large white shirt, smoothing the non existing wrinkles from my bathing suit. It was a once piece cobalt blue suit, with a halter neck and a very low back. Since Blair's death, I had lost over twenty pounds, so everything I'd bought after my release from the hospital no longer fit, forcing me to shop for new clothes, which included five new bathing suits for this trip. After chasing the tiny tropical fish which tried to nibble at my toes and fingers; I did a bit of snorkeling and then I searched the beach for shells. After a couple of hours of swimming, snorkeling, and beachcombing, I spent some quiet time under the shade of the umbrella, pondering on what type of adventure I should take tomorrow. Tomas had mentioned going into town to shop, maybe I could spend some time in town shopping for souvenirs for my family and friends. But for the moment, I was content to spend the rest of the afternoon on the beach, enjoying the sun and surf. I could see why this area was so high in demand, it was a beautiful area. After getting my fill of the beach, I decided it was time to make my way back up to the house to watch the incredible sunset from the villa's balcony overlooking the bay.

I left the umbrella, chair, and the rest of the items on the beach; after all I was certain I'd be visiting the beach again tomorrow. Head down, and concentrating on making my way up the sand covered wooden steps, I took the steps one at a time realizing that going up was much harder than going down. About halfway there, I glanced upward and waved to Enid as she looked down from the rim of the terrace, watching my approach. Enid and Tomas would be off soon, after they finished up with the dinner dishes. It was a splendid day, and I stopped to take another look around at my surrounds for a few minutes more enjoying the green untamed overgrowth of my surroundings. The closer I climbed to the top, the more of the house I was able to see. The white curtains hanging at the opened French doors fluttered in and out from the ocean breeze, and I thought what a lovely picture it made. Thinking that my progress would be much quicker in my bare feet, I sat down to remove my sandals. The salt air and the exercise had increased my appetite and I'd eaten every hardy meal that Tomas had prepared, and tonight I was looking forward to dinner which would be lobster bisque, with a dash of sherry, and fresh red snapper grilled to perfection, as Tomas had described it. I resumed my ascent and was nearing the end of my trek when I thought I'd glimpsed a silhouette of someone standing just inside the doorway, just as the curtains fluttered downward. Removing my shades I stared at the opening as the curtains waved in the breeze again and saw that the doorway was empty. Maybe it had been Tomas checking to see how close I was before he put my dinner out on the table, I thought as I sped up my pace, head down, and my eyes on the steps as I carefully made my way up.

Next time I'll heed Tomas's advice and have him meet me on the road leading to the beach instead of hiking back up this hill, I thought as I stopped and put a hand on my knee. I looked upward and notice I had only a few more steps to go before I reached the landing that lead up to the veranda. I removed the hat I'd worn down to the beach, and using the tip of my long shirt, I dabbed the sweat from my brow, and as I was replacing my hat on my head, I glanced upward and almost fell over backwards, for *there* was someone standing just inside the French doors and it wasn't Tomas. The reason I hadn't been sure earlier was because he was dressed all in white, even his wide brim hat, which hid his face in the shadows, was white. His shirt was opened and the breeze picked it up and down in rhythm with the flow of curtains. I wasn't sure what to do next, until the next breeze, and it was then that I caught a hint of fragrance, and I froze, for the scent floating down to me with the ocean breeze was none other than Blair's favorite cologne, *Paul Sebastian.*

All in white cotton to signify purity…it couldn't be. "Oh my God. *Oh-my-God.* It can't be," I spoke out loud as I held one hand up to my head. This had to be some sick-minded person's idea of a joke, and it was a pretty damn sick joke. I couldn't summon up the strength to make those last few steps as I stood there with my eyes brimming with tears. I closed my eyes; as I tried to convince myself that it was all just an illusion, a ghostly vision. Because right after his death I had so much wanted Blair to be alive, and now my mind had simply conjured him up. Upon arriving here, I'd even thought about what my days and nights would have been like if Blair had been here with me in this breathtaking place with it lush green landscape and delightful ocean breezes. No pollution, clean fresh air, the bright sun, blue skies, white sandy beaches, and then my thoughts would drift to back to Sonny, who seemed to be weighing heavily on my mind these days. With my eyes still closed I took several deep cleansing breaths, it was just my imagination. There was no apparition standing in the doorway, and once I'd open my eyes things would be back to normal.

Taking my time and trying to reassure myself that I was not going insane; I counted to ten and then slowly opened my eyes. The figure was still there, minus the hat, which he now held in his right hand. My head begin to spin, and for a moment I thought I was going to fall backwards, and tumbled back down to the beach. I was having difficulty breathing, my breath catching in my throat. My knees suddenly turned to jelly, and I slowly sank to the ground, landing on all fours, panting heavily. I think I was starting to hyperventilate, for I was having difficulty breathing. I heard movement from close by, and glanced up just as he reached down for me, pulling me up into his arms. I could feel my lips moving, but no sound came from my mouth, I couldn't breathe. I started to cry as the realization of it all hit me. Moving like a large cat, Blair carried me up the few remaining steps, around the pool and into the house. I was sobbing uncontrollably now, because this had to be a dream or else I'd fallen down the stairs and I'd died from the fall. This couldn't be real- this wasn't real. Blair was *dead*. He sat down on the sofa holding me in his lap. Sonny, where are you? This can't be. This was not right.

"Are you okay? You didn't hurt yourself did you?" Blair asked, as he looked down at me with concern on his face.

I let out a loud yelp, as I jumped up and out of his lap, backing away from him. "B-B-Blair? Is-is-it really you?" I asked, as I held my hand out, keeping him away. I covered my mouth with my free hand, as Blair smiled and stood. He reached out for my hand, drawing me closer, pulling me into his arms. His lips crushed away any and all protest that I may have had.

"In the flesh," he said as he released me. "I'm sorry, I didn't mean to frighten you like that."

His voice was loud and booming in the room. I covered my ears and tried to back away. "I thought someone was playing a mean joke on me. B-B-But the fire, y-y-you died in the fire." It was incredible how long it took for the mind to accept something that I'd been wishing and praying for, for what seemed like forever.

"It wasn't me."

"B-B-But...t-t-then w-who? Where have you been all this time? If you were alive all these months why didn't you contact me?"

"I wasn't sure if you were being watched or not and I didn't want anything to happen to you, so I kept a low profile."

"Y-Y-You could've written me, or called…was it you calling and not saying anything? It *was* you," I said after noticing the look on his face.

"Baby, I just wanted to hear your voice. Aren't you even happy to see me?" he asked, as he advanced toward me with his arms outstretched.

"H-H-Happy? I don't know. I don't know what to think," I said with a shake of my head. "Blair, is it really you?" I asked again, as I reached out with shaking hands and touched his face.

He laughed. "Yes, Mia, it's me," Blair said, as he picked me up and swung me around. Blair was laughing a little to hysterically as he spun me around, and around and I was afraid that he would drop me, or worse, I would wake up from what surely had to be a dream.

"Stop, please stop, I'm getting dizzy," I said after a few seconds of spinning. When the room finally stilled, I made my way back to the sofa and sat down. I was speechless.

"Look at you," Blair said after a while. "You look like you've just seen a ghost."

"Are you?"

"No, sweetheart, I'm just joking with you," he said as he flopped down next to me. "You look good."

"What's happening here? Tell me, what is this, w-w-what is this all about?"

"I didn't die in the fire," he replied, holding his arms out wide. "You are happy to see me, aren't you?"

"I don't know." I was speechless. I didn't know what to think. I couldn't think. "Who are you?"

"Mia, it's me, Blair! But now I'm known as *Ellis Solomon*, but I'm still the same person. Aren't you happy I'm here?" he asked laughing loudly, with his arms still wide opened, I guess he was waiting for me to embrace him.

"Happy? You faked your death, then you come back here and scare the hell out of me, and you expect me to be happy to see you? I've grieved for you for almost a year, even blaming myself for your death. I've lived in anguish all this time, and here you are, alive and well and you didn't even let me know it? And you expect me to be happy? My life has been in pandemonium ever since that night of the fire, I've been in therapy for months, and I should be happy to see you?" As I said this, I reached out and punched Blair in the arm. "This is not good," I said with a shake of my head. "This was all just a *joke* to you, wasn't it? This is not good." Here sat the man I'd been mourning, and here I was behaving like I didn't want anything to do with him, and to top it off I was babbling like an idiot.

"Blair, I've prayed to relive that night, over and over again just so I could make you come with me into that tunnel. After Sonny and I received your package, and later realizing what your past was, I prayed to relive the day I made that fateful phone call to your sister telling her your whereabouts. I'm finally able to put most of that behind me now, a-a-and I've learned how to stand on my own again, and now here you show up pulling the rug right out from under me. Y-Y-You show up trying to frighten me by telling me, that the reason you couldn't contact me was because I was being watched-" I was ranting uncontrollably now.

"Mia, baby, listen to me," Blair began, as he reached for me. "There were four of us in the house that night."

"What? Blair, what are you talking about? You're not making any sense at all." This is crazy. I must be dreaming.

"Three men tried to kill me that night, and all three men died that night in the house."

I shuddered as I removed his grip. I stood and began to pace about the room. "You killed three men?"

"I didn't have much of a choice. It was kill or be killed."

I shook my head. "Unbelievable. Blair, how do you sleep at night knowing that you took three lives? I could never take another human life." What was I saying? What did I care if he killed to save his own life, my husband was alive!

"It was hard at first, but then I just kept reminding myself that if I didn't kill them, sleep would have been the least of my problems. Mia, killing isn't as hard as you think especially after your survival instincts kick in. I won't go into any details and tell you about the grisly events from that night, because I know you really don't want to hear what happened. But, I'm telling you, there was someone else in the house that night."

I stopped pacing as his statement caught my attention. "After the investigation, I was told that judging from the evidence left in the ashes; there had been two, maybe three bodies. They couldn't really tell because the fire had been so horrible, burning and melting everything in its path. Maybe there had been four intruders and one got away, oh shit! Listen to me, now I'm totally confused." I turned around and faced the French doors, staring out at the bay.

"No, three came; I know this for a fact because I found their car. It was their car that I used to get away that night. They'd been out there for a while, probably the whole afternoon, and they left plenty of evidence behind to indicate that there had been only three of them."

"Then I don't know what to tell you, Blair. I understand from forensics that they had to use some sort of shifter to find what little evidence they did find just to determine how many people died in the fire that night." There were so many things going around inside my head at the moment that I had no idea exactly what I was saying, or trying to say. And apparently, Blair didn't notice my babbling because he just kept right on talking. I shook my head, as I folded my arms across my chest. This conversation was beginning to be a bit much for me, all this talk of death and dying. I waved my hand in the air. "Blair, maybe you miscounted-"

"Because of all the smoke, the visibility in the house was practically zero, which was good for me because whoever hit me from behind came at me at an angle," Blair said as he raised his hand to demonstrate. "This caused the blow; that probably would have killed me if they'd done it right; to land more on my shoulder than my head. The blow was just enough to knock me down, and I hit my head on a table or chair I can't remember which, I couldn't see much. But, I am certain whoever it was, they hadn't been a part of Goodbyte posse."

I raised my head and looked out at the yachts moored in the bay and they all seemed to be quite festive in appearance with lights hanging from their masts. My own mood was definitely not festive and I was confused, for surely my prayers had been answered, for Blair was alive and well in this very room with me. Why wasn't I happy? Suddenly my head was killing me. All of this was just too much for me to comprehend. Blair rising from the dead, and dead henchmen, damn, this had to be a dream. "How do you know all of this? I mean, this happened months ago, maybe you're confused, lost count, oh, I don't know-" I said with a shrug and much too calm.

"Because those men would have shot me on the spot, not hit me with their bare fist."

"Then who was it, Blair?" As we talked, Blair had moved in close enough behind me for me to feel the heat from his body.

"That's why I've been undercover all this time; living on the streets in New York trying to get information on this fourth person. Even with the Goodbyte brothers in prison, that wouldn't have stopped them from seeking me out if they had known I'd survived the hit. By the way, you did good sending those notebooks to the Feds." He rubbed my shoulders, his breath warm on my neck. "I was concerned for your safety and I wanted to make sure that when I came to you, you would be safe. That's why I arranged this trip for you."

"You? You mean you arranged this whole trip? I knew it had to have been a mistake, because I hadn't signed up for any trip. So all this time you've been spying on me?" All of this was just too much information for me. I was beginning to become overwhelmed by it all. My back stiffened from his touch.

"Not all the time, just occasionally."

"Did you know that Anthony was in Atlanta?"

"Yeah, I knew. They seemed to be doing okay."

"You've been spying on them as well?"

"Not me personally, but to answer your question, yes I've had them under surveillance from time to time."

I lowered my head; my hand trembled slightly as I reached out for one of the sheer curtains hanging from the window. "Have you spoken to them?"

"No."

"So you waited until you thought it was safe before coming to me? What does all this mean; you've found out who the fourth person was in the house that night?" I stepped away from him, my arms still folded tightly across my chest. I moved closer to the opened doors, and I turned my stare to a yacht with the most twinkling lights. It had grown darker now, and I'd missed the sunset that I was in a hurry to watch earlier.

"I believe I have."

"So, was it someone the Goodbytes' had sent after you?"

"No, it was our mutual friend, Sonny."

I spun around to face him, amazed at the calmness in his voice as he made this revelation. "You're lying! I can't take anymore of this. Do you hear what you're saying? I cannot take anymore of this *shit*, Blair! I don't believe you! Why are you accusing Sonny of trying to kill you? Were do you get off reappearing out of nowhere and accusing Sonny of trying to kill you? What the *fuck* is going on here, Blair?" I asked him, all up in his face. "You're out of your mind. You must have inhaled too much smoke or maybe the blow to your head caused you to hallucinate because you are not making any sense to me at *all*. You're paranoid-"

"Mia-"

"NO!" Blair, I will not listen to one more word of your lies."

"It all fits. I called Sonny almost an hour before I woke you, which gave him plenty of time to get there well before-"

"You're lying! Why would Sonny want to kill you? He loved you like a *brother*."

"No, Mia, he loves *you* and not like a sister."

"Don't start this *bullshit* again, Blair. You're just out to put the blame on someone else for your lies. It isn't Sonny's fault, or mine or anyone else's for that matter. Your past caught up with you, Blair. That's what happened." I started to walk around him, but Blair reached out and grabbed my arm.

"I'm not blaming Sonny for my past, but he did try to kill me that night. I don't know if Sonny thought I'd hurt you in some way, or he just saw an opportunity to get rid of me once and for all. It all makes perfect sense to me now. Tell me; since I've been out of the picture, so to speak, has Sonny been pursuing you?"

Blair's face was mere inches from mine; his eyes searching mine as though he was trying to read my thoughts. "Blair, why are you doing this?"

"Has he?"

I reached down and removed my arm from his grip, shaking with anger. I couldn't believe my ears, what the hell was Blair trying to do? "Oh I see, since you haven't been around to watch us, you're trying to pry information from me on whether or not Sonny and I have any *'secrets'* from you, right?" I was shaking with anger. "What you should be trying to do is to make up for all the pain and suffering you've caused us all by putting our lives in danger because of your past. What you should be trying to do is apologize for making me, and everyone else believe you were dead all this time. That's what you should be doing instead of worrying about whether or not someone else has been sleeping with your wife while you were supposed to be *dead*. That, Mr. Freeman, Smithy or whatever the fuck your name is, that's what you should be doing!" By the time I'd finished, I was shaking from head to toe with anger.

Blair winced as I made my last statement; his stare had grown hard as he looked at me with an ugly sneer on his face. "I know for a fact that the two of you have slept together since my demise-"

"You *son-of-a-bitch!*" I shouted as I raised my hand to slap him, but before my hand could come into contact with his cheek, Blair reached out, grabbing my hand in mid-swing, preventing me from hitting him as he pulled me to him. At first I started to struggle, but I stopped, realizing that I wasn't going to win my freedom by struggling with him. We stood face-to-face, my breathing loud and heavy about the room, Blair's eyes were two slits, and his jaw was clenched tight.

"I saw Sonny when he entered the building that day you two were together, and I saw him when he left much later. So you don't have to tell me who's been sleeping with my wife because I already know who your lover is," he said through clenched teeth.

"Let go of me, Blair." Neither of us wavered, as our stares grew longer. After what seemed like hours his grip on my wrist finally relaxed and I pulled away. "Once upon a time, I gave you my all, now I can't stand the sight or the touch of you," I said as I turned and ran into my bedroom, slamming the door shut behind me. I couldn't believe what was happening. How could this be? Was I enraged with Blair or was I angry at myself? I should be embracing the fact that Blair was alive and well. But instead, here I was loathing him for being alive and here with me, destroying my psyche, throwing me off balance. How could he do this to me?

CHAPTER TWENTY EIGHT

I turned over and slowly opened my eyes, and looked straight into the hazel eyes of Blair J. Freeman AKA *Dwight Smith* AKA *Ellis Solomon*. Blair had told me on our first meeting that his middle initial stood for *Janús*, the Greek God. What he had failed to mention at the time was that the Greek God was always represented as *two-faced*. At the time I hadn't cared, but now the name *Janús* seemed to fit him to a tee.

"Good morning," he said with a flash of white teeth.

I rolled over to the opposite side of the bed and sat up. "Are you still here?" I asked as I climbed out of bed. I looked back over my shoulder at Blair. He was barefoot, wearing a pair of white shorts and a white tee shirt. "What time is it?"

"Just a little after eight. The chef would like to know if you would like an omelet for breakfast. I'm having a ham and cheese," Blair said as he flashed one of his long forgotten smiles at me.

That smile used to turn me on. Please don't smile at me. "No thanks," I said as I headed for the bathroom.

"Suit yourself," Blair said as he left the room.

An hour later, I had showered and dressed, wearing a pair of off white linen slacks and a short-sleeved coffee colored blouse, and was in the process of packing my suitcase when Blair returned to my room. "Did you forget how to knock?" I asked as I threw a blouse down onto the bed and turned to go back to the closet to remove more items. As I turned to head back toward the bed, and to my suitcase, Blair stood over the bed, glaring down at the opened suitcase. Looking up as I approached the bed, Blair reached out and removed the hangers from my hand, blocking my path. "What are you doing?"

"I'm packing my bags and going back to San Diego. This island has suddenly lost its appeal," I replied as I snatched the hangers back from him.

"Mia-" he began as I moved to step around him. "Mia, listen to me. I'm sorry. I know I should have contacted you sooner, but I wasn't sure if it was safe or not. As you said last night, I put you and your sons in danger just by sheer acquaintance and I'm sorry for that too. That's why I had to make sure that all was safe before I could contact you."

I struggled to push him away, which was like trying to push a Mack truck, and when that failed, I made an attempt to step around him, which Blair kept counteracting by stepping in front of me each time I made an effort to go around him. Finally in anger, I threw the garments that I held in my hand to the floor, and began calling him every name I could think of as I begin pummeling him about his face and chest, and then pushed at him with all my might.

Blair's arms were crossed in front of his face, as he dodged my blows. Suddenly he ducked one of my wild swings, and grabbed me about the waist, pulling me to him. His actions caught me off guard, which sent me stumbling forward crashing into him, sending us to the floor. I landed on top of Blair and continued my assault, hitting and slapping him about the face, as hot angry tears poured from my eyes. I shouted obscenities, until I was hoarse, striking him relentless about his upper body until I grew weary from it all. It took me a moment to realize that Blair had just lain there, while I had let out all of my frustrations out on him. I was straddling him, and I started to back away, but Blair suddenly sat up, pulling me to him, wrapping his arms around me, and holding me close. I struggled in his arms, trying to gain my freedom so that I could hit him again. Growing weary of this battle I finally collapsed against his chest, my body trembling from the physical exertion. It took me a while to notice that Blair was gently rocking me from side to side, speaking softly against my face. He too was shaking, as his body trembled against mine, his head against my head. I closed my eyes as my own tears slowly ceased, and I listened to his words of endearment.

"I love you, Mia. I always have from the very first day that I saw you, and I always will. I will never stop loving you, woman, no matter what you do or say to me. I pray to God you will continue to return my love and not hate me for trying to protect you. Please, baby, all I ask is for your forgiveness and I promise I will never, ever leave your side again. My life before you was nothing. Please, please forgive me."

It took us a while to notice some loud and persistent knocking coming from the other side of the door, along with my name being called, loudly. Blair held on tighter, as I lifted my head toward the door. "Yes?"

"Mrs. Freeman, are you all right?" Tomas asked, and I could hear Enid speaking in the background. I could just imagine what Blair and I must have sounded like to them.

"I'm fine," I begin, coughing to clear my throat. "Everything's okay."

"Are you sure everything is okay, Mrs. Freeman?" Enid demanded in her strong accented voice.

"Yes, Enid, I'm fine." I could hear them muttering to each other as they moved away from the door. I leaned back and stared at Blair. I gasped as I saw the damage I'd done to him. His bottom lip was split and bleeding, and he had what looked like was going to be one hell of a black eye. I took the tip of my blouse and dabbed at the blood on his mouth. "Look at you," I said as I gently dabbed at this lip. "I'm sorry-"

"A small price to pay for your forgiveness," he said as he gently pushed my hand away. I started to rise, but again, Blair stopped me by wrapping his arms around my waist. "I love you, Mia. Please tell me that you don't hate me."

"Blair, I could never *hate* you, but I don't think we could ever be together like before." This was true, I could never hate Blair. This man had stolen my heart the first day I'd met him, and there would always be a place in my heart for him, but never like before.

"Don't say that."

"Blair, it will never be the same," I had fresh tears welling in my eyes as I said this, because my love for him would never die, and it hurt me when I realized I was going to lose him again for an entirely different reason. "You will always hold the fact that I slept with Sonny against me and you will never forgive me for that. Don't deny it," I said as Blair shook his head.

"I don't blame you for that, how could I? What about how I've hurt you? Will you ever forgive me?"

I struggled to get up again, but Blair continued his hold on me. "Blair, please let go of me," I said pushing his hands away.

"Mia, don't walk away from me."

"Blair, I'm in an awkward position here," I said as I pushed away from him. He held my hand as I slowly rose into a standing position. I was already stiff from my climb up from the bay yesterday, and sitting on the floor, even if I had been sitting on Blair, hadn't helped my situation at all. I made my way over to the bed and sat down, feeling worn out, emotionally as well as physically, as Blair stood and followed me. I looked up at him and cringe at sight of the blood as it seeped from his lower lip. "Maybe you should think about putting some ice on your lip and get something for that eye."

"Maybe you're right," Blair said, wincing as he touched his fingertip to his mouth. He left the bedroom and I got up and followed him into the kitchen.

Tomas and Enid were sitting at the kitchen table and both quickly stood as we entered. "Enid, is there a first aid kit in the house?" I asked as I opened the refrigerator door.

"It's here," Tomas, said as he opened a cupboard and removed a white box.

"Here, let me look at tat," Enid said as she pushed Blair down into a chair and peered at his eye.

I found ice cubes in the freezer compartment and wrapped a few into a dish towel. Meanwhile Enid had taken what looked like iodine from the first aid kit, and after soaking a cotton ball in a capful of the liquid, Enid dabbed the cotton ball to Blair's mouth. Tomas and I watched Enid as she worked on Blair's bottom lip, before Tomas turned and headed for the fridge.

"I have a nice piece of meat for that eye, mon. I was going to serve it for dinner, but I can always go to the market and purchase another one."

"Make it two. Ouch, that stings," Blair, cried out as the steak came into contact with his bruised skin.

"I'll be back," Tomas said as he removed his apron and left kitchen.

I placed the makeshift ice bag into Blair's hand and took a seat across from him and Enid. She looked from Blair, over to me, then back to Blair.

"What tis mon do to make you so mad that you beat him like tis?" Enid asked.

"I died and made her cry," Blair answered before I could respond.

Enid stared at him for a long time as he stared back at her with his one good eye. "You love your woman?" she asked him with a nod in my direction.

"Very much. With all my heart," Blair replied without hesitating.

She turned to me. "Do you love tis mon?"

I looked down at the table to avoid her hard stare. For the few quick seconds that our eyes had met, Enid's dark stare seem to bore all the way through to the depths of my soul, and prevented me from answering her. I was no longer sure if I could love Blair as I had before. I was confused, I had finally accepted the fact that Blair was gone, and had tucked away his memory in a small place in my heart. I had come to St. Lucia to put a closure on the whole sorry affair and to start a fresh life with Sonny, and now with Blair's return he had succeeded in throwing another wrench into my life. I still loved him, but I loved Sonny as well. It was *bittersweet*. I didn't know what to say to her question, so I said nothing. But as I glanced back into Enid's dark eyes, I knew that my silence had not fooled her, for her next words made me gasp.

"Aha," she said after a few seconds had gone by. "You have a divided heart." Enid said with a quick nod in my direction as she rose and left the room.

The room was thick with silence as Blair and I sat quietly contemplating Enid's words. I couldn't look at Blair because her words had been true. The minutes appeared to drag by as the sound of clock on the wall slowly counted down the seconds. My eyes never left the tabletop, as I stared at the different variations of patterns embedded in the elaborate design of the tiled tabletop, which was of a pink flamingo amid a tropical setting of flowers. I had no idea if Blair was studying me or not, for I could not face him. Could not dare to see the look on his face especially after what Enid had said, after all, Blair would know exactly of whom Enid spoke of. But, at the time, none of it mattered, for I could never go back to Blair, at least that decision had been made. I lost track of the time, and finally looked up at the sound of Blair's chair scrapping against the kitchen floor, as he rose from the table. I watched as he threw the meat into the sink and washed his hands before coming back to the table. He reached out his hand to me and I placed my hand into his as he pulled me up from the chair. We stood eye to eye and even more time lapsed before he spoke. "Come with me," he said softly with a slight smile on his lips.

We left the kitchen and made our way out onto the terrace, down the five steps leading to the cliff then over to the stairs leading down into the bay. Our progress was slow, and neither of us spoke as we descended the stairs with Blair leading the way, still holding hands. At the bottom of the hill Blair led me to a small dinghy lying on the beach. He grabbed a length of rope and began to pull it toward the water. Once the small boat was bobbing on the waves Blair turned and called out to me.

"I want to show you something," Blair said as he held his hand out to me. "Sit here," he said holding my hand steady as I climbed into the dinghy and took a seat. Blair picked up the oars and paddled out to one of the larger yachts sitting out in the bay. As we neared the yacht, Blair steer the dingy around it until we came to a ladder, which he grabbed hold of. After tying the dinghy to the ladder, Blair steadied the craft until I had climbed safely aboard the yacht. I raised my hand to shield my eyes from the bright sun, and glanced around the deck.

"Welcome aboard the '*Janús*,'" Blair said as he walked up behind me. "This boat has been my second home off and on for years. But for the last nine months it has been my only home," Blair said as he stood on deck, beaming with pride as he waved his hand around the deck.

"Hello, Mr. Solomon, welcome back." A heavily accented voice boomed from behind us.

"How did things go last night, Shamus?" Blair asked the tall dark man, who had seemingly appeared from nowhere.

"Tings are fine, Mr. Solomon."

Shamus was so dark, that his skin seemed to glisten beneath the brightness of the sun. He was barefooted, and wearing a pair of skin-tight knee length shorts. He smiled at me; his teeth white as snow against the darkness of his skin, as he walked toward Blair.

"Mia, this is Shamus. He takes care of the *Janús* for me whenever I'm away." With this said, Blair and Shamus walked away discussing the *Janús*.

I glanced up the cliff leading back to the Villa noticing what an excellent view Blair had of the house. I imagined that the view from the bay was probably why Blair had chosen the Villa in the first place. I had no idea where he and Shamus had disappeared to, so I dropped down into one of the chaise lounges on the deck, and took in the fabulous view as I waited for Blair to return. The swaying motion and the sound of the waves lapping against the sides of the boat were very hypnotic as I stared out at the blue sea. The constant motion of the boat put me in a hypnotic daze and the next thing I knew Blair was standing over me with a foamy tropical drink in his hand. I sat up and slowly got my bearings, and as I looked around I saw that we were no longer in the quiet little bay but out in the open water with no land in sight. "Where are we?" I asked, reaching out for the glass, realizing how thirsty I was. Blair turned to a small table and picked up his own glass before answering.

"To us," he said as he held his glass out to me.

"Blair-" I begin, but before I could say more, Blair leaned over and placed his finger to my lips as he smiled down at me, his glass hanging in midair before my face.

"To us," he said again.

This time I clicked my glass to his and raised it to my lips. It was a Piná Colada, with bits of pineapple floating in the glass. I was parched and very hungry as I remembered that I hadn't eaten any dinner the night before nor breakfast this morning, and from the looks of the sky it was probably well after lunchtime by now.

"We are in the middle of the Caribbean Sea," Blair finally said. "Damn, what a view! Isn't it stunning?" He asked, as he waved his free high hand above his head, as though he had created the crystal blue waters and breathtaking sky that lay before us.

I watched him as he said this, not quite used to seeing him the way he was. It would take a while for me to get used to the new Blair, for he was sporting a mustache with a full beard, and his hair had grown out into a small shapely Afro. "As long as you can get me back to dry land, it's lovely. But if you don't know how to steer this thing back to land, then it's noting but a lot of water to me."

"Don't worry about it; I'll get you back to land. Would you like a tour of the yacht?"

"Not really. Blair, what are we doing out here?" In the middle of nowhere I thought, as I took in the view.

"Talking. This is the only way to get you alone and to make sure you won't run away from me," he said as he kneeled down beside me. "Remember that night we talked, that first night at your place and you told me you were searching for forever, do you remember when I told you I wanted the same thing?"

"That was a long time ago, Blair, before you faked your death."

"Can we just get past that for now?"

"How can I? Faking your own death is not something that can be taken lightly. Like it or not, Blair, life goes on and I, of all people know that oh so very well. It's called moving on. The clock on the wall doesn't stop ticking and wait for us to catch up with the rest of the world. Life goes on, Blair; regardless of what is happening inside of us. I couldn't afford to wait and see what would happen next. It was a struggle, but I had to live to get to this point in my life. If I had stopped living, I would have lost my mind. You died, and I mourned your death and I stored your memories here and in here," I said as I touch my head and heart. "I've put a lot of effort into getting on with my life without you as best as I know how, and now you reappear and you just want everything to be the way it was before. I don't know about you, Blair, but I can't do that overnight. It's going to take some time for me to get used to having *you* back in my life again. And at the moment, I'm not even sure that's what I want. How am I going to explain you to my sons, or to my friends for that matter? Should I throw a party and just before you enter, say hey everyone guess what, my husband really isn't dead after all. All this time he's been hiding from some drug kingpins that were out to kill him." I hastily stood up and almost fell down again as the deck moved beneath my feet. Blair reached out with one hand to steady me as he too stood up.

"Okay?"

"I'm okay. May we please go back now?" I asked as I rubbed my arms against the chill in the air, or was the chill caused by the thought of being alone with Blair? I wasn't sure which of the two the cause was, but the goose bumps on my arms made me regret following Blair out to his boat in the first place.

"Just give it some time, I promise you'll get used to it. Are you cold? Come on, I'll take you down to the main deck."

Once we'd reached what Blair called the main deck, I was feeling warmer and was able to balance myself against the up and down motion of the sea. The yacht was larger than I'd thought, with two large bedrooms, two bathrooms, a living area with all the amenities of home, a kitchen, which Blair called a galley, with a eating area all on the middle deck, and two smaller bedrooms, a bath, and storage spaces below deck.

"This is nice," I said as I took a seat in the eating area. Blair disappeared into the galley, and returned with a large pitcher and refilled our glasses. "Where's Shamus?"

"Topside." Blair replied as he settled into the chair next to me. "It feels good to have you sitting here with me. You'll never know how long I've dreamed of this moment. Watching you yesterday coming up that hill," Blair closed his eyes, seemingly at a lost for words. "Mia, I've missed you so much. I know last night didn't go very well and when you stormed off into your room, I had been tempted to follow you, but at the last minute I decided against it. It wasn't easy for me to stand on the other side of that door. I was torn about whether or not I should join you, because all I wanted was to be with you, and not being able to touch you was very difficult for me. I had to take a long walk into the night to stop myself from entering your room. After I'd returned from my walk I went into the kitchen to find something to eat. Your dinner was still on the table, so I heated it up, and tried to enjoy the meal," Blair said with a shrug.

"I hope it was good," I added thinking about the meal that Tomas had prepared for me.

"Not really. I couldn't enjoy it all that much, thinking about you all alone in the other room. Later I decided to make sure you were okay, thinking you'd had enough time to quiet down and was ready to talk to me. I didn't hear any sounds coming from the other side of the door, and after a few seconds I cracked the door opened and peeked in. The light from the hallway shone into the room, and there you where, sleeping like a baby. I peered down at your lovely face and my heart felt heavy from the load that I knew you had been carrying since the night of the fire." A sob caught in his throat, and he lowered his head. "Mia, my love for you is stronger than it has ever been. I don't blame you for sleeping with Sonny but I do blame Sonny, and as much as you don't want to hear it, Sonny was in the house that night and he was out to kill me."

I shook my head, about to protest as I started to rise from my chair. Blair reached out and grabbed hold of my hand forcing me to a stop.

"It had been touch and go for me that night, and if it hadn't been for Orpheus I would not be sitting here with you tonight. Somehow, Orpheus found me in the smoke filled room and the wetness from his tongue on the back of my neck saved me from a fiery death, because I would have been burned alive that night. The oxygen mask I was wearing would not have made a difference for I was unconscious. Orpheus had been beyond saving. He'd been shot by one of the men sent to kill me, and he was also pretty banged up from whatever else he'd gotten into that night. So after Orpheus had revived me, I carried him out of the house and away from the fire, and that's when I made my own escape into the night, disappearing for the second time in my life."

I slowly sank back into my chair, as the hair on my arms stood at his story. Seeing that I had resumed my seat, Blair released my hand, and took a quick sip from his glass as he continued.

"My biggest regret was not being able to contact you, and now, more than ever, I wish I'd gotten back to you sooner. You have to understand my predicament, I had to be sure that the other side thought I was dead. But most certainly, I had to be sure that no tail had been placed on you, and no harm would come to you or the boys. Now," Blair began as he reached out and covered my hand with his, "it's time for me to confront Sonny."

I shook my head as I looked away from him.

"Mia, I love you, and your sons mean the world to me, I love them like my own. I'm sorry about everything that has happened, and I wish I could take it all back; but it's done now and there's nothing that I can do to change the chain of events. But I can promise you one thing; beginning *now*, you, and I will never be apart again. Mia, you are my *lifemate*, and I am yours, and you know this as well. I realize that things are not going to be like it was before, but in time it will be better. I promise it will be much better for us. Not that what we had before was bad, but its just going to be a whole lot better, you'll see.

"The first thing I want to get out in the open is to tell you about my life. Something I should've done a long time ago, because now I know your love for me would not have changed one iota because of my lifestyle before I met you."

"I read your journal, remember?"

"I know, but I want you to hear it from me. The night of our party, something didn't feel right to me, but I couldn't quite put my finger on what it was. I've never felt comfortable in a crowd of people before, whether they be friend or foe, so I kept putting it off as party jitters, and starvation," he add with a quick smile, "but the nagging feeling just wouldn't go away. I couldn't wait until the night ended so that I could enjoy my wife again. Earlier I'd noticed how preoccupied you'd been with the phone for most of the day. Although you had denied that you were expecting a call, it seemed like every five minutes you were picking up the phone and then hanging it up, or asking whether or not the phone had rung. But never in a million years would I have thought that you had called *Lawanda*."

I flinched as Blair said this. "Blair, I am so sorry I placed that call to your sister...I didn't know, if only I'd known-"

Blair patted my hand. "Not your fault. I should have told you. Anyway," he said taking a deep breath, "after everyone had gone home and after I'd returned from letting the dogs out, Orpheus wouldn't settle down and I thought it was because he was picking up the scent of the party goers. I came back in and after we'd made love, I waited awhile until you'd fallen asleep. I got dress and took a walk around the house. That's when I spotted a car that had no business being parked where it was and it was then that I realized what was exciting Orpheus. Every action I took that night was preplanned, right down to the second. I let Eurydice in and then I started the fire with methane," he waved his hand to still my question, "in the back bedroom. I woke you, got you dress and lead you to the fireplace. Seeing you disappear into that tunnel was very difficult for me, one of the hardest things I had to do that night was watching you disappear from my sight. I didn't want to let you out of my sight, but I couldn't have you there with me, not knowing if I could keep you safe. I pushed the lever of the fireplace, which closed the opening and prayed to God to watch over you.

"After seeing you to safety, that's when the adrenaline kicked in, and I was ready to kill or be killed. Earlier I'd called Sonny from my cell phone, before I started the fire because I knew the phone lines leading up to the house had been cut. I told Sonny where he could find you, and if I knew Sonny, I knew you wouldn't be alone for too long once you'd reached the ravine. I told him that his friend needed him, and the area where you could be found. This was one time I was glad Sonny loved you as much as he did. I had my silencer on my gun, and I put soot from the fireplace on my hands and smeared some over my face, to cut down on the glare. I grabbed my oxygen mask and headed for the bedroom door at a low crouch. By the time I'd gotten into the hallway they had already entered the house. I knew what I had to do, because I had no desire to be taken, dead or alive. The hallway leading into the other part of the house was engulfed in flames by then. It was a hot, angry fire, spitting out rolling balls of flame. That was because of the methane that I'd used to fuel the fire. I'd placed containers of methane throughout the house to ensure the consistency of the fire. It attributed to the intensity of the fire, which would burn and melt anything and everything in its path. I took the first one out before he even knew what had hit him. The bullet found its mark in the center of his forehead. I drug the body into the hall, depositing it close to the inferno, guaranteeing that nothing but ashes, if that much, would remain. I continued in my stealth mode, searching for the other two, with you constantly on my mind. I knew you had a long walk ahead of you, and I kept praying for your safety. It was hard to concentrate because I kept thinking about you. One minute I wanted to join you, and the next I was convinced that you'd be okay. If I wanted to keep my promise to you, I would have to keep my mind on the job before me. The fire was burning quicker than even I had anticipated and the explosions were loud, ripping through the house. I knew if I wanted to get out of there alive I would have to get a move on. I caught a movement from the corner of my eye, and I turned and took out the second henchman. After depositing him close to the burning flames, I continued my pursuit for the third and final assailant, and when I found him, I took him out as well. I was getting ready to leave when something hit me from behind, sending me crashing to the floor and then I lost consciousness. And that leads me to my other story."

"Blair, you don't have to do this." I could never stop loving him, but would I be able to forgive him for his deception? I gave Blair's hand a squeeze as he spoke with tears in his eyes as he proceeded to describe his life to me, growing up in New York with a heroin addict for a mother and a prostitute for a sister. As I listened to the sequence of events of his life, from having the love of a doting, and caring grandmother, to being shipped off to an uncaring mother and sister, I began to better understand why Blair had done what he had did.

Blair talked well into the night, with me questioning him from time to time. I was shocked and saddened by the poignant tale he shared with me, and I cried for the child who was sustained merely from the memories of his grandmother. By the time Blair's story had come to an end, we were drained from the long day and hungry as well. By the light of the moon we ate thick ham and cheese sandwiches piled high thick slices of tomatoes and romaine lettuce and topped off with a slathering of spicy mustard. We washed it all down with ice cold pineapple juice as we sat around the table and talked some more about the events of his life.

It had to have been well after midnight before my first yawn overtook me. Before long, Blair was also yawning followed by two more of my own. "I think I'll call it a night," I said as I rose from my seat. I picked up the used paper plates we'd eaten our dinner on and the used napkins and headed for the galley. "Which bedroom is mine?" I asked Blair as I tossed everything into the trash compactor. I was already heading for the back of the yacht.

"*Our stateroom* is the larger of the two," Blair replied as he followed behind me.

"*Stateroom?*"

"*Stateroom.*"

"Not bedroom?" I asked as Blair shook his head. "Oh," I replied as I entered the *stateroom*, thinking I didn't care what it was called as long as it had a bed and a pillow to lay my head on. It had a bed, and man what a bed. Judging from the size of the platform bed, it had to be a California King and it was beckoning me with its comfortable looking comforter and large fluffy pillows, making me want to dive right into bed, clothing and all, for I was just that exhausted. "What do you call that?" I asked pointing toward the large bed which sat situated on a raised platform centered in the room.

Blair smiled, "our bed."

"I see," I replied as I look longingly back at the bed.

"Don't worry, you'll pick up on the terminology," he said with a laugh.

"Right...don't you think we should start slow and sleep in separate bedrooms- I mean *staterooms?*" I asked as I turned around to face him.

"Hell no. I am not spending another night alone."

Even though Blair had put more ice on his lip it was still slightly puffy, as well as his eye. He stood before me appearing comical with his blacken eye and swollen lip, trying to give the appearance of defiance. "Well you certainly worked this out, I don't have a change of clothing, or a toothbrush," I said as I walked away from him and sat down on the bed. I bounced up and down a couple of times testing it out.

Blair laughed, and then let out a loud moan, placing his hand to his mouth.

"What's so funny?"

"Does this remind you of our first night together?" he asked heading for the mirrored walls.

I smiled as I remembered the night Blair spoke of. "Full circle."

"With one difference," Blair said as he slid the mirrored wall apart revealing a walk-in closet full of clothing.

"Wow," I said as I approached the closet and pulled out a pair of slacks. I put the slacks away and pulled out a few more items of clothing, inspecting the sizes before coming to the conclusion that Blair had indeed been observing me for I had dropped a couple of dress sizes since the fire and the outfits Blair had chosen for me would be a perfect fit. Built-in drawers took up one end of the closet and I opened each drawer, inspecting the contents, finding an assortment of lingerie, scarves, socks, and belts. Looks like Blair thought of everything this time, I thought as I left the closet.

"Toothbrush and everything else you will need can be found in the head," Blair said as nodded toward a closed door with an intricate detailed painting of a peacock on it. The entire main deck, which Blair had explained to me later, consisted of the galley, living area, and the two main staterooms, were richly done, reminding me of an Arab castle own by a rich Sheikh right out of one of those movies like Lawrence of Arabia, or Sinbad the Sailor. There were hidden niches, nooks and crannies with large potted plants or plain colorful pots, some of them as tall as me, filled some of the crannies. Most of the walls were of a shiny wood of some kind, and if I had to guess I would say teak, being the walls were similar to what Blair had in the master bedroom at what used to be our home in Alpine, I'll go with teak. But I knew wood about as well as I knew ship terminology. What part of the walls that weren't wood was painted in bright colors of gold, aqua, or red, and large rugs covered most of the elaborate tiled flooring. I guess I was the harem.

"Don't tell me, you mean the bathroom, right?" I asked as I stepped into the large room, with its gold faucets and sunken tub and beautifully tiled floor. In another corner stood an opened shower, minus a shower door with at least seven showerheads stationed strategically on two walls and a larger one hanging from overhead. Mirrors graced every wall in the room, and pocket lights dotting the ceiling gave the room its warmth. As I was changing in the bathroom, I took a quick peek in the cupboards, and I discovered a blow dryer, electric curlers, mousse, gels, and a full line of cosmetics, all in the shades I normally wore. Blair was nowhere in sight by the time I left the bathroom and I was in the bed, tucked under the silken covers when he finally returned to the stateroom. "How long have you been planning my kidnapping?"

"Is that what you think I did? Kidnapped you? I can't kidnap my own wife," he said as he removed his clothing.

"Is Shamus still driving the boat?"

"My mouth hurts so don't make me laugh. It's a yacht, sweetheart, and you don't drive it. Right now we're anchored; I've set the alarm-"

"Alarm? We're miles from land why would you need an alarm?"

"That way no one can board without my knowledge, actually I have a very sophisticated security system for the *Janús* designed by me. Look at this," Blair said as he picked up what looked like a television remote control and pushed a button. Part of the paneled wall directly in front of the bed slid back to reveal four monitors. "There's a monitoring system up at the helm too."

Helm? I was leaving that alone for I was too sleepy to even process that one, and anyway, I wouldn't remember any of this mess in the morning. "But why would someone want to come aboard."

"Pirates, baby-"

"Pirates?"

"Not like Captain Hook-"

"I know what a pirate is, Blair," I replied as I slid deeper under the covers, surrendering my body to the fluffy pillows and sheets.

"You have nothing to worry about."

I think I was asleep even before Blair finished his sentence. It must have been a combination of the drink, and all of the excitement of the day. And to top it all off, the boat felt like one big waterbed with its constant up and down motion. I would have slept the whole night through if it hadn't been for Blair. I awoke to him nibbling on my ear, and then my neck and I could feel his hardness pressed against my back.

"Baby, I've missed you so much," he whispered as his hands caressed my body.

I thought I was prepared for this, but the moment his hands began to work their magic, my body turned traitorous. My mind was saying no, but my body was saying yes, *hell* yes. I reached around and stroked his back as he became all too familiar to me once more, and I realized just how much I'd missed him too. We used to be like one when we had laid together, our movements synchronized.

A few seconds later, I was flat on my back, legs spread eagle on the bed with Blair on top of me, his hands in mine, his chest on my chest, his stomach on my stomach, our thighs and legs lined up as we kissed. I could feel his hardness against me as my legs worked their way from under his and we rocked with the boat as he entered me.

"I've missed you," he said with his mouth hard against the side of my face.

I was hungry for him, as I ravaged him with my lips. "I've missed you too," I said between kisses, as I arched my back to meet him.

"You feel so good, baby, *so* good."

"Oh, Blair," I said as I writhed beneath him. Suddenly he stopped, and I opened my eyes and looked up at him as he looked down at me, his blacken eye and distorted lip making him look sinister in the gloom of the room. "Don't stop," I said as I raised my head to give him a kiss. He pulled back and pressed my hands down onto the mattress.

"Did you miss me?"

"Yes, oh yes, Blair, I've missed you so much."

Blair moved his hips, grounding himself into me, making me moan with desire, and then suddenly he stopped. I brought my legs up higher around his waist and rotated my hips.

"Does that feel good?"

"Yes, please don't stop." I said as I lifted my hips from the bed. He repeated his earlier moments and then stopped again. "Blair!"

Blair lowered his head, tenderly cuddling me, as he kissed me about my face and neck. His face came to a rest between my breasts, and then he planted little kisses about my shoulders. I squirmed beneath him. "Does that feel good to you, baby?" Blair asked as he nuzzled my breasts. "You want me to do that again? Ooh, you taste so good, so good. Did you tell *Sonny* to stop?"

My eyes flew open at his words. It was as though he had poured a glass of cold water on me, making me come face-to-face with reality. "What? *What did you say?*"

"Did you ask Sonny to stop?"

"*Get up. Get the fuck off of me,*" I said through clenched teeth as I struggled to wiggle from beneath him. Blair grabbed my hands, pinning me down on the bed with his body.

"Did he feel good too? Did he feel this good or better?" he asked as he grounded into me.

"You *son-of-a-bitch*; let me up!" I was growing angrier by the minute as I twisted and turned my body from side to side, in a vain attempt to try and get away from him.

"I'm your husband, Mia. Don't I get to fuck you too?"

"Get off of me, Blair!" Instead of releasing me, Blair brought my hands together and held them over my head in one of his. With his other hand he grasped my chin and brought his mouth down to mine with so much force that I cried out in pain. Just as quickly as it had started, Blair released me, rolling over, and out of the bed.

I lay upon the bed trembling with anger. I could taste blood in my mouth, and I wasn't sure if it was mine or Blair's. Using the back of my hand I wiped the taste of blood from my mouth never taking my eyes from his shadowy figure as he grouched beside the bed, his heavy breathing seemed to fill the room. Blair moved closer to the bed, I bolted straight up and scooted over to the other side of the bed and away from him.

"No," Blair said as he reached out and turned on the bedside lamp. "I would never hurt you, Mia. I could never hurt you."

"How dare you! I should have known you'd pull some shit like this! I told you back at the house you would do this! It's too soon for us to be together, Blair!"

"No. No we can be together, we can make it work. I know we can. It's just, all this time I've been jealous of what you and Sonny had, and now- now that I know it's tearing me apart."

"I see." I laughed out loud and Blair looked over at me like I was deranged. "So, what you're trying to say is, it's okay for you to fake your own death, and then conveniently come back to life and expect everything to be peachy-keen? But when your wife, who thinks you're fucking *dead*, Blair, finds comfort in the arms of another man, it tears you apart? Like I give a shit, Blair J. Freeman, or whatever the fuck your name is!" I was laughing and crying at the same time, as I said this. Blair reached out for me, but I quickly jumped out of bed, moving further away from him.

I was standing on the other side of the bed now, my back up against the wall and as far away from him as I could possibly get. I had a feeling this was going to happen. Blair would never get over the fact that I'd slept with Sonny, and I was angry with myself for allowing Blair to touch to me, but I was even angrier with Blair. "Yeah, right, and just who the hell are you to tell me what to do? All this time I've been kicking myself, and blaming myself for your death! Crying myself to sleep, night after night, and for what? You weren't even dead, and now here you come popping back into *my life*, and the first thing you want to know is who I've been fucking? So, you want to know if I asked Sonny to stop. Well, the answer to your question is no! *Hell No!* Do you hear me, Blair? I didn't ask him to stop!"

Blair was kneeling on the floor at the edge of the bed, and he rose to his feet when I said this. "Don't talk like that," he said.

"Blair, get over it- okay? Shit happens." I may have said too much, for Blair had me by the shoulders in the blink of an eye and I hadn't even seen him move.

"Where did this all come from?"

Even though he had told me that he would never hurt me, I was too afraid to move. I probably looked like an owl, with my eyes round with fright. What was I going to do out here in the middle of the damn sea with an angry and supposedly dead Black man? "All wh- what?" I asked as I summoned up saliva to wet my parched mouth.

"The foul language, and the hitting?" he ask touching his face.

"I don't know, maybe you bring out the worst in me."

"This is not going the way I expected it," he spoke in a quieter tone.

"I don't know what to tell you, Blair."

"Tell me I'm a fucking asshole for saying that about Sonny. I can't believe I said that to you. All this time I've been thinking it, but to say it out loud...I'm sorry," Blair said with a shake of his head as he gave me a heart wrenching smile. "I love you. Do you love me?"

I hesitated, no longer sure if I loved him or not, but I did feel something for him. "Blair, regardless if I love you or not, I can't change what has happened to us. I know what you want to hear. You want me to say that I'm sorry for what happened, but I can't. When Sonny and I slept together you were *dead* to me, Blair, and I am not sorry for what I did." Blair pulled me close and held me in his arms as I tried to pull away from him. "I feel sorry for you, Blair, because you are in so much pain about this whole sorry mess!" I spat out. "But what is done cannot be undone. If we want to continue in this marriage, just as I have to live with your indiscretions, then you'll have to live with mine." I was finally able to free my hands and I placed my hands to each side of his face as I let out a loud sigh. "Blair, I don't think you can do this, and I'm not sure I want to," I said looking into his eyes.

"I can-"

"No, you can't, and tonight proves it." I squeezed my eyes shut to hold back the tears, as my voice caught in my throat, as I release him. I was so worn-out, drained. "Every time you look at me you will see Sonny."

Blair's eyes seemed to tear up, but in an instant they appeared dry. I noticed how he worked his jaw, as he fought to speak and with a shake of his head, he was once again back in control of his emotions. With the back of his right hand Blair seem to chase away the imaginary forces that prevent him from allowing his tears to flow, as he again shook his head in denial. "Mia, you are everything to me. When I met you I knew from that moment you would be the one for me, and that we would always be together." He raised his head upward and loudly took in deep breath of air. "Baby, my life is nothing without you. You have my heart. You are my life and I would do anything for you, Mia, anything, just name it." Blair caressed my back and held me to him.

My head was throbbing from all of the emotion that was flowing through my body, and with fatigue setting in I could barely stand as I leaned my head against his chest. I spoke barely above a whisper as my voice came out hoarse and haltingly. "I'm exhausted, Blair. I'm sick of all the yelling and I just want to go to sleep. I'm sorry but I don't know what to say to you. All this time I've prayed to relive that night over again. And I've prayed for a second chance to make you enter the tunnel with me. I didn't care what it took; I wasn't leaving without you, if only I'd been given a second chance. Blair, in this lifetime, we don't get too many second chances but for whatever reason, God has blessed us twice, and I believe whatever happens tonight will make or break what is left of this marriage. We've been given the opportunity to do this again, if we want to, but I refuse to feel guilty about anything I've done because I've done nothing wrong."

"Mia, you shouldn't feel guilty, and I'm sorry if I made you feel that way. You're right, it's my problem, and I'll just have to deal with it. Baby, I'm not going to lie to you, it hurts like hell knowing the two of you made love"-

"Blair-" I raised my head, and leaned away from him.

"No. No, don't deny it, the two of you made love," Blair said holding up his hand to silence me. "Sonny has always loved you, Mia, and I know for a fact he has wanted you more than anything else in this world. The proof lies in his actions; the man wanted me dead. So as far as Sonny was concerned, it was love. Maybe to you it was just a way of being comforted, but to Sonny it was love. You were very vulnerable at time, Mia. You needed to be held and to be loved. It doesn't mean you love him, does it?"

"Blair, listen to you. Listen to what you're saying, and then ask yourself; what good is all of this? You're standing here assuming just because it was a difficult time for me I didn't know what I was doing. Well, here's a news flash for you, Blair, I knew exactly what I was doing. It takes two you know?"

"Okay, you may or may not have known what you were doing, but still you have to look at the situation. It was bound to happen. Baby, it happened just like it did before remember? But this time instead of the two of you stopping before you went too far...you probably thought, what the hell, right?"

"Blair-"

"Mia, all I'm trying to say is, I don't blame you for what happened, but I do blame Sonny. He knew. He knew all along that after I was no longer around, he was going to sleep with his *precious* Mia."

"Why are you talking like that?"

"He knew this, Mia. Sonny has known he was going to make love to you since the night of the fire when he left me for dead."

"Blair, stop this! I will never believe that about Sonny. I don't care how much you hate him for what he and I did; I will never, ever believe Sonny would attempt anything like that. This whole...this mess is never going to end," I said holding my hands in the air. "You are never going to forgive me."

"Forgive you for what, Mia, for being human? Remember we are *lifemates*. We are in this together, for the rest of our lives. It's like you said before, we'll have to learn to forgive and forget, and what I did was wrong too," Blair said with a chuckle. "God knows that I've done so much wrong in my life that I should be on my knees every *blessed day* asking the man upstairs for his forgiveness, and I do get down on my knees, Mia, every single night, to ask for forgiveness! And if God can forgive me, then I can certainly forgive you. Mia, what you did, was only human, and I can't hate you for being human. For you see, I am the one to blame. None of this, *none of it*, would have happened if I'd just confided in you in the first place. Mia, I wanted to tell you about my life so many times before. Every day I thought of a different reason not to tell you or I would somehow convince myself that it wasn't the right time. It was literally killing me not to confide in you, for every time I looked into your eyes, every time I kissed your beautiful lips, every time I held you in my arms, I wanted to yell out loud, *this is who I was before I met you!* Believe me, Mia, this shit was killing me and I am the blame for all this mess. I knew I could have trusted you, but to this day I do not know why I did not share everything about me in the beginning. I don't know why, God help me, I should have told you everything when I had the chance," Blair said with a shake of his head. "Lord knows, we all make mistakes in our lives, and what we need to do is to learn from them and figure out how not to make the same mistakes, or heaven forbid, bigger ones." Blair knelt before me, with my hand in his. "Mia Freeman, will you marry me?"

I raised my other hand to my chest, as fresh tears ran down my face. I could hardly speak, the words stuck in my throat. Once I had loved this man, dearly, but it was not going to work. I can't go through this again. It will never work. We would never be able to recapture that spark, and all the passion we once had not so long ago. Blair wrapped his arms around my knees. I lay my hand on his head as I spoke, "I remember the first time in Las Vegas, and how right it all felt then. That time, and every other time after that we were always in harmony, and each time you where inside of me, Blair, I just wanted to keep you there forever." Blair stood and wrapped his arms around me, as our tears mingled. I leaned away from him, my tears clouding my vision, as I looked into his face. I really hadn't looked closely at Blair since his return, and only then did I see the worry lines that creased his forehead, and I reached out to smooth them away. We stood there staring at one another before Blair reached out for my hand bringing it up to his lips.

"Blair, when I thought I'd lost you forever, the feeling of *us*, the two of us, the bond that we once shared went away with you. Even now, with you here I can't feel you anymore. I'm happy you are whole, and alive again and my love for you is still strong, yet, I can't feel you anymore. That's what I want, Blair, I want that feeling back, that feeling of *us*. But I know deep inside my heart, it will never be the same."

Blair shook his head, and with one swift movement lifted me into his arms and carried me back to bed. We talked some more, well into the wee hours of the morning until we fell into an exhausted sleep in one another's arms, and in the morning just before sunrise, we made love, but I knew we would never be the same again.

CHAPTER TWENTY NINE

Blair and I spent the rest of the week out at sea, talking and listening to each other regarding our lives as we discussed our future. Talking was always the easiest part of a conversation, listening was another matter altogether. Some days our discussions went well into the early hours of the mornings, as we made sure the other understood exactly what the other meant. Conversation this deep made for long frustrating days and nights, but it was worth every tear and sleepless night as we tried to reach an understanding. We never reached a conclusion, for it would take longer than a few days to work out our differences. One of the biggest issues for me would be living on the run or as Blair had put it, on the *lam*, for the rest of our lives. Things weren't great in the bedroom either. I don't know if it was me or Blair, but it was just not the same.

We hadn't spent all of our days on the *Janús* in deep conversation; we'd also enjoyed eating marvelously fattening meals, swimming in the clear blue waters of the Caribbean Sea, and just lounging around and being all out lazy. I discovered that Blair was an excellent captain and fisherman as well; catching most of the fish we ate at dinner. Occasionally we would come across some of the local fishing boats and we would buy lobster, shrimp, clams, and oysters from them to supplement our store of food.

Blair had been in the area off and on for years, and he knew the surroundings very well. He even gave me a quick geography lesson, as we cruised around the 27-mile long island, venturing out into the Atlantic Ocean and back again. He also made me aware that the Eastern side of the island was located in the Atlantic Ocean, while the Western region was located in the Caribbean Sea. Like I really cared? Interesting? Yes. An important element needed to work on building a healthy relationship? No. For my life, as I knew it, was falling apart and here he was giving me geography lessons. Maybe this was Blair's way of coping with the actuality that our marriage was no more. We were equally guilty of running away from our problems.

In a way, I'd had a great time on the *Janús*, even though Blair and I were in this constant struggle for clarity regarding our relationship, and how we were going to go forward with our lives as a couple, we'd still had some memorable days out at sea. During our time on the *Janús*, there had been occasions when we had been optimistic, happy, and carefree, and this brief interlude allowed me to reflect on our early days together- before marriage. It was bittersweet, for I would always love Blair for the person he is, but my heart was no longer in this relationship. I was sorry when our outing came to an end, for it had been an adventure, one that I would always keep near and dear to my heart.

My original trip to the island had been for one week and I was well into my third week when I realized that it was time to go home and face the music. Earlier in the week, I'd placed a call to Atlanta to inform my sons of my extended stay. I didn't tell them the reason why, because I felt sharing this piece of information over the telephone would not have been appropriate. I wasn't sure if I wanted to explain Blair's inexplicable rise from the ashes, so it was best that we wait until I was certain it was something I wanted to do. At the time I placed the call to Anthony, he had informed me that Sonny had called him and was inquiring of my whereabouts. Sonny had been under the impression that I'd made a stopover in Atlanta before returning to San Diego, so I had Anthony call Sonny and inform him that I'd decided to remain in St. Lucia for another week. I also given Sonya a call to inquire about the temporary agency, and was happy to find out that all was well. I really didn't have any major concerns about the agency, because there was no doubt in my mind about Sonya's capabilities when it came to running the office. I just didn't want Sonya to think I'd deserted her.

I expressed my concern to Blair about my clothing and other personal effects I had left at Pilgrim House and how my reservations at the Villa had been only for a week, and Blair had informed me he was the proprietor of the Villa. So everything was just as we had left it. Now, the one thing left to do was to make flight reservations for my return trip back to San Diego, but my biggest concern was trying to convince Blair that there was no need for him to confront Sonny. I dreaded the thought of the two of them together.

Blair wanted me to return to San Diego with him aboard the *Janús*, but I begged off, explaining how I wanted to confront Sonny alone. It would take too long to get home via the *Janús*. The sooner I handled this situation with Sonny, the quicker things would go back to being normal, well at least for some of us. We'd been back on the island only one day, and were in the bedroom of the Villa discussing my return trip back to San Diego. For some reason Blair refused to let me out of his sight and had taken to hovering around me at every turn I took. The only time alone was when I was in the bathroom, and he was adamant about me not seeing Sonny without him.

"Mia, I don't understand why you can't wait until I get there? If necessary I can let Shamus bring the *Janús* to San Diego, and I can return to San Diego with you."

"Blair, Sonny and I are just going to talk, not have sex."

"That's not what I was thinking. I was thinking more along the lines that I didn't want you to be alone with him when you questioned him regarding the night of the fire. I mean, you even said yourself that when you and Sonny finally met up that night, he had more soot and ashes on him than you did, and he had supposedly just arrived. That alone is reason enough for me."

"Blair, can we do this my way?"

"No. Mia, I see no reason for you to return to the States at all. With a computer you can run a business from anywhere in the world. We can just hang out on the *Janús* for the rest of our lives. We won't have to worry about your sons, because we can take trips to Atlanta any time we feel like it, and they can even vacation with us aboard the *Janús*." As Blair said this, there was a light rap on the bedroom door. "Yes?"

It was Enid. "Mrs. Freeman, there's a gentleman here to see you."

"Thank you, Enid," I said as dropped the blouse I had in my hand down onto the bed. Blair and I shared a questioning glance, "are you expecting anyone?" I asked, as I edged toward the door. Blair shook his head following along behind me as I left the room. We still hadn't confided in anyone about Blair's return, so I pulled the bedroom door close behind me, before following along behind Enid, and as we came to the foyer, Enid turned left for the kitchen, and I continued into the living room and once there, I almost fainted dead away. Standing with his back to me, at the opened French doors staring out at the view was Sonny Steward. His broad back framed by the vivid blue sky, wearing one of my favorite tropical style shirts. I inhaled deeply, thinking this was where he was supposed to be. Not Blair and I wanted to reach out and stoke Sonny upon his back, and lean into him, my face against his back and place my arms around his waist.

But before I could do anything, Sonny swung around to face me, making my heart race.

"Mia," he said as he rushed forward with arms outstretched. "You look great."

I returned his hug, excited about seeing him again, but shocked at seeing him *here*. "Sonny, what are you doing here?" I finally asked.

"Well, when Anthony called and told me you was staying for an additional week I decided to join you," he replied with a grin on his face. "I love this place," he said as he turned back to the opened door. "Now I see why you don't want to come home. Look at this place, what a beautiful view," Sonny said, as he stepped out onto the terrace.

I walked over to where he stood, staring out at the bay, excited about him being here, but afraid for him because I didn't know what to expect from Blair once he discovered Sonny's presence. I turned to look over my shoulder, expecting to see Blair. "Why are you here?"

"I came to see you. We're still friends right? Can't friends visit one another?" Sonny asked as he sat down on the railing grinning like a kid.

I wanted to yell at him to leave, run away while he still had the chance, but instead I took a deep breath. "Sonny, I have a question to ask you," I said, suddenly nervous at what his answer might be but just as anxious to have this all out in the open and done with so I could send him away, even though I didn't want him to leave.

"Shoot," he replied, as he folded his arms across his chest, with that same grin upon his face making him look much younger than his thirty odd years.

I took several deep breaths and turned my head to look out at the bay, and away from his boyish expression. I looked out at the calming view, the clear crisp blue skies, the palmed hills, the aqua colored sea, and the white-sandy beaches. I took another deep breath, thinking it was now or never. "I don't know how to say this, but, ah-"

"What is it?" Sonny asked with a look of concern, as he jumped down from the railing. He reached out, placing his hands on my shoulders and turned me around to face him.

"Sonny, the night of the fire, when...ah, when Blair was murdered," I raised my head and looked him straight in his eyes. His love for me was radiant in his beautiful eyes. "Did you by chance go up to the house that night, I mean before meeting me down at the ravine?"

Now it was Sonny's turn to look away, as his eyes shifted to the left, and then to the right. He was doing everything in his power to avoid my gaze, before he moved away. "What? Why are you questioning me about that night?" He asked turning his attention back to the bay.

"Because, when you and I finally met up at the ravine, you were covered with soot and ashes and you supposedly had only just arrived and had driven straight to the ravine to meet me." I reached out, and laid my hand on his arm. It hurt me to ask him that question, because I'd seen his answer in his face just before he turned away. I was positive of what his answer would be, but more importantly; I knew why he had done it. I couldn't stop myself, for I had to hear the truth from him despite the fact that part of me wanted to send him away, but I couldn't. "Sonny," I said softly, as I gave his arm a squeeze, "did you go up to the house that night?" The arm beneath my hand seem to turn hard as steel, and the tears that had stung at my eyes began to fall in earnest, as I silently prayed for him to tell me no. Then I could just send him away, back to the California. Now that I had asked the question I really didn't want to know the answer. I didn't care, for it no longer mattered because Blair was alive and well, but in a way, I guess I wanted to prove to Blair wrong so I needed Sonny's answer.

Time stood still as I waited for his reply. I could no longer hear the birds in the sky, or the sound of the waves from the beach. Nor could I hear the sound of the pots and pans rattling in the kitchen, or Tomas' singing drifting down the hallway as he prepared our midday meal, for it was if the rest of the world had disappeared and only Sonny and I remain.

Sonny snatched his arm away from me and turned on me, "So what kind of shit question is that? Is that what you think happened, Mia? So is this what you've been doing all of this time, thinking about why I was covered with so much ash that night?" His fist hit the railing with a loud whack as he said this and I jumped back, openly crying.

Earlier, I'd convinced myself that Blair was wrong about this, but now I knew what Sonny's answer would be. Be still my heart. Please be still, I silently prayed. I didn't know what to do with my hands. At first I began to fan my face before folding my arms across my chest, as I repeated the question to him, but I certain what his answer would be. "You were at the house that night weren't you, Sonny?" My breath came out in little puffs. I wanted to reach out and take him in my arms, to tell him it no longer mattered what happened that night because Blair was alive and well. But I made myself back away from him, and when the back of my legs bumped up against one of the deck chairs, I slowly sat down. It was then that I realized how tense I was, as I tried to relaxed my shoulders. I repeatedly clenched and unclenched my hands into fists. I stopped clenching my hands, after I became conscious of what I was doing, and placed my hands flat on the arms of the chair. I lowered my head to my chest, closed my eyes, and took in several long slow deep breaths in a vain attempt to calm myself. I was visibly shaking, and I wanted to scream. Scream at Sonny to leave, go away. Forget the fact that I and even asked the damn question. Just go home!

I raised my head and discovered that Sonny had turned his back to me. Flashbacks of our lovemaking, assaulted my thoughts, along with remnants of the good times we'd had together when it had been just the two us, and it hurt. It hurt so badly that my head began to throb. Sonny would never do anything like that, not Sonny. Not my friend, my best buddy, he couldn't do something as inconceivable as that. I wanted to tell him how much I loved him. Then the next moment I wanted to hit something, to scream. Jump up and down and run down the cliffs and into the sea, away from all of this silence! A wave of fierce inescapable dread shrouded me as my tears distorted him from my vision.

It surprised me that I was now sobbing out loud, so loudly that when Sonny finally spoke, his voice was barely above a whisper. So low that I could scarcely hear him because of my weeping, and I silently pleaded for him to lie to me, but I knew he wouldn't. I had finally asked the right question and Sonny would tell me the truth. With the back of my hand I angrily brushed away at the tears that streamed down my face as I looked over to where he stood. What I saw made me want to disappear in a puff of smoke. Sonny was now facing me, staring at me with so much pain and grief on his face that it tore deeply at my heart.

"You're right, I was at the house that night," he spoke softly. "When Blair called and told me that you needed me- we- I thought he had...hurt you in some way," Sonny said as he reached out to touch me, but I leaned back in the chair away from him. He pulled his hand back as though he'd been stung, and his face crumbled right before my eyes. "I- I remembered what happened the last time, and I knew you would be down at the ravine, so I went to the house first. I had no idea that others where there in the house that night. I didn't know what was going on at the time," he said with a shrug of his shoulders. "All I knew was Blair said you needed me and that was enough. Not again! He was not going to lay another hand on you after that night, regardless of the reason!"

I think I did something between a laugh and a sob, as I shook my head. I raised my hand and lean even further away from him. "You mean you could've saved Blair's life and you didn't even try?" I turned away from him, for I could no longer stand to see the painful look upon his beautiful face. My own heart was breaking with his confession to me. I'd always known that Sonny loved me, but I never knew that it was of this magnitude. So great was his love for me, he would've actually taken a human life. But the greatest pain of all was I still loved him, despite all that he had tried to do to Blair. Maybe if Sonny had succeeded in what he had set out to do this moment would not be as painful to me, because I would have never known the truth. But Sonny's attempt on Blair's life had failed, and Blair was alive and well. Sonny knew how much I had loved Blair, and in his mind he had been successful in murdering Blair, and now that I knew the truth, Sonny knew he had ended my life as well.

Sonny shook his head from side to side, as though to clear his thoughts as he continued to speak. "The house was engulfed in flames, and smoke was everywhere. I saw a movement...and I don't remember much after that, until I was outside at the ravine with you. It was because of you. Mia, it was all because of you. We- I couldn't stand the thought of him hurting you again. God forgive me," Sonny said as he broke into tears. Sonny made no attempt to staunch the flow of tears as they streamed down his face. "I'm so sorry, I didn't know what all was going on that night, If I'd known-"

"What did it matter? That's why Blair wasn't able to escape that night. It was because of you. You were the one responsible for making sure that Blair would not be able to leave the house. Oh, Sonny, why did you do it?" Even though I knew Blair was alive and well, the thought of knowing that Sonny had left Blair for dead was too painful for me to bear. And it was even more painful to me because of my love for him.

"For your love. For you, Mia, you're all I've ever wanted. I did it for love. It was because of you."

He came toward me, his steps haltingly, as though his feet weighed a ton, and he reached out for my hand. I snatched my hand away from him. "I love you Sonny, but you *tried* to take away from me the most important thing in my life at that time," I cried as I placed my hand to my heart. "Once, a long time ago you gave me life and then you took it away. How could you do that to me, Sonny? If you loved me as much as you say you do, how could you do that?" Sonny lowered himself in front of me and again he reached out for my hand. I stood up and backed away, knocking the chair over in the process to get away from him. "You'd better go."

"Mia, please don't do this, okay? C-C-Can't you see that you are the most important person in my *life!* It should have been us anyway...together, the two of us!"

It was perfect timing, for just at that moment Tomas came out to ask if my guest would be staying for lunch. I quickly turned to the bay and shook my head. "He's leaving," I replied, before taking off in a run down the steps that lead to the edge of the cliff. I had to get away; I was so confused and hurt. I never thought in a million years that Sonny would have been capable of doing anything like that, and to think that I'd called Blair a liar. I was standing there allowing the sea breeze and the warmth of the tropical sun to dry the tears from my face. From the corner of my eye a movement from a nearby bush caught my attention and I glanced in that direction. "How long have you been there?"

"I followed you and Enid out and when I saw who it was I went around back through the kitchen and out the back door," Blair said a he rose from the boulder that he'd been sitting upon and joined me.

"You heard?" I asked, on the verge of tears again.

"Everything."

"I'm shocked," I said, as Blair wrapped his arms around me.

"About what?" Blair asked as he held me close.

"You didn't jump out and try to kill him with your bare hands." I replied as I let lose a flood of tears.

"I knew you wanted to confront Sonny alone, but, if it's any comfort to you, it took every ounce of will power I had to keep from jumping out and breaking his mother fucking neck," Blair replied with so much loathing and vehemence in his voice that I crumbled in his arms as I sobbed against his chest.

"Oh, baby, I'm so sorry," Blair said rubbing my back. "You don't have to cry. I wasn't going to kill him for doing something I probably would've done if the circumstances had been different."

"So much talk of killing and death- no more, Blair, please no more," I finally got out as the tears raked through me. It hurt so much for me to hear Sonny's confession. He words had ripped my heart right out of my chest. I didn't know what to do any more for I still loved him. It was true, once he had given me life, and he had also taken it away when he had tried to take Blair from me. Blair was here with me and now Sonny was gone, what do I do? Oh, God help me, what do I do now? My heart was dying, the pain from it all was making me weak, I couldn't speak, I couldn't see, as I went limp against Blair, no longer able to stand on my own. I just wanted to die. God help me. God, *please* help me.

Blair tightened his hold on me as we slowly sank to the ground. "Mia, I know Sonny is your friend, and I know you're hurting right now because of what he did. I don't know how to take away the pain. The man loves you, Mia, and I'm sorry the way this whole damn mess turned out and if I could, I would turn back the clocks to change everything, to make everything as it was before. But, baby, I can't. A lot has happened to you these past few months so you go right ahead and cry and I'll be right here, holding you."

CHAPTER THIRTY

Well, after my visit with Sonny, there was no longer a need for me to make air reservations back to San Diego so I and made the trip back with Blair aboard the *Janús*. The main reason I had been in a hurry to get back was to confront Sonny, but his unexpected visit to St. Lucia had rewritten my agenda. Although I had tried to hide my feelings about Sonny from Blair, it was very difficult being in close proximity to him for the time it took us to get back to the California coastline. Early on in our trip, Blair would leave me on my own, making excuses to help Shamus with this or that, but as time wore on I believe Blair eventually grew weary of my constant crying and moping about. No matter how hard I tried to hide from him on the 120 foot yacht, Blair would always search me out to include me in on dinner preparations, or have me look at charts, anything to get me to interact with him and Shamus. Even at a cruising speed of 12 knots Blair said it would take about two weeks for us to reach the California coastline. But it was a continuous struggle for me to live in the moment, for all of my thoughts were of how alone Sonny must feel, for I was feeling that same loneliness. I couldn't put the painful memory of his last words to me out of my head, and the look on his face would remain with me forever. Whenever I thought about our conversation that day, my heart ached all over again, as I remembered how Sonny had reached out for me and I had turned him away. How could this be? A few months before I'd been praying to have Blair back in my life, now I was trying to imagine what Sonny was doing? I guess that old saying was right, be careful for what you ask for.

While in route, Blair and I discussed the issue of the temporary agency and we agreed Sonya should formally have the title as Senior Manager. Once we'd reached San Diego, I was only there long enough to help Sonya interview for additional office support. I also met with Jeremy and made sure all was well with the pool and lawn business. Blair decided it would be time to sell off the pool business soon, and that I should give Jeremy a chance to make the first offer. I explained to Sonya how I would be taking some time off to continue with my recuperation. I left a post office box number in Atlanta for my forwarding address, even though I wasn't permanently residing in Atlanta, and made sure that Sonya and Jeremy had my current email address as well. I was also assessable via my cell phone.

Since Maurice and Anthony would be remaining in Atlanta, Blair thought that it would be a good idea to place the condo on the market, furniture and all, but I resisted because I wasn't sure if I was ready to part with my past so soon. I still hadn't shared with my sons about Blair being back in the picture. I thought it would be wise to wait until we could all meet face-to-face before tackling that issue.

I found out through Sonya that Macey had given birth to a daughter whom Macey had named Chandra, after her aunt who and passed away. Claudia and Macey had grown close over time and Claudia had given Macey a baby shower. I guess my invitation got lost in the mail, and it would have been inappropriate of me to send a gift since Macey had made it quite clear that she no longer wanted to be friends with me, and I for one, can't say that I blamed her.

Claudia married her counselor friend, and the two of them have settled in the Los Angeles area. I didn't attend her wedding, but she was registered at my favorite department store, so they did receive a gift from me.

With Blair back in my life and with him making all the moneymaking decisions in the background, I was considering opening another branch of Harris and Freeman in Atlanta. Our list of things to do continued to grow, and eventually we'll get around to taking care of everything on our list. But our first priority was the biggest of all to undertake, and that was our attempt to bring some normalcy back to our life. For it had become a daily struggle for us, trying to live together as husband and wife. Being back in a relationship with Blair took a lot of effort. We had some good days, but we had plenty of rough nights as well. We were aware that our relationship would need time to heal if it was going to work.

I couldn't help it, but it seem to me that I was in a constant state of numbness, going along with whatever Blair suggested and I knew it was because I really didn't want to be with him, but somehow I thought it would be for the best. I let him handle everything because I wasn't able to accept reality. Sometimes I would wake in the middle of night and think it was all a dream.

CHAPTER THIRTY ONE

It had been one month since my meeting with Sonny in St. Lucia, and much to my despair, Blair and I where back aboard the *Janús* much too soon for my taste. We were cruising along the Washington coastline as we headed for the Seattle area. Originally, we had been on our way to the Hawaiian Islands to spend the winter. All was well until I became ill, so we decided to stop off in Washington for a week or two so I could visit a doctor.

Glancing out at the many islands we passed on our way inland made me anxious and I couldn't wait to get back on dry land, for the constant motion of the yacht was causing me horrific motion sickness. I thought it might be due to an inner ear infection or some other malady, so on first dock; I found a doctor online and made an appointment to be seen as soon as possible. It was a three day wait before my appointment, and by the time Blair and I pulled up in front of the doctor's office in a rental car, I was as weak as a newborn baby. Although we had gotten a suite in a hotel, the motion sickness was still ever-present. In fact, it was so bad, that up until my appointment, all I could do was lie in bed flat on my back.

Blair sat with me in the exam room as the doctor examined me. Following a barrage of questioning on my recent activities, and drawing enough blood to fill a bucket, the good doctor pronounced that my vertigo may well be due to an inner ear infection. After being given a set of instructions on what not to do, I was given a prescription for Valium and another one for motion sickness, and was sent on my merry way. Because of the jarring of the car was making me nauseated each time we hit a dip or bump in the road, Blair dropped me off back at our room and after making sure I was settled in, he went to find a pharmacy to have my prescriptions filled. By the time he'd returned I was fast asleep, totally exhausted from the days ordeal. I awoke sometime in the middle of the night to find Blair hovering over me. After making sure that I had been doused my allotted medicine, he made me drink plenty of liquids before I drifted back to sleep, and I didn't wake until a day later.

It was sometime around nine in the morning that I was awakened by the ringing of Blair's cell phone. Two others, besides me, had access to Blair's number, Shamus, who was still aboard the *Janús*, and the doctor's office. As I glanced around the room, I spotted Blair sitting at the small table with a newspaper spread out on the table before him. While Blair spoke on the phone, I got out of bed and started to make my way to the bathroom. Blair rose from his chair and came forward as I inched my way across the room.

"H-Hold on, please. Baby, you okay?"

I nodded my head as I eased through the bathroom door, closing it behind me, and I didn't exit until after I'd showered and brushed my teeth. I was feeling much better as I exited the bathroom wrapped in the white fluffy robe that the hotel had provided to find a sober looking Blair sitting on the bed. "I don't know what was in the medicine the doctor gave me, but I am feeling so much better, and I'm starving," I raved as I stopped before him. "Don't tell me you're getting sick?" I commented as I reached out and felt his brow.

"I'm fine," Blair replied as he patted my arm. "That was the doctor, he wants you to discontinue the medication and he wants to see you this afternoon to go over your test results."

"Discontinue my meds? Did he say why? Whatever he gave me it worked-"

"Mia-"

"My stomach feels a little woozy, but that's probably due to the fact that I haven't eaten anything in a while," I continued on as I headed for the small kitchenette to find something to eat.

"You're pregnant."

I stopped in mid-stride, spinning around on the ball of one foot to stare at Blair, who still hadn't moved from his place on the bed. "What did you say?"

"The doctor said you were pregnant. He wants to run more tests this afternoon to see exactly how far along you are."

I was frozen in one spot, mouth hanging open, neck stiff and one hand hanging in mid air. "No," I finally spoke, shaking my head. "That's just isn't possible."

"I thought you were on the pill?"

"Blair, let's not go there, okay? It's not like I planned any of this–oh my God." I pulled out a chair and quickly sat down.

"What?" Blair asked as he rushed to my side.

I looked up at Blair, my mouth dry. "What time is my appointment?"

Blair leaned closer peering into my face, his hand rubbing my arm. "Mia, what is it?"

I had to tell him. There was no beating around the bush with this kind of news. I had to tell Blair that there was a huge possibility that it may not be his child. My mouth suddenly went dry at the thought of bringing this bit of shocking information to his attention. I looked up at Blair still hovering above me. I swallowed, hard, and thought about getting up to get a drink of water. I was stalling for time not sure what his reaction would be, and then I just blurted it out. "It may not be yours."

Blair continued to rub my arm, as he knelt down in front of me. "I thought about that."

"It could be yours."

"You'll have to get an abortion."

"Blair, there is a possibility that I could be carrying your child."

"It doesn't matter if the child is mine or *his*," Blair started. And I noticed he had some difficulty saying Sonny's name. "You know how I feel about bringing children into this world. I've told you before that I don't want any children. And if I remembered correctly, you didn't want any more kids either."

"I know, and I felt exactly the same as you, but now that I'm pregnant," I shrugged my shoulders, "if you want me to keep the baby I will. Blair, you don't have any children. Baby, this is a Godsend."

"No kids, and I damn sure don't want a child that will remind me of your little tryst with *him*."

I flinched, for his comment was like a slap in my face. But you were *dead* I wanted to yell out to him. "Even if I'm the *Mother*?"

"Mia, I didn't mean it like that. I'm a fugitive, okay, running from the bad guys, and the law. Once they find out that I'm still alive they will not stop searching for me. Just because I got rid of the Goodbyte brothers doesn't mean they are no longer looking for me. The only way to leave the kind of business I was in, is to die and I'm not dead yet. When I left I didn't just take my last pickup, I took the cash to a money laundering drop off were I was supposed to do a switch. But instead of leaving it I took every last dime that was there as well. I *murdered* people, Mia. I stole their money and I killed to acquire what they owed me. I took out two…three major families," he said with a shake of his head, "and when you take out one, there are twenty more up and coming drug bosses waiting to take their places. Lawanda had a son; he should be old enough to run the family now. How do you think he's going to feel when he finds out that the man who put his father and most of his immediate family behind bars for the rest of their natural lives is still alive? If you had not sent the information I left to the FBI, they would have come after you as well. What you did was to buy yourself some time, because they *will* come after you. You told Lawanda you were my *wife*, and she will *never* forget you. Oh, I'm sure she's happy as a lark right now because she believes me to be dead, but there is still the issue of the missing money. You understand what I'm saying now, baby? Changing my name, growing breads, shaving my head, and hiding out on a boat for Gods sake! I have fake identi-fication, and enough aliases to last me for the next twenty years. My name isn't Blair anymore remember? It's *Ellis, Ellis Solomon*. And this is all just a temporary fix, because I will always be a wanted man. What will we name this kid? Will his last name be *Smith, Freeman, Solomon*, or one of the many other aliases I'll have acquired by the time the kid reaches twenty? Now you tell me what kind of life would that be for a child? We'll never be able to settle down in one place for longer than two years, hopping from state to state, country to country, changing our names and living a lie for the rest of our lives." Blair stood and walked over to the small settee across the room.

I took in every word Blair had spoken, but as I sat there processing the information, what he was *really* saying finally sunk in and I was beginning to get an understanding of what our life would be like. We would be hunted everyday of our lives, looking over our shoulders unsure if we're being followed or not. I wondered how often had Blair done this before. "Blair, how many *aliases* do you have? How many times have you been married and how many other wives have you faked your death with?"

Blair looked taken aback by my questions and as he reached out for my hand a look of hurt spread across his face. "Mia, I swear to you on my grandmothers' grave that you are my first and only *wife*! You are the only woman I have ever loved. I hate the way we have to live our life and I hate the fact that I brought you into this *shit!*"

"What about the Goodbyte brothers, do you believe one day they will come looking for me?"

"Maybe, maybe not," he said with a shrug and much too calm for me.

"Blair, what if the shoe was on the other foot, you're now one of the Goodbyte brothers, what would you do? Would you come looking for the wife of the man who took money from you?"

"I took a lot of their money. The amount I got away with was an embarrassment to the Family. Someone would have to be made an example of."

"How much money did you take?"

"Baby, I'm not talking about a couple of million dollars, I'm talking about *hundreds* of millions of dollars. I could spend a million dollars a year for the next twenty years and still not have to worry about the next twenty years after that."

"You're just saying this to frighten me, and anyway you took the money, not me."

"No, I'm not-"

"But, how will they know? I'm back in the condo-"

"Freeman, Lawanda knows I went by the name *Freeman*. She may not be the brightest person in the world but the Goodbyte brothers didn't get as powerful as they are by being dumb. They may be stupid, but they are criminals and they have criminal minds."

"They're locked away in prison," I said as I stood up and began to pace about the room.

"How popular do you think the name *Freeman* is San Diego, California?"

I stood there thinking about what Blair was saying. He could be right. I didn't want a child, but I was pregnant and to me that was a blessing. He was also right about the kind of life we would have to live. It was bad enough for the two of us, but what kind of *lifestyle* would that be for a child? Always being uprooted, changing schools and last names and moving around. I wasn't even sure I would be able to endure that kind of lifestyle. "What about all of our plans, buying some land and having a home built?"

"And we can do that. We'll be safe enough for a year or two, and then we'll have to move on," Blair said as he lowered his head. "I'm sorry, but the kind of life we'll be leading will not be the right environment for a child."

"What about your child?"

Blair raised his head and looked at me. "For any *child!*"

"So, what you're saying is, being on the run with you I'll have a chance at a long and healthy life. But if we stay in one place, eventually we will be caught?" Blair nodded as I continued on, "But, I didn't take the money, you did!"

"Doesn't matter, we're married and you are in jeopardy whether you care to acknowledge it or not," Blair said point blank with no emotion at all in his eyes.

I looked away from him, staring across the room at the heavy drapes that covered the arcadia doors leading out onto the small balcony. In a way, what Blair was saying was the truth, but shit, I couldn't do what he was asking of me. I also knew that eventually I probably would end up resenting him for jeopardizing my life, and the life of my children. I knew what Blair was asking of me, to spend the rest of my life with him always on the run. To abort my pregnancy, to forfeit the life I was carrying and I wasn't sure if I wanted to do that. "Blair, I would never feel right about terminating my pregnancy, but I'd understand your reasoning a whole lot better if we were absolutely certain that it was *not* your child. I could understand why you wouldn't want this baby, but the odds-"

"Mia, have the baby, I don't care," Blair said with a loud sigh.

"No, I think the two of us should decide-"

"Okay, then get rid of it!"

"Blair, just listen to me, please-"

"Mia, you already know how I feel."

"Remind me again."

"I don't think I can do this."

"Meaning what?"

"Mia, I can't go through with this pregnancy."

"I see. So, if I decide to go through with the pregnancy, you want nothing to do with me or the child?"

"I didn't say that."

"Blair, it's my child too." I rushed on before he had a chance to stop me, "It isn't about the lifestyle we would be forced to live, and the running from the law and shit, it's about the fact that this could be Sonny's child, and you wouldn't want anything to do with that."

"That has nothing to do with it, Mia, and you know it," he said as he stood to face me.

"Oh please!" I was shaking as I held my ground, trying not to get into a shouting match with him. If Blair didn't want anything to do with this child, then he wanted nothing to do with me. "Blair, this is my child too, remember?"

"I'm not ready for this. Mia, please don't make me choose."

"*Choose*? Choose what, me or my child? At least give me the option of making my own choices. You behave as though I did this on purpose! *Like I get knocked up every day!* I want to know why you are being so hateful." Is this the man I thought I was still in love with?

"You shouldn't even have to ask me that question. Okay, let's say you have the child. You mean to tell me you're going to drag a baby around the world with you?"

"I didn't say I was keeping the baby."

"Then why are we standing around having this fucking discussion!"

"Damn you, Blair."

"Already been there and back, baby."

"If I had slept with any other man but Sonny and became pregnant we wouldn't be having this conversation!"

"You said it, I didn't," Blair said as he brushed past me.

I followed along behind him. "Blair, wait. Why?"

"Do I really have to say it?"

"Oh, right, Sonny wanted you dead, so you're taking it on out on his unborn child? Come on, Blair, get over it, okay? You're alive."

"Oh, so it is Sonny's child?"

"I don't know!"

Blair held up one hand. "I'll tell you what, okay? You are not going to have this child. How do you think watching *his* child grow in your belly is going to make me feel, huh? Mia, the son-of-a-bitch loves you, and he tried to kill me. Does that about cover everything?"

"What makes you so sure it isn't yours?"

"Because the doctor said you might be around twelve weeks. You do the math, okay?" Blair said as he turned and walked away.

I followed along behind him as he headed for the kitchenette. "Then why don't we just wait until after my appointment before we decide?"

Blair shook his head. "I've already decided."

I reached out and grabbed him by the arm, forcing him to stop and to face me. "Blair, no matter what, this baby is a part of me."

"I can't do this."

"What?"

"I cannot let you have *Sonny's* child! I'm tired of competing with him, okay? And I'm *not* going to do this anymore!"

"Compete! What are you talking about? Blair, this was never a competition between you and Sonny!"

"Subject closed!"

"No! It isn't closed! Let's talk about this, let's get it out in the open, now! Right now!"

"Mia-"

"Blair, what if I told you that I couldn't live like this! Running from the law, always looking over my shoulder, living a fictitious life? Not being able to tell anyone the truth. What would you say to that? What would you do?" I blurted out. The room grew quiet as we stood face to face. I knew the kind of life we'd be forced to live and I thought I would be able to accept it. But not until Blair had spoken out loud what I had been thinking all this time did I realize exactly how much I'd have to give up. Too much.

"You're not serious, are you?" he asked. I didn't have to answer his question, for he saw the answer in my eyes. "I don't believe you're doing this. You're in love with *him*, aren't you?"

"I loved you with all of my heart, but when I thought you were dead-"

"Don't! Don't say it. What about all the crap that we went through in St. Lucia? I thought everything had been all sorted out... exactly- we- we were working on making everything better. And now this," Blair said as he pointed to my abdomen. "And now you're telling me it won't work? Mia- Somehow I knew you'd do this. I'm a fool for believing we could've picked up where we left off."

"I thought I was ready to live the kind of life you've been living, but after hearing you say out loud, what I've been thinking, I realize it's a lot to ask of me, of anyone, Blair. It means I will have to lie to my sons, no wait," I said, as I pressed two fingers gently to his lips, as he began to protest. "I'll have to lie to my friends; to everyone I've ever known. We won't be in one place long enough to make new friends, or how will we be able to trust anyone? How do you change your name, how do you do that? Blair, I like who I am, and I like my name."

Blair touched his hand to my two fingers. Holding them there as he started to speak. "How do you know you can't do it if you've never tried?" he whispered.

"Look what it did to you. You lost one family, your mother and your sister. Then you gain another one, an instant family, and look what happened, you lost us too," I replied speaking in a much softer tone, as tears filled my eyes. "I have something for you," I said as I picked up my purse from the table. Inside was a small black box containing my wedding ring, and the two necklaces. I removed the box and turned to Blair, holding the box out to him. Blair pulled me into his arms, holding me tightly.

"Oh, baby, I love you so, so much, my love," Blair said as he held me. "I never realized how selfish it was of me to ask you to give up everything you love to be with me. You're not that kind of a mother; you would never abandon your children. I'm not going to lie to you, but I knew it was going to end this way. I'd convinced myself, that we could make it work. I will always love you," he said as his body shook against mine.

"Blair, I'm so sorry. I want you to know this has nothing to do with me not loving you, for I will always love you, but I cannot do what you ask of me. I'm sorry, baby." It was true, for I would always love Blair. My love for him would remain forever in my heart. I raised my head to the ceiling as my own tears flowed down my face and I prayed for God to help me get though this hurdle.

CHAPTER THIRTY TWO

Two weeks later I was lying in the same bed in the same hotel room Blair and I had shared, grieving all over again. I'd taken a cab to the doctors' office the afternoon of our argument and upon my return, Blair was no longer there. We'd decided it would be best that way, and on my first night alone I'd had my doubts, but as time went by I was sure I'd made the right decision. I'd asked Blair what was next for him, where would he go and what would he do now? His answer had been wherever the *Janús* took him. Now that business had picked up, I offered to pay back the money he'd loaned me to start the agency. But Blair just shook his head and said it was money well spent. He advised me to invest it wisely and not to worry about him because he was set for life, not to worry. How could I not worry, I would always be concerned for him. Blair told me to legally change my name back to Harris and leave the San Diego area and not to trust anyone, not even the authorities because you never knew who was on the take. Then he had smiled a strained smile and told me to take the name of Steward.

Upon returning to my room, I'd noticed the small black box I'd given to Blair which he had left on the table, and upon opening it, I noticed Blair had only removed his necklace with the locket. My wedding ring and the silver necklace with the diamond heart remained along with a note from Blair, stating I would always hold his heart. It had been hard on me losing Blair all over again and more so after my miscarriage three days after his departure. In the beginning, the nausea had mimicked my earlier illness so I never thought anything of it. But when the cramping had started late one night, and after stumbling into the bathroom, and upon seeing all the blood, I knew what had happened. I was back at the doctors' office the next day, and he had confirmed my suspicions. I was a total wreck, racked with guilt and blaming myself for the lost. I lay in bed trying to convince myself to get up and move. To pack my bags and head back to California and that eventually, the pain in my heart would subside and my life would go on. But the motivation was not there, and the days just kept adding up. I wasn't sure if I was grieving for Blair or because of my miscarriage. I kept telling myself, all I needed was one more day to recover from the shock, but one day had turned into two weeks. I'd thought about calling my sons, but I didn't want to upset them. I hadn't spoken to them in fourteen days, because I didn't quite know what to say to them. I didn't return any of their calls either. I knew I would have to call them, but just the thought of hearing their voices and I would break down all over again. I'd even thought about calling Sonny, but after our last meeting I doubted if he would ever speak to me again. The thought of reaching out to Sonny and to have him slam the phone down in my ear would be just as devastating to me as losing my child.

Blair called the hotel every other day, leaving messages for me. His first message was to inform me he would remain in the area until after I'd left, to make sure I was safe, and for me to call him if I needed anything. His calls were always the same, always about my welfare and with each call ending with instructions for me to call him if I ever needed anything. I never returned his calls either, so Blair wasn't aware of my miscarriage, but it really didn't matter because that would not have changed anything, for I did not want the lifestyle Blair was forced to live regardless of my love for him.

I was trying to will my body to move, just as there was a knock on the door. In spite of the *"Do Not Disturb"* sign hanging on the doorknob, the maid still knocked on the door every day. "GO AWAY!" I shouted as I picked up a pillow and threw it at the door. I'd learned on the first day, if there was no response from inside the room, housekeeping would use the master key to enter. I rolled out of bed and retrieved the pillow I'd thrown at the door, tossing it on the settee as I made a beeline for the bathroom. The face that stared back at me in the mirror was enough to encourage me to wash my face, and then I thought what the hell and hopped into the shower, and afterward I felt a lot better. I felt so good I called up room service and ordered a big breakfast.

After breakfast I called downstairs for a cab to take me to the nearest shopping mall. It was gray and raining outside and even though I had replaced my island clothes for some of the clothing Blair had stored aboard the *Janús*, they were still not suitable for this kind of weather. I couldn't walk around in Seattle in December with sandals and linen pants.

I spent the rest of the day shopping and even had dinner out. After being dropped off back at the hotel, I had a Bellman help me with carrying my purchases up to my room. The thought of a long hot shower before bed was very appealing to me, so I decided to leave the unpacking until morning. But before I had a chance to kick off my shoes, there was a knock on the door, and in my mind, I pictured the *"Do Not Disturb"* sign swinging from the doorknob. What now, I thought, pulling the door opened.

"Mrs. Solomon?"

I let out a little scream, before my hand flew up to my mouth and I wanted to leap for joy and throw myself into his arms. But I didn't move, not sure of what his reaction would be, after all, I'd sent him away. We stood there, neither of us speaking. I was so happy to see him I had to keep my feet from doing a little shuffle as I backed away from the door. I'd thought about calling him on many occasions, only to change my mind over and over again. Now here he stood in the flesh. He didn't seem angry; the look on his face was more of concern. His head was slightly cocked to one side, and he wore a slight smile upon his face, which seemed a bit strained and he looked exhausted. His clothing was wrinkled as though he had slept in them, which was so unlike him. "Hi," I finally spoke, my voice squeaky to my ears.

"Hi." He replied, his voice booming in comparison to mine.

"This is a surprise."

"May I come in?" he asked.

I nodded as I stepped back to let him enter. Sonny stood with his back to me, as he looked about the room before slowly turning around to face me again. "Blair called, he said you needed me. He told me everything. Mia, why didn't you call me?"

I shook my head, my eyes shifting from his face and then down to the floor. "I don't know. I guess I thought you wouldn't come," I said with a shrug.

Sonny reached out for my right hand, giving it a gentle squeeze. "Have I ever not come when you've called?"

I shook my head. Oh baby. "No. But after our last conversation and me not telling you Blair was alive, I thought you wouldn't come," I replied, as I glanced upward at him with an intent look.

Sonny nodded, as he lowered his head, gently rubbing the back of my hand. "Yeah, and after speaking with Blair I now understand why you did that, but, baby, I'm here now." As he said this, he took me in his arms. "I'm beat," he said releasing me and making his way over to the table. "Care if I sit down?" Sonny asked as he pulled out a chair. "I got Blair's call this morning around nine, and I left right after his phone call. I'd been up since six this morning. I took the first flight I could get out, had a two hour layover in LA, then the plane had some kind of mechanical problem. We had to change planes in Sacramento. I was frantic, because I wasn't sure if you'd still be here. I left you a message during my layover, did you get it?"

"No, I just got in. I was out shopping for some warm clothing and I haven't had a chance to listen to my messages." Actually, I had noticed the light blinking, but thought it was another message from Blair.

"Blair is a high tech kind of guy, seems he had everything all planned out."

I followed Sonny over to the table and sat across from him. "I guess so," I replied with a shrug, as I tried to keep my tears at bay.

"Blair said you had something important to tell me. Although he shared everything else with me that had happened since his *alleged* death, and while the two of you where in St. Lucia, he wouldn't tell me what was so important. Blair told me you asked him to leave. Said you two had a disagreement which had involved me. Blair wanted me to tell you that you were right. His lifestyle is not the life for you. He said you deserved much more than he could ever give you. He told me to take care of you. Mia, I know how much you loved Blair, and it must have been a really big disagreement for you to send him away. So, before you say whatever it is you have to say, I want you to know I have never stopped loving you and I'm here for as long as you want me."

I reached out for his hand, my eyes misting up even more at his tender words. My heart seemed to be beating furiously in my chest at Sonny's words and his touch. "That is so sweet of you," I said as I looked down at his hand. "I don't know how to start."

"Mia, you know you can always talk to me," Sonny replied as his lips curved upward in a languid smile.

His smile, no matter how slight, had been enough for me to open up to Sonny, freeing up my heart and allowing me to tell him everything. About how Blair had appeared in the opened doorway at the Villa in St. Lucia, and how he had accused Sonny of trying to kill him. How Blair and I had tried to reconcile our marriage. About how hurt Blair had been upon hearing of my infidelity with Sonny, and about my pregnancy. I was eye-to-eye as I told Sonny the last bit of news. "I had a miscarriage eight days ago, and it was your child." Sonny nodded but didn't speak as I continued on. "I'm sorry about the baby, I don't know what happened. I guess it wasn't meant to be. Blair knows nothing of my miscarriage, because I haven't spoken to him since the day he left."

I looked away from his intense stare, unable to read his expression. Sonny said nothing as I shared the events of the recent days to him. He only shifted his position in the chair as he gave me his full attention. I was trying to figure out what he was thinking as he sat quietly listening to me. His face showed no emotions, no shock upon hearing that I'd been pregnant, or my miscarriage. He didn't speak until after I completed my story.

"Mia, I'm sorry to hear about your miscarriage, and I want you to understand I would have supported your decision regarding our child, whatever it may have been. I know it's too soon, but if you want to have a child we can do that," Sonny said as he rubbed my arm. "The time away from you has hurt me more than I thought it would, and the idea of never seeing you again almost drove me mad. There is no way I could ever explain to you the pain I felt when I thought I'd lost you forever. I want this to be a new chapter for us. I want to take you home, to start our life together."

I took several deep breaths, as my eyes begin to tear up again, and I had to blink several times to will away the tears, because there was so much more to say to him. The decision to send Blair away had been easier said than done, and it had not been because of my lack of love for him and I wanted Sonny to know this before we walked out the door together as man and woman. "Sonny, before we go, I want you to know that I did not send Blair away because I no longer loved him. It's important for you to know…a part of me will always love him. Sonny, you have to understand, in the beginning I prayed for one more chance to be with him and after my prayers had been answered, I came to realize it was no longer Blair's love I was praying for, because I was praying for you love. At first I was in denial, telling myself it was his lifestyle, but I was wrong. Somehow I got the idea in my head that maybe," I shrugged my shoulders, "since Blair was back things would go back to being the way they were, but I was only fooling myself because things between Blair and I could never be the same," I said with a shake of my head. "No matter how hard I tried, it wasn't going to work anymore and it had nothing to do with the lifestyle Blair is forced to live. It was me. After you- by the time Blair came back into my life all I could think of was you and it was then that I realized that it was *you*, that I loved. Sonny, you are all I ever wanted, and no one else. I remembered what you said about how every time you kissed Macey, you were actually kissing me and when the two of you lay together in bed, I was right there beside you. I now understand what you meant by that. Because that is exactly how I've felt these past few weeks. I didn't appreciate what you were telling me then, and after your visit to the island I was afraid I'd lost you. It was *very* difficult for me to hear you speak of that night. I know how tough it was on you to tell me the truth about what really happened, for until that day I never truly understood how great your love for me was. I've tried to deny my feelings for you, and I've always known a bond existed between us, and no matter how far apart we where, we would always be together. I'd gone to the island to say my goodbyes to Blair and to make a decision about the two of us, and I had made up my mind to return to you the day Blair popped back into my life. For you see, Sonny, I've been waiting for that special someone to come into my life, and all this time you where standing right there in front of me." As I said this, Sonny stood and came around the table to stand next to me. I rose from my chair, and looked up into his piercing violet eyes. "Blair tried to frighten me by telling me I might be a target for those thugs we helped to put in prison. He said they believed him to be dead, but they are still searching for the millions he took from them and someone would have to be made an example of."

Sonny's mood seemed to change, and he gave the impression of being no longer aloof as he was when he had appeared at the door to my room several hours ago, as he sat up straighter in his chair, giving me his full attention. But maybe Sonny had just been exhausted from his trip. "Mia, about that night, I want you to know what really happened-"

"No, Sonny, I don't care about that night, and I don't want to ever mention it again," I said as I raised my hand in the air.

"Okay, well, Blair mentioned something about the Goodbytes' and he also suggested that you sell the company and move away."

"What about you, do you think I should run?"

"Well, Blair did have some valid points, but, Mia, I don't know what to tell you. How do we know they won't come looking for you?"

"I believe Blair was trying to frighten me into staying with him."

"No, I don't think Blair meant to frighten you, but he does have some valid points.

"Sonny, I don't know what to do."

"Mia, we've all been through a lot and you and I have a lot of catching up to do, and a few major decisions to make, which can wait until we've returned home. Anthony and Maurice are worried sick about you and they are waiting to hear from you. Let's go home," he said as he rubbed my arm.

"I know I should have contacted them, but I was in an unhappy place and I didn't want to drag them down with me." I stood there chewing on my bottom lip, unsure of what to do. Should I sell my condo and move away, or stay and take my chances? I guess Sonny thought my mind was elsewhere, because he started to go into this whole charade about how he didn't care if I was still missing Blair.

"I told them I was coming to get you, bring you home. Mia, I know you still care for Blair, and I don't mind, as long as it's just a *very* small part of you," Sonny replied, grinning for the first time since he'd entered the room. "I didn't want to leave you that day in St. Lucia. I was afraid if I left, I would never see you again. Days after my visit, I thought of nothing but you every single day. I kept questioning if I'd did the right thing, because I was terrified of the idea of not having you in my life, and the infinite fury I'm feeling for Blair over what he did is diminished only because of the fact that you are back in my life. Mia, you have to understand, baby, you're my blood, my water, my drug, my nectar, and my light on a dark night-"

I gasped, stepping away from him. "How did you know-" I asked startled at his words, for I had said those very same words to Blair, but I had never spoken them to anyone else.

"Mia, a long time ago I held you in my arms as your life slipped away, and I spoke those words to you because I thought I'd lost you. You don't remember that night, do you?" Sonny asked as I stared at him.

"Vaguely, I heard someone speaking, calling me from the darkness. It was you? All this time I thought it had been a dream. I hadn't realized it was you calling out to me, calling me back. You've never mentioned it since. You joke and you talk about other aspects of that night, but you've never spoken those words to me again, why?"

"I don't know why. You never said anything," Sonny replied as he studied me with intent curiosity.

"I only remembered a couple of lines, and I thought it was from a book I'd read or a song I'd heard. Is there more? Say it for me."

Sonny nodded, as he slowly walked toward me. "I am drawn to you like a mosquito to warm fragrant flesh, like a fish to cool clear waters, like an addict to their fix, like a honeybee to a flower, like a moth to a flame. Mia, you are my blood, pulsating through my veins, my cool drink of water on a hot day, my drug when my body is burning for a fix, my nectar when I'm craving something sweet and special, and my light on a cold dark night whenever I'm feeling alone. I shall be your knight in shining armor. I am your knight shining armor, forever and always," he finished, as I stepped into his opened arms. Now was the time for closure, healing, and acceptance of Sonny's love.

It had taken me years to realize what my heart already knew. I'd been searching for my one true love, and he'd been right here beside me all this time.

***

897591

Made in the USA